I Kinda Do

Cara D. Smith

Warning

This is a work of fiction. Names, characters, businesses, places, events, and incidents are either the products of the author's imagination or used in a fictitious manner. Any resemblance to actual persons, living or dead, or actual events is purely coincidental.

The following story contains mature themes, strong language, and sexual situations. It is intended for mature readers.

Dedication

For Isaac and Steven.

One more time, for the people in the back!
The following story contains mature themes, strong language, and sexual
situations. It was written for a mature audience.

Contents

Chapter 1

Fern

Monday Afternoon

"Fern, when you get a minute, would you please box up Felicity's belongings?" Mr. Chambers's voice sends a shiver down my spine. I was so focused on the laundry, he managed to sneak up on me. His voice always does that to me—deep with a hint of gravel that warms me all over—when he catches me off guard. Like now. It drives me nuts. It's a good thing I've been in Texas long enough to become immune to the accent.

As if I haven't heard that before . . . "Right away, Mr. Chambers," I nearly whisper, nodding my head so he knows I hear and obey, though my hands keep folding on autopilot.

She'll be back. She always is. She's kind of like a fungus in that regard. I've lost track of the times I've packed her shit, only to turn around and unpack it two weeks later because she changes her mind, and he's let her. When she comes back, we'll all pretend she was only away on vacation for the benefit of Mr. Chambers's daughter, Veronica. *And if she finds out I haven't followed her rules while she's away, it'll be my ass out the door.*

One of the things I've discovered during my years of cleaning houses is that men will ignore or forgive just about anything for a woman who's good in the sack. Felicity must be able to suck start a Harley because he keeps letting her back into his life and his bed. She *must* have other redeeming qualities, but she hides them well.

Mr. Chambers speaks again, reminding me that now is not the time to fall down the 'Felicity is a bitch' rabbit hole. "Thank you, Fern. When you've finished, let Len know. He'll dispose of everything."

Dispose of everything? He says it like he's talking about the trash from Saturday's party, not thousands upon thousands of dollars' worth of clothing, and God only knows what the hell else that succubus has acquired on his dime in the last six years. She definitely does *not* shop at Target.

I freeze with my arms out wide, the towel I'm folding stretched between my hands. Inadvertently, my eyes snap up to lock on his in utter amazement. I'm breaking the rules—the ones he doesn't know about, and I'm not allowed to speak of unless I want another spiteful bitch to ruin my life again. But he's being ridiculous.

"Is that a problem?" Mr. Chambers asks. His jaw clenches, a warning sign that I'm irritating him

Gulping, I figure I might as well break every rule in the book. *In for a penny . . .* I drop my arms and the towel, giving him my full attention. For the first six months I worked here—before that bitch moved in—he and I were almost friends. Surely, he'll forgive me a little honesty for old time's sake? "No, Mr. Chambers. It's just . . . That's a lot of stuff to toss in the garbage."

One corner of his full mouth kicks up into a smirk, and I swear my heart speeds up. Yeah, Mr. Chambers is *hott.* Two t's because one just isn't enough. His combination of dark hair and blue eyes is my personal kryptonite, and always has been, though I've learned what's on the outside doesn't matter. He has to go the extra mile and be tall on top of that. Being vertically challenged myself, I have a thing for tall guys. His strong jaw is shaded with stubble, which is out of the ordinary for him. He must be taking her latest outburst harder than usual. It looks good on him, though.

"You're right." His smirk becomes a full-blown smile that makes my mouth go dry. "I don't care what happens to her things. Donate them if you'd like. While you're at it, if you take a liking to anything, consider it yours. Just have it all out of my house by the end of the day. Please."

His smile flips a switch in my head. My mind immediately snaps back into work mode and reminds me of the rules. Like a good little bitch, my eyes drop to his feet. "Right away, Mr. Chambers," I murmur. Felicity would be so proud. Well, probably not under the circumstances.

Hopefully it sticks this time . . . This is the first time he's ever kicked her out. Maybe I'm a bad person, but I'm going to enjoy donating her shit. *I* don't want any of it. I'm not cleaning houses wearing Chanel and Versace.

"No," he says, a hint of irritation creeping into his tone. "I'm sick of this, 'Mr. Chambers' crap. You didn't do that when you started here. I don't know why you can't remember my name anymore. It's Mason."

I fight a smile. Before Felicity moved in, I almost felt like part of the family—Ronni's aunt or something. Afterward, she served as a wall between all of us. If she's really gone this time, maybe things will change again. *Don't get your hopes up.*

I can't resist a bit of teasing. It'll probably be the last time because she'll be back, but just this once . . . "Right away . . . sir."

My cheeky risk is rewarded with a rusty laugh. There's no stopping my smile this time. It's been far too long since I last heard that sound. Ronni usually keeps him rolling, but even she, who is the center of his world, is unable to coax so much as a chuckle from him lately.

"Fern! I'm home!" Ronni calls. I cringe at the sound of the door slamming behind her—a new habit of her's I've been working to break.

"Thanks, Fern. I need to go have a talk with Ronni. I'm off for the rest of the day. Let me know if we're in your way." He doesn't wait for my reply before he turns to go.

With no one to witness my impropriety, I curl my lip and mutter a stream of obscenities aimed at Felicity. I thought I was going to lose this gig the day the Wicked Bitch of the West moved in; I swallowed my pride and did what I had to. *I'd do it all again.*

The list of rules I received the day after she infested Mr. Chambers's home runs through my mind like end credits for a movie, narrated by her, in a voice like the whining of a thousand mosquitos. *"This is my house now. You'll do things my way. Don't look at him. Don't speak to him unless he addresses you specifically. Don't contact him unless it's an emergency, and you can't reach me. Never be alone in a room with him. And no touching. You will address him as 'sir' or 'Mr. Chambers.' He's your boss, not your friend. Understood?"*

Felicity was happy to let me continue working here, so long as I pretended to be invisible. Or maybe it's that she didn't have the power to fire me. Not wanting to clean up her own messes probably had something to do with it, too. And she had no interest in taking care of Mr. Chambers's little one.

I need this job too much to let her get to me. I've got bills to pay, and I'd have to take on three other gigs to replace the income from this one. Mr. Chambers is the heir to Chambers Freight International, the largest shipping industry in the world—a veritable empire. He extends the company's generosity toward their employees to his personal employees as well. I may be more of an independent contractor, but I'm included in that blanket generosity.

I also *like* this job too much, despite his girlfriend's manipulative tendencies. Following her rules sucks, as does being the perfect little subservient twat she wants me to be because she thinks she's better than me, but I can do this. Even when she's not here to keep me in line. I can do anything I set my mind to. *For Ronni.*

That little girl makes this job my joy. She needs *someone* here to act as a buffer. Her father hasn't realized that Felicity's outer beauty masks the ugliness within. She only lets it shine through when he's not around. There was a time when I could have told him, before WBotW moved in, but that ship has sailed.

***

Singing softly to myself to ease the loneliness of this big house, I make my way upstairs with a basket full of folded laundry. Ronni and Mr. Chambers must be in the back yard playing, because the house is quiet. He's a good dad like that. *Yet another thing that adds to the hott factor.*

My current earworm always makes me smile, which is good since it's requested so frequently. It's still crazy to me that people will tip someone else to sing for them at a karaoke bar, but it is what it is. The owners encourage it because it feeds the theme they've got going on. I can't complain. I get paid to have fun.

Ronni's room is a disaster zone. Without Felicity here to undermine me, I can see to it she picks up her own toys tonight. Ronni will do it without making a fuss the first time I ask because she's a unicorn like that, but Felicity always stops her if she hears me ask and insists it is my job to do it. While I am paid to keep this place clean, a child needs chores. Mr. Chambers agreed with me on this point when he hired me. Since he tries not to interfere with the "relationship" between his girlfriend and daughter, he lets Felicity have her way. All I can do is grit my teeth behind my smile.

It takes concentration, but I manage to make it both ways through the minefield of toys without breaking myself or anything. I make my way down the hall to restock towels in the guestrooms since some of Mr. Chambers's friends stayed over the weekend. In the master suite, the bathroom light is on, and the door is wide open. *That's odd.* However, Mr. Chambers isn't usually home when I'm doing this. He must have forgotten to turn it off before he went out to play with Ronni. I put the towels and washcloths away and hit the switch on the way out. The sooner I put his clothes in his closet, the sooner I can complete the familiar task of packing Felicity's crap. There might be some boxes in the garage.

My mind runs away with me, cataloging the things of hers I need to locate and box up. I turn the corner into the closet on autopilot, hit a wall, and bounce off. "Shit!" I lose my balance, stumbling backward. The basket lands on the floor with a clatter when I fling my arms out to steady myself. I reach the tipping point and keep right on going. Before I hit the ground, strong hands catch me 'round the middle and pull me to my feet. My brain finally catches up. That wasn't a wall.

My face heats up. I'm sure I'm the color of a damn traffic signal. I can't believe I ran into him. I do this same task, at the same time, in the same order, every Monday, and it never changes. I could do it with my eyes closed. But he's home today, which changes everything.

"I'm so sorry, Mr. Chambers!" Not only did I run into him, I cussed in front of him too! *So freaking professional!* "I swear I don't talk that way in front of Ronni!"

The ability to form complete sentences flees my brain once the warmth of his hands seeps that far. He's still holding me by the waist. We haven't as much as shaken hands since Felicity moved in. I forgot how warm his hands are. And I'm way too close to see his feet, so my eyes are fixed on nothing but bare skin stretched tight over hard muscle.

Mr. Chambers doesn't have abs for days like so many guys on TV. Felicity used to give him shit about it. He'd always tell her he likes chocolate and booze too much for that nonsense. I'm on his side because that would probably make him too damn perfect for his own good. *Stop it!* My eyes screw shut in an effort to stick to the rules. I do *not* want to be caught checking him out.

His chuckle makes me shiver. "Easy, Fern. It's alright. It's my fault. I realized you didn't know I was here when I heard you singing. I should've said something, but I didn't want to scare you." One hand leaves my waist to tuck a wisp of hair that's escaped my ponytail behind my ear. That little touch makes me break out in goosebumps. *Please, God, don't let him notice.*

It's one thing to check your clients out on occasion—I'm only human. It's another thing to do something stupid enough—even on accident—that he figures out how easily he can get under your skin. Nothing good ever comes of that. I watch just enough TV to know that. I won't do anything to risk losing my time with Ronni. That might break me. No one can ever replace my little girl, but having Ronni in my life lessens the pain.

"I should have been paying more attention." As an argument, it's weak. And it sounds weak because I mumble it to his navel like the whipped little bitch Felicity made me. I'll never forgive her for that, but it's as much my own fault as it is hers. I let her do this to me.

"It's alright," he says softly.

We're in a small, dark space, he's half-dressed, he's still holding on to me, and we're all alone. If someone walked in right now, they'd get the wrong idea. Someone like Ronni. Or Felicity, who has a tendency to pop up where you least expect her like the mold she is.

Mercifully, he lets his hands fall away. *Am I imagining the way his fingers trailed to prolong the contact?* No. I mean, yes. I'm imagining things. Why would he do that? It's all in my head.

Chapter 2

Mason

Who knew Fern could sing? I'm still blaming that random factoid for my standing here like an idiot until she ran into me. I didn't want to scare her, but I didn't want her to stop singing or be self-conscious about it.

Fern has worked here for years. I should know these things about her by now, but she doesn't share much about herself. Ronni probably told me once, but I was probably too absorbed in something that seemed way more important than it actually was to listen.

If Fern wasn't standing here, I'd smack myself in the damn forehead. Instead, I rub the back of my neck to rid at least one hand of her lingering warmth. The solution to my current problem is literally right in front of me, at least the temporary solution. If she can help, it'll buy me a little more time to figure out how to juggle my job and Ronni without Felicity. "Fern, could I ask you for a favor?"

"Mr. Chambers?"

Two words. That's all I get. *I swear she thinks that's my only name.* The way Fern ogled me would be flattering if she ever fucking looked me in the eye anymore. It's not so much that she's checking me out as it is that she is trying to look anywhere but my eyes. *Still, she is enjoying the view.* Her eyes got huge when she saw I didn't have a shirt on. I can't help the way my chest puffs out or my abs flex, trying to stand out through the layer of poor food choices. *It's nice to be appreciated for a change.*

"Mason," I say, correcting her for the umpteenth million time. I get enough of that formal bullshit at work, but I can't get her to break the habit. "If it's not an imposition, could you be here to help Ronni get up and dressed for school in the morning? I know you probably have other plans, but I'm desperate, and I'll pay you double."

She smiles at the carpet, and a wave of envy crashes through me. Fern has a lovely smile. It's a pity I don't get to enjoy it more. "I clean for the Thompsons in the morning, but they won't mind if I'm a little off schedule. I'll let them know this evening." Her smile fades and she bites her full bottom lip.

That innocent little action gives me not-so-innocent thoughts. I'd like to do the same thing to that lip. *It hasn't been that damn long, Mason. Get a grip.* Next thing I know, I'm going to be fantasizing about the woman next door. She's old enough to be my mother, but that doesn't stop her from flirting every time we see each other. And she's not subtle. Ronni needs to spend the weekend with my mother. I need a night out and some no-strings fun, but not with the cougar next door. If I can remember how the hell picking up women works. Monogamy is a bitch of a habit to break.

Focus, Mason. "If it's a problem—"

She shakes her head quickly and her bottom lip springs free. "No, not at all, Mr. Chambers. Just planning logistics."

"Logistics?" What kind of logistics could she need to plan? She comes here, she wakes Ronni, feeds her breakfast, makes sure she's dressed, and walks her to the car. After tomorrow I'll have a better plan. *Maybe her car is low on fuel?* She leaves here late, and I'm asking her to get here early. I'll have Len check . . .

She parts her lips to speak, but the words are slow to come, and they're soft when they do. "I was figuring out which bus I'll need to catch to get here on time."

The bus? Is she serious right now? "Is your car in the shop?" Sure, some people choose to utilize public transportation, but I can't imagine doing so if you make a living going from one house to the next to clean.

Her head sways side to side. "I don't have a car. It won't be a problem, though. I won't let Ronni down."

Shit. Guilt floods me for even asking. It seemed like such a little thing until she pointed out the extra effort. It's nice to know she's so devoted to my daughter, though. You can't buy that kind of thing. "Be sure to give Len your address before you go home, and I'll have him pick you up after he drops me off."

She blinks a couple of times. "But Mr. Chambers, who will be here with Ronni?"

Shit! That puts my plans in the blender. Ronni would still be asleep and is old enough, and responsible enough, to be alone for the thirty minutes it would take. Surely that's all it would take. But if she woke up, she'd probably be frightened. Fern is right; that's not acceptable. I need a plan B. It's easy to overlook how much you rely on someone until they're gone.

Running my fingers through my hair, I grab a handful and pull. *Think, Mason.* I could send Len to get her *before* I go to work. That would require him to get out of bed extra early, though, and the man is already up before the sun because I insist on being the first person in the office every day. *Gotta prove I'm dedicated.* I don't want to mess with his schedule any more than I have to. Morning is the only time in a day that is truly his own.

Mom is always an option. She could come stay, and I wouldn't need Fern to reschedule her entire day. But I'm not ready to face Mom yet. She is a big part of the reason I kept Felicity in my life for so long, and she's bound to be upset with me. Felicity is everything Mom wants for me. Good pedigree. Good manners. Pretty. *Fuck, that makes her sound like a dog.* That's not far from the truth, though . . . But a dog would have at least been loyal. If Mom had her way, Felicity and I would've been married years ago.

Another alternative occurs to me, but it's crazy. I shouldn't even ask, but I'm in a tight spot. "Could you stay here tonight? I can have Len take you home to get anything you need when you've got a minute. You know we have space. I'll pay you for every hour you're here, too."

Her lashes flutter over her pretty green eyes, and I know a moment of fear because asking obviously crossed a line. It's not necessarily inappropriate—a lot of single fathers in my position have live-in help. It's not something we've ever done, though. Fern works here, but I'm not exactly her boss. She's entitled to a life outside of work, like everyone else.

"S-sure," she says, catching me by surprise. Her reaction indicated the opposite answer was forthcoming.

A bubble of hopeful excitement rises in my chest. This will solve my most immediate problem nicely and buy me some time to plan for next week when I return to work. "Really? You don't mind?"

"No, Mr. Chambers. I don't mind. Heck, I'll get to sleep in," she says with a conspiratorial giggle that's so cute it makes me want to hug her.

So I do, laughing to myself at her surprised yelp. "Thank you so much!" I'm crossing another line, but I'm so damn relieved to have that taken care of. I've cleared my schedule as much as possible for the rest of the week in case Ronni is upset about Felicity, but there's a meeting first thing tomorrow morning I cannot miss.

Something about the way she kept herself so stiff in my arms before makes me think it's been far too long since anyone over the age of eight has given this woman a good hug. Lord knows I could use one right now as well. Since I'm already on the wrong side of the line, I hold her until she relaxes and melts into me. Even then, I don't let go.

Fern doesn't hug me back, but I didn't expect her to. She's probably thinking I'm certifiable. Hell, she's probably about two seconds from telling me to find a new nanny. *Nah.* If she was going to quit, she would have done so years ago, probably over something stupid Felicity did. Anyone who loves Ronni as much as Fern does is used to random hugs. They're a staple in this house.

The front door slams. I grit my teeth in annoyance. Fern jumps like she's been shot. She tenses but thankfully doesn't pull away. I'm not ready to let go yet. She smells good. Not shampoo or perfume, just her. I like the way her silky curls slide against my skin where her ponytail is draped over her shoulder, and her eyelashes tickle a bit when she blinks. The warmth of her breath on my chest gives me goosebumps, which makes no sense at all. She fits against me perfectly—short enough to fit under my chin without me having to crane my neck. She's an interesting combination of soft and hard, her body mostly too firm to give under my arms. She's all muscle. Not only that, but for some reason, I'm confident that everything is going to be okay right now. I wasn't sure before. It might not be if I let her go.

"Mason?" my younger brother calls from somewhere in the house.

"Uncle Austin!" Ronni calls back. Her running footsteps let me know she's bought me another minute to get my shit together.

Fern tenses again. As much as I don't want to, I let her go. Bad things are going to happen if I hold her any longer. It is seductive. Addicting. There's no room in my life for addictions.

She actually glances at me for a second, her eyes guarded. In the dim light of my closet, they're more gray than green, but they're still big and round and lovely. Even if they seem a bit worried and confused right now. *That makes two of us, Fern.*

"Sorry, it's already been a shit week," I mutter, rubbing the back of my neck again. Now that I've let her go, I can't believe I did that. It's a sexual harassment suit waiting to happen. I can't randomly grab people for a hug, even if they need it. Especially not because they need it. That defense makes it sound even worse.

It doesn't matter that Fern's part of the family here as far as I'm concerned. The fact is, she's *not* family, and she works here. I can't treat her like my kid sister. *But God, she felt good.* That's definitely not a thought I've ever had about my sister . . .

Her entire face softens and she smiles at me. Not at my feet, at me. "It's alright. Ronni always says—"

"Hugs are magic," I finish for her, grinning.

Still smiling, she nods. "People need a little magic every now and then," she murmurs. She takes my hand and squeezes. It's over in a blink, but still surprising coming from her. "I'll help with Ronni; however I can, Mr. Chambers."

I swallow my irritation and correct her again. "Mason." Her normal, carefully neutral façade settles back into place, which tells me more than anything else that I'm fighting a losing battle. I don't know what exactly happened to build that wall she hides behind, but some mighty fucking fine craftsmanship went into it. "If I want someone to call me 'Mr. Chambers' at home, I'll conduct meetings here. And I appreciate your help, Fern. It means a lot."

"Mason!" my brother shouts again. There's a note of desperation in his voice this time. "Come save me from your demon spawn! I don't want to have a princess tea party! I don't look good in tutus!"

Fern's mask of professionalism shatters, and she actually giggles. The smile she gave me before, while genuine, was a mere shadow of the one I'm enjoying now. It knocks ten years off her, not that she ever really appears old. She should be so carefree all the time. *I wonder what happened to put the weight of the world on her shoulders?*

She's never told me more about the family emergency that led her to work here. It's not my place to ask. I've already crossed too many lines with her today.

"Coming!" I call back with a chuckle of my own. He's probably already in a tutu. And if he is, I'm taking a picture. Blackmail material is always handy to have, and God only knows how much he has on me after eight years of parenting.

Unable to help myself, I grab her shoulder and give it a gentle squeeze. She's bailing my ass out and I need her to know how much I appreciate that. *If only she could bail me out of everything so easily.* Austin could only be here to talk about the alterations to my schedule that will require him to shoulder more of the load this week. Meaning this little break with Fern will probably be the second-best moment of my day, right after Veronica's happy squeal when she discovered me home so early.

Fern glances my way briefly before stooping to retrieve the basket of clothes, but the laughter in her eyes is gone again. I bend to help because Austin can handle Ronni for a few more minutes, but she waves me off with a small smile. "I've got this. Go rescue him. But if he's in a tutu, I need footage."

And she's back! That's the Fern I hired. Taking her at her word, I grab a shirt and meander toward the hall, in no rush to bail my brother out. I've got too much on my mind.

The day we met, she looked me square in the eye, smiled, and shook my hand. She was captivatingly confident and had more personality in her little finger than some people do in their whole bodies. As hung up as I was on my new girlfriend, Felicity, even I could see Fern was something special.

Fern took this house by storm, whipping it—and me and Veronica—into shape in her first week, and things have worked like clockwork since. She fit in seamlessly, more friend than employee. I looked forward to coming home after work and hearing all about her and Ronni's adventures. We'd talk and joke about everything and nothing at all before she left for the night.

Overnight, everything changed. No more jokes. No more teasing. No long talks. She welcomes me home and makes herself scarce, then I'm too busy with Felicity and Ronni to coax a real explanation from her. But Felicity isn't here to distract me anymore.

A hint of a memory teases the back of my mind, and the words come back to me. *"Mason, she can't get too comfortable here. And you can't let yourself or Ronni get too comfortable with her being here. Do you really think she'll work for you forever? How is Ronni going to feel when she moves on to bigger and better things? I just think a little . . . decorum will resolve those issues before they are issues."*

The bottom drops out of my stomach. I don't know why this is coming back to me now of all times—maybe because I know the real Felicity now and am questioning our time together—but I'm glad it did. I let Felicity convince me she was right and agreed when she offered to handle it. If she said something to cause this change in Fern, it's as much my fault as it is hers because I didn't have the balls to contradict her or the heart to have a discussion with Fern. If Felicity is the reason for the change in Fern, it's just another one of her games, and I'm through playing it.

Another conversation untangles itself from my memory, more like a continuation of the same conversation a few days later. I mentioned Fern's odd behavior to Felicity. *"She seemed pretty upset on the phone a few days ago, but she didn't want to talk about it. I'm sure she'll be alright. Just give her some space."*

And I did. I trusted Fern to come to Felicity or me if there was anything we could do to help her. She never did, and I never wanted to pry. Her distance gradually became the new normal. I let this happen, but I can make it right.

Chapter 3
Mason

"What's going on?" Austin asks before I shut the door to my home office behind us. "It's not like you to up and take a week off. Some warning would've been nice."

I eye the bar on my way by, sorely tempted, but if I start now, I won't stop until I'm shitfaced. I don't drink like that around Ronni. I lost the luxury of a late afternoon bender when I helped bring another life into this world.

Instead, I fall into my chair and drop my face into my hands. "Hell if I know. I just had the second-worst weekend of my life, man. I *accidentally* learned that my girlfriend had plans in motion to send my daughter to boarding school without my consent." I pause, expecting some sort of reaction to this news, but he doesn't speak. Either he heard about that train wreck through the grapevine, or he recognizes that I need to get things off my chest and will grill me on it later. "The bitch forged my signature on the papers! And she cheated. Again. And, because every shit sundae needs a cherry on top, Granddad invited me to lunch the next day to tell me I have to be married before he will retire. Oh, and that if I'm not married in a reasonable amount of time, he'll promote you!"

That's the real kicker. Austin doesn't want to be CEO. He'd probably sell the company, and I will not be the reason that the family business falls to pieces or sells out to the highest bidder.

Austin sighs, irritated about something. I peer across the desk between my fingers to find him frowning. *The bastard knows something.* Sitting upright, I raise my eyebrows and wait him out. He'll cough up better under the silent treatment than he will if I pester him.

Sure enough, in about two seconds, his mouth opens. "Granddad wants you married before you're thirty." He grimaces and hurries to continue, the rest of the words spilling from his lips in a rushed jumble. "Originally, it was married with children, but you went and put the cart before the horse there. We had dinner last night. You're not the only one on the hook here. He informed me that he'll expect the same of me if you don't come through."

Old fashioned bastard. I work my ass off, day in and day out, to prove to him I'm ready to take the helm, and none of that matters because I'm not married. I suppose I should be fucking thankful Ronni counts even though she was born out of wedlock.

A sigh escapes me. That's unfair. Granddad's not a bad guy; I'm only irritated with him because I didn't see this stipulation coming. Instead of clinging to it like a shield, I release my anger. "Is the age thing his requirement, or did Mom put a bug in his ear? I swear Mom will jump on whatever train gets us to the altar at this point."

She might be their daughter-in-law, but my mother and my dad's parents have always been close. They got closer when Dad died, and Mom stepped up to help fill his shoes until I was old enough to do so.

He snorts out a laugh. "Probably a little of both." He casts a longing look at the bar before adding, "Mom's going to be pissed when she finds out you publicly humiliated Felicity. She'll never marry you now."

Yeah, dumping her in the middle of brunch at the busiest restaurant in town probably wasn't the best idea. I know he's only ribbing me, but damnit! It's too soon. "I publicly humiliated *her*? She cheated on me twice that I know of, quite publicly the second time. Marriage hasn't been a likely outcome for years. I wasted too much of my life waiting for something I should have known was never going to happen—waiting for her to grow up. She doesn't get another chance. I don't get why it matters to Mom so much. Shouldn't she be more concerned about my happiness than my marital status?"

"Quite publicly?" he asks, the drama outweighing everything else for the moment. "What did she do, kiss him in a club?"

I snort out a laugh, amazed he doesn't know yet. The whole damn world probably knows by now. That's what happens when you're dating a self-proclaimed internet celebrity. "You haven't seen? They were caught fucking beside a dumpster in an alley behind some dive bar. She was recognized, of course. Len came back from lunch today with five different gossip rags, all of which had her on the front page. Can't get much more public than that. I broke up with her before I even knew about it because of the boarding school thing."

"I mean, at least she wasn't *trying* to be public about it." He doesn't laugh, though. I figured he would. I did. Loudly. Bitterly.

Six years down the fucking drain. I forgave Felicity the first time She cheated. We hadn't been together long when it happened, but it took me longer to find out. I was so wrapped up in her—the idea of her—that I believed her when she said it would never happen again. I was even stupid enough to move her in here afterward, thinking it would fix things. And I let her come back every time she made up some reason to be mad at me and left for two weeks, on my dime.

Those papers also claim her dad cut her off shortly after we met because she wouldn't join their family business. Austin doesn't need to know that, though. I might not want anything to do with her, but I'm not going to spread rumors even if they make me doubt our entire relationship. *Was she only here for my money?* She grew up accustomed to the finer things in life. No matter what she says, I know she doesn't make enough as an influencer to maintain the lifestyle she wants.

"I've suspected for a while now. Things have been different."

He tilts his head to one side. "Different how?"

Fuck it. Fern will be here tonight and can help with Ronni. She'll forgive me if I get drunk and pass out. I can tell Ronni I'm not feeling well, which won't be far from the truth. I push to my feet to pour us both a drink. When I return to my seat, I savor a few sips before I can make myself say the words. It's hard to admit, but I need to get it out so I can heal. "To start, we haven't had sex in over a year. Haven't even shared the same damn bed. She wouldn't let me touch her."

He lets out a long, low whistle and shakes his head. "No wonder you've been so tense lately." If it were anyone else, I'd probably be annoyed. He doesn't mean anything by it, though. He's only trying to lighten the mood.

"The past two months, she's spent most nights away from here. She'd leave once Fern was gone for the evening; I'm guessing she waited that long to keep up appearances."

"But why?"

I throw my empty hand in the air. "Fuck if I know. I did something wrong. Felicity wouldn't tell me. Said I had to figure it out on my own before she could forgive me."

He wets his finger before running it around the rim of his glass to make it sing. "Why didn't you end it sooner then?"

"I don't know." I sigh and try to find a way to explain how little things that didn't seem like a problem at the time escalated over the years. "She wasn't always this way . . . It just got steadily worse, and I didn't notice until she was gone. Her mind games had me convinced that it was all my fault—whatever '*it*' was. I still don't know what I did to deserve it, but since it was my fault, and she wasn't leaving, it was something we could work through. It's hard to throw away that many years, man."

"People have left longer relationships for less." He abandons making music with his glass in favor of drinking from it.

He has a point, but I don't have to like it. "That's not me, though."

"'Don't throw it out, fix it,'" he says, quoting our grandfather.

"Exactly."

"You can't fix everything, Mase. What are you going to do now?"

"Hell if I know," I say again. "Fern is staying over tonight to get Ronni off to school tomorrow. I'll have it figured out before I go back to work next week."

His eyebrows slowly climb his forehead. "You're going to figure out the whole marriage thing in a week?"

I scoff at the absurdity. "No. You asked me what I'm going to do now. I'm going to figure out how to smoothly transition Ronni to life *sans* Felicity."

"If that little twerp has taught me anything, it's that kids are resilient. Don't worry about her. Worry about you, asshole. Besides, what did Felicity actually *do* anyway?"

A bitter sneer pulls up one corner of my mouth. The rest of my drink disappears in one swallow, burning all the way down. "She was here to get Ronni off to school in the morning."

"That's it?"

I eye the bottom of my glass, contemplating another round. I might've overlooked how much I relied on Felicity's help, as minimal as it was, but I also failed to notice how much she *didn't* do until I was confronted with what her absence meant for us. "That's the majority of it, but it was crucial. Felicity has a career, too. We had a knockdown drag-out about it a few years ago. Let's see . . . Ronni was . . . five, six?

"Felicity got bored with waiting around for her after school and left. I don't know what the hell she was thinking. Ronni came home to an empty house. Felicity said that it was unfair of me to expect her to put her life on hold and that she has dreams, too. After that, I renegotiated the contract with Fern. She comes in the afternoons to clean and cook and stays until I get home so I don't have to worry."

"Fern is good people."

I nod absently, my mind upstairs with her in my arms again. "Yes, she is." I don't know how I'd manage without her.

One corner of his mouth turns up, so I brace myself for orneriness. "Dude, she's fine. First time I met her was at that housewarming party Mom insisted you *had* to throw." I fight not to roll my eyes. It would be more accurate to say that Mom threw me a housewarming party because she invited people I didn't know. Which is why I asked Fern to come, both to enjoy the party and to have an extra set of eyes on my kid. *Paranoia, thy name is Mason.* "I thought she was one of Felicity's friends. A bitchy one, though, because she wouldn't flirt back."

Reflexively, my hands curl into fists. The thought of Austin flirting with her pisses me off. It's not a rational reaction at all, but it still happens. She can date if she wants to. He glances down at my fists and grins.

"Fern isn't bitchy, she is professional . . ." The need to defend her is confusing, so I shut up before I say something I'll regret later.

"You should've been tapping that for the last year," he says under his breath as he sits back and crosses one ankle over the other knee.

I shake my head, in awe of his stupidity. "If I had been, I'd be no better than Felicity. And at risk for a whopping sexual harassment lawsuit." I sink into the leather-covered cushion behind me. Now that he's said it, my mind is going there.

It's not hard to imagine her wet and wanton—for me, not him. I've never let my-self view anyone else that way before, out of loyalty to Felicity. There's no reason not to now, but maybe not an employee.

"You said Felicity has been fucking around for at least a year." I open my mouth to argue, but he holds up a hand. "Don't try to deny it. She wouldn't have cut you off if she wasn't getting it elsewhere. You should've kicked her out and moved fine little miss Fern in and played house. Problem solved."

I'm shaking my head even as the scenario he's outlining plays out in my head. "There's still the problem of the lawsuit. My love life isn't my biggest concern right now," I say to forestall whatever smartass comment he's ready to fire off. "My biggest concern is how I'm going to get Ronni to school when I'm gone before she gets up most mornings."

He shrugs. "Change your schedule. Or hers."

I shake my head at him again. It's not that easy. If I change my schedule, I don't have enough time in a day to get everything done. If I change her's . . . "Do you have any idea how whiney she'd be every day if that happened?"

He taps his chin a few times, mulling it over. "You said Fern is getting her up in the morning?"

"Yeah." I'm not sure why his brain suddenly seems to have failed him, but Austin can be flighty sometimes. He was probably too busy imagining her naked to process what I was saying at the time.

"You said the two of you have changed your contract before, to better suit Ronni's schedule, right?"

I pause before answering, wary of where he's going with this "Yes, twice, ac-tually. When I first hired Fern, she was here all day. After Ronni started school full time, I figured Felicity could handle watching her after school since she was typi-cally home anyway but asked Fern to continue cleaning and cooking."

"Seems to me like that's the answer to your problems right there. Change it again. Have Fern here every morning."

He makes it all sound so damn easy! *Nothing* is ever that easy. I can't ask her to up and change her life again. She's already rearranged it for me twice. "What am I supposed to do, ask her to move in here?" I ask. "The woman is already here for seven hours a day. Any more and she might as well live with us."

He shrugs. "Why not? You obviously trust her to take care of your daughter, and with the contents of your home. She wouldn't have to commute anymore." A suggestive smile lights up his face. "And when you can't take it anymore, she's right down the hall."

I groan and let my head fall back, visions of Fern filling my head. "You were reeling me in until you threw out that last bit. I'm not going to sleep with her."

"Why not, too good for her?"

I sit forward to glare at him because he knows better. The smirk he's wearing only serves to further piss me off. "That's not it at all!" Vee, my first love, the mother of my child, was an orphaned waitress, for fuck's sake. "Fern is a contracted employee. That makes her off-limits. You know this. I know you do. Don't dip your pen in the company ink."

"So marry her! Solve all your problems at once," he says with a laugh at his own joke. "Then she's not an employee, she's your wife. You don't have to pay her anymore. Just give her a credit card and turn her loose. And I'd like to point out, she doesn't work for the company. She works for herself and has a contract with you. No company ink here."

Look how well that turned out with Felicity . . . I moved her in, gave her a credit card, and she went wild. "Ha-ha. Very funny. I'm glad my problems are a source of amusement for you. Maybe I'll refuse Granddad's terms and step aside. You know who the next in line is, right?"

Even though it's an empty threat, it shuts him up. He cuts off mid-laugh to glare at me. "Oh no, you fucking don't. I'm not taking that bullet for you, dickweed. Work there? Fine. Whatever. Run the place? You can fuck off straight to hell. You'd best get your ass on Tinder and get to swiping. Mail-order bride. Contract bride. Whatever it takes because I'm *not* sitting in the hot seat."

It's my turn to laugh now. Growing up, there was never a doubt we'd follow in Dad's footsteps. We'd work for Granddad, then for Dad when he took over. But Dad died young, leaving me next in line to run the shipping company my great-grandfather started. Austin is more than okay with being the spare to my heir since our sister has no interest in the family business. Responsibility has never been his forte. His reaction is precisely what I expected of him.

"What the fuck is a contract bride?" I ask, genuinely curious. The term isn't one I'm familiar with, but the others are.

He shrugs carelessly. "One of my exes has a friend who was a contract bride. Her husband needed a wife, she needed money and a place to live. He agreed to help her if she helped him. They got hitched and signed a contract stating that, at the end of however many years, her debt to him would be paid in full, and she'd receive a generous sum in the divorce. It sounded like a good idea until the dumbasses went and fell in love."

"Hmmm . . ." He's not wrong; that does sound like an uncomplicated solution. Emotions make relationships complicated. There wouldn't be any in that sort of arrangement. *Lord knows I need something uncomplicated in my life.* And I'd know up front she was only in it for the money. "How does that even work, though? Did they live together? And did they insist on fidelity? Or did they sneak around?"

Austin scowls at me as if I just stated two plus three equals eight. "No, you moron. They. Fell. In. Love. From what Carly said, they fucked like rabbits. That was their choice, though. She said she read the contract once. It clearly stated both parties were expected to remain faithful to their spouse, but fulfilling the marital duties wasn't required or some bullshit like that."

His disgust makes me grin. *The consummate playboy.* "Something to keep in mind when I strike out on Tinder." He might play it casual, but I'm sure the idea is repulsive to him—not marriage, but a contracted one.

He surprises the hell out of me when he nods. "People have been arranging marriages for centuries, Mason. Love is a luxury."

One I have no interest in. I had my shot at love and have since accepted that I cannot love again. I thought I could learn to, given enough time. Felicity proved me wrong. Love isn't everything, though. Mutual respect and friendly affection are acceptable substitutes until they cease to exist. "Love might be a luxury, but a relationship without affection or sex is torture."

He shrugs and fidgets with his glass again. "I don't think it would be so terrible if you at least enjoy spending time with the woman. Or if you don't have to spend much time with her. You're already used to having an empty bed and blue balls anyway."

Stunned, I stare and wait for him to laugh and give the joke away. He doesn't, though. "It sounds as if you think I should do this."

Chapter 4

Mason

Austin nods and tosses back the last of the whiskey in his lowball. "I do. Let's weigh the pros and cons here. Pros: You're married. You take over the company. Everyone wins. When it goes down the shitter in five years, you're not upset because it was all a business arrangement with an expiration date. Ronni has a mother figure in her life for that time. She'll be a teenager by then anyway and won't take it so rough—if she even likes the woman—"

"Just stop right there!" What the hell is he even thinking? Objectively, it sounds great for someone else. Not for me, though. "I can't bring some woman into Ronni's life out of the blue. First of all, she'd know it was a hoax. Second, she needs stability. She needs a family, a mother, not someone to pretend to be for a few years because she needs a big payday."

Austin scoffs. "Because Felicity was the picture of stability." He gets up, snatches my glass, and walks to the bar. "That is like the only damn con to this arrangement, Mase. That and the no sex, but I'm sure that wouldn't be a problem long. She'd get horny too, and I'm secure enough in my manhood to be comfortable admitting you're sexy."

Squeezing my eyes shut, I groan and pull at my hair again. My brother called me sexy. This day can't get any more fucked up. "Don't ever say that again. I don't care how secure in your manhood you are. That's just weird. You're my brother."

"Just keeping tabs on the competition."

My eyes fly open and I stare at him. "Competition? I'm a twenty-eight-year-old single father. You're twenty-four, single, and free as a bird. What competition?"

He meanders back to his seat, saying, "Hey, girls like single dads. They turn their panties into puddles watching you assholes play with your adorable little devil spawn. Sometimes, I want to borrow Ronni to pick up chicks."

"I will kill you." I might even mean that. He's not using my daughter as a tool for debauchery. That is not the sort of instability she needs in her life. I never let her see me behaving that way, and I do my best to shield her from his string of short-term flings.

He laughs my threat away. "That's why I've never asked. Hell, I bet even your *'professional'* Fern gets all hot and bothered watching you take care of Ronni. Wish I was around some time to help her out with that since you obviously won't."

"You have got to stop talking about her that way!" I spit the words at him through clenched teeth. But is it the potential lawsuit, or the idea of him with her that bothers me more? I'm not sure I want the answer anymore. Fern has been a staple in my life for six years now. She's gorgeous, but I've made it this long without lusting after her. I'm not going to start now. *Too late.*

"You have got to remember Fern is a sexual being, not a robot. As uptight as she is, she probably hasn't had her world rocked in a good long time. I'm just saying, I'd volunteer to help her out if she was looking for someone to fill the position."

I tip back my whiskey and run through the stats from the last meeting until the tightness in my pants dissipates. "I am very aware that Fern is human, Austin. For the love of fuck, would you please stop talking about her and sex in the same sentence?"

"Because you want to boink her?"

"No, you asshole! Because I don't want her to fucking quit!"

"Because you want to boink her."

"So help me God, I will reach across this desk and slap some sense into you. I don't—" I can't make myself finish that sentence now. Saying I don't would be a lie. I haven't entertained such thoughts of Fern since the day we met. Until my asshole little brother sat here and talked about flirting and fucking and her.

He grins and taunts me. "Say it. Come on, chickenshit. Say you don't want to lay her on this desk and plow her 'til she screams your name! I know I want to, and I have no problem with admitting it. Where's she at? Her cheeks turn a really pretty pink when she's embarrassed. It's fun to make her blush."

I grab the edge of the desk to keep from shooting to my feet. "Leave her alone. I swear to God and all that is holy, I'll have you here washing my clothes and sweeping my floors if you make her uncomfortable enough to quit. You have no idea how hard it is to find someone reliable and trustworthy enough to look after Ronni."

"Gee, someone like a mother?"

His statement brings my brain to a screeching halt. I narrow my eyes at him, suspicious once more. "What are you getting at?"

"You need a wife. Ronni needs a mother. Look at that, you've got a Fern that already fulfills half of those requirements. She washes your clothes, sweeps your floor, cooks your meals, takes care of your kid. Find some leverage, put your ring on her finger, your dick in her box, and—"

I slam my fist down on the desk. "Enough!"

In the silence that follows, the smug bastard leans back in his chair and grins at me. "Thinking about it now, though, aren't you?"

Yes, thank you very fucking much . . . He's pushing this too hard. He came in here with an agenda. None of this is chance. "That was your plan all along, wasn't it?"

He shrugs again and kicks his feet up on my desk for half a second until I shove them off. Scowling at me, he waits until he's comfortable again to shrug. "Maybe. She's single. I've asked her out a time or two, but she always blushes and politely blows me off."

I swallow hard. *He did* what? I have no right to be pissed, but I am. The reason eludes me, but it doesn't matter. Before I say anything I'll regret, I take a deep breath and count to ten. "What does that have to do with anything?"

"She doesn't date—and don't even try to argue that. She flat out told me. That means she's available."

My pulse pounds in my ears. "So, you came here to convince me to ask Fern, the one reliable constant in my daughter's life aside from myself, to be my contract bride, simply because you know she's not in a relationship?"

"That's part of it," he says, unperturbed by my obvious disdain for his plan.

I scrub my face with my hands, wishing I could somehow take back this entire conversation. "I fucking hate you." Not true. Not at all. I love my brother. I only don't particularly like him right now. This master plan of his is ridiculous. And I'd love to punch him for asking her out.

Austin crosses his arms behind his head and leans his chair back to balance on two legs. "Only because you can't stop thinking about her naked now."

"How could you do this to me? How do you not see how wrong this is?"

"'Cause I love you. It isn't wrong if you're both willing. And I don't want to end up CEO of Chambers Freight."

All I can do is shake my head. He's asking me to rob myself and Fern of our chances to find happiness so he won't run the risk of shouldering some responsibility. I could do it to myself, but I can't ask anyone else to give up years of their life like that. It would be neither right nor fair.

"But why Fern, for God's sake?"

"Because she's put up with Felicity's uppity bullshit this whole time, so you know she's dedicated. And she loves your little girl like her own. I'm only a visitor here, and I've seen that, so I know you have. And because I've noticed the way she peeks at you when Felicity isn't around, and you aren't paying attention. Trust me, she'd like for you to lay her across—"

I slam my fist on the desk again. "Would you please fucking stop? When I leave this room, I have to go spend time with my eight-year-old daughter. I would like to do so without a fucking tent in my pants!"

He leans forward to point at me, and the front two legs of his chair slam into the floor. "Hah! Gotcha!"

"And you're wrong about that. Fern won't even look me in the damn eye. She hasn't for years. I swear she thinks my name is '*Mr. Chambers,*' and she *refuses* to call me Mason. She won't stay in the same room as me for more than a minute unless there are other people present. I'm afraid I've done something to offend her, but don't ask me what it is, or why she didn't quit because of it."

Austin wrinkles his nose. "Oh well. If I'm wrong about that part, I'm wrong. I don't think I am, though. As I said before, you're used to sleeping in an empty bed with blue balls anyway."

"I won't have a wife who can't stand to look me in the eye. For that matter, I won't have a wife who won't share my damn bed. I'm old fashioned that way, I suppose."

His eyes light up. "Actually, the habit of spouses sharing a bed is a new one among the wealthy. Being able to afford separate bedrooms used to be a mark of wealth. Only the poor had to share a bed with their spouse."

"Then I'm not that fucking old fashioned after all, I suppose!"

Austin laughs. Rat bastard. How can he do this to me? How can he expect me to fuck up a good thing? "Get out of my house!" I point toward the front door for emphasis.

"You don't mean that. You're just pissy because I'm right." He rises and saunters to the bar again, a glass in each hand though I never noticed him take mine.

That's the sad part. He's not wrong. Fern does most of the things a wife would do. That's what I pay her for, and she's damn good at her job. He is also right about her devotion to Ronni. When he puts it that way, she's probably the one woman in the world who would be suitable for the job. I'm sure there are others who would learn to adore Ronni as Fern does, but none would have the instant connection the two of them did. Would it be such a stretch to go from one contract to the other? I'm already paying her to do everything but sleep with me. Regardless, I can't ask Fern to give up her chance at real love. It wouldn't be fair to her.

I could give her a good life . . . We might not have love, but she wouldn't lack for anything else. It would be all too easy to dote on her. She could quit her other jobs and do something she enjoys. Austin has proven I wouldn't mind having her in my bed, so she wouldn't lack physical affection if she wanted it. I can imagine her small body tangled with mine, her legs around my waist, heels digging into my . . .

"Dammit, make it stop!"

He smiles as he sits again and offers me a bottle of water, but there's nothing innocent about it. He's not even attempting to pretend anymore. "Make what stop? The mental picture of her tits bouncing and her curls fanned out across all these papers here?"

I massage my temples, hoping that doing so will somehow erase the images. "Yes, you asshole. Six years she's worked here, and I've never once had a thought like that about her! Six fucking years!"

He drops his chin and stares at me. "There's something wrong with you. I've thought things like that about her every damn time I've seen her. You wanna know what I think it is? You didn't let yourself consider her that way until I planted the seed. You didn't want to when you met her because the new hadn't worn off things with Felicity, and you were still a little hung up on Vee. And she was working for you; therefore, it was 'wrong' even if you removed Felicity from the situation."

"Of course, I didn't! She's my fucking nanny! Do you know how hard it is to work with someone when you can't stop wondering what they look like naked? Or what they tas— No. Not going there. I'm not. Stop fucking laughing at me!"

A soft knock at the door pulls a groan from me. Thank God the desk will hide the situation I've got going on in my pants because it's Fern out there. Len knocks with more authority, and Ronni beats on the door with both fists. Only Fern would knock so unobtrusively. *That word fits her to a T.*

"Come in," I call, glaring my brother into silence, threatening a slow, painful death with my eyes.

Fern opens the door just enough to poke her head into the room. "Sorry to bother you, Mr. Chambers," she says, her eyes fixed firmly on the floor between the door and the desk. "The steaks you wanted are marinating in the fridge, and I've lit the grill so it'll be hot when you're ready. Ronni's room is clean, and she's doing her homework. If now is a good time, I'll ask Len if he is available to take me home?"

She turns her last statement into a question. It's so hard to keep my voice normal now that I keep imagining those big curls in my hands while I . . . *Fuck you, Austin.* "Whenever works for you. I'm not going anywhere today." If she notices that the words sound strained, she doesn't react at all.

My brother gives me his trademark crooked smile, which only makes an appearance when he's up to no good. He turns around in his seat. "Miss Fern, do you happen to have an extra steak? If so, maybe I'll stick around."

I'm silently willing her to say no, but she won't. With Felicity gone, there's no reason we won't have enough for him.

She smiles at him, actually *at* him, which makes me insanely jealous, and says, "Absolutely, Mr. Chambers." Her eyes drop to the floor before she addresses me once more. "Ronni asked to help, and she knows where all the sides are and how to warm them when you gentlemen are ready."

"You won't be here?"

Her lashes flutter, and she meets my confused gaze with one of her own. "N-no, Mr. Chambers. It'll take me at least a couple of hours, I think." She takes a deep breath and lets it out slowly, and plasters on a smile that's as real as a three-dollar bill.

"Why so long?" It can't take that long to shove a few things in a bag and walk out the door again. Hell, I do it all the time for business trips.

Her smile disappears. "I- I . . . I really don't know how long it'll take. I don't live nearby, and since I always take the bus, I don't know how long the drive will take. And I've got a few things I have to take care of when I get there."

"Why not wait until after dinner?"

Panic flashes through her eyes for a moment before she explains, "By the time I'm done with cleanup and whatnot, it'll be pretty late. I don't want to keep Len waiting that long. It's fine, Mr. Chambers." She hesitates, something else on the tip of her tongue, and it's not, "I'll clean up everything when I get back." But that's all she gives me.

She closes the door behind her before I can press the matter, and I'll look like a fool if I chase her. *Who the hell turns down a steak dinner? And what was that panic about?* She's not an herbivore; I've watched her eat a cheeseburger like it was manna from Heaven. *God, that was hot.* Even I took notice of that.

Instead of chasing her down to demand answers, I go to the kitchen with Austin hot on my heels, pestering me with questions that I ignore. I'll put her steak aside and grill it when she returns. Problem solved.

I yank open the refrigerator door and find the sides she was talking about, all my particular favorites. As promised, three steaks are marinating in a container, but there's not another to be found anywhere. *Why only three?*

Since Ronni helped Fern cook, I dash up the stairs to her room. She'll know where the other is.

"Hey Rice," I call as I walk through the door. She hates it when I call her Rice, but she started it by pointing to a Rice-A-Roni box in the supermarket one day and declaring it was her name when she was first learning to spell. "Why did Fern only put three steaks in to marinate? There should be four. I couldn't find another one."

Ronni looks up from her homework and blinks at me slowly. "Because that's all we have?" she says as if she can't believe I even have to ask. *God, help me. She got her mama's sass.*

I shake my head. "There should be four. She told your uncle Austin there was enough for him to join us for dinner."

She rolls her eyes with all the drama of a teenager and turns back to her homework. "Fern hasn't eaten dinner here in ages, Daddy. Felicity said she couldn't anymore."

I barely hold back my growl. "What? Why? If she wasn't going to eat, why were there three steaks?" I know for a fact that meals were part of our arrangement when we re-negotiated her contract hours because she would be staying so late. I insisted. It's the least I can do. She hasn't been at the table, but I never thought anything of it.

Ronni's head comes up long enough to roll her eyes at me again. I'm not sure where she picked up that habit, but we're going to have to have a talk about it soon if she doesn't knock it off. *Like hell, you aren't . . . Felicity did that all the damn time.* She smiles guiltily at my glare. "The third steak was supposed to be Felicity's.

Fern was going to put it in the freezer, but she said it was a good bet Uncle Austin would be here for dinner."

I can't argue that. Austin loves food but hates to cook. Sometimes, I think he stops by at dinner time just to be invited to stay.

Ronni looks over my shoulder to grin at her uncle. It's short-lived, though. "Felicity was mean to my Fern when I wasn't around to stop her. I tried to get Fern to eat with us a few days ago, but Felicity heard and called Fern into the office. I know it was wrong, but I listened outside the door to make sure Fern didn't need help.

"She said only family and guests get to eat with us, not the help. And she couldn't eat in the kitchen, either, because it is not your responsibility to feed her. Then, she said something about Fern needing a reminder about the rules and went on and on about how Fern isn't supposed to talk to you, or look at you, or be alone with you."

My blood boils. I came up here for answers, but I didn't expect her to be so enlightening. I want to dismiss what she's saying as jealousy, but it's not like before when she would make up ridiculous reasons to be upset with Felicity, and there's nothing for her to gain from getting her in trouble now. Ronni never wanted to share me with Felicity, which led to many petty disagreements between the two of them.

Or so I thought. I was the first one to suggest that Veronica's possessiveness was the root of their problems when I introduced her to Felicity and they didn't hit it off. That became the explanation for everything after that. But what if I was wrong all this time? What if the things I dismissed as fabricated bids for attention actually happened the way Ronni said?

Ronni doesn't give me time to pursue that train of thought. "I asked Fern what Felicity was talking about, but she told me Felicity was doing what she thought was best, and I should forget about it. But I heard Felicity tell Fern if she broke the rules, she'd fire her. And she'd tell all her other clients she caught her sleeping with you. I thought that was ridiculous. Fern doesn't sleep here; she has her own house. And if she did, why would she sleep in your bed? But Fern told me not to mention it to anyone, not even you. And she *never* tells me to keep anything a secret from you. I didn't tell, though, because I was afraid of getting Fern in trouble. But Felicity is gone now, so Fern can't get in trouble for any of that stupid stuff anymore. Right, Daddy?"

"Right, Rice." My heart sinks into my toes. Felicity was belittling my most important employee right under my nose. And, for some reason, Fern took it on the chin like a champ and kept going.

Ronni scrunches her nose, and her mouth draws into a sad frown. "Daddy, you'll fix it, right? Her tummy talks a lot at night. She always tells me not to worry and that she'll be fine, but it makes me sad because I don't think she eats dinner. She told me once that she goes to bed as soon as she gets home."

I'm so disgusted I could be sick, but I have to pull myself together and hide it from Ronni, or she'll figure out she should've told me, and I would have stopped it all. If that happens, she'll be even more upset. I can't fucking believe Felicity would do that to Fern. *The woman is a fucking saint to have stuck around.* "Fern probably eats on her way home, but I'm going to fix it, Ronni. Thank you, baby girl. Finish your homework now, okay?"

"'Kay, Daddy."

The figurative Great Wall of China Fern keeps between us makes perfect sense now. She spent the last five and a half years walking on the razor's edge of my ex's jealousy. She's probably too afraid I'll take Felicity back again to get comfortable, no matter what I say, because I always have in the past. And I allowed Felicity to distract me all this time, so I never noticed until she was gone.

I thought that I was the only one suffering because of Felicity, but I was clearly wrong. I don't know how, but I'll fix this. Felicity will never set foot in this house again, and Fern's days of walking out my door hungry are over.

Chapter 5
Fern

There's something satisfying about seeing Felicity's things in boxes at a consignment shop. Len navigates toward my apartment without any input from me once we've completed the drop-off. It's like he knows where he's going. I wouldn't be surprised if he does. Len just knows things. Since security is part of his job, I suppose it makes sense.

This presents me with a problem. I can't have Len dropping me off at my door; it'll bring me nothing but grief on several fronts. He'll get all protective. He'll tell Mr. Chambers, who will want to know why the hell I'm living in a shitty apartment in a dangerous part of town. There's also the reason this part of the city is unsafe. Mr. Chambers's hundred-thousand-dollar car will draw attention. If one of the local thugs sees *me* in it, they're going to get ideas.

I've done a decent job of flying under the radar here. Things were a little dicey at first but smoothed out once some of my neighbors adopted me. Having them helps when I miss my parents and my two sisters. I do little things to help them out because it's just what I do, and someone needs to help them. In return, they look out for me. If the gang targets me, they'll have a swarm of their loved ones chasing them down, *las chanclas* at the ready.

I spend at least an hour putting out little fires after I get home from the Chambers' every evening. My super gives me a break on the rent because I take care of half of the things he's too lazy to do. *Totally worth it on every level.*

But I can't let Len or this car get within sight of my apartment.

I sit forward and lean against the back of the seat in front of me. I wanted to ride up front, but he insisted I should sit in the back like a right proper lady. *Hardy har har.* "Hey, Len? Turn right up here, 'kay?"

He doesn't as much as glance my way in the mirror. "Your address is the other direction," he says in his soft, rumbly voice.

"Yeah, I know." *Obviously, I know. I live there.* "Look, it's not a good idea to take this car into my neighborhood, okay? I don't care how big of a badass you are, my friend. Let's just park it somewhere safe, and I'll walk. I won't be long, I swear."

"Out of the question. If it's not safe for the car, it's not safe for you. Mr. Chambers would rather you return in one piece than the car."

So much for reasoning. That simple statement warms me inside as much as it infuriates me. Len is stubborn as the day is long, though. *And mistaken.* But once he has something in his head, there's no changing his mind. So I sink back into my seat and pray the bangers are all busy elsewhere.

He completely ignores me when I tell him to wait in the car. I expected nothing less, but I hoped telling him instead of asking him would make a difference. After all, he's used to taking orders from the person in the back seat of this car. I guess some things aren't ingrained. Or maybe my voice isn't deep enough.

So a five-foot, ten-inch tall hunk of tall, dark, and scary muscle follows me from one apartment to the next while I do my thing, displaying the patience of a saint, especially with the ladies. They lose their shit when he answers their rapid-fire Spanish in rapid-fire Spanish. By the time we get to my door on the top floor, he's acquired a heaping plate of tamales, some candies, more compliments than I care to count because he took care of things I couldn't, and ten times as many hints that I'm single and grandmother approved.

I fit my key into the lock, talking to him over my shoulder all the while. "Okay, I'll be right out. Wait here."

Of course, he shoulders the door open and follows me on in. There's not a damn thing I can do to stop him unless I want to resort to violence, and I don't. I actually like Len, just not very much right now. Not only that, but my chances of besting him in any sort of physical altercation where I'm unarmed are zilch. It would most definitely not be a fair fight, and the odds would not be in my favor, so I'm not going to pick it.

"Or come on in," I say on a sigh. My cheeks are already heating up. My place is nothing spectacular. I don't spend enough time here to care. That doesn't mean I like to let people in to judge. Most of the time, I find my lack of material possessions oddly freeing. I could carry everything important to me out of this apartment in one trip and never look back, just go where the wind takes me. Of course, it would be the wind because my bank account won't get me far at all.

Other people don't see things the way I've learned to, though. They pity me because I don't have things—any things, really—and because this apartment is atrocious. It might *look* horrendous, but it's as clean as hours and hours of scrubbing my hands raw can make it, it's warm, and it's dry.

Besides, I've been squirreling away ten bucks here and there to pay a deposit on a nicer place. The money I'll make tonight will put me closer to making that a reality. Rent will be higher, so I'll have less money to put toward my bills, but I'll be safer and won't have as much travel time, so I can take on more houses to make up the difference. Maybe even start saving to go back to school.

Len frowns but seals his lips.

I glance around my living room, analyzing it through a stranger's eyes. I have a bean bag chair, a laptop, and a laptop tray I Frankensteined a leg back on with scavenged parts. If Len makes it as far as my bedroom, he'll find a mattress on the floor covered with black sheets I bought at a second-hand store—black because all the others had questionable stains. I'm sure these do too, but I can't see them, and that's enough for my peace of mind.

My kitchen, at least, has a full range of appliances and a table and chairs. Because they came with the apartment. I don't have the money for luxuries *and* bills.

"I'll be five minutes," I say again.

"Why?" he calls after me as I rush down the hall. The more time he has to think, the worse off I'll be. I need to hurry.

"Because it won't take me long to pack what I need? I'm kinda low maintenance," I call back.

"Why do you live like this?"

I shrug, then remember he can't see me. "Things cost money."

"Boss pays good."

Mr. Chambers does pay good, but I still don't make enough. "Got more places to put money than money to put in them," I say, hoping that'll be the end of it. And it is. He doesn't say another word until he bids me a good night outside Mr. Chambers's mansion.

I sigh to myself and try the door. It's open, so Len taps the horn and drives away. He lives in a little house next to the garage. He's let me in numerous times since Felicity confiscated my key years ago. I can't prove it, but I swear she messed around on Mr. Chambers the entire time they were together. Cheaters are always paranoid. She was either afraid I'd catch her, or that Mr. Chambers was sneaking around with me. The help is always the first to catch the blame because we're easily accessible and apparently desperate for a good lay . . . *Fucking bitch.*

When the front door closes behind me, Mr. Chambers's voice echoes from the kitchen, "Fern?"

"Yes, Mr. Chambers," I call back, groaning inwardly. I hoped to slip in unnoticed and finish up my work for the evening without another odd encounter. He asks too many questions now that his head isn't buried up Felicity's ass. Shouldn't he be doing whatever it is people with families do after dinner these days? Watching television or playing board games, reading books?

He steps out of the kitchen and smiles at me. "Have you had dinner?"

I blink stupidly and fight the wave of anxiety that comes any time I have to talk to him. Belatedly, I smile. "I'll clean up the kitchen now, Mr. Chambers," I say, hoping to deflect. I don't want to lie to him.

His smile fades away. "Did you eat?" he asks insistently.

I swallow hard and hold my head high, focusing on his chin instead of his eyes. It at least gives the illusion I'm meeting his gaze. "No, Mr. Chambers."

The smile powers up again. *Gah, that smile should be illegal.* "Good, we waited. Why don't you go put your things away? I'll put the steaks on."

"But—" He *what?* Why in the hell would they wait for *me?* It's been hours! Even if it didn't take as long to get there by car, it's still well past Ronni's dinner time. And there's not enough to feed all of us. I only bought three steaks.

His smile disappears faster than his paycheck when Felicity goes shopping. "We went to the store. There's plenty, and you're not going hungry."

My face must have given me away. *Oh shit.* It's gonna hit the fan now. I'm not sure how, but he knows. He'll fight with Felicity when she comes back. She'll take it out on me. "Yes, Mr. Chambers," I murmur meekly, my eyes glued to his feet. Maybe he doesn't know *everything,* and this is mostly salvageable.

"Mason," he says, more than a little annoyance giving the word some bite. "Ronni thinks she's going to die of starvation, so hustle up."

"You shouldn't have waited," I whisper to myself.

He makes an unhappy sound, and I cringe. I didn't mean for him to hear. I track his feet as he crosses the foyer and stops in front of me. "You should have told me what Felicity was doing years ago."

How does he know? What *does he know?* I swallow hard and wait for him to leave.

Instead, tips my chin up with gentle fingers until I'm sucked in by his gorgeous eyes. Tingles dance across my skin, originating from the points of contact. His eyes leave mine to focus on my lips, and I could swear he's about to kiss me. And I'm not so sure I'd stop him. *What the hell is wrong with me?* He closes his eyes and lifts his chin instead, letting out a deep breath.

"She's not coming back, Fern. And Ronni told me about the rules. No more. Never again. You are family here. Go put your things away and join us for dinner, please."

"Yes, Mr. Chambers," I whisper meekly. I can take my time and get my head on straight since it's currently impersonating a Tilt-A-Whirl. As much as I want to believe Mr. Chambers has finally had enough, I don't dare to get my hopes up.

"Mason." It's more of a growl of irritation than a word at this point—the *'Mr. Chambers'* thing has always bothered him, but we've spoken more in the last six hours than we usually do in six weeks. At this point, it's become a splinter he keeps bumping but can't rid himself of. I could lay off, but some small, petty part of me enjoys his irritation.

I nod noncommittally and take a step toward the stairs. It'll be a hard habit to break.

"I want to hear you say it," he whispers harshly, stopping me in my tracks.

Sweet Jesus! My heart beats hard enough, I'm surprised it's not making my ribs rattle. Maybe following those rules wasn't such a bad thing after all. They prevented situations like that almost kiss when I wanted to close the scant distance between us. I've never thought things like that before. Until today, anyway. Check him out? Sure. Consider acting on it? Hard pass.

"Mason," I repeat, my own whisper a match for his. Saying his name like that . . . I can imagine saying it exactly like that somewhere soft and private while . . . *No! Stop it!* There's no room for things like that in my head. I'm better off alone, at least until my bills are paid. Until then, I'm just a burden. Unbidden, my thumb reaches to toy with the wedding rings I had to pawn years ago.

Widows don't need wedding rings. It's not my voice that bounces around my brain this time, but *hers.*

"There we go."

I glance over my shoulder to find myself the recipient of another one of those smiles.

It slowly fades away to be replaced by a sad little frown. "I'm so sorry. You never should have had to deal with her shit. She wasn't your boss."

My poker face is in grave danger of slipping, so I face forward again. She knew what she was doing and how to play us both. I could have tattled, but I didn't want to put him in a situation where it was her or me. Ronni is worth everything I put up with.

"No, but she is a very convincing liar. Please, Mr.—*Mason*," I emphasize his name, hoping my deliberate use of it will catch his attention and make him listen. I have no right to tell him how to live his life, but he needs to hear it. And I need to say it. Otherwise, I'm as much at fault as he is if she comes back. "For Ronni's sake, don't let her come back this time."

"I swear it."

"Ronni hates her," I continue, so happy to finally get this off my chest.

"We've talked . . . I'm sorry I didn't realize that before. Felicity will never set foot in this house again."

Relief on behalf of his sweet little girl makes my shoulders sag. I hang my head and take a deep breath. A warm hand squeezes my shoulder, urging me to turn, and I comply to find him waiting with open arms and a rueful smile that I mimick in a moment of perfect understanding.

Oh, what the hell. The man just found out his relationship was one big lie. He can use all the hugs he can get. I step forward, consciously accepting this one rather than allowing it. He sighs, and one big hand cups the back of my neck to guide my head to his chest. I don't fight it. I should, but he's so warm and so solid, and I'm so stupid like that. With a deliciously lazy slowness, he combs his fingers through my ponytail, each stroke melting my brain until it's the consistency of pudding.

"Thank you for staying. I know you only did it for Ronni."

"I'd do anything for Ronni, Mr.—" I bite off the words at the last second. Using his name doesn't feel right, and calling him *'Mr. Chambers'* irritates him, so I won't call him anything. We've covered a lot of ground in the last few minutes. The dynamics of our professional relationship have changed now that he's learning the extent of Felicity's control issues, and I need to figure out what this means. Maybe we can be friends again. *That's all this is. Friends.*

Chapter 6

Mason

Len hurries into the back yard through a cloud of smoke from the grill. He nods at me and slows his steps. His head swings left and right like he's looking for something, then he speeds up again. This is not normal Len behavior. Nothing gets to him, so why is he acting paranoid?

I turn and survey the yard myself. Nothing and no one is out of place. It's Austin, me, the grill, Ronni's play set, and patio furniture. I make a full circle, but the only suspicious thing is Len. He continues to glance about until he stops beside me and shoves his phone in my face.

"What am I looking at?" I ask, relaxing because the picture he's showing me doesn't seem to be an immediate threat. Yeah, it's a shitty part of town, but what of it? Is he suggesting we need to donate more money to community restoration? I can talk to Granddad about it tomorrow. However, the apartment complex in the picture doesn't appear to be sturdy enough to withstand a stiff breeze. It's a lost cause. Tearing it down before it goes on its own and someone dies is the best course of action.

"You told me to take Fern home." For all that he's acting strange, his reply is as gruff as ever.

"Uh-huh. What's that got to do with this?"

He glances over his shoulder toward the house once more. "That's her home. Scroll through."

His words cut through the list of ideas I'm creating to attempt to make up for years of Felicity mistreating Fern and upsetting Ronni, including VIP passes to

Disneyland for the three of us. Assuming Fern would enjoy a trip with Ronni. And me.

"What?" I snatch the phone from his hand and swipe through the photos. Most of them are of the building's exterior, but there's also one of the lobby and a hallway.

"You're joking, right?" The last picture is one of an empty room with carpet so stained and dingy that if guessing the original color was a drinking game, someone would probably die of alcohol poisoning. In addition to the cringe-worthy flooring, there's some lovely wallpaper—if you're into circa 1970 home accents—peeling from the walls. A mostly-flat beanbag chair and a weird little table that was the recipient of a back-alley leg transplant round out the overall wretchedness of the room.

From the corner of my eye, I watch him shake his head. I can't rip my eyes away from the screen long enough to acknowledge him. "No, I'm not. She's living in the heart of gang territory. The only reason she hasn't been found dead somewhere is that she made friends with the elders in her building and looks after them. I had three women old enough to be my grandmother dropping hints about what a fine wife she would make. I asked her about it. I quote, 'Got more places to put money than money to put in them.'"

"Shit." I should have known this. Her address should have been on her application. *It was, she's moved.* "This is . . ." I want to rant and rave and throw things. It kills me that someone I'm responsible for in a roundabout way is living in such terrible conditions.

"Unacceptable?"

"Yes. Definitely. No one should live like this."

"I agree. I have space . . ."

It would be a tidy solution, but the idea of them living together pisses me off, like the idea of her and Austin. Especially after his comment about what a good wife she'd make. Such things didn't bother me before my brother proposed his harebrained scheme. *Thanks, asshole.*

I don't own her, though. She can do as she pleases, but I've got to do something to get her out of that situation before she ends up dead. Eventually, she'll step on the wrong toes, or someone will see harming her as a power play.

"I'll think on it," I say instead of outright dismissing his suggestion. After the talk with Austin earlier, this all feels like it's happening by design.

Speaking of Austin . . . The asshole sidles closer and takes Len's phone. After glancing through the pictures, he glares at me and lifts an eyebrow as if to say, *'I told you so.'* His suggestion would solve a lot of problems. That still doesn't mean marrying her is the right idea.

"I'll talk to her after dinner."

Len nods his approval and takes his phone.

I know what he's going to say, but I ask anyway because I picked up extras. "Would you like to join us for dinner, Len?"

"Thanks, but no, thanks, Boss. Fern's friends sent me home with homemade tamales. I just came to show you the pictures."

Chapter 7

Mason

There's something in the atmosphere over dinner I can't quite place. It's familiar—like it should have been here all along, but I'm just now realizing it hasn't been. Ronni insisted on eating in the dining room instead of the kitchen, and she set out the fancy china. She put me at the head of the table, where I always sit, but the other three places are all set on the same side so she can sit between Austin and Fern.

When she drags them in, holding each by the hand, she puts Fern immediately to my right. I regret that Len opted not to join us. I wanted him here to diffuse the tension. Since Austin knows Fern's living situation, he's doubly determined to prove to me a contract marriage would solve all our problems. Hers. His. Mine. The only time he shuts up about it is when someone else is nearby, but I'm sure he can find a way to sneak in some pointed comments.

Surprisingly, he keeps it to himself, and dinner passes without mishap.

"So, Fern . . . What's this cake I keep hearing so much about from my darling niece?"

Ronni's eyes get as big around as silver dollars and light up. "Sheet cake? Please, Fern?"

Fern makes a show of checking her watch—an archaic fitness tracker she's always worn. *I'm amazed it still works.* "Rainbow, it's after eight o'clock. You need to be in the bath."

"Please? Daddy?" Ronni turns her silver dollar eyes my way, begging me to make an exception.

"You have school in the morning." I wouldn't mind this once, but I don't want to undermine Fern.

"Damn," Austin mutters, barely audible under Ronni's, "Awwww!"

Fern bites her lip, waffling. "I'll make you a deal, Ronni."

My daughter immediately perks up and is ready to offer her soul in exchange for whatever Fern is about to promise. "What's that?"

Big green eyes turn my way, seeking something from me. What, I do not know, but I raise my eyebrows in a silent query, waiting for the details. "Cake for breakfast?"

Ronni's whole body crumples. "Dad will never go for that." She's right, but I hold my tongue and let it play out. I can't resist the pull of Fern's eyes. I'd probably take Ronni to breakfast in a chocolate shop if she asked me to right now.

Fern correctly interprets my silence for permission. She turns back to Ronni, leaving me dazed, lowers her voice, and takes on a conspiratorial tone. "Your dad won't be here for breakfast."

"Then . . . who?"

Fern's wide eyes dart my way again, afraid she's made a mistake. I wanted her to be here when I told Ronni so we could both enjoy her excitement. If Fern is going to get credit for cake for breakfast, I get this. "Fern will, and I am okay with cake for breakfast this once."

I'm not sure which excites her more. Ronni shoots to her feet and jumps up and down. "Really?"

"Really."

"Yes!" The word is squealed at the top of her lungs, loudly enough to shatter eardrums. She hurries to me and throws her arms around my neck before covering my face in kisses. She releases me to give Fern the same treatment, forcing me to lean with her or shake her off because she isn't letting go. Fern tries to turn sideways in her seat but isn't fast enough, and Ronni pulls her off balance. Fern flings an arm out, grabbing my shoulder to keep herself from falling. We find ourselves in a group hug that feels way too damn right.

Over Ronni's head, Austin is watching us with a superior smirk on his face.

I clear my throat and disengage from the tangle of arms, even though it's the last thing I want to do. "But you have to go take your bath now."

"Okay!" She gives us each one more hug and kiss and runs upstairs, still cheering to herself.

Fern sighs happily and stands. "Gentlemen, I have a cake to make. Thank you for dinner. It was wonderful."

Her praise fills me with an overwhelming sense of contentment. She gathers dishes, but I jolt to a stand and take them from her. "Then we'll clear the table. You did most of the cooking, after all."

"Go ahead. We've got this. After all, I did ask you to take on extra work," Austin says smoothly. He stands and gathers his plate and Ronni's.

"If you insist," she says with a smile. Still, she doesn't leave until her hands are full.

I gather faster and follow her out. I don't want to be alone with Austin. He's going to say things I don't want to hear.

He steps into my path and skewers me with determined eyes. "That's the one," he whispers. "Even if you don't love each other, you'll be happy together. Ronni would never know you're not a 'real' family. Every night could be like that."

"You're insane," I say under my breath. "A contract marriage is not what Granddad has in mind. He wants me to have a *real* family, like ours."

"He didn't specifically say you can't. He never has to know. You three play house quite well. And you'd make a beautiful family."

Vee . . . My heart breaks again for that once-in-a-lifetime love I can never hope to experience again. We had the world by the ass until the condom broke and we got Ronni. Life was a new kind of perfect after that. Until a nurse rushed my screaming daughter from the room, and another shoved me out with no explanation. Vee hemorrhaged. And I didn't even get to tell her goodbye. I was a twenty-year-old single father with a broken heart and no idea what I was doing.

He's right, though. It would be so easy, dinner proved that. It was flawless—like we've been parenting her together for years. But I suppose we have, in a roundabout way.

"You're right." Admitting it nearly chokes me. "But you're wrong. How can I ask her to throw away years of her life when her Vee is out there somewhere?"

Serious isn't something Austin does, so his somber expression surprises me. "Maybe *you're* her Vee? And maybe she's your new Vee?"

I recoil, the words stinging worse than a slap. I can never replace Vee. Losing her destroyed me. I can never love another woman like that again; I proved that with Felicity. Without another word, I shoulder my way by. This conversation is over.

Smiling at Fern after my brother's verbal slap in the face takes some work, but I dump the dishes in the sink and try my best. It's not her fault. I can't lash out at her.

Fern is different since that conversation by my front door, more confident in my presence. She smiles back and turns her attention to measuring the flour and sugar she'll need for the cake my mouth is already watering for. *But is the cake or the woman more tempting?* The voice in my head sounds suspiciously like Austin's. Even more disturbing, I'm not sure if I can supply an answer I like.

Austin follows me in and takes over a barstool opposite where she's working, leaning forward on his elbows like an overeager kid to watch her. His innocuous questions go in one ear and right out the other, and her answers barely register because I'm waiting for him to throw me under the bus. But also, because Vee now weighs heavy on my mind.

Veronica Anne Brown. Vee for short, because her hated given name was *"too fancy for an orphan."* Growing up in an orphanage sucked the happy-go-lucky out of her, or so she said, leaving her cynical. She also said I was idealistic enough for both of us, and that was why we worked well together. She kept me grounded, but

I helped her fly. I fell in love at first sight, but convincing her took some work. *I'd do it all over again.* Eighteen months together, then she was gone.

She would want me to be happy now, but she took that part of me with her.

"Daddy! I'm ready for my story!" Ronni's familiar call pulls me from my reverie. I shove thoughts of Vee firmly into the back of my mind where they reside and excuse myself. Once Ronni's story is read, I can talk to Fern about her living arrangements. Austin is at least right about that, even if that wasn't his idea. Fern needs a better home, and I need help. I can't focus on either thing with Vee in my head.

***

Ambling into the kitchen, I catch Fern teasing my brother. "Can I trust you to follow simple instructions?"

"Maybe . . ." He somehow manages to make that single word sound flirty, and I want to deck him for it. *He's lucky she's here to stop me.* For the life of me, I can't find a reason for the relieved look he sends my way when I sit beside him. He loves to flirt, apparently with her, so why is he happy I'm here?

Fern glances my way and grins. "Oh good, there are two of you now. Two men should be able to replace one woman. One of you come stir this."

It's so unlike her that I don't know what to make of it. No, not unlike her . . . This is how she was *before.*

"Or maybe you can't . . ." Her laughing eyes snap up to spear me in place. Whatever my brother said to her while I was gone got her to open up more than two hugs and my promises that Felicity is gone for good managed to do.

Austin beats me to the task at hand. He stands behind her, leaning around to see instead of taking the space beside her like a logical person. In an instant, blood is pounding in my ears. The air fills with tension, all of it mine. *You have no reason to be pissed. You don't want her.* There's no reason not to let them . . . Nope. I can't finish that thought.

Fern shuffles closer to the stove. She doesn't protest, so I watch passively while he folds his big hand around hers on the spoon and lets her guide him. He's not *technically* doing anything inappropriate, but it's all intentional. The bastard is doing it to taunt me, and I'm letting him. I hate every second of it too.

"Um . . . I promised Ronni that I would tell her *'good night.'* So the cake is ready to come out of the oven, and the icing is nearly done. You just need to add this," she jerks her chin toward a bowl full of chocolate chips and some sort of nuts, "to the pot and stir until the chocolate has melted. Then pour the icing on the cake and spread it evenly."

Her directions are delivered quickly, sounding a little rushed. As soon as she's done, she sidesteps around Austin and nearly runs from the room. It takes everything I've got not to chase her, and I don't even know what I'd do with her if I caught her. *Lies.*

"Damnit, Austin! I needed to talk to her about her living arrangements!" I get the oven mitts and hit him over the head with them before taking the cake from the oven as she directed, shutting it off while I'm at it.

His smile is evident in his voice when he says, "That's what you say, but what I hear is you needed someone to awaken your inner caveman and make you realize you've already claimed your woman. Truthfully, I think you claimed her six years ago and have been in denial all this time."

I watch the frosting he finished ooze across the cake like it holds the answers to the universe. "I'm not a caveman. She is not mine. I claimed my woman, and she died. End of story."

"It had better fucking not be *'end of story,'* bro. I've told you; I'm not taking your place. You'll get hitched before you're thirty if it's the last fucking thing I do." He sticks a fork in one corner of the pan and scoops up a bite. He at least has the good sense to blow on it until it stops steaming before he pops it in house mouth. "Mmmm . . . Fuck you. I'm keeping her."

"Need I remind you she's a human, not an object to possess?"

"Tell yourself that, caveman."

Chapter 8

Mason

Tuesday

My stomach rumbles for the first time today, managing to time its demands to fall between the swish of the windshield wipers and the rolling thunder, so the only competition the sound has is the rain beating on the top of the car. I was too anxious to eat breakfast, though Fern's offer to cook was hard to turn down. I'm not used to someone else in the house being awake when I leave. And usually, if someone does happen to be up, they're definitely not smiling. It was a nice change.

The stab of hunger breaks me out of my mental review of my meeting long enough for me to glance around. Len will have me home soon, and I can eat lunch. As soon as the storm will allow anyway. The driving rain makes it difficult to see through the windshield clearly, even with the windshield wipers on high, turning the residential neighborhood we're passing through into abstract art. My eye is drawn to flashes of white ahead. *What the hell?*

It's not lights. Whatever it is, it's moving. But what is it? I shift around, searching for a better angle, and scoff. There's a jogger on the sidewalk. The white flashes are the soles of their shoes. *Who in their right mind jogs in a thunderstorm?* The blurry silhouette is unidentifiable in the driving rain, but something about the figure seems familiar.

Len shakes his head and sighs. "I told her to call me," he says softly as we pass. He presses the button for the caution lights and slows down to pull over, stopping a few car lengths ahead of the jogger. "Sorry, give me a few minutes to talk her into the car."

"What?" I don't know anyone who would be out in this weather. I'm not opposed to his helping a friend, though, and I'm glad he knows that.

He points behind us with his thumb. "That's Fern. This is her route. That's why I came this way."

You have got to be shitting me. Lightning flashes across the sky chased immediately by a clap of thunder, triggering an overwhelming urge to shake some fucking sense into her and get her in the damn car to keep her safe. *Dad reflex.* Women are referred to as mother hens when they try to take care of their people. There's no such term for a man; we're just overbearing. If my people are safe, I don't give a rat's ass what they call me.

"I've got her," I tell him. I can't imagine why he thinks it'll take some time to talk her into a ride. She's a smart woman—most of the time.

"If you insist. I won't fight you to stand out in this mess and try to outwit her." He hands an umbrella over the seat and wishes me luck. Hopefully, I don't need it.

I'm soaked to the skin in the seconds it takes to open the umbrella. I don't take my eyes off Fern, though. Her head is down in a futile attempt to keep the rain out of her eyes, so she doesn't notice me until she's close enough to reach out and touch. Once she does, she skids to a stop and backpedals to a safe distance. There's no fear in her eyes when they meet mine, just determination and a healthy dose of fight, though her hands fly into a defensive position in front of her face.

"Goin' my way?" I have to shout to be heard over the storm, so it doesn't come across nearly as playful as it was in my head.

I watch her gasp, noting the way her lips part and her chest rises because the sound of it is lost in another clap of thunder. "Mr. Chambers?" Again, no sound, but I've watched her say the words often enough, I'm familiar with the way her lips move to shape the words.

"C'mon, Fern, get in the car." In case she didn't hear me, I hold my arm out in an invitation to join me. Comprehension smooths away the lines at the corners of her eyes.

She looks around warily, but nods. As soon as I open the door, she practically dives into the back seat. I follow too soon and land halfway in her lap. She shrieks and giggles and shoves me, successfully sliding herself away since she's not big enough to move me.

"I'm glad I didn't bet you now, Boss," Len says. I meet his eyes in the rearview mirror, confused by his statement. "I was gonna bet you fifty that it took you ten minutes to talk her into accepting a ride."

"Off-f-f-f, L-l-l-len," Fern says, fighting to get the words out through the shivers racking her body.

"What?" I ask.

Len chuckles and checks for oncoming traffic. "She's politely telling me to eff off."

"I s-should've-ve-ve s-s-s-stayed out-t-t-tside."

"No, you shouldn't have. It's not safe." My suit jacket isn't dry, but it's at least warm. I shrug out of it and drape it around her narrow shoulders.

She quickly wiggles around until she's adorably engulfed, but the shivering doesn't subside. Taking care of her results in the same sense of satisfaction that comes from caring for my daughter. However, if I were dealing with Ronni, I'd pull her closer to stop the shivers. I have the warmth to share.

I pushed my luck far enough with Fern yesterday. Things were different this morning. Better. We might be on the right track to being friends again, but a hug here and there isn't cuddling in the back seat of a car. Even if we aren't alone, and she is freezing.

We're not far from home now. I'll still feel guilty, but she'll be fine.

"Th-Thanks for s-stopping."

"Anytime," Len says. "Why didn't you call?"

"You were b-busy!" She must be getting warmer because her stuttering is subsiding, taking some of my guilt with it.

"You could have waited!"

They lock eyes in the mirror, as much as he can while driving anyway, and I know he's in for it. "It's not your job to ferry me around!"

He flings a hand skyward. "Special circumstances!"

"It wasn't storming when I took off!"

"Don't hand me that! It's been thundering for the last hour! Thunder means you keep your scrawny rear inside and phone a friend. Not take your chances."

This has the makings of an old argument, one where they each know what the other is going to say next and can drag on for ages. My siblings and I have some of those. Since I'm on Len's side, I decide to chime in, just as Mom did when we were younger. "Knock it off!"

That earns me nearly identical scowls. "Fern, you should've waited. For that matter, *I* could have waited. I'm in no hurry. The point is, you can always call Len for a ride."

Fern crosses her arms over her chest and turns her glare on the window. The rest of the short ride home is quiet. Even the rain slows down so as not to make too much noise.

Len gets out to open her door and takes her hand to help her from the car, as he would for any other woman. "Told ya so," he says with all the maturity of a toddler.

I straighten up in time to see him stick his tongue out at her, which surprises me more than their argument. He's not exactly the playful sort. Competent. Steadfast. Intimidating. Those are all words I associate with Len. Not playful. *Is he* flirting?

Over to the top of the car, I watch her reach up and gently pat his cheek. Something suspiciously akin to jealousy flares to life in my chest, until she withdraws her hand and fakes a jab at his solar plexus. She was only lulling him into a false sense of security. He catches her wrist and uses her hand to pat her on the head.

"There, there, little one," he says over her growl as she struggles to stop him. "Everyone has to be wrong sometimes."

She flips him the bird with the same hand once he frees her, and flounces away.

Smirking, he asks, "Still not gonna call, are you?"

She doesn't look back. "Not unless I'm dying!"

I wait until the door to the house closes behind her. "I didn't know the two of you were such good friends."

Len frowns at me and takes his time to answer. "Fern is everyone's friend, but *she* only has acquaintances, with few exceptions."

What the hell is that supposed to mean? Fern surely has many friends. "I don't understand."

He shrugs, turning toward the side door of the garage. "If you can't figure it out, you don't deserve to be her friend."

Fern

A door closes, causing me to jump. *No one can hurt me here.* There's a reason those goons waited until I was away from here to approach me. They don't want to be seen near this place. Sighing, I check the mirror once more. My lip is a little swollen, but with a bit of luck, no one will notice.

The familiar sharp raps of Mr. Chamber's Oxfords on the kitchen tile stop just inside the door, where he always takes his shoes off. *He's been out there for a long time.* Len probably unloaded all of his best 'Fern is so stubborn' stories on him.

Think happy thoughts. "There's a towel in the dryer!" I shout while I run down the stairs. My cheerful tone comes across a little forced. *Too happy! Dial it back!* I don't need Mr. Chambers paying too much attention to me right now. He's more perceptive than I gave him credit for being, and my bravado from the car won't save me if he looks closely. I need a plan before I tell him what happened.

"Thank you, Fern," he calls back from the direction of the laundry room. The dryer stops when the door opens.

"No problem!" *Better.* I remember the time and frown. "Have you had lunch?" I don't know his schedule outside of when he leaves and returns, but it's lunchtime, and he's here, so probably not. I'm going to have to adjust to him being home this week. I open the refrigerator and make a note of the contents in case he's hungry.

"No, but I'm starving. What are we having?"

"Options are BLTs or last night's leftovers. Whatever you don't have now will be dinner. I need to leave early tonight." If I can get to my apartment while the sun is still up, I'll be a little safer.

"Sandwiches are fine, thank you."

Perfect! Leftovers won't take long to reheat. "I'll let you know when they're ready."

"No need. I'll come back after I change."

***

Something behind me creaks, startling another jump and a shout from me. I whirl around to see Mr. Chambers wincing from the kitchen table. The noise that surprised me was the wooden chair adjusting to his weight.

"Sorry, Fern. I didn't mean to scare you."

I wave away his apology. It's not his fault I'm jumpy today, but I don't want to tell him that. Doing so might lead to questions I'm not ready to answer.

"How was your meeting?" I ask instead. It feels odd to ask him such a personal question after all this time, but I want to shift the conversation away from me. I risk a quick peek at him and am rewarded with a smile that tells me it was the right question to ask.

"Great, actually! We got the contract!" I don't need to see his smile; I can hear it in his voice.

His enthusiasm draws a smile from me. "That's wonderful!"

"I was worried I'd say something to ruin our chances, but I think I made Granddad proud today."

"Proud-*er*, maybe," I say absentmindedly while I put the finishing touches on his lunch. Plate in hand, I turn to take him his plate and find him smiling at me. "He's always been proud of you. He tells me so every time I see him."

If his smile gets any bigger, his face will crack. Something does a cartwheel in my chest. Heeding that warning, I hurry back to the counter to make myself a plate. I like it when he smiles at me, but I like it better when he smiles at other people so I can actually admire it.

"How was your morning?" he asks when I join him. I take care to sit to his right to hide the swollen side of my lip. "Did Ronni give you trouble?"

"She was great, of course."

"Good! And the rest of your morning?"

I look down and away to hide my face. "It was great." The lie doesn't come easy, but they never do.

Before, if he even noticed my reaction, he *probably* would've written it off. But things have changed. He abandons his food in favor of watching me like a hawk, his folded arms resting on the table. "Fern? What's wrong?"

"It's nothing." I'll have to tell him eventually. He has every right to know. But I'm still trying to process it all and find a solution that doesn't involve me being fired. If I can stall him just a little while longer . . .

"Has anyone ever told you you're a terrible liar?"

Only everyone I've ever fibbed to. I fight a smile with middling success. "I'm fine," I say.

"I'm a decent problem solver, you know?"

"I know." But so am I, most of the time. I've worked too hard to see my plans fall apart now.

"I'd like to help. Why don't you tell me about it?"

I smile wryly at my plate. "I'm not really the *'talk it out'* type."

And when I have a bit of free time, I'll make my way down to his basement gym and take up my problems with his heavy bag. Felicity never revoked my permission to utilize the equipment. She even helped me find a place to keep a couple sets of workout clothes.

"I didn't think you were. You seem more like the *'grin and bear it until you can break stuff'* type."

He's not right, but he's close enough to surprise me. "I don't break things. I hit things."

I quickly turn away from him, surprised with myself for admitting that. I don't talk about me. I talk to my clients about them, their families, their homes, inconsequential small talk, but never about myself. When you reveal those little pieces of yourself, you're giving them little bits of your soul. They own a part of you, and you start to care about them. Then they die, and you lose them and a little bit of yourself.

Mr. Chambers says, "I have siblings, Fern. I can take a few hits. I want to help you, and if that means letting you blow off some steam, that's alright."

I push away from the table and hurriedly gather our dishes. If I ignore him, maybe he'll go away. I'll talk to him when I'm ready, not a minute sooner, and not until I've had a chance to deal with this. Luckily, I've been saving to move. I don't have all the money I need yet, but I'm out of options.

I can't keep my mouth shut, though. "There's a perfectly good heavy bag downstairs!"

"That's not the same, and we both know it. It doesn't share your pain."

I never said I was in pain. He's making assumptions, trying to get me to admit to something. "You're fishing."

He leaves the table to lean against the counter next to the dishwasher. "I think I caught one. What happened?"

Life would be easier if I never trusted anyone. That's the problem, though. I remember what it's like to have someone to share my problems with, someone who would listen objectively and tell me I was making a mountain out of a molehill. And I miss that.

"You don't have to deal with this alone."

"Why are you doing this?"

"Because it's not fair when things are one-sided. I came to you when I had a problem. I want you to trust me enough to do the same."

And your problem got me into this mess. That's not fair at all. It's not his fault, it's mine.

He claps his hands, startling me out of my skin, and sidesteps to the stove to grab a pair of oven mitts. He puts them on and holds up his hands like he's wearing a pair of practice pads. "Right here. Talk and hit."

Have it your way. One hit, and he'll change his mind. Those mitts aren't thick enough to protect him. I jab as hard as I can, expecting the momentum to carry his hand back into his jaw, but he redirects the strike up and away.

"Five years of Karate," he says in answer to my surprise. "Talk."

I watch him for a long moment, debating. This is an olive branch. His way of attempting to rebuild bridges Felicity burnt. Maybe we're better off as we are. Neither of us tried to fight for our friendship. *No, I didn't try. He did.* I let it happen because fighting would've meant him choosing, and I'd lose. Which would mean losing Ronni, too.

Now, I'm afraid that what remains isn't strong enough to bear the load he's asking me to share. If it can't, well, I can't blame him. *Sometimes, bridges have to be built from both sides and meet in the middle.*

"Ten years of Muay Thai." I pair the sentence with a couple more jabs, testing him to see if he can really take it before I open up. "I live in a rough neighborhood."

"I know. Len showed me pictures last night. I wanted to talk to you about it, but you went to bed."

I growl at Len, not that he cares because he's not here to hear. I expected him to tattle, though, and I was prepared to reassure Mr. Chambers that I'll be moving soon. I didn't know how soon, but I do now.

"Right, well . . . guess there's nothing left to say about that then."

"So, what's going on?"

I skip to the relevant details and give him the Cliff Notes version, punctuated with punches. "Some of the gangsters followed Len and me last night. A couple of them came back here this morning, looking for me since I didn't go home. They approached me outside one of my other jobs and tried to scare me into stealing some of Felicity's jewelry for them." I put everything I've got behind my next strike to drive my following statement home. "That didn't go so well for them."

After a rage-fueled flurry of strikes, I stop to catch my breath.

He twitches his hands. "You good?"

I shake my head because if I try to talk, I'm going to do something stupid, like cry.

"Get it out. I can take it."

I cut loose again. That apartment might not be much, but it's my home. I've always known where I would lay my head at night until now. And to top it off, as soon as he isn't busy catching punches and can think about it, he's going to fire me for putting his daughter at risk. There's no guarantee they won't come back and try something, even if the gang can't get to me anymore. I made him and Ronni targets.

"You weren't running because of the rain, were you?"

I'm panting too hard to speak, so I shake my head. Just because two confronted me doesn't mean there weren't four more waiting in a car. *But I still ran back here, bringing the threat with me.* Ronni's safety should have been my priority. I failed them both.

My arms burn. Sweat pours out of me in rivers. Muscle memory is the only thing saving my form because my mind is elsewhere; I'm moving on autopilot. The first time a strike falters, he closes his hand around my fist and uses it to pull me close.

"Okay?" He makes it a question, seeking consent like he did the second time yesterday. Ronni is right; hugs are magic. I'm beyond their help, but that doesn't mean I can't help others heal.

I wave my other hand toward myself, indicating my general state of sweaty disarray. "I'm a mess."

He tosses the oven mitts on the counter. "I don't care. That's some heavy shit, and you need a hug." One arm hugs me tight while the other goes to the snarled mess that is my hair. "Better now?"

"Yeah. Thanks." And I am. It's good to have it off my chest. I can't relax, though. The other shoe will drop any second.

"So, now what are you going to do?"

I sigh because I don't have a whole plan yet, and that bugs me. "I'm moving. I've got some cash to pay a deposit, but I don't know where I'm going to go."

"I do."

A small spark of hope takes hold in my chest. Mr. Chambers knows a lot of people. His friend Gabe is a Realtor; perhaps he has a rental property open.

"Oh?" I tip my head up to look at him, pulling my hair because his fingers catch on a tangle. Guilt makes it hard to look him in the eye.

He steps back to lean against the counter and crosses his arms over his chest. "That's what I wanted to talk to you about last night. At the very least, you'll stay here again tonight. But I wanted to ask if you'd consider living here?"

"What?"

His eyebrows shoot up. "What part do I need to clarify?"

"I expected you to fire me, not offer me a place to crash."

"Why would I do that?"

"They wouldn't be targeting you if it weren't for me. And I came back here today knowing they could be following me again!"

He frowns. "That's true. But you're overlooking something: without you, they can't get to me. You're not going back there. I'll send Len to retrieve your belongings later. And Fern?"

I swallow a knot in my throat. "Yeah?"

"Where would you have gone if not here?"

I hang my head, hiding from the damnation I'm sure to see in his face once I confess my own cowardice. "I don't know. This is the safest place I could think of."

He tips my head back with a finger under my chin and smiles at me. "Exactly. We have a security system. One button closes the gate and shuts them out. And if they do get in, you let them take anything they want. You and Ronni are irreplaceable, but I can buy more stuff."

Why is he so reasonable? Doesn't he understand the danger? "But—"

He silences me with a finger to my lips. "Stop trying to find a way to blame yourself for this. We'll discuss it more over dinner. Right now, we need to file a police report."

I scoff at him. What good would that do? It's just one more thing on a mile-long list of crimes, and it might make the target on my back bigger. "They can't do anything. And I have no proof, anyway."

"It's more about due diligence than anything. And the security cameras might've caught something. Go wait in the office, please. Len and I will be right in." He nudges me toward the hall, and I'm too dazed to argue. I make it two steps before he calls after me.

"Fern?"

I stop and wait.

"Thank you for trusting me."

I nod and put one foot in front of the other. Hopefully, doing so wasn't another mistake.

"I'm proud of you."

Four words pull the rug from under my feet. No one has said that to me in years. I haven't done anything to deserve it in years. I'm not sure why I deserve it now. "Thank you," I whisper so he won't hear my voice break around the tears I'm holding back by a thread.

Chapter 9

Fern

Tuesday Afternoon

A knock on my door wakes me. "Fern?" I was expecting Mason's voice, but that's Len. *Something's wrong!* Did the gang send more people? Did the ones I met earlier press charges? Can they do that? I mean, they assaulted me first. I scramble out of bed and run to the door.

"Boss said he doesn't want you going back to your place, but you need some closure. If you want to go, we need to move now. He just left to pick up Ronni, and he'll argue if we're not gone before they get home."

He's right. Mason might have good intentions, but I need to do this to make peace with the situation I've found myself in. And if he goes alone, there's no one to watch his back. "Let's go."

There are three big guys crammed like sardines into the back seat of Mason's SUV, leaving the front open for me. They nod in sync when I climb in and look back at them. Len waits for me to buckle in before he throws it into reverse and backs out.

"They all work for Mason?" I ask, tipping my head toward the back seat.

"No. They're here for his peace of mind." His tone also tells me we're not talking about them anymore. I can be smart, sometimes, so I let it go. "What happened?" he asks.

The strangers in the back, all decked out like extras from the *Men in Black* in their black suits, ties, shoes, and sunglasses, shift almost imperceptibly, betrayed only by the slightest rustle of fabric. I suppose they should be reassuring, but they make me twitchy. I don't want them to get hurt on my behalf. Nothing I have is worth that. I also don't like the nagging suspicion we're about to be attacked by an alien life form wearing a human as a Halloween costume.

I give them the same abbreviated version I gave Mason earlier. "I've always been careful not to tell anyone who I work for so they can't try to strong-arm me into ripping him off," I add when I finish relaying the pertinent details.

Len makes an unhappy, growling noise. "We'll keep you safe while you get your things out." Knuckles crack behind me. They're a lot more confident about their chances than I am. He chuckles after a quick look my way. "Don't worry, even gang bangers have a bogeyman. They will never bother you again."

I'm sure he means it to be comforting, but it's not. It's really not.

Mason

Ronni and I lock eyes through the open window of my car. Smiling brightly, she breaks into a run and throws open the door. I watch as her face falls before she slowly climbs in.

"What's wrong, Rice Monster?"

"I was hoping Fern was hiding to surprise me."

Since Ronni usually rides home with Mrs. Sampson, I can't imagine that Fern has ever done such a thing. "Why would you think that?"

She shrugs. "I was just hoping. She'd do something like that to make me smile."

I almost invited Fern along. Seeing the footage of the thugs on the security cameras and filing her report wiped her out worse than the actual altercation. I've had a breakdown or two in my life. I know how you feel when you make it through to the other side. She needs her sleep. "Speaking of Fern, keep your voice down when we get home. She's is having a rough day, so I sent her upstairs to nap."

Her mouth puckers into a pout. "Okay, Daddy. But if she's not feeling well, why didn't she go home?"

I'm not ready to have that discussion with my daughter. She's not unfamiliar with the uglier aspects of the city, but it would break her heart to know what Fern experienced today. Besides, it's not my story to tell. Hopefully, I can distract her with her plans for the evening. "Hey, I have a surprise for you! You need to pack an overnight bag when we get home."

She sits forward to ask, "Are you going out of town again? Can Fern stay with me instead?"

"No, honey. I'm not going anywhere. You know I always warn you before I leave. You're staying with your Gigi tonight."

She slouches back into her seat. In the rearview, I watch her cross her arms and turn her head to look out the window. "Oh."

"Oh? You love staying with Gigi."

"I do, but it's more fun when I don't have school the next day so I can stay up late and watch movies and bake cookies. Can't we ask Fern to stay with me instead?"

As if there's ever a time my mother doesn't spoil Ronni her rotten . . . "Maybe next time."

"Why am I staying with Gigi on a school night? That almost never happens."

I can tell her the truth, or I can deal with the inquisition and let her talk me in circles before I tell her the truth. *She learned from the best.* "Because Fern and I are having dinner tonight."

She sits forward again, stretching the seatbelt to the limit and craning her neck. Her wide, innocent eyes are a sharp contrast to her mischievous little smirk. "Like a date?"

I brake harder than necessary for the approaching stop sign, eliciting an angry honk from the car behind me and a giggled squeal from Ronni when she loses her balance and falls back into her seat. "No, Veronica. Fern and I are renegotiating her contract."

"What's that mean?"

It's my turn, so I consider my answer while I navigate the corner. "Fern and I have an agreement about the duties I pay her for. We're just making some changes."

"But she'll still be there, right? You're not . . . letting her go?"

Her use of the term she must have learned from me makes me laugh. "No, Rice. She'll still work for us."

Guilt eats at me. She might be a kid, but she should get a say in who shares our home. She has to live with them too, and it didn't turn out so well for her last time. I let out a deep breath and ask, "How would you feel if Fern moved in with us?"

"That would make me so happy, Daddy!" She launches into an explanation of the various merits of having Fern as a housemate, most of which have nothing to do with me. I'm only there to pay the bills and bankroll their various adventures.

As great as it is that she's excited about the prospect, I can't quite name how her enthusiasm—and my exclusion from the fun—makes me feel. It hurts a little.

She waxes poetic about the slumber parties they'll have, in my room because it's the next best thing to a movie theater, for blocks before I come in as more than a walking credit card. "But you don't get to pick the movies, Daddy. Fern and I will take turns."

"Uh . . ." I clear my throat and shift in my seat. Austin's suggestion is still pinging around my brain, giving me all kinds of ideas. And now Ronni is providing more. "I think I'll leave the sleepovers to the two of you. I'm probably too boring for sleepovers. You can't braid my hair."

She shrugs and picks up where she left off. The subject carries us the rest of the way home.

"Keep your voice down," I remind her once I've closed the back door behind us.

She frowns and whispers, "If Fern isn't feeling well, why didn't she go home?"

Damn. I should've known Ronni would circle back to that when I didn't answer before. "She's not sick. She just had a rough day, and I told her to stay so she doesn't have to come back for dinner."

Ronni stops and turns to frown at me. "But it's not Cassie's birthday."

"Who is Cassie?"

My eight-year-old manages to convey more with one slow blink than the most eloquent poets in history could with any combination of languages. Apparently, I'm a fucking idiot. "Fern's daughter."

The words ricochet around the empty space between my ears for a few seconds before they penetrate the two brain cells that reside there. I sink into the chair I never pushed in after lunch and let the guilt have me. I had no idea. That makes me asking her to stay last night extra shitty. And asking her to extend her hours years ago. She's never said a word about a family. *Is she that desperate for money?* She's a smart woman, an excellent worker. She could find a better paying job, so why hasn't she?

Maybe the father has custody? I wouldn't be surprised considering her living conditions. We have the space for both of them, though, if she accepts my offer to live here. I love kids, and Ronni will enjoy having a new friend just down the hall. They have to be close to the same age because I would've noticed if Fern were ever pregnant.

"I didn't know Fern has a daughter, honey," I finally say.

"She doesn't anymore," Ronni says as she slowly shakes her head. Her big blue eyes well up with tears, and one rolls down her porcelain cheek. "She died the day she was born."

Chapter 10

Fern

The trip back to Mason's is quiet, providing the perfect opportunity to make peace with what just happened. Packing my stuff took less than ten minutes and only one trip to the car. That's all the time it took for a crowd to assemble in the parking lot once word spread that I had dared to show my face there again. But they disappeared quickly after a good look at something one of the wannabe-*MIB* showed them. I wasn't allowed to see, and curiosity is *killing* me.

Len and his buddies gave me a better gift than that, though. Yeah, I've got some things that I'd rather not lose. But it wouldn't be the end of the world. The big thing was the opportunity to bid my friends farewell. It was a long, drawn-out, tearful process, even though they're all happy to see me leaving a dangerous situation. They might love me, but they've all made it clear they think I'm a fool for living there. They're probably right, but it was the best option at the time. Luis, the super, didn't ask for *favors* on top of rent.

Once the car is unloaded, I hug each and every one of my guards, even Len. It's a bit like hugging brick walls. Even tough guys need a hug every now and then and, as ridiculous as it is, none of them hesitate.

It also kills a little more time before I have to go inside. Standing here right now, staring at Mason's door, the only thing I want to do is get back to my routine. It's hard to believe he'd really offer me a place in his home. It's too good to be true, so there must be a catch. That possible catch has my stomach in knots.

I could carry everything I own inside in one trip, but Len insists on doing it for me. He and his buddies follow behind me and wait while I try the door. It's locked, but Len puts down the bag he's holding and pulls out his key, stalling my knock.

Before he can fit it into the lock, the door opens from the inside. Mason's eyes rake over the men huddled protectively around me, and he dismisses them to look from Len to me, then back again.

"Need to get her a key, Boss."

I hold my breath. Len knows I had a key, and what happened to it. So, why tell Mason that?

Mason frowns. "I gave her a key when I hired her. Remember it clear as day."

Len nudges me and nods when I look his way. After our encounter in the kitchen, looking Mason in the eye isn't so hard to do anymore. Swallowing hard, I tell him the truth. I'm sure he already suspects the answer anyway. "Felicity took it."

"For fuck's sake," he whispers softly enough to keep Ronni from hearing since she's hovering behind him, stealing peeks at the wall o' muscle behind me. His eyes narrow, and he turns them on Len. "A note? Really? You could've called to tell me what was going on!"

Len shrugs. "It was that or argue with you. Imagine how you'd feel in her situation. She needed closure. My friends here kept her safe and ensured that she will remain so." He catches me looking at him, asking a million questions with my eyes, and shakes his head. We're still not going to talk about who these big bastards are.

Mason listens patiently and nods his understanding with a sigh. His eyes drift across the goon squad behind me, but he must decide that Len wouldn't let anyone on the premises who posed a threat, because he steps back. "Come on in. Len, would you take her things upstairs, please?"

Len squeezes my shoulder before he gathers my things and motions his troop of suit-clad muscle to wait.

"Mom should be here soon," Mason says as he ushers me inside behind Len. Ronni scampers before us, chattering about how excited she is.

I consult my watch and sigh in relief. It's not too early to hide in the kitchen under the guise of cooking. "I'll go start dinner."

"About dinner . . ." He doesn't continue, so I stop and glance back to see him running his hands through his hair, sending his curls into disarray. He only does that when he's nervous or stressed. He grins shyly and rushes to say, "I thought we could go out. I made reservations. But I can cancel them if you'd rather stay in. Or if you don't have anything to wear. Or I could make a couple phone calls and get a shop to open. Lord knows they've taken enough of my money to owe me that."

I appreciate his consideration for my situation, but I have to bite my tongue to keep from laughing at him for getting all tripped up. "It's fine, Mason. I've got a couple dresses."

***

This is so weird. Mason and I usually talk business during my work hours; he's never suggested dinner before. I suppose this situation is different—more personal. I smooth imaginary wrinkles from the bodice of my dress and wander about the patio, hoping that moving will stave off memories of the last time I wore this dress. It's not my favorite of the two I kept, but it's more appropriate for a business meeting than the other. I kept it for sentimental value; Aaron bought it for me the weekend we were married.

My foot slips out of my shoe, but I catch my balance before I can fall. Hopefully, I won't have to walk much wherever we're going. My only pair of heels isn't right for the occasion, but the one thing of Felicity's that I kept is a darling pair of Louboutin pumps that I couldn't make myself part with, even though they're a size too big.

"You look lovely, Fern," Len says. He has no idea he just saved me from a never-ending spiral of increasingly dark thoughts. I'm not going to tell him either. I don't talk about it. "Would you please stop pacing, though? You're making me dizzy."

"Thank you, Len." *For more than you know.*

The door opens. I whirl around in time to see Mason step out of the house. His eyes go wide when they land on me. "Wow," he says through a wide grin.

Wow yourself. His gray suit has a hint of green to it. It's totally something I would have picked out. I like things that only appear to color inside the lines, but upon closer inspection, prove to be a little unconventional. The olive green and navy blue striped tie he paired with it helps set off the color of the suit. Now that we might be living together, I really need to stop noticing how attractive he is. *But why? I'm emotionally unavailable, not dead.*

"Th-thank you?"

He grins again and nods as he eyes me up and down again, lingering over my hips and my chest. I can't help my blush. No one looks at me like that anymore. *He's not used to seeing me dressed up. That's all it is.*

It's almost as if we planned our outfits to complement one another with me in this peach-colored lace dress. It's shorter than I like in the front, but the high-low hem means I don't have to worry about my ass hanging out. The V-neck is deep, but not to the point it compromises modesty.

He extends his elbow, and I recognize the gesture, but it takes me a blink to remember what the hell to do with it. I slide my hand into place so as not to appear rude, but I barely touch him. My grasp is so light I can hardly feel his warmth clinging to the soft fabric of his suit jacket. He walks me to the car, not seeming to mind that I'm a little slower than usual in my second-hand heels.

Len opens the back door for me, and I manage to maneuver myself into the car without flashing either of them. When the door closes behind Mason, I plaster on what I hope is a genuine smile and act like everything is fine. It's not, but I can pretend until everything makes sense again.

"Let's get business out of the way now, so we can enjoy dinner, hmm?" Mason asks conversationally. "You need a home. I need someone to take care of Ronni in the mornings. It seems to me like we can help each other out here. Can we agree on that?"

I don't know that he actually needs someone to see Ronni off to school anymore. I learned this morning she's mostly done it herself for years. Still, she shouldn't be alone.

I agree as pleasantly as I can.

"Perfect. The purple room will be yours." *Fucking dammit. Why that one?* That's the room Felicity moved into when she decided to punish Mason for Lord knows what. "Do you have a driver's license?"

"Yes." It's an odd question, but since he knows I take the bus, I suppose it's a fair one.

He nods briskly. "I will provide a car, and you will take Ronni to school every morning. The car will be yours. Once you've dropped her off, you can do whatever it is you need to until time to pick her up. Will this arrangement be a problem for you?"

That seems too good to be true, but I make the decision to trust him. "No, I'd love that. Could I maybe take her to the park after school on days she doesn't have homework?" That would be so nice. And maybe I can put aside a little money each week to take her for ice cream.

He frowns, and I prepare to be shot down. "Fern, as long as she gets her homework done before dinner, you are free to do anything you'd like."

My heart leaps into my throat and beats out of control. "Okay!"

He smiles. "I trust you to take care of my daughter as if she were your own, just as you always have, Fern. You have a credit card for groceries. It's also for any expenses related to her, fuel, meals out—which means yours, too—clothes, things she needs for school."

"Um . . . Felicity has that card, remember?" His slow scowl has me shifting nervously in my seat, so I rush to explain since he's obviously forgotten, "She told me you wanted her to keep it and would give it to me before I went to the store every week."

He closes his eyes for a long time and grumbles under his breath. "Of fucking course she did." When his eyes open, he smiles at me. "Excuse me, please. I need to cancel that card." He takes his phone from his pocket and taps the screen a few times before holding it to his ear. Someone answers surprisingly fast, and he provides the necessary information.

I don't mind the extra responsibilities he's asking me to take on at all. It seems like a fair trade for knowing I have a place to lay my head at night that isn't occasionally in the middle of a gang war. Depending upon how much he wants for rent, I might be able to pay my bills off a little faster than expected. *Or save to finish my degree.*

"That's settled," he says contentedly, bringing me back to the here and now. "You have a home. I don't have to worry about my daughter. Everyone is happy."

"But—"

He cuts me off with a confused frown. "Have I forgotten something?"

"We haven't discussed rent and utilities."

He waves dismissively. "Consider it part of the wages for the extra work I'm asking you to do. Having you there isn't going to cost me anything more."

Is he serious right now? I relax a little. I was expecting rent to be a deal-breaker.

Something he said finally registers. "Part?" I whisper, not daring to hope. Is he still going to pay me *and* let me live there?

He turns his head away from me a little and tips it to the side. It's the same look he gives Ronni when she's telling wild stories he can't quite believe, and it's one of the most adorable things I've ever seen a grown man do. "Part," he says slowly. "As in, in addition to what I'm already paying you, so we're clear. I feel like we're not on the same page here. Maybe not even in the same chapter."

He doesn't wait for me to reply. "You thought I was going to consider housing to be your wages, didn't you?"

When I nod, he closes his eyes and mutters under his breath.

The car stops. "We're here," Len says.

I look out the window. The stupid mistake I've made finally hits me.

Chapter 11

Fern

In awe, I stare at the beautiful building while Len helps me from the car, and do some mental math to figure how much money I have in the bank. I might have eighty bucks. If I'm lucky. What if that's not enough? With few exceptions, I pay my own way in this world. I learned the hard way that nothing good comes from relying on others. I'll figure something out. *There's always a credit card . . .*

"What's that look for?" Mason asks in my ear.

I was so lost in thought, I didn't notice him come up beside me. I jump, lose my balance, and stumble out of one of my shoes. He chuckles even as he steadies me. I nearly fall over again when he kneels on the sidewalk to slip my shoe back on my foot. His little frown warns me that I'm busted, but he doesn't comment on the bubble wrap I've got stuffed in the toe of my shoe. Instead, he palms my calf to support my leg, making it easier for me to balance. It's an odd sight to see, and somehow so intimate that I'm blushing all over. *If anyone saw us like this, they'd think we're lovers.*

For some reason, my treacherous mind takes the opportunity to note how easily I could throw that leg over his shoulder to give him better access to the promised land. *Where the hell did that come from?* Sure, I've entertained the occasional smutty thought about him before. He's gorgeous and good with kids. It happens sometimes, but never with him right in front of me, touching me. Until recently.

His fingers linger when he lowers my foot to the ground, triggering goose-bumps and a rush of heat that causes a flood in the promised land. *This can't be happening.* I hold perfectly still, afraid that squirming will give me away.

"Thank you," I whisper.

I just have to get through tonight. After this, we won't be spending so much time around each other, and I can go back to life relatively free of dirty thoughts centering on him. *Thank God.* I could not look Ronni in the eye if I was wet for her father. Luckily, this is the first time I'm encountering this problem, and she's nowhere to be seen.

I should be happy. This is surely a sign I'll be able to move on someday. Maybe. I'm only a shell of a person now. I have nothing to offer to bring value to a relationship. Even if I could move on, I can't inflict myself upon someone hoping for love that I can't give him.

"No problem," he says lightly, brushing imaginary dirt from his knees before he rights himself. "Well?"

"Hmm?" I can't remember the question now. It was carried away on a tide of lust.

His lips stretch into a cocky smirk like he *knows* what he did to me. "What was that look about?"

Look? Oh! My real dilemma reclaims center stage, where it should have been all along. I can't tell him I can't afford the place he chose for dinner, though. I'll have to make do. "Oh! Uh, nothing."

He grins mischievously while he takes my hand to place it on his arm like it belongs there. Something makes me glance over my shoulder at Len. He's watching us with a superior smile I can't decipher. When I catch his eye, he winks at me before climbing back behind the wheel and driving away. *What the fuck was that all about?*

✳✳✳

Mason orders wine for both of us without consulting me. I don't drink much as a rule. There's also the little matter of the expense. I'll make it work. I always do.

I still haven't settled on anything when the waitress returns for our orders. I squirm in my seat while he orders surf and turf, and try to hide behind my menu when he and the waitress both turn to me.

"What are you stuck on?" he asks.

The price tag. "I don't know! It all sounds so good!" He doesn't seem to notice the edge of panic in my voice because he smiles at me.

"Order whatever you'd like. My treat."

I swallow my sigh of relief, but subconsciously wonder what it'll cost me in the long run. Regardless, when the waitress suggests the shrimp alfredo, I go with it. Sometimes, people can do something just to be nice. They don't always have motives.

Once she's gone, Mason watches me over his wine glass and says, "So, we're going to be living under the same roof. Tell me about you."

"Oh!" I laugh awkwardly. It's an unexpected topic of conversation, but in keeping with his recent behavior so I shouldn't be surprised. It's like we're picking up where we left off when Felicity moved in, but we're not the same people we were then. "Where to start . . . ?" *More like how do I get out of it?*

He helps himself to the bread in the basket between us and asks, "I know you're from Nebraska. What brought you to Texas?"

That's easy enough to answer without costing me anything. "College. And teenage rebellion. I wanted to get as far away from home as possible, and a new state and city life seemed so glamorous back then." The glamor wore off quickly, though. Television doesn't do the gruesome side of city life any justice if they show it at all.

His grin tells me he understands, and possibly even that he understands the disillusionment that comes with age and experience. "What did you major in?"

There's no easy answer to this question. The truth will lead to more questions, I can't lie, and not answering isn't an option. I used to be so proud of the path I chose, but now, it's just another painful memory. "Nursing. I wanted to be a Nurse Practitioner, to be exact."

His eyes widen. "So, when you said that you were first aid certified on your application, you were putting it mildly?"

I grin at him. "Yes. And I keep up with my certifications." I save all year to afford to do so, but it's worth it. I like the peace of mind that comes with knowing I haven't forgotten anything and am ready to jump into action should something happen with Ronni or anyone else.

"Good to know." He puts his glass down and leans back into his chair. We watch each other across the table. When I don't look away immediately, I'm rewarded with a smile. "So, how did you go from studying to be superwoman to cleaning houses?"

The day we met, I told him I was taking some time off due to a family emergency. He didn't ask, so I didn't elaborate. He *never* asked. I finally worked up the nerve to talk about it after he told me about Ronni's mother, but it was too late then. He found out about Felicity's fling, then she moved in. It took a long time for it to come up again, but here we are.

Maybe it's because he told me he's proud of me, and I need that kind of support in my life, but I don't need to be drunk to say, "Car accident."

His eyes go wide. "I had no idea," he says softly. "What happened?"

I'm not sure if he means with the accident, or after. Car accidents are pretty self-explanatory. I shrug. "Dropped out."

"No, with the accident? I have a feeling that something Ronni said this afternoon will make more sense once you tell me."

Tears spring to my eyes. I don't talk to Ronni much about my past. Not this part of it anyway, so I can't imagine what she's told him. Once, when she was five,

I told her about my daughter. She wasn't old enough to retain that information. The idea that she might've remembered all this time chills me to the bone.

He doesn't know what he's asking of me. This isn't a little piece of me, but if we're going to do this friendship thing again, I have to answer his trust with some of my own. "Let's back up a little . . ."

"Alright," he whispers. His eyes settle on me, and the weight of his gaze leaves me grounded—and oddly drunk—enough to get through this.

I take a deep breath through my nose, which isn't as centering as I hoped it would be since I'm assaulted with the woodsy smell of his cologne. I allow myself another deep breath for the hell of it because he smells good. "I was married before."

Mason chokes on a sip of wine. "I'm sorry," he says, mopping himself up.

"We met in college. I turned him down for months before I finally agreed to a date, and we eloped a year later. I was twenty at the time, Aaron was twenty-five. Our parents weren't thrilled, by any means. Mine said I was too young. His mother thought I was a gold digger." My eyes roll of their own accord. I never cared about his money. I didn't know he had money until I met his mother. "My birth control failed, and I got pregnant on our honeymoon."

Mason winces sympathetically.

I swallow hard and will my voice not to shake. Talking about it all hurts in a way that thinking about it doesn't anymore—probably because I never speak of it. "I convinced Aaron to go home with me to try to make peace with my parents a couple months before the baby was due. It was a quick trip because we were between semesters, and we had a lot we wanted to get done before I delivered. I barely had time to change my name because we were so busy with school, so we never had time to add names to bank accounts and all that. And we wanted to find a house of our own.

"It was late when our plane landed here, nearly midnight. I fell asleep in the car on the way home. I was told a drunk driver came into our lane, clipped the side of our car, the car behind us hit us, and we rolled several times.

"I was knocked unconscious and suffered a few minor lacerations, but nothing life threatening. I barely even have scars. The stress sent me into labor early, though. I woke to find out my husband passed at the scene, and my baby died en route. The trauma of the accident caused placental abruption, and they couldn't get me to the hospital in time to save her."

Mason's hand inches across the table. When I don't object, he wraps his fingers around mine, reminding me that I'm not alone, no matter how I feel. "You okay?" he asks.

I nod and hide my other hand in my lap so he won't notice the beginnings of a tremor in my fingers. "Aaron's mom insisted on planning the funeral even though she lives out of state. She assured me she'd take care of everything, I just needed to go to the funeral home and pay for everything with my credit card, and she'd pay me back when she got here. I thought maybe she realized that I really did love her son, so I didn't question it."

Mason smiles, likely thinking her benevolence to be a good thing. I envy his naivety. "Then I had to pay rent, the utility bills came in, and I knew the hospital bill wouldn't be far behind. I called her because Aaron's bank account defaulted to her since we never put my name on it, and I didn't have the money to cover his half of everything. She told me to put it all on my card too. She promised to cover every last cent of it, even my hospital bill. I opened new cards because my old ones were maxed, and I maxed those out, too."

White-hot rage the likes of which I haven't experienced in years burns through my sorrow. My voice gets sharper with every word. "When she got here, she didn't say a word about a check. Bringing it up felt rude at the time. I mean, she was here for her only child's funeral. So I waited, but she never said a word. After a month, I called her. She laughed at me and said I married him; I was his next of kin. It was my debt."

A look of wide-eyed horror replaces Mason's smile. I can practically see the questions pinging around in his head, but he keeps them to himself, for now. They'll come up, sure as the sunrise.

I take a deep breath and release my anger along with it. "So I dropped out of school after that semester because I couldn't afford to finish my education and pay the bills. Not even with my scholarship. I had to go to work full time. Someone advised bankruptcy, but I was afraid of what it would mean for my future. I was young and dumb and didn't comprehend the scope of it all at the time. I didn't understand refusing wasn't the better option, and I'm too proud to do it now. Don't want it popping up on a background check, either. It might cause someone to change their mind about hiring me, make them think I'm desperate, and would steal from them or something."

Mason squeezes my fingers tight enough it hurts, but I don't mind. "Why didn't you go home?"

I look down at the hand in my lap and curl it into a fist. He needs to know the truth if I'm going to live with him but admitting it sucks. "My family . . . doesn't know about the debt. They think I got my CNA and work nights at a hospital. Which was almost true, but it was too much—too many memories. Going home would make me a burden on them because they'd try to help. So I stay away and email every week so they don't worry."

It's the only lie I've ever successfully sold, and I hate myself for it.

"How long ago was this?"

"They died almost seven years ago."

"And it's still not paid off?"

I shake my head. My cheeks heat up, but I refuse to be embarrassed. I didn't ask for this. This is what trusting someone got me. This is why I don't trust easily anymore.

He throws his other hand over his eyes as if that'll make whatever I have to say any easier to hear. "Jesus, Fern! How much?"

I shrug because I really don't know. "I stopped looking at the big picture. I take it one payment at a time."

Chapter 12

Mason

He needed a wife; she needed money . . . Austin's explanation of a contract bride is still ricocheting around my brain when Len parks the car in the garage. I barely remember the rest of our dinner because of that constant distraction echoing through my mind, eroding my resolve. But a restaurant is no place for the discussion I want to have, so I had to wait patiently.

Fern doesn't question me when I steer her toward the patio door. She lets me lead her outside and immediately turns her eyes to the sky. The happy expectation melts from her face. "No stars."

The back yard does an excellent job helping you forget we're in the middle of a city thanks to the trees and the little flowerbeds that Ronni 'rescued' from the landscaping crew to tend herself. I didn't think *'rescued'* was the right word for it, but they're thriving. *How much of that is Fern's doing?* There's nothing I can do about the stars, though.

I sit across from her to give her some space. I've done a shitty job of showing it at times, but I can respect personal boundaries. Something about her makes me want to be closer. It's no excuse, but I can't seem to help myself, and she doesn't demand that I do. Fern is a healer. A giver. Maybe that part of her is a siren's call to the broken pieces of me.

After hearing what she's suffered, I'm itching to be close to her. But it's not all about me.

She angles her face away from mine, hiding half of it in the shadows. "Why are you looking at me like that?"

I don't have an answer I'm ready to give her.

He needed a wife, she needed money . . . It's like something from a movie. I need a wife. She needs money. *She needs a whole helluva lot more than money.* She needs stability and security, someone who has her back, admires her for the tough decisions she made but also knows how and when to protect her.

I sense a kindred spirit in her. Someone who has loved and lost, only she lost it all. More than I could ever comprehend. Not only the love of her life, but her child, her present, and her future. *But I could fix that.*

"Mason? Are you alright?"

I could make her an offer. If anyone understands that it's not so easy to move on after the loss of a loved one, it's this woman. Fern wouldn't expect something from me that I can't give.

She lost a family. I lost my girlfriend. We could be the answers to each other's questions. I could give her a doting husband and a daughter who adores her. She could give me a wife who would always have my back, as I would have hers, and a mother who would move heaven and hell for my daughter. We might not love each other, but we could work. *Fuck Austin for being right.*

All it takes is a few promises and a legally binding contract. A contract doesn't have to be written by an attorney to be legally binding. It was Austin's idea. He can help us. That keeps it more or less private. The fewer people who know, the happier we'll be.

My family will love her. She's incredible with Ronni. She and I can probably be great together too, once we figure things out. *There's no reason not to do this.*

"Fern," I begin hesitantly. This situation requires some finesse. She doesn't have to accept my proposition, but I need for our working relationship to remain intact if she doesn't. Ronni will never forgive me if Fern quits. "I do not doubt you can do this yourself. I'm sure you don't *need* help, but I would like to help you with this debt."

That seems like a good starting place. She's definitely a strong, capable woman who wouldn't approve of *anyone* presuming she needs saving. She wants to be a nurse—a hero. *Sometimes, even the heroes need a hand.*

Her smile is soft, the sort of smile that comes with a gentle letdown. "Mason, you're already helping me more than you can imagine."

"I think I can do better than that, and you can help me."

The smile disappears. She's all business now. "What do you need help with? Is it something else with Ronni?"

"Sort of." *God, how do you propose a loveless marriage to someone you barely know, but can't get by without?* "Look, there's no easy way to do this. It's going to sound crazy no matter how I word it."

Fern purses her lips. "Alright."

"I'm assuming you know what an arranged marriage is?" While I speak, I study her face for minute changes that might clue me in on her feelings about my question.

Instantly, that wall slams back into place. I didn't even realize I managed to bulldoze through it until it came back. I'm not going to get a thing from her that she doesn't want me to now. "Yes?" she says, drawing it out into a question. "Is that what you were and Felicity were supposed to be?"

"No!" I sigh and pass a hand over my face. *How can I make her understand?* "In the spirit of honesty, I thought I was in love with her. I wanted to be, I tried, but I wasn't. The truth is, I'm not sure if I'll ever love anyone again. I've sort of given up on the idea. Which brings me back to my problem. I have a daughter who needs a mother, and I have a grandfather insisting I get married before I'm thirty or he'll give the company to my brother. Austin doesn't want it. He'd probably sell it, but I've been training for this my whole life."

Her chin lifts in an understanding nod. "Ahh, so you're hunting for a contract bride." *How the hell does she know what a contract bride is?* It's a fair enough question, so I ask her. She shrugs it off like it's no big thing. "Books. It's a trope in romance novels."

"You read romance?" I ask, incredulous. She seems too jaded, and wouldn't stories about happy couples rub salt in the wound?

She shrugs one shoulder this time. "Sometimes. A girl's gotta have some sort of romance in her life. It's not happening to me, so what's the harm in living vicariously through the written word from time to time?"

That highlights the flaw in my plan. Feelings. Romance. Sex. *I can give her romance without love.* Hell, dinner was romantic, and we're just friends. Thanks to Austin, I'd be lying if I said I wasn't interested in her in a sexual way. When I was helping her with her shoe, it was all I could do not to kiss my way up her leg and bury my face between her thighs. That doesn't require love either, though. *I should know.*

"Fair enough." I reevaluate how I'm sitting to ensure she won't notice what remembering the way her skin felt in my hands does to me. "And yes, I suppose that is exactly what I'm 'hunting' for."

One arched brow lifts. "I'm not sure how I can help you with this, Mason. It's not like I'm rubbing elbows with eligible bachelorettes on a regular basis. I mean, one of my clients is single and well off, but she's also seventy-eight and can barely walk."

I laugh because she means for me to. *That's the problem.* I *am* familiar with them all, and I'm not interested in any of them. I haven't been truly attracted to anyone since Vee died. Until I met Fern. That's the cold, hard truth I've been trying to ignore.

My attraction to Felicity was purely physical. I appreciated her body; she appreciated mine. Sort of. *She enjoyed my bank account more.* This connection I feel with Fern was never present in my relationship with Felicity. It's not something that can be forced. I tried.

Austin was right. I remember the day I met Fern. In Technicolor. She walked in, looking like the two-point-oh version of the love of my life, and it was a punch in the gut. Vee was beautiful in an unconventional way. Fern though . . . no one in their right mind would deny she's gorgeous. I didn't want to hire her because of that. It would be like having a ghost in the house. The way she interacted with my daughter trumped all that. She was the best woman for the job. I was able to ignore it all this time . . . Until Austin took it upon himself to stick his nose where it doesn't belong.

"I don't need your help *finding* the bride. I want you to *be* the bride."

Her eyes widen. She shifts around, leaning forward to look me in the eye. "Are you *drunk?*"

I mirror her, leaning forward to get closer. I have to remind myself not to stare at her lips. "No, I'm sober. And yes, I know it sounds crazy. Think about it, though. You love Ronni. She loves you. She'd be your step-daughter. You'd never have to worry about anything again. You could quit cleaning and go back to school if you wanted."

"What?" She whispers the question, cutting me off before I can finish extolling the numerous benefits of this arrangement.

I grab onto the benefit that probably seems the most desirable to her. "Consider it a sign-on bonus." If I speak about it as a job, she might be more likely to do it. I'll do whatever it takes to get her on board. Now that the hard part—asking— is done, I want this. "Your debt will be paid in full. You can do whatever you want with your time while Ronni is at school."

She brings a hand up to cradle her forehead, effectively hiding her eyes from me. "Oh, sweet Jesus, you're serious."

I nod, but she's still avoiding eye contact. "I am. I'm not going to pretend I've spent a lot of time thinking about this because I haven't. It doesn't matter how long I think about it, though. I know you're the right woman, Fern. You're practically family already."

"And what do you get out of this?" She lets her hand fall away and watches me closely, judging my reaction, I'm sure.

I couldn't sleep last night because Austin's suggestion ricocheted through my brain for hours. There was also a sexy little woman down the hall I needed to distract myself from fantasizing about. I'm going to have to find something to keep me from that particular pastime now that she'll be living with me, and only one door down the hall. Or I'm going to have to spend some quality time with my imagination and my hand before I can get to sleep.

"I get to see my daughter happier than she's ever been in her life. I get to see the second most important person in her life thrive. I get the future I've always planned for."

She shakes her head, and my heart drops. For a moment, I believed she was actually going to go for it. "You," she pauses, and her eyes roam over my face and down over every inch of me she can see, "want to marry *me?*"

The blatant appreciation in her gaze has me fighting a grin. "Yes." I nod to underline how much I mean it. "Can't you see how it would be a mutually beneficial arrangement?"

Her eyebrows twitch up for a second, but her head bobs from side to side in a sort of assent. "Sounds like I'd get more out of it than you, but sure. I can see that."

My heart pounds. It's the same sort of thrill I get when negotiating deals at the office, but this might be the biggest deal of my life. "You might benefit more, but I have more to lose if you don't agree."

"Nah." She scrunches her nose and sits back. "Women would beat down your door if they knew you were in the market for such a thing." *Is that an admission she finds me attractive? Or is she merely pointing out that most women would jump at this opportunity?* "I get where you're coming from, okay? And really, I'm flattered you'd even consider me. I'm not the person you want, though, Mason. I'm nowhere near your league, alright? What're all your buddies going to think when you announce you're getting hitched to your nanny? And your family?"

Taking a page out of her book, I indulge in a blatant perusal of her face and body. "Probably that I'm a lucky sonofabitch?" She rolls her eyes at me. "Look, I know a lot of women, and I'm telling you there is no one else I'd rather do this with. I think we understand each other. We wouldn't expect anything the other couldn't give. Someone else might not be so understanding. I'm not asking for any sort of commitment right now, okay? Just . . . think on it for a while. It's not something I planned to jump into right away. I couldn't do that to Ronni. We'd have to go through the motions, date, actually get to know one another."

"Pretend to have a real relationship, fall in love," she says woodenly, turning her face toward the sky again.

"Yes." I swallow around a lump in my throat. That will be the hard part. It'll be a constant reminder of what I lost. *I can take it.* "Will you consider it, please?"

Fern studies my face for a long while before she shakes her head. Whatever thoughts she has flitting through her mind turn the corners of her mouth down in a sad little frown. *I want to fix that.* "Mason, I can't. It just wouldn't work. You need someone who isn't broken."

Someone who isn't broken? The notion about makes me laugh, but I can't do that to her. She wouldn't understand. *Or maybe she'd understand better than anyone else.*

"You know, I read in a book once that we're all broken and desperately trying to put ourselves back together. We never succeed because we don't have what we need to keep the pieces in place. We have to find the right person, the one with the glue we need, who needs the glue we have." I shrug, embarrassed with myself for putting that out there. I imagined her rejection several times while I was letting myself entertain the notion of pitching this deal last night, but never once did I imagine it hurting. "The writer said it better, though."

She quickly looks at her lap. "I love that series," she whispers. "Master Silvers is brilliant."

She's read that book? I don't get much time to read, but it's a guilty pleasure. It seems Fern and I have more in common than I thought we would. We could make this work with nothing more than a mutual love for my daughter, but we'll enjoy it more if we share some of the same interests. That's a definite bonus, and further proof she's the right person to do this with. We won't have to pretend to enjoy each other's company.

"I'm not saying we can fix each other or fall in love. I'm saying we're both broken. That's why this could work. We both understand what it's like, and this way, we wouldn't have to be broken alone. We'd have each other to lean on for the bad days."

She nods, but I take it as an understanding more than an agreement.

"So, you'll think about it?" I ask, suddenly giddy with excitement.

"I'll do it," she whispers.

My lungs stop working. "Seriously?" I whisper so softly, I'm not sure she'll hear.

"Yeah, for Ronni. And because misery is easier with company."

I want to jump up and shout, sweep her up and spin in circles, and kiss her until she's breathless, but I force my excitement down and take a deep breath. "I think the phrase you're looking for is 'misery loves company.'"

Her head shakes. "No. Misery loves company because then it is multiplied. We both have our burdens, but together, we'll lighten the load. I don't want to inflict my misery upon you. I'll be less miserable knowing I have someone nearby who understands what it is to lose love and doesn't expect me to be whole."

"Because having to pretend to be okay when you're not only compounds the misery." I know that feeling all too well. It's been my reality since the day Vee died.

"Exactly. We might have to hide it from the rest of the world but not from each other. We might not be able to fix each other, but we can maybe manage to figure out where the pieces are supposed to be and which ones we're missing."

Love might not be an option, but I know deep down I just found the best friend I could ever have because she'll never expect me to forget my feelings for Vee like I'll never expect her to lose hers for Aaron.

"So, where does that leave us?" she asks when we've both sat quietly too long. Her voice is a little husky from the tears she held back. It'll be a hard promise to keep, but I'll do my best to ensure she never feels like she has to repress her emotions.

"Friends." I give the simple answer because it's the best one right now. "Very good friends who are on the verge of being something more. We're going to do this right."

"Okay," she says, nodding slowly.

"I'll have it all figured out before our next date." I'm not sure what she expects, but I mean it when I say we're doing this right. Just because it's arranged doesn't mean I can't give her all the things that come with a traditional courtship. "After that, we can negotiate until we're both content. I still have a year and a half, and I don't mean to rush this. I'd rather use every last day I have to ensure we can both commit for Ronni's sake."

"I agree. It's the smart thing to do. People would ask too many questions; assume we've been sneaking around for years if we jumped in right off the bat."

"Exactly! We'll let this play out like a real relationship. Awkward dates and all."

She giggles, and her megawatt smile takes my breath away. "Well, Mason, you might be the king of awkward date discussions."

"I try, Fern. I try."

***

I lace my fingers through Fern's and lead her inside. "Welcome home, Fern," I say as I watch her step over the threshold, eyes lingering on those curves that are killing me. I've never been so happy to welcome someone into my home.

She smiles at me over her shoulder. "Thank you."

She struggles a bit on the stairs, likely due to the *bubble wrap* in her shoes. I didn't want to ask her about it and embarrass her right before dinner. Now, though . . . "Why in the name of fuck is there bubble wrap in your shoes?"

She lets her head fall back with her laughter. "Because they were Felicity's, and her feet are bigger than mine. My one pair of heels isn't right for dinner with a client."

It's hard to frown when she's laughing, but I pull it off. Why would she keep something of *Felicity's* that doesn't fit? "That won't do at all. Tomorrow, we'll fix that."

Her brow furrows. She opens her mouth, no doubt to argue. Before she can, I bend to kiss her cheek. It seems like the perfect end to an impromptu first date. And the perfect way to end this argument before it starts.

Confusion quirks Fern's eyebrows, and she tracks my movement with suspicious eyes. She turns her head to watch me, putting her lips in line with mine. And it's too late to stop.

We connect with a zing. I know a moment of blind panic and freeze completely, bracing for the slap I'm sure is coming. Fern's soft moan thaws me. Her body softens, melting into me. I didn't plan this, but holy shit, I'm not going to complain. The quick, chaste kiss I thought to steal hovers on the edge of becoming something entirely different, and I might spontaneously combust on the spot. It's been so long since a woman gave herself over to me like this, I can barely hold myself back from shoving her against the door and exploring her as I want to.

I'm breathing harder than a racehorse at the finish line, and my dick could cut diamonds. I could press this further, but it's too soon. I don't want that between us if our agreement fails. *I should've let her argue.* "Good night, Fern," I whisper against her soft lips.

She gasps when I pull away, and her eyes bore into my back while I retreat to my room to do something about the highly inappropriate thoughts I'm having.

Chapter 13

Fern

What the fuck just happened? Pinching my arm doesn't change anything. I'm still standing in front of the door to the damned purple room. My lips still tingle. That just happened. He just kissed me. And I really enjoyed it.

He left, though. *Was it that bad?* I should go knock on his door and demand an explanation. *For the kiss, or for his hasty retreat?* He can't do things like that! We just agreed! *Then why am I more upset that he left?*

No. I should go to bed and pretend it never happened. My fist is raised to knock before what *I'm* doing catches up with me. *Too late now.*

The door opens a bit and he hides everything but his face behind it. "Fern?"

"What the hell was that?"

He fights a smirk and mostly wins. "Well, you were married once. I'm sure you're familiar with kisses."

Well, yes, I am. But . . . Does he regret it? Is that why he left?

"But . . . but why? And why did you run away like that?" *Because he changed his mind.* I saw the panic in his eyes. "Oh, my God. You realized it was a mistake. This was all a mistake. I'll find somewhere else to live tomorrow."

The rest of my world is falling to pieces. I can't seem to make myself stop. I have to fix this. "Ronni will never know. I swear. I love this job. Please, I'd be heartbroken if I never got to see Ronni again." I don't care about the rest of it anymore, so long as I can still see her.

He throws the door open wide, and my brain kicks into overdrive, processing several things all at once. He's shirtless, and there is a pronounced bulge in his pants, which is probably why he was using the door as a shield. "Because I wanted to," he says in a low and seductive growl. My heart beats faster. My head spins. This . . . is not at all what I expected.

"Do I have your attention now?" A nod is the only answer I'm capable of giving. He sighs and rubs the back of his neck. "Look, I was only trying to kiss you on the cheek, but you moved, and I panicked. But I've wanted to do that since I met you, if I'm honest. I left because it seemed like the smarter option, as opposed to doing it again and maybe trying to convince you to take things too fast. Stopping was not my first instinct, and I don't think it was yours, either."

Struggling to keep my eyes somewhere appropriate, I gulp and take a step back. He's not wrong, and I don't like it. I didn't think about *this* before I agreed to this marriage of convenience. Intimacy wasn't even on my radar. I was thinking of Ronni. The money, Mason's promotion, that's all just fringe benefits. I'd do it without any of that so I know Ronni will never have to deal with another Felicity.

Mason leans against the door frame, watching me. Waiting for me to make up my mind. He doesn't expect me to love him. That's why this can work. He won't take Aaron's place because we're only pretending. I'm not stupid. Sex and love go hand-in-hand. I only have to carry on as I have since day one: look, don't touch. *Easier said than done.*

What just happened highlights a flaw in this plan. I liked it, and I shouldn't. I vowed to love Aaron forever when we married. He should be here now, and he's not. My body is betraying me, betraying *him.*

"Good night," Mason calls, taunting me as I hurry to my room.

I have no idea how I'm going to face him tomorrow.

My bedroom door is the first casualty of my frustration. I apply a little more force than necessary, and it slams behind me. Leaning against it, I swear I catch the faint sound of his chuckle. I'm imagining it. He's too far away and the blood pounding in my ears makes it impossible to hear.

When I stop breathing like I just completed a marathon I didn't train for, I make my way to the bathroom to clean up for bed. I need a shower to wash away the stress of the day. On my way by, I glare at the bed like it insulted my mother.

Felicity *maybe* fucked another guy in that bed. There's also the possibility that Mason fucked her there. And now, it's where I have to sleep.

Hot water cascades over my head, easing the tension in my shoulders. It's been a long day. *If only it could wash away lust.* That accidental kiss and then seeing him like that for *me* breathed new life into my frustration. As keyed up as I am, I'm doomed to toss and turn for hours unless I do something about it. But when I try, I can't get Mason out of my head, and it's not him that I want. *No, you don't want to want him.*

Groaning my frustration, I turn the water off and open the door to grab a towel. *Why is this happening to me?* Bracing my arms against the vanity, I stare into the blank nothingness of the steamed-over mirror and comb through my memories to remind myself what I lost and what I live for.

"C'mere. I've got a secret to tell you."

Rolling my eyes, I lean across the table so he can whisper in my ear. At the last second, he turns his head and presses his lips to mine.

"You said you had a secret!" He hasn't moved, but I haven't either. I should. I'm practically daring him to do it again. I'm not sure I'd mind if he did, though.

His lips curl into a satisfied smile. "That was *the secret. I've been dying to do that for months, half-pint."*

I never told him the only reason I agreed to the second date. It wasn't a secret that he wasn't really my type. I wasn't his, either. His sense of humor was so weird, and brown-eyed blonds weren't my thing. It was his sense of honor and his passion for helping people that drew me to him.

I'm not replacing you, Aaron

"Fern? Did you hear me?" Mason's voice, muffled by two closed doors, brings reality crashing down around me again. I think back, but come up blank. I didn't hear, but he's definitely concerned about something. *How deep in that rabbit hole was I?* "You okay in there?"

Reality is a bitch. There is no Aaron here. Only me and the man who inadvertently chases Aaron out of my head and makes my body come alive in ways no one has since him. Though he's not doing it on purpose, I *really* want to bash him over the head with a chair for it. *What if I forget?*

"Yeah. I'm fine," I say, raising my voice to carry to the hallway.

"'Fine' rarely means fine when a woman says it like that."

He's not wrong. "Memories." He should get it. I'm sure he has a few.

"Can I come in?" Even with a room between us, I recognize the slight edge in his tone. Mason is in his problem-solver mode again. He won't stop until he knows everything is okay.

"Just a minute!" I clutch my towel tighter and cast about for my clothes. "I'm getting dressed," I add so he doesn't come barging in.

"Sounds like incentive," he jokes, his voice brimming with laughter now. But he'll wait.

I have to fight a smile. As much as I don't want to want him, it's nice to know I'm wanted. *That's fucked up. I won't touch you, and you can't touch me, but I'm happy you want to!*

Guilt worms its way through my chest and settles in my stomach. I scramble into my clothes so I can see what he needs. "I'm decent."

He opens the door before I can, but doesn't come in. "What's wrong?"

Why does he think something's wrong? "Nothing? What did you need?"

"I heard you crying."

His bathroom is a mirror image of mine, so he maybe heard the shower running. *I hope that's all he heard.* But there's no way he heard me crying. "No, you didn't. We covered this earlier. I don't cry. It's not my thing."

"No one likes to cry, but we all need to sometimes."

"Not me." I haven't cried since I left the hospital. Granted, the shit they had me high on made me too numb to care for a while. By the time I stopped taking my script and came down off the cloud it had me on, which was *not* cloud nine, the bills rolled in, and I didn't have time to cry. "At this point, if I start, I might not stop. Best not to chance it."

He gives me a *'really?'* look, chin down, eyebrows cocked. "Fern, there are tears on your cheeks. Your eyes are all red." He holds out a hand for mine. I don't know what he's up to, but decide to go with it. He leads me to the bathroom, where he swipes up a towel and dries a spot on the mirror. "See?" he asks, pointing to my reflection.

I look to humor him. My eyes are red and swollen. There are red lines down my cheeks from . . . something. Not from tears, though. I don't cry, and I'd know if I did. *Wouldn't I?* "It must be the heat. And the water is from the shower."

"You're dry, sweetheart. You don't have to hide from me, remember?"

"I'm not hiding anything!" Why can't he drop it? *Why can't I?* Everything is perfectly fine. I lost it a little for a second, but I'm okay now. If he'll just leave me alone . . .

Mason throws his hands into the air. "Fine! Be stubborn. You weren't crying, I didn't hear you. Your eyes just sprung a leak. Completely normal."

My hands ball into fists at my sides. *Is he* trying *to piss me off?* "You're the one being stubborn! I was minding my own business. You came in here throwing around ridiculous accusations!"

"What are you afraid of?" he whispers.

What? The list is fairly long. I'm not sure he has that kind of time. Forgetting my husband and my daughter. Falling apart so badly, I can never be put back together again. Falling in love again. Losing someone else important to me.

He lowers his eyes and reaches for one of my fists and brings it to my eye level. "Tell me something, does hitting when you're upset mean you're a strong person?"

"What does that have to do—"

"Humor me."

"No?" I'm not strong because I can throw a punch, or because I prefer to work my feelings out that way. That's just my way. It doesn't mean anything, except maybe to a therapist. Really, I consider it a weakness. I've never thought of myself as a strong person, merely a determined one. And I really don't need that reminder right now.

"Exactly. Your character determines your strength. Hitting doesn't mean you're strong. Crying doesn't mean you're weak. I don't care how you work through whatever this is, but we agreed earlier that we'd have each other to lean on, and there's no reason we can't start now. So, here I am. You don't have to hide from me either way. My shoulder is no stranger to tears. I'm not afraid to catch a few dozen punches, and I don't mind a few bruises."

Bruises? Did I hit him so many times I bruised his palms? Sick with guilt, I grab his wrists and turn his hands over to see for myself, but his skin is unblemished save for callouses.

"No, here." He tugs one of his hands free to touch a faint shadow in his chest, right over his heart. It's still so light I didn't notice it earlier. Of course, other things about him drew the eye at the time. "I missed one. You were in the zone and didn't even notice."

My stomach churns. In a daze, I watch my hand reach out to touch him. Some distant voice warns me not to, but I brush it off. I did this. I hurt him.

A big hand covers mine, pressing it flat against his chest, which heaves with a sigh. His other hand cups my cheek and tilts my face to his. There's no looking away from those magnetic eyes. "Stop blaming yourself. I'm not breakable, baby. I liked that because you trusted me enough to drop your guard. We can do that any time, just promise you'll never get pissed at me and take a swing."

Numbly, I nod. I'd never do that to anyone. I'm not really a violent person by nature, but I feel so damned helpless sometimes that I have to scream and yell and hit something to feel like I'm still here. So I know I didn't die in that accident. This bruise, though, it breaks something inside me. Before I can puzzle out what's happening, a plaintive sob shatters the silence that's fallen between us. It's an ugly, broken sound, and I can't figure out where it's coming from.

Shocked, I look up at Mason. Why the hell he's crying? Am I hurting him? He's only watching me calmly, though, no tears to be seen.

"It's okay. I've got you, baby. You don't have to hold yourself together, alright? I'll do it for you."

Oh, my God. That was *me?* Another sob echoes around the room. And another. And I'm trembling both with the force of them leaving me and the effort it's taking to hold them back. I can't, though. I can't make them stop. My heart hurts more now than it did all those years ago. *How is that possible?*

"I've got you," Mason says. "I've got all night, and there's nowhere I'd rather be."

Fighting hurts too much, so I surrender and let the pain sweep me away, trusting Mason to hold me together like he keeps promising he will.

Chapter 14
Fern

Wednesday

My head is gross when I wake up, like moldy concrete. Heavy and fuzzy. It takes a few seconds to wake up enough to realize the angry buzzing on my wrist is my alarm, and I need to shut it off and get out of bed. *Why do I feel so shitty?* I don't have time to be sick.

Fear jolts me into alertness when someone sighs next to me. *What have I done?* I open my eyes and, even in the dark, I can tell I'm not home. Things are familiar, but I can't figure out why I'm here or how I got here.

I lost my home. The memory hits me like an arrow to the heart.

I live here now, with Mason and Ronni.

I flush from the roots of my hair to the tips of my toes when memories from last night assault me.

That still doesn't explain what the hell I'm doing in his bed. I have no business being here. Ever. I'll move my things in for appearances, but once Ronni is asleep, she won't know where I'm laying my head.

Mason is close enough that, if I had a light, I could count his eyelashes. It's too intimate. Too familiar. Too much, after the memory of him holding me while I broke down. I don't remember coming in here, though. Was I sleepwalking? I never have before. Surely we didn't *do* anything. I'd know if we did. I need to get away before he wakes up.

His arm is slung over my waist. It weighs a ton, leaving me no wiggle room. Wiggling would probably be a bad idea anyway. We're close enough he might mistake my motives since I'd end up grinding against his wood. Never mind that parts of me that haven't had any visitors for a very long time might get ideas as well . . . *Too late*. I'm going to have to move his arm and hope—

"Mornin' gorgeous," he says, his voice rough and rumbly from sleep. The sudden sound startles me. He notices, and his lips curl into a smile. "Sleep okay?"

No one should sound that damn sexy first thing in the morning. It's indecent. Should be illegal. Between the frustration from last night, that sound, and morning wood, I'm feeling a little stabby. I have a stubborn itch that needs to be scratched. It's not about to let me forget that I had no luck last night, and I'm not about to let him scratch it for me, so I'm just going to have to deal.

"Um, yeah. Thanks . . . Wh-when did I come in here?"

"Hmm?" he asks, stretching. In the process, he wiggles away and gives me some space. "You don't remember?"

"I don't remember much aside from feeling like I was gonna die."

"I tried to get you to lay down, and you refused because that bed is infested with, and I quote, evil-bitch-from-hell cooties."

I clear my throat and thank every star in the sky that it's dark enough he can't see me blush. "That sounds like something I'd say." It's the truth, after all.

He laughs again. The arm that's still draped over my waist shifts, and he rubs my back. "Those were your exact words. And I agree. I didn't want to lay there, either. But I was going to. I didn't want to leave you alone in case you woke up and needed me, so I suggested coming here. You said that we're both adults, and we can keep our hands to ourselves. So, here we are."

"Alright, then." I've got nobody to blame but me. Now that he's said it, I remember bits and pieces. That doesn't make me any less pissed with myself for letting myself get closer to him, for giving him a few more breadcrumbs.

"I'm going to burn that bed today. Buy a new one."

I'd love to be the one to toss the match since he's insisting I take that room. I don't want to be infected with evil-bitch-from-hell cooties. I'm not sure what his reasons are. *Her cooties are reason enough for both of us.* They might not be water-soluble. The sheets will have to go, too, just to be safe.

"Don't worry, it'll be replaced by bedtime."

I nearly sigh in relief. The little voice in the back of my head ceases its temper tantrum. Some part of me took his decision to burn the bed to mean that he assumed I would share his from now on. He doesn't get to make those decisions for me. Besides, we agreed last night to ease into things. Me ending up here last night was just a fluke.

"Maybe donate it instead? Or sell it?" No one else will have a problem with it. It's a perfectly good mattress.

The bed moves with his shrug. "Whatever makes you happy, as long as it's gone by the end of the day."

"Leave it to me." I'll call the consignment shop. Someone will pick it up.

The sound of stubble scratching skin answers me. "I got a string of angry texts from Felicity Monday morning when she figured out I was serious about it being over. She confessed to sneaking her lover in when I was gone. That bed is definitely contaminated."

We certainly see eye to eye on that. But he's forgotten something. We both did last night. "I'm pretty sure this one's contaminated, too." She surely didn't spend *every* night in the other room. "I did wash your sheets Monday, but even Lysol can't kill her cooties." *Thank God.* Waking to the smell of her *Eau de Trashy* perfume in my nose would've redefined waking up on the wrong side of the bed.

"Nope." He clears his throat and fidgets a bit. "This bed is too new. In the interest of open communication, I'll tell you that Felicity and I haven't had sex in over a year. Once she stopped sleeping in my bed, we never touched in any way. No hugs, no holding hands, no kissing."

"Wow," I say as I huff out a laugh. Given his penchant for random hugs, I bet that bothered him more than the rest. *That's probably why he's been so huggy lately.*

He groans and pulls the pillow from beneath my head in one quick yank, then he smacks me across the stomach with it. "Yeah, I know. I've heard it all now. I made the mistake of telling Austin."

Seriously? A pillow fight? Through my laughter, I manage to gasp out, "Wasn't gonna say anything!"

"You were thinking it, though!" He laughs, landing another blow with his improvised weapon.

"Guilty."

***

Mason is already in the kitchen, making a pot of coffee when I walk in. I feel like I'm late because I'm normally walking from the bus stop by now, and because I took a long shower after my workout, hoping to finish what I started last night. It was a waste of time. I've got time for breakfast, though. Not that I'm hungry. My stomach is still adjusting to three meals a day.

"Hey, what are the chances you could make us some of that oatmeal you made this time last year?"

"Uhh, refresh my memory?" I've made a lot of things for them over the years.

He turns around and leans against the counter while he waits for the coffee. "Pumpkin pie or something like that. I loved it."

I have the recipe memorized because it's one of my favorites. And it's cheap, so I eat it a lot. But . . . "Felicity said you hated it, and I should never make it again."

He scowls. "Why the hell would she do that?"

I'll never understand her. If he hated it, she would've told me he loved it so I'd make it more and irritate him. Why would you intentionally do things to make your partner miserable? "Your guess is as good as mine."

While he grumbles under his breath about batshit crazy girlfriends, I check the pantry. As it happens, he's in luck. We've got everything I need. *It's funny how fast I'm adjusting to thinking of this place as home.*

While I work, he sets the table for two and settles in with his tablet while he waits. The awkwardness I feared between us is absent. It's as if we've done this thousands of times. Unfortunately, that means I'm treated to his near orgasmic moans of pleasure while he devours his share of oatmeal.

Ordinarily, I'd be happy to know he is enjoying his breakfast. Those happy noises he's making are obscene, though. Each one of them seems to vibrate between my legs, calling attention to my frustration. He doesn't comment on my squirming. If he even notices. When he runs out of oatmeal, he gazes at the bowl like he's contemplating licking it clean. I have to bite my lip to keep from volunteering as tribute.

I've got to get away from him. It is my belief that sex shouldn't happen without love, but one could argue that oral isn't exactly sex. I might be desperate enough to buy that if this keeps up.

"So, when do you get done with your morning jobs?" Mason asks while I rinse the breakfast dishes and put them in the dishwasher.

"11:30. I'll have to adjust to all this extra time." I stop what I'm doing to smile at him, excited by a possibility I hadn't considered yet. "Maybe I can pick up an extra house or two!"

He frowns at me, causing me to question everything I said. "Fern, please remember that, very soon, you won't be in debt anymore. I'm not going to wait for the actual wedding to hold up my end of the bargain. Once the contract is signed, you can consider it paid off. You can enroll in whatever classes you want to take right away. If you want to quit your other jobs and focus on your degree, I will support you in that."

"So, what, I'll be . . ." *A freeloader?*

"My live-in girlfriend, who is a good role model for my daughter, her caretaker, a wonderful housekeeper, and the best cook," he finishes for me.

Oh, shit. I haven't thought of it in quite those terms. I haven't considered the time between signing the contract and the wedding. *What are people going to think?* He *just* broke up with Felicity.

People aren't going to know. Not until we're ready to tell them. *Right?* By then, we'll be more comfortable with things. We'll figure out a way to sell this that doesn't raise eyebrows. No one can say we haven't known each other for years. Maybe we can say once Felicity was out of the picture, we realized we have a lot in common and became good friends, and things just kind of escalated from there. It was there all along; we only didn't know it. *That should work.*

"I'll think about it," I say with what I hope is a nonchalant shrug. I don't want to get my hopes up about going back to school. A lot could happen between now and whenever we sign the contract. A lot could happen between now and whenever he decides to go to Vegas for a quick wedding, too.

"It's your decision. You can do whatever you want. Work. Don't work. Finish school. Don't. As long as you hold up your end of the bargain, I don't care what you do with your time darlin'. Ready to head out? I'll give you a ride. I gave Len the day off, and I don't want you walking for a while in case those people decide to come back. When I pick you up, we're going shopping."

Shopping? I don't have time for that. I still work here! "But—"

"The house is going to go to the dogs in one day," he says, knowing exactly what's bothering me.

Chapter 15

Mason

Fern flashes a tight smile my way when I turn into the driveway to pick her up from her last job of the day. It tells me everything I need to know. She was distracted and tense after breakfast, and she still is.

Surprising her seems to drop her guard. Maybe if I can do that now, she'll share whatever is bothering her. *How am I going to manage that?*

When she climbs in the car, I lean across the center console and kiss her cheek. She gasps like she did when she woke up, and again when I said she'll be my live-in girlfriend. Her cheeks turn pink, and she touches the spot where I kissed her.

"Hello, gorgeous. How was your morning?" I ask, reversing out of the drive.

"Hi," she says shyly. If she could see the dopey smile on her face right now, she'd probably slap herself. It's adorable, though. "It was okay. Same ol', same ol'. They got a new puppy over the weekend . . . He's not housebroken."

"Oh, shit." Translated, she had to scrub shit and piss stains all morning. That's not a great way to spend your day.

She throws her head back, laughing. "Exactly!" I wasn't trying to be funny, but I'll take the win.

"We have a slightly new game plan." She won't mind this though, I'm sure of it. "We're going to wait until Ronni is out of school to go car shopping."

Sure enough, she grins. "Okay, great."

"I figured it would be best to let my girls pick out their car together," I tell her, basking in the sunshine that is her smile. But it disappears as quickly as the sun in a storm. "What?"

"I . . ." Instead of continuing, she gnaws at her bottom lip and stares at her hands in her lap.

I guess when she doesn't expand upon it. "Need some time to get used to things?"

"Yeah."

"I understand. It's probably easier for me than it is for you." *Too easy.*

"Yeah," she says again.

"How about we make a deal?"

"Another one?"

That makes me grin. "Yes, another one."

She snuggles deeper into her seat that I'm now insanely jealous of, and angles her body toward me. Traffic demands all my attention, but from the corner of my eye, I can see her watching me. "What's that?"

"We'll never say anything we don't mean, alright? Not to sell this to each other, or to anyone else. If I call you beautiful, I mean it. When I tell you I'm happy to see you, I mean it. Okay?"

After a few seconds, she nods and says, "Alright. That sounds like a good idea."

"Good. So, you'll believe me when I say I'm excited about this."

She cocks an eyebrow at me. "Buying a new bed?"

Her skepticism makes me chuckle. I *am* excited about that, though, because I'm doing it with her. "Well, that too. But I meant our arrangement. Our contract," I add to clarify. "I like you, Fern. You're easy to talk to, and you're fun to be around now that you've stopped calling me Mr. Chambers and have accepted that eye contact isn't a flogging offense. This will be as easy as breathing because so much of it will be real."

She makes a funny face and nods hugely. "I agree. My mother always told me you should marry your best friend. This isn't quite what she meant, but hey . . . It'll work."

"I'm glad we agree. Ronni will be spending Friday night with my sister and her brood. Maybe Saturday night as well, because she never likes to leave. I'm thinking order in and discuss the contract over dinner?"

"Sure."

Best get this out of the way now, too. "I'd also like to take a look at these bills of yours. Can you gather statements for me?"

She cringes, but nods. "Yup."

"Fern." I try to say it as softly as I can. "I promise you, however much it is, it doesn't change anything. It's not like you went out and bought a Lamborghini and a bunch of Prada on credit."

Some of the tension bleeds out of her shoulders. She actually smiles a little. "You say that now," she whispers. She doesn't mean for me to hear it, but I do. I hope she never remembers how well I can hear.

"Nope," I argue. "I promise I can afford it. If I can't, I'll take out a loan. I told you I'll pay it. I don't care how I have to go about it, I will." It won't come to that, though. I could retire tomorrow, live comfortably for the rest of my life, and Ronni would never have to work, either.

Fern frowns and chews on her bottom lip again. She's driving me crazy. "You don't have to, Mason."

The sadness in that short statement washes away my good mood. I can only imagine the mountain she's been hauling around on her shoulders all these years. Now, someone has finally stepped up and offered to take it away. Why would she let me off the hook? *Is that her way of trying to get out of this?*

I sneak a few glances her way when traffic allows it. She doesn't notice because her eyes are glued to her hands, which she's dry-washing in her lap. "Yes, I do. That was part of our agreement. I want you to uphold your end."

"I would anyway, for Ronni."

I nearly miss the brake lights in front of me. Though I stop in plenty of time, she curls in on herself, bracing for impact. "I'm so sorry!" I reach for her hand, and she latches onto it without hesitation, squeezing for all she's worth.

Guilt threatens to choke me. The woman lost her husband and child in a car accident, and here I am, about to cause another because she shocked the shit out of me. "You surprised me. You'd seriously go through with this for Ronni?"

Tight-lipped, she nods while she takes deep breathes. "If I do it, I never have to worry about you marrying someone who mistreats Ronni. Getting married for love again isn't in the cards for me, but there's no reason I can't do it to protect her."

I should be offended that she thinks I'd marry someone who wasn't perfect for my little angel. But I did date Felicity for six years without noticing that anything was amiss. All in all, it's a fair assessment. I don't like it, but it's fair. "That's brutal," I tell her, my voice a little gruffer than I'd like right now since she's still upset.

She shrugs. "We agreed we'd be honest."

"That we did." I squeeze the hand I haven't let go of yet. I can't believe how badly I misjudged her motives for agreeing. Did the money matter to her at all, or was Ronni her motivation from the start? "Has anyone ever told you you're an amazing woman?"

"No!" she says much too quickly. Her cheeks flush, and I've gotta know why. "Fibber!"

I can practically see the wheels turning in her head. We just promised to always be honest with each other. This doesn't technically qualify, but . . .

Finally, she says, "Aaron did once, but we're not going to go there."

This is gonna be fun. "Oh, baby. We're going there. We've got nothing but time. Do tell." I'll sit in the car for an hour if that's what it takes. Take a wrong turn. Get lost. Find a secluded corner of a parking lot . . .

She drops my hand like a hot potato and her walls slam back into place. "Nope. Not happening. I would like to add a no flirting or sex clause to our contract."

I nearly slam on the brakes in surprise this time. *What the fuck? Is she serious?* "We're here." *Thank God.* I don't even know what to say to that.

Arguing that one out in traffic would be a bad idea. I can't imagine not flirting with Fern. She flirts back so easily. I don't understand where this is coming from, but we can talk about it later.

***

A call from work holds me up in the parking lot, but I wave Fern on so she can browse. I have no idea why she's upset, but I need to smooth it over. At least long enough to get us through the rest of the day. Some distance might help.

The problem at work is resolved quickly, and I make it inside only a couple minutes after her. My eyes zero in on Fern and a balding, middle-aged man who is leading her deeper into the store. I try not to glare at his hand on my girl's back and mostly fail.

Whoa! Not my girl. Not yet, anyway.

I practically power walk to catch Fern and the sleazy asshole who can't keep his hands to himself. I get it. Some people are naturally touchy-feely. I'm one of them, sort of. Regardless, I want to rip that guy's arm off and beat him with the bloody end.

What's gotten into me? I've never been the jealous kind. At least, not to this extreme. *She's not even my girlfriend!* It would've taken a lot more than this to bother me with Felicity, and she cheated!

The bastard grins at Fern and waves his hand toward a row of mattresses. "So, you currently have a full-sized bed? Have you considered upgrading to a queen? They don't take much more space."

"I don't take much space!" There's a smile in Fern's voice, and it pisses me off even more since it's for him, not me. *What the fuck is my problem?*

He laughs and shakes a finger at her. "One should always plan for the future, though! Husbands and babies take up space."

Yes, they most certainly do. I step between them, forcing him to step back, and sling my arm around Fern's waist, hooking my thumb through one of her belt loops, sending a clear message to anyone who glances our way that she's mine. *If I can't flirt with her, no one can.*

His eyes light up until he takes in my less-than-friendly expression. His tone doesn't change, though. He's a salesman to the bone. "See, that's what I mean! Take it from me, your husband doesn't want to cram himself into a tiny little bed every night!"

"He—"

I open my big mouth and run right over her attempt to correct him. "You're absolutely right," my eyes drop to his name tag, "Randy. I'm thinking a king size." We'll never see these people again, and it'll be true soon enough. The white lie soothes the ugly emotions coiling in my chest. I hug her a little closer to my side and kiss her temple.

Cool it, idiot. I'm doing what we said we wouldn't do. Only I'm not. I'm not technically lying to him with my words. My actions, on the other hand . . . I can't say those are a lie, either. I'm only allowing him to make incorrect assumptions.

His eyes light up dollar signs like a slot machine in Vegas. "An excellent choice! Right this way!"

Fern scowls at me with confusion clouding her pretty green eyes before she follows him like a well-trained puppy, pulling me along by the thumb I've still got hooked through her belt loop. I expected anger, either from before or for letting Randy believe a lie. Instead, she glances down, pointedly eyeing my hand on her hip, then back up at me and raises her eyebrows as if to ask me what the hell I'm thinking without missing a stride. *If I knew, I'd tell you.*

She displays none of the earlier stiffness with me as we try out the mattresses that can be had in the size I want before the close of business. I'm still worried Randy might pass out or have a heart attack over the news that price isn't an issue. Keeping an eye on him is easy. He won't get far enough away to risk anyone else poaching us.

After a few trials, I let go of my anger and try to enjoy myself. I have no reason to be mad at her for being herself and charming this guy to the point that he's eating out of her hand. She's not actually flirting with him, and he's not flirting, either. He's a salesman, trying to make a buck. I'm the only one here being unreasonable.

We flop onto the fifth choice, Fern laughing at something he's said, and a new little scenario plays out in my head. Me carrying her upstairs with her laughing over something I've said as we fall into bed together. Like Vee and I did dozens of times.

My good mood evaporates. I wouldn't be doing any of this right now if Vee had lived. I'd be happily married to the love of my life with two or three more children to chase around. *You'd want me to be happy, right, Vee? Is this wrong?*

Not every night ended with us falling into bed laughing together, though. I'm happier forgetting those other nights. I don't want to relive the times I slept on the couch because she was pissed at me over something stupid. I smiled at another girl. I didn't text back soon enough. She was so jealous and always suspicious because she thought I was too good for her. Maybe that's why I didn't catch on to Felicity's bullshit. Unlike Vee, she wasn't one to lash out at me every time. It makes my bout of jealousy even shittier, though.

"Do you want me to be an asshole to every girl I talk to in a day? Will that make you happy?"

"Only if they're pretty!" Our bedroom door slams in my face.

"None of them are prettier than you," I tell her through the flimsy wood.

"Don't lie to me, Mason!

"Vee, let me in! I don't want to sleep on the damn couch again. I didn't do anything wrong!"

Thinking poorly of Vee twists the knife her death left buried to the hilt in my heart. I loved her—love her still. I should focus only on the good times we had together. Sure, they weren't all good, but that didn't matter because we loved each other. Love like that never dies.

Vee wouldn't hate Fern, though. Well, she might if she were here, but she would approve of her now. She wouldn't want me to be alone forever. She would want me to be happy now. She's probably watching me, ready to bitch me out for squandering so much of my life with Felicity that I'm arranging a marriage because I've run out of time.

She'll never be you, Vee. She'll never take your place in my heart. She loves our little girl, though, and Ronni needs her. I need her.

"Mase?" Fern asks. *I like that.* She's never called me by a nickname before. The concern in her eyes warns me she's been trying to get my attention for a bit now. "There you are! How was your trip?"

"Sorry," I say, my voice breaking over the lump in my throat. "Thought of something I'd forgotten."

Fern leans over me and studies my face. She knows what actually happened. Her eyes tell me she does. "That's alright. What about this one?"

"Whatever makes you happy, sweetheart."

Chapter 16

Fern

Wednesday Night

"Thank you so much for everything," I whisper to Mason as we walk away from Ronni's room.

Being able to tuck her in is a dream come true. Felicity never allowed it before, not even when Mason was out of town. Ronni would beg and plead and cry, but Felicity wouldn't have it. For the first time since she moved into this house, I got to sing my little rainbow a lullaby and snuggle her while her daddy read her a story. He even does all the voices. Watching them together is the best thing ever.

Beside me, he shrugs. "You need nice things. Sometimes, I'm going to need you to go to company dinners and such with Ronni and me. There's one in a couple of weeks."

That's when things will get complicated. I don't care what he says. His family isn't going to like it that he's shacking up with his nanny. It doesn't matter if they like me or not. I've met most of them, and we get along fine. That won't keep them from being pissed off that we're suddenly in a relationship, especially not so soon after his breakup with Felicity.

I stop outside my door, grabbing his wrist to pull him to a stop. "I didn't only mean the things and the car, Mason. The home. Letting me help you tonight with Ronni . . . That means more to me than anything money could buy."

Mason sighs and slowly brings a hand up to cup my cheek, his eyes searching mine for permission. The same thrill I felt last night when his lips met mine zaps through me. My traitorous body begs him to do it again—to pull me close and hold me tight and kiss me until I'm dizzy.

"You're going to be her step-mom." The world spins, taking care of that unwelcome longing. *I think I need to sit.* "Hell, you're already her mom as far as she's concerned. Of course you should help me tuck her in at night. You got a minute? I wanna talk about something."

"Sure?" After his reminder that I'll be her step-mother, I'm a little too dazed to question much of anything, but that doesn't stop me from worrying that I've done something wrong.

He takes my hand and leads me to his room, probably so we don't run the risk of waking Ronni. Even after waking up here this morning, it's weird to be alone in his room with him. But I trust him. And I trust that I can kick his ass if he proves that trust to be misplaced.

"What's up?" I ask.

"Why were you so upset before the furniture store?"

Oh. That. That's what's got him so shook up? This whole honesty thing is going to be a pain. "I uh . . . I think flirting and sex will complicate an already complicated situation." That's not entirely honest, but it's not a lie. I don't want to want him, and I need him to stop making me want him. It's just not working out for me. I can't *not* be attracted to him. God knows I've tried.

He leans away from me a bit, his eyes wide, and blows out a breath. "Okay," he says slowly. One hand covers his mouth, and I watch his eyes dart around as he searches for the right thing to say. When he finally shakes his head, the breath stills in my lungs.

"I'm going to have to disagree with you there. I feel like a lack of both would complicate things for both of us. I can't—*won't*—have you taking other lovers. I don't share. How will we make this work if we try to ignore this spark between us?"

"Spark?" I repeat dumbly.

I thought it was just me, even after last night. He did say it's been a long time for him, too. His reaction didn't have to mean anything. It would probably be better if it *was* one-sided. He wouldn't have any interest in intimacy. My request would be a no-brainer.

He scowls. "Yes, Fern. Don't pretend you don't feel it. You gave yourself away last night when I accidentally kissed you."

I close my eyes and let my head fall back. *Fuck.* There's no way I can deny it. I might as well own it. "Yeah, but look . . . I don't believe sex should happen without love, so . . ."

His dark eyebrows climb his forehead. "So, you're telling me you haven't been with *anyone* since he died?"

"I'm afraid to be with anyone else because I might forget him!" Horrified, I slap my hands over my mouth as if that will take the words back. *What the fuck did I just say?* Why am I telling him things he doesn't need to know? What is *wrong* with me?

Mason sighs. His hands move in my peripheral vision, but I can't face him any more than I already am. That was too big. Telling him put too much of me on the line. *This is why I don't talk about the past!* First, it's a little bit here and there, then the dam breaks and it all comes out!

"Oh, baby. Come here," he murmurs. He pulls me close, and I don't fight the hug he's offering. "You're not going to forget him. It doesn't matter if you sleep with one guy or one hundred, you won't love him any less. He wouldn't want you to stop living your life because he's gone, just like Vee wouldn't want me to stop living mine. They'd want us to find happiness again."

"Happiness doesn't have to mean love, though," I say into his shirt. His heart beats a steady rhythm against my forehead. I could turn my head and listen to it, let it comfort me. But that was something I did with Aaron. Doing it with someone else feels wrong.

"No . . . But I don't believe they'd want us to live without love either. I understand, Fern. I don't expect I'll ever love anyone again. It would feel like I'm replacing her, but there's more than one kind of love in the world. I won't push you. I'll wait for you to decide you're ready and come to me. I need a confirmation you understand there's no other option anymore. I won't screw around on you; you won't screw around on me."

"Oh, I know. I don't care." Truthfully, I don't care if I never have sex again.

He heaves a huge sigh. "Alright, I can't pretend to be happy about this, and I'm sorry, but I can't stop flirting with you. It's too fun."

It's hard to shrug with him hugging me, but I make it work. "I'll deal with that."

He snorts out a bitter laugh. "Austin is going to have a field day if he finds out about this . . . I specifically told him I wouldn't have a wife I couldn't touch."

My heart sinks. It's crazy, but I want this more than I've wanted anything in a long time. Is it worth it if he's not happy, though? How will that affect Ronni? "Not too late to change your mind."

He combs his fingers through my hair in that deliciously slow way he has. The unhurried movements lull me into relaxing into him until everything he says is punctuated by the steady rhythm of his heart. "Yeah, it is. I meant it when I said there is no one I'd rather do this with. We understand each other too well, even if we don't agree on everything. You know, most people who believe you should wait for sex say you should be married first."

Moot point. "Most people love each other before they get married."

He laughs again. "People have been arranging marriages for thousands of years. Love is a luxury. Sex is a basic human need." He exhales deeply and hangs his head, letting his forehead rest against the crown of my head. "I will respect your wishes, but I can't promise you I won't try. No means no, but I will flirt, I will tease, and I will probably tempt you from time to time. You're going to be my *wife*, Fern." Those words from his lips make my heart stutter. "There's nothing wrong with sex between husband and wife, even if they don't love each other. Hell, it happens all the time. Don't you want babies?"

Damn, he's got me there. Yes, I want babies. "Well, yeah. Someday . . ."

He lifts his head to arch a brow at me, a slight smile teasing the corners of his eyes and mouth. "You *do* know where they come from, right?"

The tension between us snaps like a guitar string stretched too tight. Shaking with silent giggles, I bite my lip in a last-ditch effort to hold them back. It's no good, though. As corny as that joke was, it was perfectly timed. I give in and let my laughter ring out from the depths of my soul.

Still wearing that little smile, he leans back to tap my chest, over my heart. "I don't expect to own this. I get that I'll always take second place to him. It's the same with me; Vee owns my heart, and she always will. But when you're ready to spare a little real estate in there for me, I'll be waiting."

Looking me in the eye, he slowly leans in. I watch him close the distance between us, reading his intention in his eyes. I should turn away. This is crazy. It's too soon. But I want to feel that rush again. *Was it only last night?*

He's not going to do it. He's only bluffing, waiting to see what I'll do.

He stops. We're a twitch away from kissing, but I won't be the one to back down.

I allow myself the smallest of smiles because I was right, but disappointment floods my heart. *What is wrong with me?* I shouldn't want this.

The smile in his eyes is pure wickedness. I would swear in front of a judge that he knows what he's doing to me. He moves a bit closer. My stomach swoops with excitement. I tilt my chin up, ready for the warmth of his lips even as I question my sanity, and that same thrill from before shoots straight to my heart the instant his lips touch mine.

Just like last night, I turn into a giant pile of putty in his hands. He moves to pull away much too soon. I follow him, going so far as to push onto my tiptoes when he doesn't stop, desperate to maintain the connection. He's too tall, though. My head might feel like my brain is made of cotton, but I'm not crazed enough to climb him.

When I open my eyes and blink at him, I find a bitter smile aimed at me.

"You can say you don't want me if it makes you feel better, but you and I know the truth, Fern. You wanted that."

Though it's not a question, I absently nod my head. "Yeah."

My voice snaps me out of my daze. *What have I done?* Fueled by panic, I turn away and hurry to my room before he can try to push my resolve to prove a point. He wouldn't be taking anything I don't want to give him, but I can't. It's not mine to give.

I rush through my bedtime routine and fall into bed. The scent of fabric softener clinging to the sheets is enough to drive me crazy. I'm already so sexually frustrated I'm going to explode. Now, I'm wrapped in sheets that remind me of the only man I've actually wanted since Aaron died, and that's precisely why I can't have him.

I surrender and slip a hand into my panties. Nights with Aaron play out in my head while I tease the sensitive little pearl that holds the key to my problem. Nothing fancy. I'm a pro at getting the job done fast. Pleasure ceased to be part of the equation for me years ago. It's about getting my fix and going on with life. Like the last two times though, nothing happens.

Irritation causes my concentration to slip, and when it does, Mason strong-arms his way into my mind. It's his hands on me. His finger inside me, finding that sweet spot that isn't always easy to wake. For him, though, it comes to life. It's him squeezing my breast, pinching my nipple. It's his name I groan into the pillow when my orgasm hits me like a damn freight train. And it's him I want to hold me while I cry myself to sleep because I got off thinking about him.

Mason

Sleep has me in its clutches, but I swear I hear my name. Becoming a parent means learning to detect even the faintest cry for help, or call for Daddy. But I heard my name. Ronni doesn't call me by name. Ever.

Sitting bolt upright in bed, I wait and listen. My ears strain hard enough to pull a muscle if such a thing were possible, but the call doesn't come again. But is that . . . ? Someone is crying.

Out of habit, I run to Ronni's door first. After all the false alarms I've responded to, I've learned to run down the hall without making a sound. I've also learned to keep her hinges oiled so they don't give me away when I open the door. She's breathing deeply, lost in dreams.

I tap softly on Fern's door. *What if she didn't hear?* Instead of knocking again and risking waking her if she's asleep, I push it open a couple of inches to listen. She lets out another muffled sob. *I don't think so.* No one cries alone in my house, my girls, least of all. Even if all I can do is hold her hand, she won't be alone.

"Fern?" I call softly so as not to scare her. With Ronni, I'd crawl in bed. This isn't Ronni, though. *No, it's the woman I'm going to marry.* But she has boundaries, even if I do a monumentally shitty job of respecting them sometimes. I can't climb into bed with her without giving her the chance to say no and mean it. Last night was a one-off, not a blanket invite.

Tears and misery choke her voice. "Go away."

There's an odd, squeezing sensation in my chest at being dismissed so easily when all I want to do is help. "Can't do that, sweetheart. I promised you I'd be here for you to lean on. You can't do that if I go away, so do you mind if I join you?"

"Thank you, but I'd really rather be alone." I peer into the darkness, toward the sound of her voice, but there's not enough light for my eyes to pick her out. She doesn't sound like she should be alone. She sounds absolutely shattered, worse than she was last night. Maybe last night gave her the strength she needs to face whatever it is. For whatever reason, that's disappointing to me. Probably because we agreed we'd never have to be alone, but now she's telling me she doesn't want help. *What if she's changing her mind?*

Defeated, I do the only thing I can without possibly driving a wedge between us. She might take it the wrong way if I ignore her wishes to be alone and decide I can't keep my word. "If you change your mind, you know where to find me. I'll save a place for you."

"Thank you," she whispers, her voice tight.

She's not thanking me for the offer. I'm certain of that. She's thanking me for backing off when I want to charge in. *Charging in would be easier.*

With the door closed between us, I cross the hall and slide down the wall, landing hard on my ass. Waiting. Hoping. If she calls for me again, I'll be right there. I won't give her time to change her mind.

My ass is numb before I surrender and go back to bed, trusting her to come to me for whatever she needs when she can't handle it alone anymore. The sheets are cold when I crawl between them, and I realize that some of my disappointment stems from sleeping alone again. Sharing my space with her was wonderful, even if she did fall asleep as soon as she laid down. Waking up with her was, too. I hoped it would happen again.

Sighing, I collapse onto my stomach. The sheets smell faintly of her. My hand slips across the soft fabric, finding nothing but emptiness. Taking things slow suddenly seems to be the most idiotic idea I've ever had in my life.

Chapter 17

Fern

Thursday

Ronni thinks she's sneaky, or maybe that we're oblivious, but Mason and I see the way her eyes keep bouncing back and forth between us. She smiles every time we speak to one another.

"Have some more coffee, Fern. I'll clear the table!"

"Uh, okay. Thanks, Ronni." She loves to help out, but I wasn't expecting her to this morning.

Mason shakes his head when I catch his eye. "Better hurry, Rice," he says, checking the time. "You need to leave soon."

"This is so cool!" she says, bouncing on the balls of her feet, tipping the stack of plates in her hand until the flatware on top threatens to slide off. She stills and rights the pile in the nick of time.

"What's that?" I ask her.

"Having you here! Getting to ride to school with you!"

"You're not going to miss the carpool?"

She stops loading the dishwasher to look at me and scoff. "Well, maybe a lit-tle," she says with a small frown. "But I'd rather ride with you." My heart goes squish.

"Do you ladies mind if I join you this morning?"

Oh, please, no.

Ronni cheers her assent. Her enthusiasm isn't as infectious as usual. I'm not mad at Mason, but after last night I'm on edge around him. He doesn't know why

I was crying, but I'm sure he's going to question me about it as soon as we're alone in the car.

I put on a smile and keep my eyes on my coffee. It's better to get it over with than to dwell on it all day.

***

Ronni is still running backward toward the school, smiling and waving when Mason pounces. "Sleep okay?"

It's a perfectly innocent question, but he's already asked me that today. He's trying to trick me into talking about last night. I know it's going to happen eventually, but I'd rather he ask outright than tiptoe around it. "No better than the last time you asked me."

He laughs softly. "I deserve that. I'm just . . . worried. Is everything okay?"

My eyes twitch his way, but don't make it far before they snap back to the road. I was always a cautious driver, but the accident made it worse. "I'm fine." It's mostly true. I'm embarrassed and angry with myself for what happened last night, but I'm fine. "Did you need to go somewhere, or did you just want to get out?"

We're stopped, so I peek his way and watch him look around at the surrounding neighborhood like he's forgotten where we are. "To get out. Hey, I know it's out of the way, but if you have time, there's a nice little coffee shop over by CFI. Can I buy you a drink before work?"

I'd rather gouge my eye out with a rusty fork than keep myself in this situation longer than necessary, but refusing his request seems unnecessarily bitchy when he's trying to be sweet. "Thank you, I'd like that."

"Can I ask you a question?"

"You just did."

He makes an unhappy noise. "If you don't mind, there's a personal question I'd like to ask you."

I bite my tongue to keep myself from telling him that I don't like personal questions. It's true, but why get picky at this point? "Shoot."

"Are you happy?"

My mind blanks out. That's so far from what I was expecting that I don't know how to answer. And so incredibly sweet, I think I feel a cavity coming on. My first genuine smile of the day that isn't Ronni induced takes me by surprise.

For a simple question, it's not as straightforward as it seems. That's why he labeled it personal. He's asking about more than how I'm feeling right this second. He wants to know if I'm having second thoughts, or if I'm content with my choice despite my misgivings.

We still have a few bugs to work out, but the reward is worth the time and effort to me. "Yes, Mason. I'm happy. You?"

"I'm happy. Thank you, Fern." He holds his hand out for mine.

His words bring me an odd sense of fulfillment. We're in this together, no matter how different it is. I hate taking my hand off the wheel, but I don't want to leave him hanging either. His fingers are sure and strong when they close around mine. At this moment, holding his hand feels right. His lips are warm against the back of my hand.

Since we're already discussing it, in a roundabout way, this is the perfect time to bring up something that's bothering me. "I want to pay you back."

He's quiet for a beat too long. "What are you talking about?"

"My bills." I risk a glance his way, but he only cocks a curious brow at me, so I spell it out. "Look, it's my debt, and I want to pay it. It will take me a while, but without such steep interest rates, it shouldn't take as long."

He sits quietly long enough I start to fidget. We reach another stop sign, so I chance another look. He's wearing an intense scowl that makes my insides coil and squirm. Slowly, he shakes his head back and forth.

"Why are you glaring at me like that? Stop shaking your head!" I snatch my hand away to shove his shoulder, trying to get him to stop it. He makes a show of rocking to the side, into the door, and sitting upright again.

My playfulness at least earns me a grin. "I've looked through the binder you left on my desk. I've gotta say, I'm impressed with the way you've managed everything, considering you have no background whatsoever in finance.

"Not gonna lie, it was more than I was expecting." *I knew it was too good to be true.* He grabs my hand again and squeezes it. "That doesn't change a damn thing. I didn't know it was remotely possible to make a funeral cost that much."

Memories of the day rekindle the grief that's always waiting to catch me off guard. "It was quite the spectacle," I whisper. "Mrs. Williams did nothing small."

"I've noticed. This is essentially a business arrangement. You're selling me a chunk of your life—seven years—in the form of your hand in marriage. If you pay me back, you're not making a damn thing from this. So, thank you, but no. I'm not going to dictate what you can and cannot do with your time, but I am telling you right now, I won't accept a single penny from you."

My argument dies on my tongue when he spells it out like that. It almost sounds like he owns me for the duration. Technically, he does. Once my debt is erased, I'm bought and paid for. "Where did you get seven years?"

He's apparently given this a lot more consideration than I have. I tend to focus on the here and now too much to think about the distant future. "A year-and-a-half to date and plan the wedding. Five years married, plus a few months so as not to raise eyebrows by filing for divorce at the five-year mark."

That seems like a lifetime, and no time at all.

"That a problem?" he asks when the silence becomes protracted.

I shake my head. "No, just a surprise."

Chapter 18

Fern

Friday Evening

The doorbell rings. It must be the food unless Ronni forgot to pack something. "I've got it," I call to Mason, putting my ancient laptop aside.

I smile when I find Austin waiting on the other side, three boxes of pizza in hand. "Delivery!" he says in a sing-song voice.

Laughing, I step aside to let him in. Austin spends more time here, so I know him better than I do their sister, Nicole. Calling him a friend might be presumptuous, but he always goes out of his way to make me smile. "Hello, Mr. Chambers. He's in his office."

He rearranges his features into a comical scowl and shifts the pizza boxes to one arm so he can hug me with the other. "Cut the crap, Fern. We're siblings now." He lets me go and steps back. "Your face!"

I can only imagine I have a deer-in-the-headlights look going on right now. "That's going to take some getting used to." I knew Austin was aware of the arrangement, of course, but somehow I imagined him against it. Or against me. "You're really okay with this?"

He smirks and jerks his thumb toward his chest. "I'm the one who gave him the idea. I didn't really think he'd do it, but you were always the logical choice. I'm glad he basically admitted I was right by asking. I get to rub his nose in it! And I'm helping draft the contract. Mason and I have been researching what needs to be done to make it legally binding for the last two days."

"Oh." The cold hand of uncertainty wraps its fingers around my heart. Some small part of me wants to believe Mason picked me because there is something special about me. I know better. Mason only asked because he knows I won't be sacrificing a chance at a real relationship by agreeing, but I want to believe it all the same. Even if it's a bad idea.

Austin grins again and nudges me with his elbow. "Cheer up! We're supposed to be celebrating! You're getting married, and I'll no longer be competing against the hot single dad for the ladies. I'm telling you; he doesn't even realize how high he's set the bar. Women think they're getting him only to be bummed when they learn they're going out with the wrong Chambers."

"Well, then I suppose we should get on with it." I raise my voice to carry into the other room, "Hey, Mason! Dinner is here!"

With Austin's quip about women getting the wrong Chambers still buzzing around my brain, I can't resist the urge to tease them both a bit. "The delivery boy is kinda cute. I think I'm gonna keep him!"

Austin unceremoniously dumps the boxes off onto the drop station by the door, almost knocking over a lamp, and sweeps me into his arms, dipping me back dramatically in true Austin fashion. "I fucking love you. That's it. I'm calling this off. You're marrying the wrong brother. I object. Strenuously."

Mason clears his throat, and I look to find him glaring at us, framed in the office doorway. "Get your hands off my girl," he says when Austin turns a sly smile his way. Glare intact, Mason steps into the foyer.

Surely, he knows there's nothing to be jealous of. It's only a joke. Austin is never serious about anything. I search Mason's face for signs that he's about to crack—a twitch in the corners of his mouth, a hint of laughter in his eyes—and come up empty-handed. Austin took my weak joke too far, but Mason is pushing it to the limit.

"Hey, nothing has been signed yet," Austin says. "She could change her mind. She's a catch. I've been waiting for you to realize that for years. You're lucky I have zero interest in settling down, or I would have stolen her from you sooner." For one heart-stopping moment, I think he's going to kiss me on the mouth and ignite World War III to prove his point, but he turns his head and plants one on my cheek.

Mason's lips press into a hard line that I recognize from the furniture store when he joined Randy and me. He's not faking it; he's pissed. This needs to stop right now.

My heartbeat cranks to eleven when I realize I can't escape Austin's hold on me without hurting him, or maybe myself. I need to get away from him and diffuse this situation, though. Austin seems oblivious to the warning signs, which are practically flashing like neon now. There's a twitch in Mason's jaw, and his brows are so low over his eyes it's amazing he can see. All signs point to angry.

Mason growls another warning and stalks closer. "I'm not stupid," he says, smiling at his brother. *Maybe I'm wrong. Perhaps he is only yanking Austin's chain.* "The real reason is that you live in fear of what Ronni will do to you when she finds out you broke her Fern's heart, and what I'll do to you for hurting both of them."

Austin shrugs carelessly and stands me up, but he doesn't let me go. "Guilty as charged."

Mason's eyes zero in on Austin's hand on my waist, and his smile disappears. His voice drops an octave and becomes pure menace. "I repeat: get your hands off her."

"Temper, temper!" Austin smiles a crooked smile at me and winks. "Someone sounds a little jealous, don't you think?"

Mason says, "Someone sounds like he wants his ass kicked."

My mouth goes dry. I scramble away from Austin and put myself between them. Mason would never hurt me, but I face him so he doesn't think I'm taking Austin's side. "Mason," I say to draw his attention. I might as well have whispered for all the good it did.

"No, someone wanted to see how bad you've got it. I'm pretty sure Usher wrote a song about you."

"Stop with your stupid fucking games, Austin. You have no idea what you're talking about!"

The tension in the air is strangling me. I've got to stop this. "Come on, guys. Knock it off. Mason, Austin is just teasing you. You know that. Austin, I'm not sure what the hell is up with your brother. Sorry."

Mason continues to glare at his brother over my head.

Austin laughs. "Oh, that? No worries, Fern. That was the mating dance of the Neanderthal. I'm surprised he didn't communicate in grunts and two-word sentences à la Tarzan. I threatened to take his shiny new toy, and he threw a temper tantrum like I knew he would."

Mason edges another step closer. "Look, you need to back the fuck off, okay? I'll admit you had a great idea, and Fern is absolutely the best person for the job. But you don't know everything, so you need to butt the hell out."

Austin cocks his head to the side. "What don't I know?" he asks without a hint of his usual cheerfulness.

"Never mind. Let's eat. We can talk about the contract after dinner." Mason holds out a hand in a silent demand for mine, and I have a sudden vision of being caught in a tug-of-war between them.

"I do my second-best work with food," Austin says.

I thought Austin was kidding about the whole Tarzan thing, but I'm not so sure anymore. I'm also not sure how I feel about this possessive streak of Mason's. I'm only kind of his. Still, I give him my hand and let him pull me to his side.

Oblivious to his brother's eruption-level anger, Austin prattles on. "My best work is in the bedroom, though. Put the two together, and . . ." He pantomimes a bomb exploding around his head, presumably indicating it's mind-blowing.

Ordinarily, I'd give him shit. Rile him up. Tell him it's not his mind he's supposed to be blowing, but hers. Doing so right now would be equivalent to dropping a lit match in a barrel of gasoline, given how worked up Mason is. I'm fairly positive that having Austin offer to blow my mind wouldn't be good for anything right now. Even if it is just a joke.

Mason

"What don't I know?" Austin whispers when Fern excuses herself to the bathroom.

I hold up my finger, listening for a door to close. I'd bet big she only left the room to diffuse the situation. Even knowing that she was joking couldn't stop me from seeing red at the sight of him holding her. And the things he was saying . . . *What if she decides she wants a shot at a real relationship with him? Or with anyone?*

That's been my worst fear since she ran from me after our first real kiss. The one that wasn't an accident. We're too close for her to bail on me now.

Despite what he says, he's not truly interested in her, or he would have tried harder before. *It was a joke.* They see each other on a somewhat regular basis and have always been friendly. They're going to be family. I'm sure she, at least, is trying to work out the new dynamic. He's not her client's brother anymore. He's her boyfriend's brother. Later, her brother-in-law. They're testing the waters to figure each other out. Nothing more.

I swallow my pride and prepare to confess. And apologize. Austin and I don't keep secrets, and if anyone can help me find a way to sway Fern, it's him. I told her I'll respect her wishes—and I will—but she's going to kill me without even trying. "Look, I overreacted . . . I'm—"

He waves away my apology before I can say it. "Forget it, Mase. I knew what I was doing. I baited you."

What. The. Fuck? "Why?"

"So, you'd see it's real."

I cross my arms over my chest to resist the urge to play Whack-A-Mole with his head. "That what's real?"

He backhands me lightly on the arm like he does when he thinks I'm willfully ignorant. Unfortunately, he's right half the time. The other half, I'm just ignorant. "That you have real feelings for her, dumbass!"

"Of course I do. We're friends."

Austin sighs. "Whatever, you stubborn sonofabitch. I'm only trying to get you to understand you have genuine feelings for Fern, but you're too scared of falling in love again to give anyone else a real shot."

Sighing, I rub the back of my neck because he's not totally wrong. There are some feelings there. I haven't figured out what they are yet, but he doesn't need to know any of that. "You heard Ronni. Fern spent most of her time avoiding me as much as possible because of Felicity's rules. How could I have these supposed feelings for her? Over the last few days, I've grown very fond of her. You were right before. She's . . ."

"Perfect for you?"

I choose my words carefully to put an end to the discussion and move onto the real problem. "Perfect for this situation. I think we'll make this work once we've figured everything out. There's a problem, though."

"What's that?"

I hesitate. It's personal, but I need his help. "Fern doesn't want sex to be part of our arrangement."

Austin rolls his eyes. "So, what? It's not like you need a contractual agreement to boink her. What, did you want to schedule it? Mondays, Wednesdays, Fridays, and twice on Saturdays?"

"No, you dumbass. She doesn't want to have sex! She doesn't believe in sex without love."

He scratches at his jaw. "So, give it a few months? I'm sure she can learn to love you eventually . . . I mean, I know you're a dickhead, but . . ."

I sigh and shake my head. "She has her own Vee." That's the only explanation I can give without giving too much away. "He died years ago."

Austin watches me, probably waiting for me to laugh and tell him I'm bullshitting him to get even for his little stunt. Finally, he shakes his head. "You two are truly a match made in heaven. Perfect for each other. Both in love with ghosts. This is better than *Romeo and Juliette*. Star crossed lovers, my ass, they don't have anything on you two."

"Please, don't mention it unless she brings it up." I punch him in the shoulder for good measure, just hard enough to sting. "And keep your fucking hands to yourself. I wanted to rip the arm off of the last guy who put a hand on her and beat him with the bloody stump."

"You realize what's going on here, right?" he asks.

"I have a permanent case of blue balls and no chance of getting laid? Lack of sex is making me crazy?"

"Yeah, we'll go with that until you're ready for the truth."

What the hell does that mean? "That *is* the truth."

He rolls his eyes. "I'd also like to point out that a handjob isn't sex . . ."

"Good thought . . ." I could make do with that for a while. Until she changes her mind.

Somehow, I doubt she'll agree, and that I can keep my mouth off her. She specifically said sex, but she probably meant all forms of intimacy are off the table. "Doubt she'll go for it."

"Why not? It's a win-win. You both get what you need."

Because Fern doesn't like it when I turn her on. That's when she runs away. "I don't know," I lie. It's not a first—me lying to my brother—but it hurts every time. The answer is simple, but it isn't. She's afraid she'll lose control. If she loses control, she might succumb.

Austin grins at me. "Well, figuratively speaking, you're fucked. Enjoy monk-hood."

"The idea was for you to put your brain in gear and help me think of a way to convince her the world won't end if we get horizontal!"

"Yeah, I know. But I'm going to enjoy watching you work for it for a change. The challenge will be good for you."

"Hello, Satan. Who invited you?"

Chapter 19

Fern

Laughter is my cue that it's safe to rejoin the guys. They haven't moved much, still standing in front of the door, but Austin clutching his stomach like he's about to bust a gut from laughing. Mason, on the other hand, has his fists balled at his sides like he would *like* to bust him in the gut.

Uncertain of what I'm about to walk into, I stop on the last stair and watch. If they're not done beating their chests, I'll hightail it back upstairs. My presence probably won't help if Mason is still on edge.

"Hey Fern," Austin calls. His face is still red, and his smile is big enough it probably hurts. *Surely, he wouldn't be smiling if they were still pissed at each other?*

"Hey." I raise a finger and flick it back and forth between them. "We all good here?"

"Yeah, we're good," Mason says.

"Grab your laptop," Austin tells Mason. "We work while we eat. I have plans tonight."

"I swear to Christ if you get grease all over my laptop . . ." I don't catch the rest of Mason's threat because I yank open the cabinet to get out plates for dinner.

Austin strolls in with the pizzas. I've seen them eat, so I don't even question why there are three. Mason brings up the rear and shoves his laptop is to his brother's chest hard enough to make his breath whoosh out in a soft, "Oof!"

"As requested," Mason says, grinning and clearly pleased with himself.

"Asshole," Austin shoots back.

"Yeah, yeah. Let's get to work." Mason walks around the bar, lines up the pizza boxes, and opens them one by one. "What the hell, Austin? They're all the same . . ."

"Well, yeah." Austin sounds confused. "Meat lovers is the best. Don't pretend it's not your favorite."

Mason flings his hand my way. "And what about Fern?"

He shrugs. "I figured she could pick off the bits she doesn't like."

"Reasons Austin is single for two hundred, Alex," Mason mutters as he stacks five pieces of pizza on a plate and turns to me. "I'm sorry my brother is an idiot," he says solemnly before he takes a big bite.

"I'll live." I shrug my indifference. "Honestly, I'm just excited to get pizza that wasn't a dollar-fifty from the freezer section of the grocery store."

Identical stares come to rest on me. "But . . . that's not pizza," Austin says, waving a slice at me from the other side of the bar.

The weight of their gazes makes me squirm uncomfortably. "Eating out is expensive, so I don't." Buffets can be cheap at times, but I never allow myself to indulge. It only makes me miss it more.

"That is insane!" Austin whispers. He turns to his brother. "You're going to fix that, right?" Since Mason's mouth is full of pizza again, he nods. "Good. Let's do this. Start with the basics: when does the contract expire?" While he waits for an answer, he opens the laptop and wakes it.

"Seven years from today," Mason says without pause.

Austin doesn't comment, but his fingers fly over the keyboard. "Got it. And at the end of that time? Divorce? Renegotiate? Reevaluate?"

Mason watches me while he answers for both of us again. "Reevaluate. We shouldn't make decisions now about what we might want in the future."

Okay, I can agree with that. I nod my assent when Austin glances at me for confirmation. "That seems reasonable." For all I know, we could be happy with the arrangement and want to continue, because why ruin a good thing? *Anything with Ronni is a good thing.*

"Okay. Seven years together in exchange for . . . ?"

"Fern's debts will be paid in full, effective immediately."

I brace myself for Austin's reaction. Sure, Mason didn't volunteer any information about the source of my debts, but that could be worse. Austin is free to imagine all sorts of things. Will he now worry that I'll spend his brother into debt as well? But he merely blinks and looks at Mason over the screen.

"You might want to expand upon that . . ." Austin tells him.

"Like?" Mason asks.

"Did you do *any* reading? Cap on how much you're willing to shell out for this debt. Housing, all that."

Mason snorts. "Yes, I read. I just . . . forgot it all. Her debt will be paid in full. And she lives here, duh."

Austin massages his temples. "For the sake of the contract!"

Mason's shirt hikes up a bit when he lifts his arm to rub the back of his neck while he thinks. The exposed sliver of skin is oddly distracting. I force myself to look away before I get caught staring. "Oh . . . Um, for as long as the contract is in effect . . . fuck, I don't know! I had this all planned out, and it's just gone!"

He turns to me and raises his eyebrows, but I shrug because I don't know either.

"Damnit! It's Friday. I shouldn't have to think this fucking hard." He blows out a breath, puffing out his cheeks as he does so, and stares at the last slice of pizza on his plate.

Mason turns his head and locks eyes with me. His smile is soft, and so are his eyes. It's an unreadable expression, as indecipherable as the emotions in my chest, sprouting like seeds in the spring, from the warmth directed at me. I might not be able to define it, but I kind of like it. "We'll effectively be in a relationship once we sign, and will be married within eighteen months. I'll keep a roof over her head, food on the table, bills will be paid—including tuition if she wishes to continue her education—and insurance. I will cover anything she needs or wants, within reason. Any income she has during this time will be her own. In exchange, she is to care for my daughter as her own, ensure she gets to and from school, and handle any appointments and extracurricular activities when I cannot. She will continue to keep the house clean as she has always done. Does that cover everything?"

It's like a book—the next seven years of my life in black and white, possibly in a numbered list. I hate the way it sounds. He's doing so much for me. In exchange, I'll sign a couple contracts, say some vows that have an expiration date, wear his ring, and live a cushy life for a while. *No, not a book* . . . It's a bit like adopting a dog . . . An adoption contract and a collar with a tag to tell the world that this creature belongs to someone. I know what he'll say if I argue, though, so I hold my tongue and resolve to be the best fake wife ever.

"Should be sufficient," Austin mutters, typing furiously. His eyes are glued to the screen, which gives them an eerie glow. They're the same shape as his brother's, but the blue isn't as vivid. It's tamed by a hint of gray. One would think it would make them dull, but they're every bit as unique and beautiful as Mason's bright blue.

Though Austin is four years younger, they're similar enough to be twins. Austin is a little lighter than his brother all around, hair, eyes, and skin tone—though the latter could be because he doesn't spend as much time out of doors. If I asked, I'm sure he'd have a joke about spending most of his time in bed. Now that I am comparing them side-by-side, his face is a little softer, too. It could be the age difference, or that life has been kinder to Austin in general. He might lose some of that softness when he's older.

I feel eyes on me and turn to find Mason watching me intently. He smiles, and his eyes dart to my empty plate and back pointedly. I'm not sure I have an appetite right now. The next seven years of my life are about to be determined. It'll be a life of comfort and happiness, I'm sure. *Hell, it sounds like an all-expenses-paid vacation.*

Plus dental. It's surreal, though. Here we stand, calmly discussing something monumental as if it's nothing at all.

"Anything else?" Austin asks. "You haven't addressed the possibility of children. Are we leaving that open for interpretation, or are we spelling it out here?"

My heart pounds. Neither of us answer. We're too busy staring each other down, trying to communicate without words when we don't know each other well enough to do anything of the sort. This is when I should speak up, but . . .

Blithely, Austin continues on, "Let's face it, Mason, if you wait until this is over to have more, you're going to be in your mid-thirties and Ronni will be a teenager. If it's something you want, you're probably going to want to get on that soon." He flashes me a crooked smile I only see from the corner of my eye and says, "No pun intended. I'd never call you a 'that.'"

"Such a charmer," I tell him, rolling my eyes so he doesn't miss the sarcasm. Even as I do, my attention remains fixed on the man I've agreed to marry. *"Don't you want babies?"* His question keeps popping into my head at inopportune moments, like now. It, more than anything, made me rethink things. But I'm not a damn broodmare. If we decide we want children later, so be it. It's not fair to make that decision right now.

"Fern?" Mason asks, his voice raw from whatever he's holding back. "I'm not a heartless bastard here, darlin'. I'm not going to force you into anything you don't want."

My eyes slide away from his because I know what he's going to hear when I say, "I don't really feel it is something we can decide right now. That would be dictating life beyond the contract. Well beyond, because you're absolutely nuts if you think I'll give up custody rights."

Mason closes the distance between us and slides his hands down my arms to hold my hands. "Do you think we're going to come out of this hating each other?" I make the mistake of meeting his eyes, now bright blue whirlpools of sadness that pull me right in. *Does he actually care what we think when this is over? It's just a means to an end.*

I shrug a little. I've lost too much sleep in my life worrying about *'might'* and *'maybe.'* If I've learned anything from the mess Mrs. Williams dropped on my head, it's that there's very little in life I can actually control, and I shouldn't waste the headspace on the things I can't. "We can't know what will happen. Truthfully, I can't foresee either of us doing anything to cause hard feelings. No one ever goes into anything like this expecting to hate each other, but this isn't normal.

"We're not doing this because we're crazy about each other. We're doing this for convenience. We both stand to gain from it. We might stand to lose from it. All we can really do is hope it's worth it in the end. For all we know, we're going to be just another statistic. When our time is up, we shake hands and go our separate ways. Hopefully, our lives will be better for our time together."

"So," Austin says, drawing it out, "if kids happen, they happen. If they don't, you'll both deal. Got it. But neither party can be mad about either outcome because it was not spelled out clearly at the time the agreement was made. Agreed?"

Mason gives me a little shake. "Talk to me, Fern. You were adamant the other day that you wanted it in writing sex would not be expected of you. I'm not complaining if you've changed your mind. I stand by what I said that night. This is your chance to spell it all out, though."

"As long as we're both clear that I reserve the right to refuse service to anyone, for any reason, at any time—"

Austin cuts me off. "Oh, that's going on here. That's fucking hilarious. Are we talking about pussy or a restaurant?"

I roll my eyes at him. "This from a man who probably can't tell the difference."

"Touché! God, I like you. Where have you been all his life? And, for the record, I can, too, tell the difference. At a restaurant, food goes in my mouth. Pussy—"

I cover my ears. "Yeah, got it! Thanks for that . . ."

Mason is shaking with suppressed laughter now, but he leans to kiss my forehead. "Baby, no means no. But I'd better be the only person you're turning on the 'Welcome, please come in,' sign for." *So considerate . . .* "In the interest of honesty, when it is a yes, I'm going to treat it like an all-you-can-eat buffet." *And he had to go and ruin it.*

"Fucking caveman . . ." I grumble to myself, borrowing Austin's new favorite nickname for him. It takes all I have not to squirm in anticipation. I have a good imagination. It's not hard to conjure images of that little scenario.

"Yes!" Austin cackles, reaching across the bar to fist bump his brother. "That's what I'm talkin' 'bout!"

"You're both horrible. Are we done here?"

"Oh, no. We're just getting started, sweetie. Buckle up, buttercup. You're in for a long ride."

"I wish that's what she said . . ." Mason mutters, following it with a wistful sigh.

I shake off Mason's hold on me and press the heels of my hands into my eyes. "I need alcohol. God, I've never needed alcohol as badly as I do right now."

He wraps his long fingers around my wrists and gently pries them away from my face. "Seriously, though, Fern, I want you to want me. I'm okay with waiting until you do."

I can't help my smirk. I try, but it wins. "Whatever you say, Cheap Trick."

"Fucking yes! This keeps getting better! Tell me you have a sister!"

"I have two. One is married. The other has a boyfriend. If you touch either one of them with a ten-foot pole, I will cut your dick off and feed it to you."

"Ooooh, feisty! Challenge accepted. It might be worth it to have your—"

"Finish that sentence, and I will kill you," Mason says with a deadly calm that's slightly terrifying.

Austin must agree because he doesn't say another word about it. He clears his throat, smirks at his brother, and that's the end of it.

Mason turns back to me. "This isn't what you said you wanted. Have you changed your mind?" He brings one of my wrists to his mouth and presses a kiss over the pulse point there, holding my gaze while he does so. Involuntarily, my eyes flutter shut. I let out a breathy little sigh. Lean a little closer. Will him to do it again. *Damn you, Mason!*

I have to swallow a few times and take a couple of deep breaths before I can safely speak without sounding all worked up. "I've . . . given it thought over the last few days. You made valid points and, upon further reflection, I realized I shouldn't let my current opinions dictate what may or may not happen in the future."

"So, to put it bluntly, you realized seven years is a helluva long time to go without sex."

"Amen," Austin says.

Huffing out a sigh, I nod. "And that I am placing a lot of importance on an act that could spontaneously happen under the influence of alcohol and mean absolutely nothing."

His eyes narrow for a moment, but quickly brighten with a smile. "You're worried you'll cave, and I'll think . . ." His cheeks flush, and oh, sweet Jesus, he's adorable when he's shy. I kind of want to kiss him just to see if he can get any redder right now. "Okay, yeah . . . That . . . I see your point there. That could be major."

"Someone give me the Barney version of that, please? I was with you until Mason turned into a freshman again."

There's no way to prepare myself for the ridicule, so I yank off the Band-Aid and get it over with. *I've been doing that a lot lately.*

"I don't believe sex should happen without love. However, as Mason kindly pointed out, once this is signed, he might as well be the last man on Earth because his is the only dick I get. Under those terms, if I get drunk and decide I don't care anymore, is he going to wake up the next morning, afraid everything has changed because I love him? Same thing goes if we do decide to have kids. Love wasn't part of this bargain. While it might not seem like it'll change anything right now, that might not be true later. What if he doesn't reciprocate? That's a lot of pressure to put him. And on myself, because it might not be as easy to talk about in the future."

"God, you two overthink. Get drunk— or don't. Fuck like rabbits either way and fuck the consequences. You'll be married. There are literally no consequences that would be an issue, not even a baby."

"You try getting married to a friend and see how much shit you obsess over that's never crossed your mind before," Mason fires over his shoulder.

"Well, since I like bed-hopping too much to consider getting married in the first place, that won't be a problem for me." Austin clears his throat. His eyes dart back and forth between us. "We might want to add something in the event one of you bails. Say, if Fern leaves before the contract is over, she pays you back. If you leave, she doesn't owe you anything, and you're obligated to pay the remainder of her tuition, if applicable."

I swallow hard. I never considered what would happen should this fail. It seems fair on my end. I'll put most of my income in a savings account from now on, just in case. I won't let Mason continue to pay my tuition, though. If this falls apart and he finds someone else, I don't want his generosity towards me to come between them. She might not understand.

Mason presses his lips together while his beautiful eyes search mine. "Okay, but not in full. Her debt will be divided by the number of years we've agreed to, then multiplied by the number of years remaining on the contract."

"Why are you being so nice about it?" It seems awfully suspicious to me. Typically, there's a penalty for breaking a contract—a bigger penalty than that. If I back out at any point after this is signed, he's not getting his end of the deal. So, why should I get any of mine?

"Because if you're unhappy enough to want to leave, I don't want you to stay and make us both miserable because of the money. If you do leave, I want you to leave in a better situation than the one you're coming into this from. I want you to be able to support yourself without resorting to living in a roach palace somewhere and skipping meals to make ends meet."

Tears well in my eyes. That's probably the most considerate thing anyone's said to me in a long, long time. I don't consider the entire arrangement to be an act of kindness. It wasn't kindness that sparked it. He recognized we were both in a position to help the other out. This, though, it's pure generosity on his part. He doesn't have to give two shits about what happens to me once this is over, but he does. *Because he truly is a good guy.*

He's giving me a parachute, which makes the whole thing a little easier to handle.

There are maybe two feet between us, but when I step forward, he widens his stance to make room for me. It's like he knows what's coming, or maybe it's wishful thinking on his part. His arms circle my waist right away. When I take his face in my hands, he smiles and follows my lead, letting me guide his face closer to mine so I can kiss his cheek. "You really are an amazing guy, Mason," I whisper. Something ugly and knotted in my chest tries to choke me to keep me from asking, "Are you sure about this? All this? There's got to be someone out there who'll—"

He cuts me off with a quick kiss on my lips that makes my heart pound. "I have the someone I need right here. This is what I want, Fern."

"God, you two are going to give me diabetes. Fucking stop it already." In disbelief, I lean to peer over Mason's shoulder at his brother, who shoots me a cheeky wink before pushing away from the bar to stalk out of the room. "Be right back. It's time to sign your lives away."

Chapter 20

Mason

"You need to eat," I whisper into Fern's hair. *Damn, she smells so good.* Unable to help myself, I nuzzle my nose into her hair and sigh contentedly. If it weren't for my pain-in-the-ass brother, this would be perfect. I could stand here all evening. *I've missed holding someone.*

Her head shakes a little. "Can't yet. I need to do this first, or I might be sick."

"Are you feeling okay?" Under the guise of a kiss, I press my lips to her forehead to gauge her temperature. She doesn't feel too warm.

"Yeah, just nerves. This is . . . life-altering shit, Mason."

She's not trying to make me laugh, but I do. It's huge, and yes, life-altering, and she's calling it shit. "Yeah, I guess it is."

"So why are you so calm about it?"

Good question. "Because I'm doing the right thing for you and Ronni, and I'm meeting Granddad's requirements on my own terms."

"How can you be so certain?"

Another good question. I shrug while I try to find a good answer. "Because it'll make Ronni happy. Making her happy makes both of us happy. So, we'll all be happy together, and the rest will sort itself out."

"Yeah," she whispers.

"If you two don't stop it, people are going to think you like each other," Austin says when he comes back into the kitchen.

Fern jumps and pulls away, but I'm not letting her go this time. Not for him. "I'm allowed to like giving her hugs. I'm marrying her. Someday."

"You've mastered putting the cart before the horse, dickhead."

I glance at him over my shoulder and smirk. "Maybe someday, I'll learn." It's working out okay for me so far, though. Not great. Great would have been not losing Vee. But maybe . . . No, the very thought is blasphemous.

"If you two are done feeling each other up, sign here. Then, Fern needs to eat, and you both need to get changed. We're going out."

"I beg your pardon?" My ideas for celebrating do not involve dressing up. After her little change of heart—and her reaction when I kissed her wrist—they involve undressing if I can push my luck that far.

"You heard me. Our friends are going to some club. Speakeasy or something like that. We're going, too."

Fern's voice is a mouse-like squeak. "Easy Speak?" She takes great pains to keep her face turned away from mine, even as I lean around to try and get a glimpse. Something has her tense. *How does she know this place?*

"Yeah, that might be it. I've never been. Someone Gabe knows was there a couple of months ago, and he can't stop talking about one of the performers there. I think he said they call her the Killer Queen. The rest of us decided to check the place out tonight. I decided it would be a good date night for you two since you're kid-free. It's semi-formal; you'll need a tie, Mason. It's like a throwback to a Prohibition-era speakeasy, I guess."

"Fern?" I ask, concerned there's something wrong. If she doesn't want to do this, I won't make her. I will pester her for an explanation once Austin is gone, though. I know it's not the dress code. She's got plenty of clothes—and shoes— now.

She clears her throat. "I've been there." She shrugs like it's no big deal. Somehow, I doubt that's the whole story. She'll tell me when she's ready, though.

"Dude, let her go. You can grope her on your own time."

"This is my own time! You're the one who made plans for us!"

"Suck it up. It's do or die time."

Sighing my irritation, I hug Fern to my side and turn to read over the contract, hating that I didn't write it myself. I doubt Austin would sneak anything in to screw with us—after all, this is in his best interest, too. I asked him to do it for Fern's peace of mind, though. He's a neutral-ish party.

It all seems straightforward enough, and in line with everything we've read, so I take the pen he's holding and scrawl my signature on the line.

Fern doesn't hesitate, but she reminds me of the scene from *The Little Mermaid* where Ariel is signing the contract with the sea witch because of the way she leans away as she does so. When she hands the pen back to Austin, our witness, she heaves a huge sigh that seems much bigger than anything she should be capable of.

"You okay?" I ask, watching her closely. She's a little pale. *Is she coming down with something?*

"Yeah. Just . . ."

"Yeah." I get it. It's huge. I just signed away seven years of my life, and she did the same.

Our eyes lock, and her giggle comes out of nowhere. That giggle quickly becomes a genuine laugh that's as beautiful as she is, and I find myself joining in. The color comes back to her lips and cheeks, and even though she's a little wild-eyed right now, I can't help but wonder if this is a preview of our wedding day. I can almost see her in white and a veil. Outdoors. In the spring.

Impulsively, I grab her face and kiss her. "Seemed like the thing to do to make it official," I whisper when our lips part.

"I'm gonna be sick," Austin mutters. He answers my glare with a smile and a wink. *Of course!* His jokes, his smartass comments, they've all been designed to keep things from getting overwhelming. *Guess I owe him.*

I nod my appreciation and turn back to my new girlfriend. "Food, or you really will be sick."

She cocks an eyebrow at me. "You're not the boss of me!" she says, sounding just like Ronni when Nicole's eldest starts issuing orders, but grabs her plate anyway. "Will the cleaning lady get pissed if I expedite the process and eat while I get ready to go?"

Typically, I don't allow food upstairs. But this is her home, and she's the one who cleans it, so she can do whatever the hell she wants. There are two slices left in the second box, so I slide them both onto her plate. "I'll text her and ask."

Her laughter continues to ring in my ears, even when she's out of sight.

Despite Austin's insistence we dress up, he's wearing jeans and a tee. "Why do we have to change if you're going like that?"

He parrots my question in a mocking voice and rolls his eyes. "My suit's in the car. I'll go get it."

***

Austin barges into my room with a bag and changes while I figure out what the hell to wear. I still kind of want to make him pay for springing this on us. I was looking forward to an evening alone with Fern.

"I dunno what the hell you're thinking about that has you smiling like that, but save it for later, or you're going to be horny all night."

What the fuck is his problem? "Why the hell are you so pissy with me?"

"I'm not pissy. I want you to be happy."

"I am happy."

"You'll both be happier once you've fucked and got it over with. It won't be such a big deal anymore."

"You're an idiot." I sigh at him. "Fern deserves a night out, though, so we'll go. How's this?" I turn away from the mirror and hold out my arms to let him inspect my outfit, black slacks, shirt, and vest, and a gold tie. It should complement anything Fern wears. He frowns for a second before latching onto my sleeve. "What the hell are you doing?" He unbuttons it and folds it back, then rolls it.

"Trust me," he mutters. "I've been perfecting the art of picking up chicks for years while you've been boinking the shrew from hell. I don't pretend to understand why, but they go gaga when you show off your arms a bit. Rolling up your sleeves is like our equivalent of letting their hair down."

Is he serious right now? "Uh . . . I don't *need* to pick her up." I know who she's going home with.

He smacks me across the chest, so I take over rolling up my sleeves. "Yes, you do! You owe it to yourself and to her to make an effort. Just because it's done now doesn't mean you shouldn't try to make it . . ."

"Special?"

"Yeah."

He's right. I told myself the same thing the night I pitched the idea to her. Romance, dates, all that.

"Just because she's a sure thing doesn't mean you should treat her like she is. Treat every date like it's the first."

"When did you get so wise?"

He shrugs. "Failure teaches you what to do right."

"Yet, you're single?"

"Haven't found one worth the effort yet."

I'm not sure a club is the right place to find who he's searching for . . .

Fern's door is still closed when we leave my room. Austin checks his watch and mutters to himself about high maintenance women. It almost makes me laugh. She is about as low maintenance as she can get. He follows me to my office and helps himself to the bar while I stash the contract in my safe.

Grinning to myself, I sit at my desk and wake my computer. The websites I need are already loaded. When Austin arrived, I was in the middle of adding my bank info to Fern's credit card accounts. A few minutes later, the printer whirrs to life and churns out one payment confirmation after another.

"Not wasting any time, are you?" Austin asks.

"Nope. I want to see her relax tonight." I wave the stack of papers at him. "This should do the trick." With nothing else to do, I grab a drink of my own, and we head to the family room to wait.

Austin clears his throat. "I've briefed the guys. I didn't give them the particulars, just that you're a thing now."

"And how did they take it? I'm not putting Fern in a situation where they're going to make her uncomfortable because they're condescending bastards."

Since we all get together here once a month to drink and bullshit, she knows them all. None of them have ever given me a reason to think they'd be anything other than kind to her; in fact, they treat her like family. But I'm feeling overly protective of her now.

"Mason, they've all met your nanny. The general consensus is it's about fucking time."

I knew they didn't like Felicity much, but if they had such strong opinions about it, why didn't they say something? *Whatever. It doesn't matter anymore.* "But they'll be nice?"

"Yeah. And if they aren't, do you actually believe Fern will pull her punches? She can run with the big dogs, Mason. Don't worry about her."

The tapping of heels on the stairs triggers a fit of nerves that makes no sense. It's Fern. She'll smile, she'll say something sassy, I'll laugh. We'll go. *There's no reason to be jittery.*

She steps out of the stairwell, and I forget how to breathe. Austin and I both scramble to our feet, just like our grandmother taught us to do when a lady enters the room. Oxygen doesn't matter, but manners do.

Austin wolf whistles at her. "Have mercy! Worth the wait." He elbows me in the ribs, but I'm still speechless.

Her cheeks flush with his praise, and it makes her even more enticing. If Austin hadn't mentioned that the place we're going is Prohibition themed, I might not recognize her dress as being a nod to the era. The hem is cut diagonally, longer on one side than the other, and the—borderline indecent—shorter side is covered by some sheer, beaded material that wraps around behind her to the other hip, skimming the floor and leaving the other leg exposed. Since the skirt is longer on that side, it's not too scandalous, though. *Damnit.* As if that isn't enough skin on display, the neckline plunges damn near to her belly button. Every inch of it shimmers in the light, and the plum color makes her creamy skin glow. The very sight of her has my hands itching to reach for her.

I can't recall seeing Fern with makeup on, not even when we went to dinner. If I have, it's never been done up like she's got it now. Her eyes appear twice their normal size and capable of reversing the pull of gravity. I sense myself moving her way, leaning, straining to get closer because I can't take my eyes off of her. Whatever she slicked on her pouty lips shines in the light and promises the next time I kiss her will be a little messy. *Just the way I like it.*

She clears her throat, embarrassed, and asks, "Are we driving?"

"The guys rented a limo. They wanted to impress the ladies. They thought it might work on this Killer Queen we're hoping to see."

Fern's whole face flushes now. She turns away without comment. "You look nice," she says shyly.

Somehow, probably because Grandma ensured that manners are second nature, I find my voice. "Thank you. I could say the same, but it would be an understatement." I hold up the stack of papers to lure her to my side. "I have something for you."

A crease appears between her brows, but she floats across the room to join me. She takes her time to read over the first confirmation from top to bottom, barely breathing. I find myself holding my breath along with her. She flips through the rest quickly and looks at me with suspiciously watery eyes and that bright, beautiful smile.

"I don't know what to say," she tells me.

"There's nothing you need to say."

A honk put an end to our conversation, but when I help her to her feet, she squeezes my hand. Coming from her, that's a big gesture. When Austin has his back to us, she stops me to lightly touch her lips to my cheek, careful not to leave a mark behind. *I'd wear it proudly, baby.*

"Thank you," she whispers.

"No, thank you."

My three childhood friends watch for us through the open window of the limo and cheer when Austin steps outside. The sound cuts off abruptly when Fern follows him.

"Holy fuck," Ryan mutters. "Is that *Fern?*" And then the catcalls begin.

To my surprise, the growl I fight down is more out of concern for her—I don't want them to embarrass her—than jealousy.

Fern's entire face, her neck, and her chest flush pink. It's a good look on her, but I'd rather be the reason for it. Austin climbs into the back and holds out a hand to help her in.

"Sorry to crash your guys' night out," Fern says, gazing around the car from the edge of her seat. "I can stay home, really."

"Don't be absurd!" Austin waves away her concern with the hand that's not accepting the beer Chris is passing him. "Without you, this is a sausage fest."

"But if the objective is to pick up girls—"

He smirks. "The objective is *always* to pick up girls."

"Won't I kind of be . . . impeding the process?"

"Nope." He shakes his head confidently and takes a swig of his beer. "I've got this down to a science. A group of guys walks into a bar, and all the girls evaluate us, wondering if we're safe or if we're going to harass them. A group of guys, plus one girlfriend, walk into a bar, and our threat level drops dramatically because a girl wouldn't go out with a group of guys she doesn't trust. And if she feels safe, we must be okay. So, brother dearest," he pauses and salutes me with his beer, "thank you for taking one for the team."

"He's not wrong," Chris tells her, "but he is so full of shit he stinks. Other groups of guys might give girls a bad vibe, but that's never been a problem for us. We're too . . ."

Ryan sighs and rolls his eyes. "What he's trying to say is, we're all stupid rich local celebrities. We make a point not to associate with the sort of people who would make a lady think twice about associating with us." That's probably sugar-coating the truth a bit, but a fair assessment.

We're all well off, come from good families, and have good jobs, which make us semi-public figures—at least on a local level. Bill Gates is stupid rich, not us. And no one asks us for autographs, so the whole local celebrity thing doesn't work in my mind. Yes, our names are known, but that doesn't make us celebrities.

She grins at Ryan. "Austin tells me we're going to Easy Speak?"

"We're going to find their Killer Queen and see if she is in the market for a King. Or two," Gabe says grandly, waggling his eyebrows. He doesn't mind flaunting his wealth to get what he wants. That gives him a bit of a flare for the dramatic, but I'm sure she's already aware of that. He's always larger than life.

Beside me, she tenses a little. "I have it on good authority she isn't," she tells him gently through a forced smile. Her sudden cautiousness puts me on high alert.

He narrows his eyes at her. "You know her?"

Her right shoulder lifts a fraction of an inch and drops. "As much as anyone really does. She's . . . private."

Kinda like someone else I know.

Excited now, Gabe leans forward, crowding into her space. She doesn't react, so I force myself not to when I want to pull her away from him. "Is she as beautiful as Logan says?"

"Logan?" she asks.

"Cousin of mine," Gabe says, waving it off like it's no big deal. "He was there like a month ago when she was singing. Says he's been back every week since, but she hasn't returned. I think he's full of shit, so I'm going to debunk the myth of the Killer Queen if I have to go to this dive every damn week."

"I see," Fern says carefully. "Well, I'm not into girls, but I tend to think we're all beautiful in our own way. Can't help you there, sorry."

"What's this place like?" Chris asks her. "I never heard of it before."

"Um . . . It's . . ." She chuckles nervously. "You've gotta see it. It defies explanation."

"And what does she do there?"

"Oh! She sings. It's a karaoke bar, but there are a few people who swing by regularly to put on a show, feed the whole vibe. They're not exactly employees, so they sing for tips."

Just how much time has she spent there?

"And she's one of those?"

"Mmhmm."

Chapter 21

Mason

The limo stops on a side street that is too gloomy for my liking. It's not safe to be walking on a sidewalk so dim anywhere anymore. There are plenty of street-lights, but more than half of them are out. The window across from me is in line with an alley, and every dumpster in sight is overflowing. Their combined aroma hits us all as soon as the door opens, causing an array of reactions from my companions, the politest of which is Fern's wrinkled nose. Trash clogs the gutters as well, rounding out the neglected vibe. This is the last damn place I'd put any sort of reputable establishment. All the same, there's a line around the block to get in.

"How have we never heard of this place?" Chris whispers to himself before he climbs out. *Chances are, we wouldn't have heard anything good.* Like the gentleman he is, he turns and offers Fern his hand to help her. I quickly maneuver in behind her so the other fuckers can't ogle her ass. *My ass to stare at.*

Once we're all out, Fern takes my arm and leads me to the door, almost pulling me along, though she doesn't seem to be walking any faster than usual. Still, her excitement is palpable. *She loves this place.* Her earlier apprehension had me second-guessing the decision to come, but now I'm glad we did.

The bouncer does a double take when we walk up. I wait for him to call out one of our names. That'll say a lot about what kind of night we're going to have. If he recognizes Gabe, he'll never let it drop that *he* got us in. The rest of us will be a little lower key about it. I won't say shit. Ryan probably won't either.

His eyes go wide, and so does his smile. "Fern! Good to see you again, baby!"

Baby? What the fuck?

She gives him a shy little wave and stops walking. "Heya, Teddy. How're you tonight?"

"Good! Good! Glad to have you back." He eyes her hand on my arm before his gaze slides away to take in the rest of the group. "We gonna do our song?"

The poor lighting can't hide her blush, but she nods. "Always. Come find me on your break?"

"Well, in that case," he unhooks the rope, but toys with the hook instead of letting us pass. "They with you?" he asks, eyeing us all suspiciously once more. *What the hell?*

"Well, technically, I'm with them. But yeah."

"You gentlemen behave yourselves." He takes the time to lock eyes with each of us before he lets us pass. The back of my head tingles from him glaring daggers at me until the door closes behind us.

The warehouse-turned-bar has a smoky atmosphere that was probably run-of-the-mill for a speakeasy back in the day. Then, it would have been from cigarettes and cigars. Today, it's probably the work of fog machines. The place has surprisingly good acoustics considering what it used to be. There's a catwalk all the way around, already teeming with people though the night is young. In other places, that would be the VIP area and our destination for the evening.

I'm following Fern, though. She glides through the maze of round tables lining the perimeter of the room, and the throng of people milling around, making her way toward a long bar that dominates the back wall.

Once I break through the tables, I find myself on a dance floor packed with well-dressed people engaged in different dances spanning the decades. A couple is grinding all over each other next to an older couple swing dancing. It's odd to see. Fern doesn't slow. Trusting her completely, I thread my fingers through hers and gawk.

Most of the left wall is dominated by a large stage and a DJ booth. There's a guy on stage, singing some pop song that sounds vaguely familiar. Not my kind of music, though, so I don't strain my brain to figure it out

The song ends as we reach the bar, and something changes. The lights all turn yellow, bathing us all in a golden glow. It's more than that, though. The air is charged with an energy that wasn't there before. "Shit," Fern says on a sigh. I barely catch it, and only because the room seems to hold its breath at that exact moment.

The DJ snaps his fingers in front of his mic in an intentional rhythm, drawing everyone's attention. "Ladies and gentlemen, boys and girls. I have an announcement to make," he says over the rhythmic snapping the entire room has taken up now. He affects a terrible British accent and continues. "A rumor has reached mine ears. A rumor that royalty walks amongst us again! Maybe if we ask very, very nicely, her highness will show her loyal subjects a little love!" A deafening cry hundreds of voices strong rocks the room. Over the din, the DJ shouts, "Your Majesty, I have a list of petitions that require your attention!"

He trails off, and Queen's *Killer Queen* plays, and not the karaoke version. People nearby seem excited about something in our general area, but I can't figure out what.

Gabe whoops, garnering several affronted looks from nearby patrons. He pays them no mind at all, pulling his phone from his pocket instead. He taps the screen a few times and holds it over his head, likely recording the show. I turn around, dismissing him when Fern greets someone.

"Hello again, gorgeous! The usual?" the bartender asks, looking Fern up and down like he'd like to eat her alive. He's so intent on her that he fails to notice my glare. Or maybe he does but doesn't care. Looking isn't a crime, but I'd like to blacken his eye for it.

"What would you like?" she asks me after nodding at him. I give him my order, but I have no idea how he hears me because what sounds like every person in the damn building bursts into song for the chorus.

Over the noise, Gabe shouts, "I can't believe I'm in a fucking karaoke bar!"

Fern tugs at my sleeve to get my attention, then leans in close and whispers, "I'll be right back, okay? There's someone I've got to go talk to, or he'll be very cross with me. The bartender's name is Brandon. Tell him I'd like my spot; he'll take care of the rest."

Shocked, I blink at her a couple of times before repeating her instructions back to her to be sure I have it straight. *This is so weird.* I'm used to giving orders, not taking them. "Where are you going?"

"I'll just be over there." She waves toward the dance floor. "I'll know where to find you, promise."

Before she can walk away, I grab her wrist and pull her back for a quick kiss. She doesn't even have time to close her eyes, so I get to watch her pupils dilate. *The sparks are practically visible.* "Be careful." This place is packed, people are assholes, and she looks like she could jump-start a dead man's heart tonight. If we make it out of here without me hitting someone for getting handsy, I'll be amazed.

"I'll be fine."

She makes to walk away while I'm still holding her wrist, so I tug her back and kiss her again. "Sorry, wasn't done yet."

Playfully, she pushes my shoulder. Her smile is bright, but the cute little furrow between her brows speaks of uncertainty. This time, I let her go.

"Where's she going?" Austin asks.

I shrug at him. "Said she needs to talk to someone."

Ryan socks me in the shoulder; only he's built like a tank, so there's nothing gentle about it. "So, your fine-ass girlfriend cleans up nice, and she likes to hang out at a karaoke bar?"

"I'm as surprised as you guys." It's true on both counts. I never would have imagined quiet little Fern hanging out here.

The song ends, and the DJ introduces the next singer. The lights revert to the nauseating, multi-colored swirl from before. Since a guy takes the mic, I can safely assume it's not this Killer Queen the others are determined to see. I couldn't care less. I'm only here to see Fern let her hair down a little.

Brandon the Bartender taps my shoulder. "Fern want her usual place?" he asks. I nod, and he shouts for someone named Monique.

Monique is tall and caramel-colored from head to toe; at least what parts of her are visible. Since her gold sequined dress doesn't leave much to the imagination, that's a lot of her. "Follow me," she says with a flirty wink before she turns to lead us wherever the hell we're going, one hip at a time.

I hate to leave Fern behind, but the others follow her with no problem, their eyes glued to Monique's ass the whole way. *They'd follow her into a slaughterhouse and never notice her killing them.* She takes us upstairs to a corner that's cordoned off. Only two of the tables here are occupied, and they all have an excellent view of the stage. She stops next to one with a tiara as the centerpiece with a candle situated in the middle.

"I'll be right back with your drinks, fellas." She tosses in another wink for good measure.

"Thank you very much," Gabe says, managing to make himself sound like an obnoxious tool. He's practically drooling over her, which is embarrassing, doubly so considering he's newly divorced for cheating with his secretary.

I grab a seat. Any other night, I'd jump his ass about it. Tonight is about Fern and me.

Austin moves down one, leaving an empty chair between us for Fern. I'm grateful for it. She'll be more comfortable with an ally on either side. And I can relax because Austin knows he doesn't stand a snowball's chance in hell.

The lights change again, turning yellow once more. Like they did for *Killer Queen.*

"Wooooo!" Gabe pumps his fist in the air. He shoots to his feet and jumps around like a pre-teen girl at a Taylor Swift concert. Austin and I exchange a glance. Gabe is generally over the top, but he's a little extra tonight.

I don't recognize the song that plays. It sounds like the unholy bastard child of blues and country, but it's pleasing to the ear all the same. However, I do recognize the woman who sashays up the stairs to take the stage. Gabe whoops and hollers like an idiot, but the other three sit in silence. At itch between my shoulder blades warns me that I'm being watched, but I can't take my eyes off her long enough to figure out which one it is. *Probably all three of them in turn.*

The crowd loses their shit when she steps up to the mic. *I can't believe this.* She's a star here. Like the music, the words are unfamiliar to me, but she shimmies her shoulder and sways her hips and sings a funny little song about the woes of getting older and gravity's role in it.

Monique returns with our drinks. When I try to pay, she pushes my card away. "You're the Queen's guests. First round is on the house."

I point to the stage. "She's the one they call Killer Queen?"

Monique frowns, clearly confused, but answers readily enough. "Yes."

"She never said."

She shrugs it off. "I can't say I'm surprised. Fern doesn't like the fuss they all make, but she likes the tips."

"So, wait," Austin says, gaining her attention, "if I go request a song, she has to sing it?"

Monique frowns again and shakes her head. "She doesn't have to. She's more likely to sing it if you tip, but I've seen her turn songs down before, even with a couple hundred on the line."

"What won't she sing?"

She shrugs. "It's entirely at her discretion."

Austin pops to his feet and calls over his shoulder, "Be right back!"

I should probably stop him, but I don't. Whatever he's up to, I'm sure Fern can handle him.

"Fern never brings guests anymore," Monique says matter-of-factly. She eyes the empty seat next to me, then gives me a once over through slitted eyes. "You're not Aaron."

Her brusque behavior puts me on the defensive. *If she knew Aaron, she should also know what happened.* This is a test. But what does she hope to determine? I gesture to Fern's unoccupied chair, inviting her to have a seat. She only hesitates for a moment. "I'm Mason. Aaron passed away years ago."

Between one blink and the next, her face shifts from hard-eyed suspicion to outright shock. "She talked to you about it?"

"Well, yeah . . . I'm her boyfriend." *That word sounds so juvenile.* I'm not her lover, yet, or her fiancé, so it's the best word I've got for what we are.

Her hand darts out to squeeze my shoulder. "Her boyfriend?"

"Yeah . . . Why?" She's freaking me out. Why is it so hard to believe Fern and I are together? She doesn't know me.

"No, I'm just . . ." She tips her head back to face the ceiling, and I catch her murmured, "Thank you!" When she turns back to me, she smiles and pats my shoulder. "Next one's on me. Any guy who can get Fern to let go of the past deserves a free drink."

She makes to leave, but I put a hand on her arm, asking her to wait. "You knew them both?"

Her smile turns nostalgic. "Oh, he's the one who gave her that stage name. They stumbled in here one night, looking like a couple of drowned rats. Teddy should have turned them away, but he told us later that he watched the two of them caring for some of the homeless and decided that one good deed deserved another. The next time they came back, they had about twenty people with them, all med students looking to let off some steam. Most of them are still regulars."

So this was their spot . . . The revelation catches me off guard, opening the door for doubt to make itself at home in my brain. Does she only come here to remember him? Is that why she was upset about coming? Or was it because she's the one the others were here to see?

Monique's eyes roam my face. She bites her bottom lip. "I've said too much."

"No! It's a lot to take in. We're a new development. She told me about him and what happened, but not that this was something they did together."

Her shoulders slump. "She should have been the one to tell you, though. If she wanted to."

That's probably true. I smile reassuringly, hoping to ease her concern. "Fern and I don't keep secrets. It'll be fine."

This time, I let her go.

"What was that about?" Chris asks once she's gone, jerking his thumb toward the stairs.

"She knows Fern." He lets the explanation stand, and we both turn to watch my girlfriend sing. I alternate between watching her and watching Austin, wondering what the hell he has planned. There's a line to request a song, and that line is long. Probably longer than his attention span, but he surprises me and sticks with it.

The DJ's face shines with obvious delight when my brother finally gets his turn. His teeth stand out in sharp contrast to his midnight dark skin, making his Cheshire Cat smile that much more apparent, even from a distance. He nods enthusiastically and shoves Austin toward the stage.

When the last note of the song she's singing fades, the speakers go quiet instead of fading into the next song. Grinning, the DJ taps his mic and says, "Your Majesty, this gentleman claims to be a friend of yours. He requests an audience."

Smiling sweetly, she beckons Austin to join her. He runs up the stairs amid cheers from her fans. Once he's on the stage, he hams it up, waving and bowing to them. It's no surprise. Austin is a natural performer.

There's laughter in her voice when she asks, "What can I do for you, Austin?"

"How much will it take to get you to sing something for me, no questions asked?"

"Oh, sugar! You can't afford me!"

What the hell? I've never heard Fern try for sexy. Hell, her aiming to *act* sexy is a first for me. *I like it.* She's not the same person on stage that she is in day-to-day life. She's more confident up there. More playful. I wish she'd bring some of that home with her.

His feet shift, edging farther apart, and he crosses his arms over his chest. "Try me." Nothing short of her outright refusal will sway him now. He loves a challenge.

Fern steps back and makes a show of looking him over. When she turns back to the crowd, there's an edge to her smile that throttles my heartbeat up. It's more than her customary sass. She's up to something. "You know, I didn't come here to work tonight," she tells him. He only shrugs and leans away from the mic to talk to her and her alone for a moment.

"What do you think? Should I do it?" she asks the crowd. The floor vibrates when they roar their approval back at her. "I'll make you a deal, Austin. Since we're friends and all."

I'll give him this, he's smart enough to be wary of her sudden shift in demeanor. Nevertheless, he doesn't balk. "Let's hear it."

Grinning, she props one elbow on his shoulder and leans against him. "I'll sing whatever song you pick for *me* if you sing one I pick for *you*."

He doesn't hesitate. "Deal." He even holds his hand out to shake on it. *Dumbass* . . . She's apparently a karaoke queen. She's sure to know more than one song that he'll make a fool of himself singing. Apparently, the risk is worth the reward to him.

"Hold onto your hats, ladies and gentlemen." The DJ cackles into his mic. "You're in for one helluva ride." He presses a button and the sound of crickets chirping filters into the room through the speakers, accompanied by high pitched, breathy whimpers exactly like the ones I'm hoping Fern makes for me sooner rather than later.

"Did you pick a song, or a porno, Austin?" Fern asks teasingly into the mic. A siren blares in the background, stopping my heart. I know this one. Several other members of the crowd recognize it as well, judging by the excited murmur that carries up to us on the balcony.

Fern stands primly before the mic, seemingly scandalized by the racy introduction. But when the guitars come in, she throws her head forward right on cue. *Holy shit*. She does a seductive little dance while she removes the mic from the stand, then walks toward the front of the stage, one slow, exaggerated step at a time.

She doesn't need the lyrics. She doesn't miss a note. And she doesn't stop dancing. Feet planted wide, her hips snap from side to side before she slowly arches her back, her hand tracing a suggestive path from her collar bone, between her breasts, and to her hip. It's a map I'd like to follow later with my tongue if she gives me half a chance. She pivots until her back is to the crowd, giving everyone a chance to admire the hard-earned roundness of her ass. During the chorus, she sinks slowly to her knees, somehow managing to wiggle and thrust while she does so, acting out the lines. Looking like a wet dream.

The room around me spins a bit because every last ounce of blood in my body is trying to force its way into my dick. Some small part of my brain, the caveman that Austin accuses me of being, grumbles about other people ogling what's mine. The logical part metaphorically pats that caveman on the head, reminding him that no one can take her away now. Still, I'm overcome with the urge to mark her as mine in an obvious way, like a dog pissing on a tree. The kisses weren't enough. They don't mean a thing to a determined individual. I would tattoo my name on her forehead if she wouldn't kill me for merely thinking about it.

Chapter 22

Fern

I should not have done that . . . Mason is here. Mason just watched me dance around like I should be taking off my clothes instead of singing. *He's going to call this whole thing off.*

I can't take it back, though. I'm not sure I want to, either. If he can't handle who I am, this won't work. It's not like I behave that way in front of Ronni. That's probably the raciest thing I've ever done on this stage, though.

I shove the problem to the back of my mind. I can't do anything about it right this minute.

Austin is waiting his turn like a good sport. A multitude of songs pop into my head that will undoubtedly embarrass the living shit out of him. I've got to pick just the right one after a heavy song like *Follow Me Down*, though. Something light-hearted and ridiculous.

Settling on one, I skip across the stage to whisper in Desi's ear. He tosses his head back, cackling dementedly, and brings up the song. The opening notes of *Call Me Maybe* play and Austin's face flushes beet red. The crowd goes insane.

He holds out both arms and says, "I asked for it," into the mic.

A clown to the bone, he gets into the music, shaking his hips and bouncing around. I'm laughing so hard I'm leaning on Desi to keep me upright. The best part is, he has a superb voice. While he looks goofy as hell, he sounds fantastic while doing it.

Desi grins and folds the wad of bills he collected for me, then slips it into my bra.

I swat at his hands. "You sassy little shit!" Once upon a time, I gave him a black eye for that, before I learned my boobs are of no interest to him. He does it purely for shock and awe.

"Good show, Your Majesty," he yells over Austin channeling his inner Carly Rae Jepsen.

"Why thank you! I'm off duty, though. I really didn't come to put on a show."

"Then why are you here?"

I freeze. "I . . . uh . . . I'm . . ."

He points at me. "You're on a date!"

My whole face gets hot. "Guilty."

His bony arms pull me in for a hug, then he shoves me away. "It's about fuck-ing time. Get your cute little ass away from me. Your boy toy probably needs a few minutes alone with you in the bathroom after that long-distance lap dance."

Oh, shit. I imagined Mason reacting as a businessman whose company is still dealing with the scandal of his ex being caught in the act in public. It helps that CFI is generally above reproach, but if someone recorded my little performance, they could paint it in a much different light. It wouldn't look good for Mason right now.

How he might react as a man, as *my* man, never occurred to me.

The song ends. I turn around and watch Austin take his bow. His eyes find mine, and whatever he finds looking back at him tinges his smile with uncertainty. He bounds over to me like an overgrown puppy, though, and Desi takes that as his cue to get back to work.

When Austin stops, he bows. "Your Majesty! How did I do?"

I laugh because he knows he was great. "You were wonderful. The audience adores you."

"Are you uh," he glances around a bit, "done here?"

"I am."

"In that case," he says, offering his arm. I take it and try not to let worry eat me alive as we make our way back to the balcony.

Gabe greets us first, because he's already on his feet, jumping around, scream-ing like an idiot for the guy on stage who couldn't carry a tune in a bucket with a handle and a lid. Even if the bucket was in a wagon. He's enthusiastic, though, which partially makes up for it. Gabe comes to a dead stop and bows so deeply he loses his balance and tips forward, nearly cracking his head on the floor before Ryan manages to catch him.

He must have started drinking early to be that bad already. "Gabe, sit your drunk ass down before you kill yourself!" I tell him.

He rolls his eyes at me. "I can't wait to tell Logan I know the Killer Queen personally! Hey! I need a picture! Hold on!" He's talking so fast I can hardly keep up, so I have no time to prepare or protest before he shoves his phone in my face, and I'm blinded by a flash.

"Not cool, dumbass." Austin shoulders past Gabe and is flagged down by the others seated in the only real slice of sanity in this place. That leaves me to face his brother alone. *Chin up or your crown will fall.*

My stomach turns cartwheels, kicking my heart into my throat on its way over. Until now, I didn't realize how invested I am in this little ruse. He holds my life in his hands and has the absolute power to make it or break it. More importantly, I don't *want* to ruin this. Not just for Ronni's sake, either.

But he smiles and holds out his hand as I approach. Relief makes my knees a little weak. I lean against the back of his chair to keep myself upright while I pull myself together, and Mason wraps his arm around me.

Chris and Ryan clap. "That was awesome!" Chris tells me, and Ryan nods his agreement. I aim for my best smile in thanks but miss the mark. Mason's gaze is so focused I wouldn't be surprised if he could see straight through to my soul.

"I'm sorry. I was hoping no one would notice me. If I hadn't bit the bullet and gotten it over with, people would've harassed me all night and—"

Mason cuts me off to say, "Fern, that was amazing."

Relief leaves me breathless. "Oh . . ."

"What's wrong?"

His eyes drop to my hands, where I'm wringing them obsessively. "I was afraid you'd be mad. I didn't tell you, then I bailed without warning you and—"

He flashes me a smile that should be illegal because it's some sort of weapon that has the power to make perfectly rational women lose their damn minds. "I'm not sure I would have believed it if you had. I'm sorry, sweetheart, you left me speechless."

"You . . . You're not mad at me?"

He pulls me into his lap. "Does that feel like I'm mad at you?" he asks, his lips against my neck.

He's hot and hard, pressing against the back of my thigh. Dick deprivation goes straight to my head. This is the second time this week, third if you count the morning wood incident. A girl can only stay strong for so long.

"That's why I didn't stand when you came upstairs. I expect every man in here is having the same problem."

My eyes cut toward Ryan and Chris, who are watching the stage intently, then I do a sweep of the balcony. There's no privacy to be had here, which might be a good thing. It'll keep us both in check.

His lips inch their way to my ear, leaving a trail of kisses behind. When they get there, he whispers, "If I had my way, we'd hijack the limo and go home now."

My heart races at what his tone implies would happen at home. *There's always Uber . . .* The confidence boost that comes from assuming my Killer Queen alter ego overrides my reservations. "That sounds . . . nice," I concede.

He's still close enough for me to hear him groan. "I wouldn't wait until we got there, though. I'd rip your panties off and lick you until you beg me to stop, or until we get home. I probably wouldn't be able to wait until we got upstairs. I'd push you against the front door. Every time someone walks in our door, we'd both know we stood there and fucked."

I never knew dirty talk did it for me, but there's no denying the heat flooding my body. My eyes drift shut even though I'm fighting to keep them from doing just that. It's easier to imagine him carrying out those illicit little promises when I can't focus on what's going on around me. *Thank God for music.* It masks the low groan that slips my control from everyone but Mason, whose lips have traveled back to my neck.

He leaves off to whisper in my ear, "Say the word, baby. Now, five minutes, an hour from now. I'll be ready. And all that is just the beginning."

I've never wanted something so much in my life. My hands shake with the need to touch him. One little word. That's all it would take. Theoretically, it's an easy word to say. One syllable and I'm all in. I'm not ready, though, at this rate, that might change before the night is over.

"Why'd you stop?" he asks me.

It takes a second for my brain to catch up with the subject change. Once I realize I'm not crazed enough that I was giving him an actual lap dance, it's an easy answer. "I didn't come here to work. I'm out with you."

My answer earns me a kiss. "That doesn't mean you're not here to have a good time, baby. I saw you up there. You can't tell me you only do it for the money. If you want to sing, go sing."

My heart soars. I like that he's showing support for something I enjoy and that he's not acting clingy and jealous. "Will you sing with me?"

He shrugs. "Maybe. If I get to pick the song. I heard what you did to Austin."

I laugh. "He had that coming!"

"No, he has a steak dinner and a bottle of whiskey coming for that."

Austin drops into his seat. "And he'll hold you to it! I thought you'd enjoy *hearing* her sing that. I didn't know you were going to get *that* kind of a show out of it. That was spank bank material."

"Spank bank, dirty dreams, and ugly hookups!" Gabe says from behind me.

I try not to squirm in Mason's lap, but I don't like having my back to Gabe. He's weird tonight. His movements are too fast, his words too loud, and he can't sit still. He was by the stairs a moment ago. Now, he had his hands on my shoulders.

"I want a dance with the Killer Queen!"

I don't want to dance with him. I don't trust him to keep his hands anywhere appropriate. When he doesn't, Mason will get pissed. Gabe isn't his brother, so he won't go with a friendly warning. He might throw a punch. If my fans think Gabe is crossing a line, they'll back Mason, and it'll turn into a free-for-all.

I lock eyes with Mason and try to communicate my dilemma. There are questions in his eyes, but he doesn't miss a beat. "I'm going to have to go with no. I don't mind admitting I don't like to share."

"Dude, you just shared her with every schmuck in here. They're going to think about her shaking her ass and touching herself like that while they're fucking their ol' ladies tonight, and you know it."

What the fuck, Gabe?

Surprisingly, Mason only shrugs and smiles at his friend and removes his hands from my shoulders. "I can't control what their minds do, but I'm not big on seeing someone else's hands on my girl. Get over it."

Gabe's lips twist into a snarl. He shoves Mason's shoulder, but Mason doesn't budge. "Jealous bastard!"

Mason tenses, every muscle poised for action, but he takes a deep breath and slowly relaxes. He shrugs again. "At least I own it. I could've let her go if she wanted to, and then changed my mind and made an ass of myself. Instead, I'm sitting here, politely telling you that tonight, the only hands I want to see on her are mine. Get over it."

I can't believe he's so cool about it after the showdown with Austin earlier. Unless signing the contract placated the green monster. He has it in writing that I'm not going to back out.

Gabe grabs my hair and pulls my head back, standing straight to loom over me. Though he's not hurting me, rage makes my pulse throbs in my ears. Mason reaches to do *something,* but I grab his arm to stop him. If he tries anything right now, I might get hurt. This is between Gabe and me.

"Are you going to let him dictate what you can and can't do like some whipped little bitch?"

If I could get a good hit in on his nuts, I'd take it. Since I can't, I glare up at him, silently communicating a promise of pain, and he has the balls to look me in the eye. His pupils are blown out, and it's not dark enough up here to explain it. "I don't want to dance with you, Gabe. Let me go."

"Fucking stuck-up bitch!" He shoves me forward. Mason saves me from hitting my head on an empty chair.

Austin jumps to his feet. Mason is clutching me to his chest protectively, one hand cradling my head. He works his arm under my knees and stands, then puts me down behind him. Some sixth sense warns me that things are going to get ugly. I reach for Mason's arm, but my hand closes around air as Mason's fist connects with Gabe's jaw.

Gabe's knees buckle, and he goes down. His head bounces off a chair on his way to the floor.

Austin and Ryan dive at Mason, each grabbing an arm to hold him back. It's a waste of their time, though. Mason isn't the kind of guy to jump on a downed opponent.

I grab Mason's hand to check it before I go to Gabe. Other than a knuckle being busted open and swollen, he fine. Without thinking, I kiss it as I would for Ronni. She's too old for such things now, but it makes her laugh, and laughter makes everything better. But it's even more ridiculous because he's a grown man. Mason doesn't laugh, though. He watches me with sharp, hungry eyes.

I hurry to Gabe, who should be up and moving already. But he's not. Kneeling next to him, I press my fingers to his neck. His pulse is steady, though much faster than it should be, and his skin is too hot. "What's he on?" I ask, shouting to make myself heard over the music.

My question is met with blank stares all around.

"What do you mean?" Ryan asks. There's a hint of a growl to his voice that puts Mason on the defensive again. He puts himself between Ryan and me, but I'm not scared of his friend.

"He's high. My guess is coke. I need a light."

Ryan leans around Mason to glare at me, but reaches into his pocket and offers me a lighter.

"Sorry, I meant like a flashlight. I left my phone at the house."

The four of them stare at me like I've lost my damn mind, but Mason takes his phone from his pocket, turns on the flashlight, and hands it over. I check Gabe's pupillary response, which isn't worrisome. He's passed out, not concussed. And he's starting to stir.

Chris and Austin jump in to hold him down when he reaches out to push me away, but I've seen all I need to. "He's high as a kite but coming down. There's nothing I can do but slap some sense into him and suggest he seek help, but he needs to hear it from his friends."

"What the fuck is wrong with you, Gabe?" Austin asks.

"Sorry. It's cool. I'm cool. We're good. I'm sorry," Gabe says over and over.

"You're damn lucky is what you are," Chris tells him.

"Never, I repeat *never*, touch me again." I might be small, but my bark is *not* worse than my bite.

He holds his hands up in surrender. "I'm sorry! I didn't mean it! I swear!"

Ryan grabs Gabe by the hand and heaves him to his feet. "Let's go, man, before Mason kills you."

Upright, Gabe takes a step back, fighting against Ryan for a moment. A switch flips, and Gabe transforms into a different version of himself. Lines crease his face, and his eyes turn flat. Empty. He slumps forward, as if too tired to fight gravity any longer. "Tara left."

"No shit, dumbass. You cheated on her."

Ryan's comment surprises me. Gabe is *crazy* about Tara. Most of the time, she's with him when he comes to Mason's. I only saw them when I was bringing in snacks or clearing away dishes, but you can't fake the love in his eyes when he looks at her. I can't imagine him cheating.

"No, she left."

Ryan rolls his eyes and grabs Gabe's arm. "Come on. You're trashed and talking out your ass. We'll catch an Uber."

Chris takes his other arm. "I'll come, too. You might need a hand if he passes out." I'm glad that they're getting Gabe out of here, but I hate to see them go. I was looking forward to spending time with Mason's friends without Felicity breathing down my neck.

When they're gone, Mason loops an arm around my middle and pulls me tight to his body. "If he ever hurts you again, I'll kill him," he says for my ears only.

"You'll have to beat me to it." I'm not the type to let other people fight my battles for me, but I can appreciate the position he found himself in. It's a matter of respect.

Monique's bronze head appears at the top of the stairs. She surveys the area, taking in all of the occupants standing tense and ready, the hastily abandoned chairs, and asks, "Is everything okay?"

"It's handled," I tell her.

She acknowledges my statement with a quick nod. Gabe wouldn't be the first person I've bounced out of here, and she knows it. "Good. Brandon sent this." She holds out a tall tumbler that I gladly hurry to her side to accept. His timing is impeccable, and he always knows what I need, even though my "usual" could be one of six things.

"Brandon is the king," I tell her solemnly, wincing internally at my poor choice of words.

"Brandon would like to be your king," she says more to herself than to me. I don't let on I hear her, and I hope Mason didn't. We're far enough away that he shouldn't have.

I have nothing to hide, but based on the way he's acted lately, he won't appreciate it. Brandon has never kept his interest a secret. My lingering feelings for Aaron are more than he could handle. And he'd wrap me in bubble wrap and put me on a shelf somewhere, taking me down when it was time to play. I'd be a possession, not a partner.

And look at me now . . . I'm not a possession, though. Some people might think that if they knew about the contract, but that's not how Mason treats me.

Monique's eyes drift toward Mason, and mine follow. He's looking right at me but doesn't seem to notice us watching him. He's too busy watching my lips, which are puckered around my straw because I'm the kind of weirdo who drinks *everything* with a straw.

Intrigued, I exaggerate my next sip and watch his reaction. It does not disappoint. He swallows hard. His grip on the back of the chair beside him tightens until his knuckles are noticeably white. I imagine I even hear him groan, but it's all in my head because the music is too loud to allow me to pick up such a small sound. All the same, it's a heady feeling to know that I can get to him as easy as he does me just by being himself. And fuck if that doesn't turn me on, too.

A lazy grin turns up the corners of his mouth when he catches us watching him. I would be embarrassed if our roles were reversed, but he owns it and stalks across the distance between us to pluck my cup from my hands. Monique takes it from him and sways her way to our table before veering to check on the other VIPs. His grin turns into a full-blown, heart-stopping, panty-dropping smile. *This* is why I decided it was neither safe nor fair for me to insist on celibacy. I can only be so strong, and I'm already getting tired. I love that smile. Hell, I love all of his smiles, and I love being the reason for them.

His hands land on my hips. He steps into my space, holding me close enough to feel his heat and his hardness. "Will the queen dance with her king?"

Dick deprivation strikes again. I'm not entirely in control of my own actions. My lady bits mutiny and seize control of the vessel—my body. I find that I don't mind so much when he groans in response to my hips grinding against his, a feat made possible by high heels. "She can probably be persuaded if he asks nicely enough."

Chapter 23

Mason

Austin's entertainment *du jour* climbs out of the car. Before he closes the door behind her, he crouches down to wink at me.

"Alone at last," I say, enjoying the way Fern swallows hard when it hits her. One little word, and it's happening—all of it. She holds herself very still, but nothing of what's on her mind shows on her face.

She leans in to kiss me. I don't move, allowing her to do as she will, but she stops short, teasing me. I don't think it's intentional. Aaron's hold on her heart is holding her back. She'll follow where I lead but is afraid to take the steps on her own. She needs me to show her how to dance between the past and the present. I close the gap and claim her lips, and the heat between us burns away her hesitation. She gives up trying to scoot closer and climbs into my lap, making it hard not to smile.

I wind those big curls of hers around my hand as I've dreamt of doing so many times so that I can tug her head back, leaving her neck bare. It takes some effort, but I keep my lips to myself. Instead, I trail my fingers down her neck and follow the hem of her dress. "What'll it be, Fern? I'll keep my word, but I never promised to make it easy on you." I can do a lot on the trip home if she'll give me the green light.

She shakes her head to clear it, I think. Until she says, "Not here."

Would that be a yellow light? "That's not a recognized answer."

"Not here. What if—"

"It's almost two in the morning." I jerk my thumb toward the front of the vehicle. "He isn't interested in small talk, and he doesn't need directions." I push myself as upright as I can, turn, and put her on the seat before I drop to kneel before her. "Stop or go?" A little crease forms between her eyebrows while she struggles to make up her mind. I know she wants this, but the risk scares her. I push her skirt up slowly, allowing her time to stop me. When she doesn't, I test her boundaries by licking my way up her inner thigh.

Her panties are soaked through, teasing me, telling me that I don't have to strip her for a little appetizer. My mouth waters for just a taste. *Push too hard and she'll run.* The subconscious warning makes it easier to hold back. "Stop or go?" I ask again. While she debates, I suck in a deep breath, memorizing the smell of her want.

"Go," she whispers. A thrill shoots up my spine. *Yes!* I'd rather she scream it, but I'll take what I can get.

I ease her panties down so slowly she's shaking with anticipation before they're off. "Fuck, you're so wet."

It's hard to tear my eyes away from such a beautiful sight, but I want to watch her watch me. I want to see her eyes hazy with lust and pleasure. But she's hiding behind her hands.

I can waste precious time talking her into watching, or I can give her something to watch when she relaxes. My tongue presses into her wetness, and her whole body goes tense, fighting the urge to move. *That won't do, baby.* I groan when her flavor hits me, and she twitches. Sucking her clit into my mouth sends a shudder through her. Her hips roll, pushing her into my mouth. *There we go.* My dick jumps, dying to get in on the action. But not yet. I have promises to keep.

I stop to whisper, "That's it, baby. Let go." I don't want her to come yet. I've got time, and I'm going to use every last minute to drive her higher and higher. But I want her to relax and enjoy it. *Fuck my face, baby.* I take a glance up and forget how to breathe. She's got her head thrown back, and her arched back is pushing her tits forward. *I wish I had a camera.* She's dancing like she did on stage tonight.

Engrossed in watching her move while I pleasure her, I forget to ease up and push her right over the edge, headfirst into a glorious, gushing orgasm. She gasps and grabs a handful of my hair to hold me where she wants me, but doesn't make a sound while I ease her down from her high. I lap up every last drop while imagining myself buried deep inside her to feel her squeeze and pulse around me.

She never made a peep. *How disappointing.* On the edge of my own orgasm, and desperate to feel her, I sit up and turn her sideways in the seat. I'll find out what it takes to make her moan if it's the last thing I do. My zipper is halfway down when the car stops. A familiar sight greets me when I glance out the window.

"Shit! We're home, baby. Let's take this inside." Before I help her sit up, I pocket her panties. Those are my trophy, not the chauffer's. My ego is healthy enough without absorbing her slightly dazed eyes or her breathlessness, but I don't mind some extra inflation. As long as it's been, I like the confirmation that I haven't lost my touch.

I climb out and help Fern before the driver makes it around the car. He's already been paid, but I tip him anyway. He pockets it with a nod and a grin and wishes us a good evening.

Fern is unsteady in her heels, which suits me fine because she leans on me until we make it inside. She stops with her back to me and waits while I close the door. *I haven't forgotten. Have you?* She remains still while I walk around her, her eyes fixed straight ahead, and when I cup the back of her neck, she lets out a slow, steady breath. "Stop or go?" I got to her once. She'll be back for more, even if she's changed her mind now. She said it herself; mine might as well be the last dick on the planet.

She swallows hard. "Go," she whispers.

Thank God! I'm so hard I hurt. So hard, I'm not sure if I can come. There probably isn't a shower cold enough to help me if she changes her mind. She's my new favorite addiction, and I need another hit.

As promised, I pick her up and carry her to the door in two quick steps. Before we collide with the wood, I slip a hand up to the back of her head to ensure she doesn't get hurt.

Clothes are only a minor inconvenience. I've already dealt with her panties. Her skirt goes up, unzip my pants, and *voila*. She's so close, so warm. I'm a condom and one quick thrust away from paradise, but I can't do it. This isn't right.

Groaning, I lower her to the ground without sliding her body down mine. Too much contact will fray my self-control.

"Wh-what's wrong?" she asks, her voice barely louder than a whisper. Huge eyes watch me uncertainly, so I smile to ease her mind.

"Nothing that can't be quickly solved."

"What do you mean?"

Shaking my head at my own foolishness, I put some distance between us before I can change my mind. I want her now, here, consequences be damned. Later, when my brain isn't in a lust-filled haze, I'll kick myself for the missed opportunity. Fern deserves better, deserves romance. "Someday, we're going to walk through this door so worked up we can't make it another step. That night is not tonight. The first time I have you is not going to be against our fucking door."

I undo the top button on my shirt, my mission to ensure that she didn't misunderstand. This isn't a rejection, merely a redirection. We're taking this upstairs. Her greedy eyes watch for a few buttons before she pushes my hands away and finishes the job. With every button, she sinks a little lower, and I pray I'm right about where this is going, even if it wasn't part of my plan. Once my shirt is open, her hands move to my pants, shoving them off my hips and following them to the floor.

"Maybe this will hold you over then," she whispers before she wraps her fingers around my shaft. Her kiss-swollen lips follow, dragging her name from mine.

"That . . . just might do it." Her giggles add an incredible new dimension to the pleasure. "Woman, if you suck any harder, I'm going to be permanently cross-eyed." She glances up at me, and her eyes clearly read *'challenge accepted.'*

"Baby, if you don't stop, I'm going to blow." A year of dating my hand has me a little off my game. If I come now, will I be ready to go again before she gets tired of waiting?

Her eyes lock on mine again, seeming to smile at me, and she hums a little. Her eyes shoot my control to pieces, and the hum is enough to send me over the edge. I come so hard my vision blurs and spots dance around the room, groaning her name and cussing.

She stands and reaches to take off her dress. "Freeze!"

She stops, but her glare warns me that she doesn't appreciate being ordered around.

As good as that was, I wasn't ready yet. I want to feel her body around me tonight. Getting her naked will buy me some time to recover. "I've been waiting to get you out of that dress all damn night, but I'm not done with you in it yet." I motion toward the stairs. "You go on. I'll be right up."

Chapter 24

Fern

Doubts assault me the second I walk away. Saying yes was so easy when I was still riding the high of a night at the bar. I'm not that person here, though. I'm only just learning to be myself again here. I could use a little of Killer Queen's confidence to get me through until he joins me.

My trembling hands fumble the doorknob, forgetting how to grasp, turn, and push. Once I succeed in opening the door, I can't handle the sight of his bed. *It's been so long* . . . I'm pacing, my back to the door, when I feel a change in the air. I didn't hear the door open, but I know he's here.

His eyes are on my ass under furrowed brows when I look back. "Not that I don't enjoy watching you walk, but what are you doing?"

"Waiting." I finish walking to the window, putting the width of the room between us, before I turn around to face him. It takes every ounce of willpower I possess to hold my ground instead of rushing into his arms. I spent most of the evening wrapped in one, or both, of them. Funny how I didn't realize how much I enjoyed that until just now. Though now, it has less to do with being held and more to do with his lack of clothing.

His clothes are in a bundle under one arm. Under the other, there's a bottle of wine, and he's holding a pair of the stemless glasses Felicity always bitched about for reasons I never parsed out. He eyes the space between us and his face tightens. All the same, he chuckles as if nothing is wrong. "I imagined you on the bed, waiting impatiently, maybe taking matters into your own hands because I took too long. Never thought you'd be pacing."

Mason crosses to the little sitting area I've never figured out why he has and leaves the wine and glasses on the table before continuing to his closet. "Didn't think it was a good idea to leave my clothes downstairs in case Nicole brings Ronni home early for some reason."

Yeah, right. That girl won't come home until Nicole or her father make her.

I still haven't moved when he emerges again. He grins at me and shakes his head. "You're looking at me like you want to throw me down where I stand and do bad things to me, but you also look like you're about five seconds from making a break for it."

His assessment isn't far off. I press my lips together and pull them between my teeth to keep from telling him so. It would be easy to say I've come to my senses and realized taking things farther this soon is a mistake. *It doesn't feel like a mistake.*

He was right before. We're going to be married—we practically are. We're just two rings and a piece of paper shy. *Another piece of paper.*

I'm on the edge of something here—more life-altering shit. I can pump the brakes, and we can continue to take things day by day instead of jumping in head-first like we agreed to. I can cling to the past a little bit longer, or I can step off this edge and embrace the future I chose.

It's hard to hold onto a ghost.

And Mason makes me come alive again. I don't have to kick and scream to know I exist, take up space, and influence the world around me. All week long, every time I've found his eyes on me, I've felt a little more solid. He *sees* me. Until now, that only ever happens when I'm with Ronni. Or when I'm on stage, being the Killer Queen.

Downstairs, when I made him lose control with a look, something shifted. I can't explain it, but I want to feel it again. Right now. Tomorrow morning. Every day. It was as addictive as Gabe's cocaine and has the same power to destroy my life. But am I going to hide behind the ideals of a teenage girl who knew nothing of the world, or am I going to accept that the commitment we made is a suitable substitution for the love I craved back then?

Mason watches me, patiently waiting me out. Respecting my right to decide what I want. He might not respect my decision so easily if I were to tell him this isn't happening, but that possibility doesn't matter because I'm not going to do that.

Finally, I come clean. "You're not wrong."

He cocks an eyebrow. "About?"

"I do want you, but . . ."

"Well, I can't pretend I won't be disappointed if you go with option B. If you don't, I'd like to point out that I'm not opposed to floor sex, but there's a perfectly good bed right there." He smiles suddenly, a hungry, wolfish thing that cranks up my pulse. "You know, until this evening, I would have sworn you hated it when I turn you on. I'm not so sure now."

My cheeks get hot. *I should've known he'd figure that out.* "I did."

"But now you don't?"

Admitting he is right was easy, but explaining it hurts. I don't like admitting weakness, but this man has seen me weak already. And he called me strong. "You broke me."

Mason takes a step toward me but stops and changes direction, going to the coffee table instead. "Then come here, and I'll put you back together again." He busies himself with pouring us each a glass of wine.

His deliberate inattention is a small mercy. Deciding to embrace this is one thing, but having the courage to follow through is another. Walking across the room doesn't seem so deliberate without him watching me like he's the one who lacks the patience to make it to the bed once he gets his hands on me.

"Thank you." I take the glass he offers me, but don't drink. Wine sounded like an excellent idea when he walked in with the bottle. Now, my stomach is too raw to handle it.

"You're welcome." He reaches to brush my hair back behind my ear and smiles when I lean into his hand. His eyes drop to my lips for a heartbeat, but he makes no move to kiss me. Instead of asking for reassurance that I want this, he's making me prove it by letting me lead.

His eyes never leave mine when I push up on my tiptoes and lean in to press my lips to his. My throat tightens. I get goosebumps and tears spring to my eyes, but then Mason's arms slide around my waist, and I'm okay. It's the first time I've initiated a kiss since Aaron died. I suppose it's fitting to be kissing Mason now, on our first official day together, since the last time I kissed someone was on my last day with Aaron.

His lips taste like wine. I linger longer than I planned to, enjoying the unexpected surprise. Nothing hurts. I don't fall over dead. Lightning doesn't strike me down. The Earth doesn't open and swallow me whole. It doesn't feel like a betrayal. In fact, it feels incredible, like I'm buzzing from the wine on his lips. As slowly as I leaned in, I back away.

Mason doesn't so much as blink. "You call that a kiss?" he asks, his voice a little extra gravelly. I breathe out a surprised laugh, but he surges forward to take my bottom lip between his teeth, and that laugh becomes a moan. His arms fall away. Feverish hands wrap around my middle. He pulls me tight to his body, using his hold on me to lead me where he wants me until he's sitting on the loveseat with me on his lap. Seated astride him, I'm spread wide open and cradling his dick in a different sort of kiss. One little move and I can have him right where I want him. He shudders beneath me but doesn't move to break contact or to get closer.

"Not yet, Fern. Wait until we get to the bed."

"Then why did we come over here?"

"To give you time to adjust or change your mind. I was afraid the bed would freak you out." He stops and frowns. "By the way, I'm going to die if you change your mind. I need you."

There's no going back now. We crossed the point of no return when he pulled me into his lap. My lady bits have already spoken. The dick deprivation ends tonight. I roll my hips, sliding along his length, teasing us both.

Mason shudders again and grabs my hips. "I want you to dance on my dick like you danced on my face." He swallows my gasp with a kiss. He doesn't ask this time but parts my lips with his tongue. My hips try to roll again, but he's still holding me fast.

When I get a chance to speak, I nearly forget my question. "What do you mean?"

"Baby, you didn't ride my face. You danced on it like it was a fucking stage. Hottest fucking thing I've ever been privileged enough to watch." He moves closer to the edge of the couch and leans forward, pushing me back and supporting my weight easily. "I can't wait for a repeat performance, but I want to watch you do the same thing while I'm inside you."

He bends over to bury his face in my cleavage. "I've been dying to do this all night, too." Warm kisses sear a path down the skin my dress leaves bare. I close my eyes so I can focus on the delicious sensation of his lips on my skin.

When he reaches the lowest point, he stops again. "Look at me."

My head is heavy now, and so are my eyelids, but I manage to comply—anything to get him to keep going. When my eyes find his, he grins and licks his way back to my neck in one long swipe. Involuntarily, my hips jerk, seeking some relief for the throbbing ache that simple little act caused.

"That's it. Why are you so quiet? Hmm? We're going to have to fix that. I like to hear you're enjoying what I do to you."

He returns his attention to my neck and the swath of skin he's so fascinated with. Only for a moment, though. "You have entirely too many clothes on, and if I don't get you there soon, we're not going to break in that bed this time, either." Holding me tight, he stands and sets me on my feet.

I reach to push the dress off of my shoulders, and again he stops me. "I want to do it. Where's the zipper?"

"There isn't one . . . It doesn't need one."

"What, I just do . . . ?" He lays his hands on my shoulders and guides the fabric down my arms. "This," he whispers, a little awestruck. I guess he's never seen a dress so easy to get a girl out of. His eyes move over every inch of skin he slowly reveals until the dress reaches the point of no return and slips from my body without further assistance, leaving me in nothing but my bra. It quickly follows the dress, though.

"Gorgeous," he says softly.

I try to cross my arms over my stomach to hide the stretch marks and slightly saggy boobs pregnancy left me with.

"No." He grabs my arms and holds them at my sides. "Don't hide from me. Don't you dare."

Felicity frequently bebopped around the house in the tiniest crop tops and shorts she could find. *She* didn't have stretch marks or saggy boobs. She might have been a little soft around the middle, but her skin was flawless. Why the hell would he want to look at my battle scars after he's had her?

He drops to his knees in front of me with no warning. I yelp in surprise and hop back, but he catches me by the hips and holds me still while he nuzzles my belly, pressing kisses to the marks I wanted to hide. "You created life. Your body held another human being. You're more perfect for every mark she gave you."

He places another careful kiss just below my belly button. It's such a tender gesture, especially coming from someone who isn't the father of the child responsible for the changes, that my eyes water and tears threaten to fall.

His hands slide around to squeeze my ass, and he nips at my hip bone. "No more hiding." As abruptly as he sank to his knees, he stands and pulls me against his chest, tipping me back, kissing my shoulder.

My brain glitches from having so much of my skin pressed against his. *I forgot how good this feels.* I've lost a couple of seconds when I open my eyes again. He moved us without me noticing.

Mason backs toward the bed, leading me with kisses. When his hip bumps the frame, he lets me go to grab a double handful of the bedding. With one quick move, he pulls the covers off the bed. His eyes are bright with lust when they settle on me again. "I wanted to see you in the middle of my bed, naked and waiting for me."

That mouth! A shiver of excitement originates somewhere in my belly and stops between my legs. My head tilts to one side. "Is that a hint?" It's not like anyone would ever mistake me for a centerfold or anything. I'm not a model. I can't imagine why he would want to see me sprawled out like something from a magazine.

"Indulge me?" he asks, sticking out his lower lip in the second most adorable pout I've ever been subject to. *Now I know where Ronni gets it.*

Resigned, but intrigued by the idea, I sigh and climb to the middle of his bed, leaning into the pillows. I keep my knees bent in a half-hearted endeavor to hide.

"I want to see all of you." He leans across the bed and grabs my ankle, tugging my legs apart.

"Why?" The thought of putting myself on display for him makes me incredibly self-conscious. Yeah, he's already seen all there is to see, but this is different.

"More spank bank material." His eyes dare me to argue. It's not worth the breath it would take to do so. "And because a bad day at work will be infinitely better with the image of you like this to recall."

Rolling my eyes, I let my knees fall apart. "I feel ridiculous." While this is true, part of me also likes the idea of him thinking of me like this when he should be working. Not that it'll ever actually happen. Mason Chambers is far too dedicated to his job to let himself become distracted at work.

"You don't *look* ridiculous. Is spontaneous ejaculation a thing? I'm about to find out."

Somewhere, I find some leftover reserve of confidence. I stare into his eyes and slowly circle one finger around my nipple, exaggerating the movement. He's immediately captivated by the hypnotic motion, and I smile triumphantly.

I've always been sensitive to touch, so when pleasure gives way to the pain of overstimulation, I slide my other hand between my breasts, down between my thighs to coat my fingers in my wetness. He tracks my hand, watching my palm skim back up my middle. I almost forget what I'm doing when he fists himself and squeezes. But when I spread my cream around my sensitive nipple, he lunges onto the bed.

His lips wrap around my fingers, and he sucks them clean. I groan, remembering the way his mouth felt on my sex in the limo. My over-stimulated nipple receives the same treatment. The heat of his mouth is intense in a good way. My back arches, pushing my chest out, offering him better access. Urging him on.

"I'm never going to forget that. You're so sexy it hurts."

Whatever, Mason. But I *feel* sexy when he watches me like he is now. Breathless and on the edge of losing my mind with need, I ask, "Are you going to keep me waiting?

He grins and his hands set to exploring the places he hasn't touched yet. "Only until you're so wet, you're dripping for me."

I grab his hand and move it to my breast. I know where I like to be touched. Obligingly, he pinches my nipple again, which sends sparks of pleasure careening through my body like a shower of shooting stars streaking across the night sky. His mouth replaces his fingers, and his teeth threaten the little nub, introducing me to a new brand of pleasurable pain and robbing me of my ability to think.

He pushes me onto my side on over onto my belly before my mind remembers that it can control my body. I try to turn to face him, but he stops me with his body over mine. "What are you doing?"

"Exploring."

"What? Why?"

"Because it's fun."

"But—"

"Trust me, Fern."

It's hard to relax, but I do as he asks. He places a lingering, open-mouthed kiss at the base of my neck, swirling his tongue against my skin. I try so hard, but I can't keep from moaning. He hums his approval and moves to where my neck curves into my shoulder and repeats the kiss. This time, a jolt of pure lust seems to radiate from that point to every last inch of my body, and I go completely boneless. Over and over again, he kisses and licks and bites various places on my back. Nearly all of them are accompanied by that same thrill.

When he's worked his way to the base of my spine, he grabs my hips and pulls them up, off of the bed. "Just like that," he murmurs. "Perfect and perfectly wet. I like it messy, baby."

Teeth scrape over skin that isn't accustomed to touch, much less a bite. "What the hell? Did you just bite my ass?"

The pleased smile I can picture, but not see, is apparent in his voice. "Yes. Yes, I did. It looks good enough to eat."

He's had his fun; it's my turn now. I want to see him. I want my turn to touch and torture him. But he stops me when I try to roll onto my back, and I'm not strong enough to fight him.

"No. I want you just like this, so you can move, and I can watch."

"What? No! That's not how—"

His voice is dangerously deep when he cuts me off to ask, "Not how what? Not how you want to be fucked? Or not how Aaron fucked you?"

Embarrassment floods my cheeks with heat. I don't have a good answer. Aaron was my first. What we did was all I know.

He takes my failure to respond as an answer. "And are you thinking of him now? Imagining it's his hands on you?"

"No! I just . . . I know what I like." As an argument, it's lame, and we both know it. Sighing my frustration, I hide my face against the mattress. I don't want to tell him I'm afraid of disappointing him. Sticking to the familiar will be easier. "I'm not imagining him, but I like what he did," I say instead.

"That's tantamount to saying you want to fuck him again, baby."

"No!" I squirm in his hands, trying to roll onto my back again. It's wasted effort because he has me where he wants me and isn't about to let go. "I want you. But I like—"

Mason's chuckle stops my explanation. "You don't know what you like. You know what you're comfortable with. Just . . . stop, Fern. Let me figure you out. I'm not going to fuck you like Aaron did so you can pretend. Even if you say you aren't now, you can't tell me you wouldn't be tempted."

"No! I—"

He ignores me. "You were practically a kid then. You barely know what sex is. Let me . . . Just let me, baby. Let go and trust me. If you truly loved him, letting someone else in won't make you forget him. It'll make remembering him easier to bear."

Frustration loosens my tongue. All the words I couldn't say before spill out. "It has nothing to do with him, okay? I've never done it like this before. I don't know how to!" Thank God my face is buried in the sheet because it's probably doing it's damndest to hit every shade of red known to man, and maybe some that aren't.

His warm breath raises goosebumps on my back. "Get out of your head and trust me. And trust you. You only have to do what feels good. Okay?"

"Okay," I say on a miserable little sigh.

"Good." The mattress barely moves when he does, but the drawer in his nightstand opening tells me that I have a few more seconds to adapt. "That bitch!"

I jolt upright and look around. "What?"

He thrusts a note into my hands that reads, *"Fucking cheater!"*

"That was at the bottom of my box of condoms. Wait, there's something on the back."

I flip it over, and we put our heads together to read, *"I poked holes in one, or maybe two. Who knows? Best wishes on the new baby!"*

He holds up a strip of condoms that's only three packets long. "Who the hell did she think I was sleeping with? It would've been her getting knocked up." Sighing, he scrubs his face with his hands. "Now what? Unless you've got some magical way of detecting holes in condoms?"

The note was a bit of a mood killer for me, but he's obviously not put off by it. *Not enough to call it a night, anyway.* "No, I don't. I'm on the pill, but maybe we should just—"

His chin sinks toward his chest, and he cocks one eyebrow at me. "Why the hell are you on birth control if you never have sex? Isn't that shit expensive?"

I make a face at him and stick out my tongue because I'm mature like that. "My parents are super old fashioned about babies and wedlock and all that. Mom and Dad got married because Mom was pregnant with my sister, so it's ridiculously hypocritical. But yeah, I've been on birth control since I was like sixteen. They pay for it because I refused to after I moved out."

"Then you were on the pill when you got pregnant last time?"

I shrug. "I'd also been sick and on antibiotics that month. We knew better, but we didn't think it would happen to us."

His eyes roam over my body before darting back to the nightstand. "Fuck it," he says, reaching for one again. "If there is a damn hole in it, and your birth control fails, we were meant to have a kid. I want you so bad, that's a risk I'm willing to take."

"That's not really a risk at all. You're basically wasting a condom."

Mason freezes in the act of opening it. "You'd let me . . . ?" he asks, the wrapper still between his teeth, waiting to be torn open.

My heart twists into a pretzel. Once upon a time, Aaron asked me the same thing. "Not like we're going to be married or anything," I tell him, echoing the words I said so many years ago. "We're in this for a while, Mason. Might as well get comfortable."

The foil packet hits the floor, and half a second later, he's pulling me into his lap. "New plan," he whispers, his forehead pressed to mine, dominating my field of vision. I have nowhere to look but into his eyes. "I know this isn't easy for you. I wanted to give you space so it wouldn't be so overwhelming. But this changes things for me, and I'll be damned if I have your back to me the first time I fuck you bare. If you can't handle that, you—"

The intensity of his words reignites the flames the hateful note doused. My hips swivel until his hardness is pressed against me. We're lined up like puzzle pieces waiting to be fit together. Another wiggle and I can sink onto him and alleviate the empty ache inside me.

Strong hands hold me in place, keeping me from completing the puzzle that is us. "You're sure?" he whispers.

His breath comes in short, rapid pants, telling me he wants this as much as I do. He's not changing his mind; he's giving me a chance to change mine. So there are no misunderstandings; I push against him, using my weight to break free of his hold, sliding him deep inside. He groans, and I suck a breath in between my clenched teeth because nothing has stretched me like this in a long time.

"You okay?" he asks.

"Yeah." Better than okay. The only word I can think of that applies scares me because my convenience boyfriend shouldn't make me feel complete.

"Dance for me, baby. Move like you did to that song."

Easier said than done. But I close my eyes, listen to his advice, and move until I find that little spark of pleasure and chase it for all I'm worth.

"You're fucking amazing."

For a moment, I forget I'm sitting upright and lean back, trying to hit just the right spot. My mistake isn't evident until I lose my balance, but his arms shift around me, catching me before I fall. "I've got you, baby. Don't stop. Please don't fucking stop. Look at me, Fern. Don't get lost. Stay with me."

His eyes are so intense they hurt. I can't tear my eyes away, though, because he smiles in a way that says he likes whatever it is he sees looking back at him. As vulnerable as it makes me, there's a certain sort of power in it. *I feel like a goddess.* It's *me* he's seeing. It's *me* making him moan and gasp and groan and beg. Everything else about us might be arranged, but this is *real.* When we're together like this, he's mine. I own him.

I've never felt this way before. I've only ever felt owned.

"That's it, let go, baby. I want to feel you." My orgasm explodes like an atom bomb. I rasp out his name and cling to him as if my life depends on it, afraid I really will shatter into a thousand pieces of pure bliss. "Yes, that's—Fern, just like that." He babbles in my ear, telling me how good I feel. How close he is. How wet I am. What feels best for him. It doesn't matter that I'm so sensitive every stroke is its own kind of sweet torture; I'm not going to stop until he gives me his pleasure. It's mine, just like him.

Like he did downstairs, he shouts for me when he reaches the edge of oblivion. Abruptly, he turns and lays me on my back. He thrusts slowly, deeper than I thought possible and definitely deeper than I could take him like we were, whispering my name. When he's completely spent, he sits up. His eyes are wide and wild, but mine probably are, too. *It's a good look on him.* We watch each other, not saying a word, just trying to catch our breaths.

We did that. *I* did that. And nothing has changed. I don't feel like a horrible person. Of course, it would be hard to feel bad about anything right now because that was amazing. I need to get up and clean up, but I just want to lay here for a bit and bask in the contentment seeping into every bone in my body.

Mason's grin catches me by surprise. So do his hands when he grasps my knees and pushes them apart, spreading me as wide as I can go.

"That is the hottest fucking thing I've ever seen," he pants. He shouldn't be breathing so hard now. The man is in good shape. I've watched him working out every day this week. It is most certainly not that he needs more cardio in his life. He isn't a smoker either, so his lungs should be in good shape, too. *Oh, my God. Is he sick?*

"What are you talking about?" I ask. "That's like the third time I've heard that tonight. I'm losing track. And are you feeling okay?"

"Seeing my cum dripping out of you like I've marked my fucking territory." *Well, you kinda have.* "My turn," he says, causing me genuine alarm.

"What are you talking about now? Are you feeling okay?

"My turn to make you come."

Gulping, I shake my head. Here I lay, coming down off what is hands-down the best damn orgasm I've ever had, and he thinks he's going to give me another? He's joking. *Or fishing for compliments.* "Uh, in case you missed it, you just did."

"Oh, no. You used my dick to make yourself come, and I fucking loved it. Now it's my turn."

"You're insane. Lack of sleep is making you unstable. Get some rest."

"I'm not sleeping until you come on my dick again and I'm the responsible party." He slowly moves over me again. My breath catches in my throat. *He can't be serious.*

"Look, it's a minor miracle I managed to get off a second time tonight. That never happens. A third time is out of the question."

Ignoring me, he slides home again, groaning with pleasure at the slippery mess we've created. A wave of pure pleasure radiates through my body. It should be overwhelming, but it isn't.

Mason's voice is a rasp in my ear. "Fuck, that's good. Isn't it?"

My breath is still lodged somewhere in my esophagus. A nod is all I can manage.

"You let me lead the way. I'll get you there, even when you think you can't."

***

The display on Mason's phone informs me that it's after six in the morning. My body is tired and content where it's at, but my mind is in a tumult. I need to get out of here. The cuddle hormone is real, and it is a bitch. I've seen the havoc it wreaks firsthand. That's why friends with benefits never stay friends. They either convert because the feelings are mutual, or they crash and burn because only one of them falls victim to the cuddle hormone.

But I don't want to go. He's so warm, and it's wonderful to have a connection with someone again.

You're falling for it. Sighing, I disentangle myself from him and roll off his bed.

He cracks one eye open, but only just. He's as tired as I am. "Where're you going?"

"To clean up." With any luck, he'll be out cold before I'm finished.

Chapter 25

Fern

When I step out of the bathroom, Mason is watching me by the faint light of the rising sun. *Shit.* What do I do? Leaving now feels cold, but staying is a mistake. Cuddling is for people in relationships—real relationships—or maybe for people who know they'll never see each other again once they part ways. I have to see Mason every day. I can't afford to forget this is a temporary arrangement.

I shuffle to my clothes and stoop to gather what's left. He's still watching when I right myself. I flash him a smile, but my heart isn't in it. "Good night," I whisper on my way to the door. I stop and giggle at my mistake. "I guess I mean good morning." *I'm getting too old for all-nighters.*

"Where are you going?"

I stop again and look over my shoulder at him. "To bed. I've been awake for more than a day. Some of us have to work today. And Ronni will be home soon. She'll be a live wire and want to know why I'm so tired."

He scowls. "What do you mean by 'work to do'? It's Saturday. You've already said you don't have any clients on Saturdays."

I stop myself from rolling my eyes. *What else could I possibly mean, Mason?* "I have a house to clean." It was part of the arrangement, after all.

The scowl disappears. "The house isn't going anywhere, Fern. This is your home now too. You don't have set hours. You get to things when you get to them, but your life doesn't revolve around it."

I suppose he has a point. I'll have to learn to stop thinking of this place as a job now. I smile again, but it's more than an automatic response this time. "Thank you." I hesitate, waiting to see if there's anything else before I take another step.

Behind me, I hear the sheets rustle. "Where are you going?"

I keep my eyes forward and my feet moving. "To bed," I say, struggling to hold only my patience.

"Then turn your cute little ass around and come to bed," he says, sounding every bit as irritated as I feel. "What the hell kind of prick do you think I am? I'm not going to screw you and send you away like a dirty little secret. We both signed that contract. We're official."

What happened to taking things slowly? This is as much fault as his, though. I didn't exactly stop him. "Have you forgotten the little girl who will be very confused if she comes home to find her nanny in bed with her daddy?"

He has the nerve to laugh at me. Not a little chuckle either, but a full-blown belly laugh that frays the threads of my patience. I look back and roll my eyes at him. I know that Ronni is happy I moved in and that kids are resilient, but a new relationship isn't something he should spring on her so soon after his breakup with Felicity. She deserves time to adjust to the changes in her life before he adds more.

I reach for the door handle, and his laughter abruptly cuts off.

"Confused probably isn't the word for it. More like fucking ecstatic. And you're not her nanny anymore, either. You're my girlfriend. We'll take care of Ronni together, as a family."

My hand falls away from the handle. That all sounds great. Just freakin' dandy. If only it were that easy. But what if Ronni feels like I've betrayed her? Like I'm stealing her father? Is this going to damage my relationship with her? Or hers with him? Either outcome would crush me. The last thing I want is to hurt her, but ultimately, she's his daughter. I have no say. *Maybe I'm overthinking it.* "Mason, we can't just drop this bomb on her. We agreed to take this slowly to give us all time to adjust."

"Look, Fern . . ." He stops and sighs. "Yeah, I know what we said that night, but things have changed. It's not going to stay a secret forever, especially not after last night. As you pointed out, we've got years ahead of us. We might as well be comfortable."

I pinch the bridge of my nose to ward off my budding headache. It hasn't been a week yet. What could've changed for him? *Sex* . . . Does he think he needs to play nice all the time, like we did tonight, to get laid again? That had nothing to do with it. That was me knowing he wanted me as much as I wanted him, to hell with the contract. There was no one around who needed to believe I'm his girlfriend when I tried to kiss him in the car. I wanted to.

And that makes staying far too risky.

My throat hurts from fighting back tears. *I've been doing that a lot lately for someone who doesn't cry.* "You're giving me whiplash, Mason. It's okay to call a spade a spade, alright? You don't have to pretend when we're alone. Nothing has to change because we had sex and nothing has to change for us to do it again."

"You've got some wires crossed somewhere." Something in his voice causes me to turn. I've seen that wounded look in his eyes before when I chanced upon him after a fight with Felicity. *But this time, I did it.* "I'm not pretending anything. I don't care that we're going about it differently and skipping steps. You're mine, and I'm going to treat you that way all day, every day. I'm not putting on a show for anyone.

"Yeah, when we first talked this out, I thought it might be that way. I expected it to be weird, but it's not. We're friends, or we're learning to be. While we're at it, we might as well skip another step or two and learn to be an actual couple instead of tiptoeing around it for a few weeks."

'An actual couple?' How is that supposed to work? Couples don't come with predetermined expiration dates, and they usually end up with feelings. We both need to take a step back right now to prepare ourselves for what's ahead. He swings his legs out of bed and goes to his closet, so I have to raise my voice to make myself heard. "Taking a month to adapt won't hurt anything."

"I don't need time to adapt, and after last night I don't think you do either. You can't treat this like a one-night stand. Walking out that door won't change what we did."

Anger sets my face on fire. That's not what this is at all! I'm only trying to protect us both! He steps out of the closet clad in a pair of shorts and comes to me. He offers me a shirt, and I automatically smile my thanks. I don't trust myself to speak it. I might lose my cool.

"Sharing my bed afterward shouldn't bother you if coming to my bed for sex doesn't," he says. "Think about it. Are you going to sneak down the hall when you're horny? That's not fair to either of us. I won't do it."

He takes my clothes and goes to his closet again. I'm grateful for the chance to calm down before I say something I'll regret. How dare he accuse me of using him for sex when he knows what a struggle it was for me? I don't care to dignify anything he just said with a response.

I busy myself finger combing the snarls from my hair to avoid looking at him. "We can't tell Ronni yet," I say to steer us toward a safer conversation. I can't tell him how to raise his daughter, but I can hopefully make him understand where I'm coming from.

"Why not?"

I take a deep breath and let it out slowly, releasing my anger along with it. "She wouldn't understand, Mason. No one would. You just got out of a relationship, and now you're moving me in? What if she—"

"Fern, anyone who knows me knows Felicity and I have been in trouble for a long time now. They all saw it before I did. No one will be surprised if it seems as though I've moved on quickly."

I scoff. "Seems as though?" I ask, looking up at him. "I've never seen anyone less affected by a breakup."

"What did you expect?" He shrugs. "We've barely qualified as a couple for more than a year. I resented her more than I was attracted to her because I couldn't figure out why she was treating me like she was. At least now, I know she thought *I* was cheating, though I can't imagine why. We're off subject, though. Come to bed. Please?"

"Maybe last night was a mistake." We wouldn't be at odds with each other right now if I was stronger. We'd both be asleep in our separate beds, perfectly content with our arrangement.

He cups my cheek in his hand. "If it was a mistake, why do I want to do it again?" he whispers.

I close my eyes because I can't answer honestly while he's looking at me like I'm something he can't bear to lose. It puts too much of myself on the line again. "Because we're weak. And because it makes us feel whole again."

His thumb glides over my cheekbone. "Then it definitely wasn't a mistake. We don't have to tell her right away, but we agreed to be honest with each other, remember? That wasn't a mistake, and you don't want to go sleep by yourself. We both know it."

I open my eyes, but looking at him is still too much, so I look away. He's right. It would be easier if it was a mistake, and if I didn't want to stay. That doesn't make it the truth, though. "Just this once. After this, we stick to the plan."

"If that's what you want, but I meant what I said. I won't sneak around with you. I'm not going to touch you again if you can't stay with me after. I'm not ashamed of you, Fern."

I smile bitterly. "But I *am* your dirty little secret, and I don't even mean that in a fun way. That's what we have, Mason. A dirty little secret. No one will ever know the truth about us."

"No! That's not . . ." He doesn't finish his sentence, maybe because he knows I'm right.

I try to smile again, but I can't quite manage it. "It's okay. I went into this with my eyes open."

Groaning, he removes his hand from my cheek to run his fingers through his hair. "I don't want you to feel like that! I appreciate what you're doing for me. I'm trying to make sure you know that, and you don't feel—"

"Mason, feelings weren't part of the bargain. Don't worry about me, okay? I know that's not what you intended, and no, that's not how I feel. If it were only about the money, maybe. It's not, though. It's about Ronni, too. But I do feel like you're trying to rush this to . . . I don't know, prove how good it can be so you don't feel guilty?"

His expression hardens and he glares down at me. "*Guilty?* What the hell am I supposed to feel guilty about? We haven't done anything wrong. *I* haven't done anything wrong! If I'm rushing, it's because I want us all to be happy. You're too damn stubborn to let us be!"

Oh, I'm stubborn? "Fine." I'll let him have this night so he can't say I'm not trying. But deep down, I do think he's only doing this to assuage his guilt. It's not worth arguing over, though. And, the mood I'm in, there's no danger of falling prey to that pesky cuddle hormone.

I keep my head high and take a couple steps toward his bed.

"Fern," he groans. "Stop, please! I'm sorry I let my temper get away from me. I don't want you to do anything you're not comfortable with."

His apology surprises me so much I stop. It's not that I'm not comfortable with staying; it's that I'm scared of what will happen if I get too comfortable here. "What one wants to do and what one should do are often not the same thing, Mason."

He sigh, and I picture him shaking his head at me. "You do what makes you happy. I want you to stay, but you don't have to. I liked holding you that night and waking up next to you in the morning. That's all I want."

I liked that, too. And that's why I shouldn't. "Just this once."

Mason

Why is she so difficult? It's not like I'm asking her to fall in love with me. I just want to spend time with her. As an added bonus, she doesn't even have to be awake for it. "You do realize I will insist later? Once everyone knows?"

"Uhm . . . noooo?" She sounds so small I wish I could take it all back. *Letting her walk away without telling her I want her to stay would have been a huge mistake.* "I, uh . . . Figured I'd keep my room. Ronni would never know. And you don't have company frequently. I figured moving my stuff in here would suffice, but you'd want . . . me . . . to . . . keep . . . my room unless . . . someone is staying over."

She trails off when I shake my head. "No. I won't demand sex, but I draw the line at separate beds once we're public knowledge. We're supposed to be a family. We might fake the feelings for each other, but we're not faking the relationship. It's real, and I want my girlfriend to be beside me always. How horrible would it be to spend all day together knowing once the sun goes down, it's over for the day, and you're dismissed? That's not how this is going to work. I thought you understood that."

Fern climbs into bed without another word and collapses in the fetal position, her back to my side. *Fuck.* Not the fucking silent treatment. I got enough of that from Felicity. "Will you say something, please?"

"Can we just . . . not do this right now? Can we talk about it later? Once Ronni is in bed or something?"

I can't argue without being the one to refuse a reasonable request. "So long as you're not refusing to speak to me."

"I don't know what else to say right now, Mason. Let's sleep on it. Please?"

"Sure, baby." That sounds promising, at least. I fall into bed and move to the middle so when I pull her closer, we're meeting halfway. She doesn't resist and lets me cuddle her close. Everything would be perfect if she wasn't mad at me. Or if I understood why she was.

I slip my hand up her shirt and spread my fingers wide across her stomach. I'm not trying to start anything; I only want to feel her skin. She tenses beside me but doesn't move to stop me. I got my point across before. She doesn't have to hide anything from me.

Vee would have marks like these now. Would she try to hide them, as Fern did? *Probably.* She tried to hide them then. She tried to hide her stomach, too, afraid I would be repulsed by it.

"What are you doing?" Fern asks, calling my attention to the way my fingers are wandering over her abdomen, exploring those marks.

"Sorry. I was thinking about—" I stop, not wanting to admit that I was thinking about my dead lover with my current one in my arms. *But she should understand.* We agreed to support each other through times like this.

"About Vee?"

"Yes. Sorry."

"That's okay. Do you need to talk about it?"

Being angry with me won't stop her from doing what she feels is right. I kiss the top of her head and sigh. "I don't know. Maybe. I don't want to weird you out."

"You won't."

I'm not so sure about that. Felicity was bothered by the photos of Vee I had on the walls when we started dating. I didn't see it for the warning sign that it was, and I took them down to make her comfortable. Most of them are in an album now, one that Fern has probably never seen. She doesn't know.

"You remind me of her."

"Oh?" she asks, curiosity evident in her voice.

"Yeah. If I didn't know better, I would wonder if you're related. So seeing you makes it easier to imagine what Vee might look like today had she survived."

She remains silent for a long while. Finally, she asks, "Does that bother you?"

"Not anymore. It was hard at first, but it would be hard to mistake you for her now that I know you better. Sometimes, I wonder what she'd be like today. She wasn't always a happy person. Would she be now, though?"

Fern sighs and hugs my arm. "It hurts, remembering the things about them that were less than perfect."

It's hard to admit because it feels like I'm betraying her memory, but Fern's right. "Yeah. But it's good to do so. If you don't, you think no one can ever measure up."

"Yeah."

I'll show her those pictures someday if she wants to see them. I want to share that piece of past with her *because* I know she'll understand. And I want her to know that she can share such things with me. *Does she even have pictures?* My insides twist. She might not.

"Fern?"

She jumps a little, and I feel bad for pulling her back from the edge of sleep. "Hmm?"

I hesitate, considering leaving it until morning because she's so tired. But I've already woke her up, so I might as well ask. "Do you have a picture of your daughter?"

"Yeah, on my phone. I can't look at it, though. I can barely recall her little face, but she just . . . doesn't look right in the picture." The pain in her voice cuts me deep.

My heart breaks for her. But I know someone who might be able to fix this picture. "Can I see it?"

She yawns and stretches. "Yeah, remind me some time. It's on my phone, and I don't want to go get it."

My curiosity isn't going to let me sleep until I do this thing. "Do you mind if I do?" She grunts, and I take it as assent. It'll only take me a minute.

She yawns again when I settle in behind her and pull her close to me once more. "You're crazy."

"Sorry, I've got this in my head now. It was going to keep me awake."

She unlocks her phone and puts it back in my hand. "There's a folder in the photo gallery labeled 'Aaron.' It should be the last one."

"You're turning me loose with your unlocked phone?" I don't know many people who would do that.

"Go crazy, I've got nothin' to hide," she says, fighting a yawn to get the words out.

"Sweet dreams." I kiss the top of her head and delve into her pictures, feeling like a voyeuristic creep even with permission. I scroll by dozens of folders, all neatly labeled with Ronni's name and the occasion. It's strange to see. Ronni isn't her daughter. But it's further proof that I picked the right person because she loves my child so much.

Seeing a younger version of Fern smiling next to a man who could only be Aaron takes me by surprise. He's tall, not just compared to her—everyone is tall compared to Fern—and his round face is dominated by a lopsided smile. Blond hair hangs loosely to his shoulders in the first picture, but it's short in the last ones; when they went to meet her family. Fern looks so happy, and it's not only the pregnancy glow, though she's as gorgeous as I knew she'd be. Knowing those pictures are from their last days together gives me the chills. *I'll take care of her.* It's strange to feel compelled to make a promise to a ghost.

The last picture, little Cassie, tries its best to pull my heart out through my throat. She's perfect. It's hard to tell on a newborn, but I think she got her mother's mouth, and definitely her dark curls. Fern's right, though. Her little body is blue and lifeless. I suck in a shuddering breath and try not to think of all the little moments Fern didn't get to experience the day her daughter was born. Even in the chaos of Ronni's birth, I got to hear my daughter cry. I got to hold her tiny little hand. Give her her first bottle.

"Fern?" She jumps again and grunts. "I'm so sorry, sweetheart. Is it alright if I send Cassie's picture to Nicole?"

She tenses. "Why?"

"Nikki's a photographer. She might be able to touch up the picture and make it . . ."

Fern rolls in my arms and stretches to kiss my cheek. "I'd like that. Thank you."

"Don't thank me yet. It's not done. But if you insist, I accept kisses."

She kisses me again, and then I watch her doze off with a smile on her face.

Chapter 26
Fern

Saturday Afternoon

"Daddy?" Ronni's voice hits my ears like an electric jolt. "Fern?"

Oh, shit! Oh, fuck! Damn it all to hell! I don't have an adequate supply of cuss words. How did we not hear her come through the front door, let alone come in here? *I knew this was a bad idea!*

"Rice!" Mason bolts upright in record time. His voice is all rumbly from sleep, just like last time I woke up here.

She's standing just inside the door, her aunt Nicole right behind her, looking back and forth between her father and me. Ronni goes into full-on pout mode and cranks it up to eleven with a whine. "Why did you have a sleepover without me?"

I take my time sitting up, making sure I'm still covered. *Thank God he got me a shirt.* This is awkward enough without us being naked.

"We were talking, and we fell asleep without meaning to. You and I do that sometimes, don't we?" *Oh, he's good.* That was smooth. She loves it when that happens, but he's usually in her bed when it does.

"Yeah, but it's past lunchtime . . ."

"Fern and I were out late last night, Rice. We stayed up past our bedtimes and talked too long, so we slept too late."

Her eyes widen. "You went out? Together?" I might be wrong, but she sounds excited . . .

Mason winces. "Yes, Rice. I . . . uh . . . decided Fern and I could use a night out and a chance to get to know each other better."

Nicole scoffs and says under her breath, "Is that what they're calling it now?" Ronni might not understand what the hell she walked in on, but Nicole sure as hell does. And she's glaring a hole in her brother's head. Her disapproval—and disappointment—are plain to see, written all over her face in bold. All caps, too.

Ronni's squeal could shatter glass. "Was it a date?

Mason exhales deeply. "You know what? Yes. It was."

I stop breathing. Surely he's not going to tell her everything.

Ronni frowns, and her eyes bounce between us, scrutinizing our faces. "Why don't you look happy then? Aren't you're supposed to be happy after a date?"

What the hell is going on here?

"We're tired," Mason says.

Her little face falls. "Did you not have fun?" Her voice cracks. I can practically see her heart breaking.

He throws me a wide-eyed look, a cry for help that I don't know how to give, before turning back to her. "Oh, honey, we had the best time."

"I'll bet you did," Nicole mutters.

I hold out my arms and beckon Ronni over. I've remained quiet because she's not my daughter, and he should handle this how he thinks best. I just can't anymore, though. I need to hug my Rainbow. I hate to see her sad.

She climbs up and right into my lap. "What's wrong, Rainbow?" I ask as I comb my fingers through her messy curls.

Before she answers, she bursts into tears. "Oh, Ronni." I sigh, rocking her side to side. "There's nothing to cry about, sweet girl. Tell me what's wrong."

Mason scoots closer and wraps his arms around both of us. *This shouldn't feel so good.* He rests his chin on my other shoulder and rocks with us.

Between her sobs, she tells me, "You're s-s-supposed to be happy! I-I-I-I-If you're h-happy, you'll b-b-b-be Daddy's n-new—" She breaks down too hard to finish her sentence, but I get the gist of it. For whatever reason, she *wants* us to date. She's not upset at all. Well, at least not that we went out.

"Why do you think we're not happy?" Mason asks her.

"Because you don't *look* happy!"

Mason's arms contract, hugging us both. "Honey, you scared us! We thought we'd be awake before you got home. We didn't plan to sleep all day. We weren't going to tell you about our date because we didn't want you to get too excited."

"Why not?"

"Because one date isn't much in the grand scheme of things."

"But Fern slept in your bed! You told me Felicity slept in your bed because you were dating. And one other time, you said dating someone meant they were your girlfriend."

Oh shit. Does she have to remember *everything?*

"It was an exception, alright?"

I feel a little guilty because I know it has to be hurting him to blatantly lie to her, but it's better this way. For now, at least.

The miserable little thing in my lap sniffles. "But—"

"Ronni, please," Mason stops her. "Go play. We'll talk about this more later, alright? I need to talk to Aunt Nicole so she can go home."

"Yes, Daddy." Ronni sniffles again before she scoots off my lap and shuffles her feet all the way to the door, only stopping when Nicole squeezes her shoulder.

The door closes behind her, and Mason drops his head into his hands. "Fuck!"

I silently agree with him and breathe a sigh of relief. That bullet is dodged for the moment.

Nicole waves a hand toward me and asks her brother, "Are you *fucking kidding me?*"

Shame burns me up from the inside out. *What* were *we thinking?* This will never work. His family won't approve.

"What?" he asks.

"Oh, don't play coy!"

I envy Ronni's dismissal. *No one said I have to stay.* Mason grabs my arm when I try to slide away and out of bed, keeping me in place. Apparently, I have to suffer through this with him.

"Don't stand there judging me!" he says, struggling to keep his voice down. "It was an accident!"

She waves toward me again. "So, you *accidentally* slept with the woman your daughter regards as a mother? And don't even act like you didn't know that. The whole damn world knows that!"

Under different circumstances, her words would mean the world to me. I don't feel I deserve them right now.

His hands fly up. "That wasn't the accident! Ronni finding us like this was!"

It's a relief to hear him defend us rather than blaming it on alcohol. He said he's not ashamed of me, but that was before his daughter and sister found us like this.

Nicole points at him. "That right there! That's why I'm judging you, dumbass! For being stupid enough to believe your eight-year-old wouldn't figure it out! They don't miss anything, Mason! And because I can't believe you'd risk losing Fern for a little fun! Ronni would be devastated!"

"Were you not listening? It's not like that! I wasn't lying to Ronni. I didn't tell her that Fern and I are together now, but fuck, Nicole! It's a delicate situation!"

Mason! I don't know how to react. I can't believe he just blurted that out.

Nicole shifts her weight to one foot and plants her hand on her hip. "So, wait, you're actually doing this now? You're together, together? Not just . . . ?"

Mason scoffs at her. "We're not doing the friends-with-benefits thing, if that's what you're asking." He wraps his arm around me and slides me into his side. "We're a couple."

He sounds so damn . . . proud! He'd make a killing if he worked in sales. Eskimos would buy ice from him. No one will ever know this isn't real if I can sell it half as well as he can.

Nicole nods to herself and paces. "Right, well . . . You've got to tell her before Monday. It'll sound better if she tells all her friends she found her daddy and his girlfriend asleep in the same bed than it will if she tells them it was her daddy and her nanny. And trust me, she'll tell."

Mason starts to argue, but Nicole shuts him up with a look. "One of the kids in Mallie's class told them all about how she found her new daddy putting his pee-pee in her mommy's hoo-ha. Give it a week; you'll hear about it, too. This," she swivels her finger back and forth between us, "I approve of. And may I say, it's about damn time. I disapprove of the sneaking around. If you're serious, own up to it. Otherwise, maybe you shouldn't be doing it."

I hide my sigh of relief. The plan might be ruined, but knowing that Nicole approves somehow makes it easier to deal with. Maybe it doesn't matter if people know after all.

Mason throws his head back into the headboard with an audible *thunk* and groans. "It's just . . . new. Very new. We're not sneaking around. We only didn't want to tell her right away."

She narrows her eyes at him, not that he can see. They hone in on him with laser-like precision, boring a hole in his head. "How new? And I'll know if you lie."

"Like this week new. Last night was our first date."

"You two haven't been sleeping together all this time?"

I hold my breath. If she thinks that, others probably do, too. Will they believe us, or will they label me a homewrecker?

He sits forward so fast I'd think he'd been stung if I didn't know any better. "*What?* No! How could you even think that? I haven't been with anyone but Felicity since Vee died. Until last night. This morning, to be precise!"

"Well . . ." She winces and ducks her head. "I really didn't, but one did wonder sometimes. Out of the blue, Fern went from being, well . . . Fern, to being too professional. And Felicity glared daggers if either of you so much as blinked in the other's general direction. Speaking of this morning, what in the hell are you doing sending me a picture of a dead baby at a time when sane, child-free people are only awake on a Saturday because they're putting their pee-pee in a hoo-ha? I fucking bawled for an hour right off the bat this morning, you big fucking jerk!"

He's probably lucky she doesn't have anything to throw at him, and that she didn't get it in her head to cross the room and beat the shit out of him. If he sent it with zero explanation, he might deserve it. "That's the only picture Fern has of her daughter." He opens his mouth, then abruptly closes and kisses the top of my head. "She was stillborn. I was hoping you could maybe make it . . ."

There's no easy way to say it. Tears sting at my eyes, but I'm getting good at stopping them. He's so sweet to think of something like that for me.

Nicole waves her hand to stop him, sniffling a few times. "I'm on it." Tears roll down her cheeks when she turns to me. "I'm sorry, Fern. I had no idea. She's gorgeous. What's her name?"

"Cassie." It's been so long since I've said it out loud it sounds rusty and grates on my ears. I clear my throat and try again. "Cassandra Rose Williams, after her grandmothers."

"Oh, baby," Mason whispers. Since he has the whole story, he has some idea of how much it hurts to know I named my daughter after the woman who did her best to ruin my life more than it already was. He pulls me into a hug and rests his chin on top of my head while he holds me.

"Leave it to me," Nicole says, sounding more like herself. "And I'll make you a deal. If you tell Ronni the truth right now, I'll take her home with me for another night. But you also have to keep my brats some weekend. I need a night with my knees behind my ears, too."

"Nicole!" Mason groans, lifting his chin to bury his face in my hair instead. "I did *not* need to hear that. You're my little sister."

"Oh, please! Like I need to hear all the stories you and Austin swap when you think you're alone!"

"Austin's, maybe. Not mine! I don't kiss and tell!" He kisses the top of my head before asking, "Whaddya think? Should we tell her?"

To avoid being scandalous gossip at school Monday morning? Yes, please . . . Obviously, the situation with Ronni isn't what I feared. What can it hurt? *Plenty.* "She's your daughter. It's your decision to make, and I'll respect it."

Mason

My heart is trying to break through my ribs. Fern's anxiety is evident in the way she's clutching my hand like a lifeline. I thought giving her time to get dressed would also allow her time to come to terms with what we're about to do. *I thought wrong.* It only made things worse.

I raise my hand to knock on Ronni's door but pause. "Ready?"

"As I'll ever be."

I rap lightly and wait. Instead of calling for us to come in, she opens the door. Her eyes slide from my face to Fern's, then down to our clasped hands. Her gaze flies back to mine, a new hope shining within.

"Rice—"

She throws her arms around my waist. "Why didn't you just tell me?"

I pat her back and look to Fern for help. Finding none, I sigh and give her the only explanation that comes to mind. "It's complicated, honey. We wanted to keep it a secret for a little while. It happened very fast, and adults can be funny about things like that."

"But it's not complicated at all." She points at our hands. "See, you're already doing it. You hold hands. You kiss. You fall in love. How is that complicated?"

I glance at Fern to see her fighting a smile and losing. "That's not the complicated part, Rainbow. It's complicated because other adults won't understand our relationship since your daddy just broke up with Felicity."

Ronni rolls her eyes. "Daddy and Felicity didn't fall in love. They didn't kiss enough or something." She narrows her eyes at me. "You better give Fern lots of kisses."

Fern manages to turn a laugh into a cough. Ronni's gaze is far too intense for me to find humor in her words.

"Yes, ma'am."

Chapter 27
Fern

One week later

Aaron kisses my forehead, each cheek, my nose, and my lips like he does every time he leaves. "Love you, half-pint."

"Fern? Baby, I'm here." The mattress dips beside me, and warm arms engulf me. "What's wrong?"

My heart leaps into my throat. It was only a dream. It's not Aaron holding me, it's Mason.

Waking up in his room is disorientating again. It doesn't take me as long to get up to speed this time, though. All the same, I'm still a little off-kilter. It has more to do with my dream, though. Or was it a nightmare?

"Just a dream," I whisper both to myself and to him. After so much time spent in his arms, the scent of his shower gel is comforting enough that my tension eases. "How long have you been up?"

"Ten minutes. I was going to make you breakfast, but I heard you crying when I got out of the shower."

"Just a dream." *If I repeat it often enough, maybe I won't feel so guilty.* I'd love to snuggle closer and bask in Mason's solid, steady presence. That's a terrible idea, though. He wouldn't mind, but it's not a luxury I can afford if I want to make it out of this with my heart intact. And it's confusing to seek comfort from him with Aaron so heavy on my mind. That dream felt so real.

"Tell me about it?"

I hesitate, uncertain if I'm ready to share this. Mason is the closest thing I have to a best friend, and I need to talk about it, so he wins. "I was talking to Aaron,"

I whisper. "He told me I need to let go. He told me he loves me like he was saying goodbye, then I woke up." And I hurt like I lost him all over again.

His hand stills. "I had a dream like that. Two days later, I met Felicity at a party. She was there with some friends, and they called her Fee. I thought her nickname was a sign or something, so when she called and asked me out, I went."

"That's why you kept trying to make it work," I whisper. It's nice to finally understand why he put up with her.

"Yeah."

"It felt so real . . . Like he was right beside me, whispering in my ear. He told me I need to be happy." My throat constricts. I don't know how to be happy without feeling guilty about it. I'm caught in the middle of a tug-of-war between the two.

"You do need to be happy. You deserve to be happy. Maybe . . ." He sighs, followed by the scratchy sound of stubble on skin. "I sound like an asshole, but maybe you need to listen?"

He's not wrong. Everyone I know has been telling me I need to let go for years now. I didn't have a reason to before, but now I have this thing with Mason and Ronni. I owe it to both of them to let go of the past so I can be present and ready for the future. "Maybe I'll go visit soon . . . Talk to him and Cassie. That sounds silly, huh?"

Warm lips press against my shoulder, and goosebumps spring up in response. "Not at all. We used to visit Vee all the time."

"Maybe next time, when I say goodbye, I'll actually mean it." Panic suffocates me. How can I let them go? They're my family.

"Whenever you're ready, sweetheart. If you'd like, I'll go with you." He kisses my shoulder again.

"You would?" Having him there might be a little weird, but I am always so lonely when I go. That's why it's always hard to mean it. I can't let him go when their memory is the only thing that keeps me from feeling lonely.

"Absolutely, baby. Remember, we always have each other to lean on."

"Yeah . . . I'd like that."

***

Mason reaches across the table to take my hand. "What's on your mind, sweetheart?"

He's been hovering since I woke up. On the one hand, I appreciate it. On the other, I don't know how to react. The dream stirred up feelings I thought I was past now. Marathon sex with Mason didn't bring them to the forefront, but one little dream about Aaron and I'm suffocating under the crushing weight of the guilt I feel for moving on. And for their deaths. That guilt will never leave me, though. If I hadn't asked to go home, he and Cassie would be with me now.

But letting someone else into my life, even if it's not a *real* relationship, suddenly feels like a betrayal. I think of Aaron less and less every day, but it took my dream to notice. Mason is slowly taking over.

"Just homesick." It's only a little fib. Harmless. And mostly true. "I wish I could talk to my sister."

Mason cocks his head to the side. "So, call her?"

"I can't . . ." I have to swallow hard before I can explain. "I don't have enough minutes on my phone for long calls. Just for emergencies."

Comprehension blooms in his bright blue eyes. He stands up and hands me his phone. "Then you will use my phone to call your sister while I do the dishes. And when you're finished, we're going out to get you a new phone, and you can call her whenever you want."

"You don't need to do that! You've spent enough on me!" I don't try to give his phone back, though. I will use it to call my sister, but I don't *need* a new one.

"Yes, I do. I won't have you cut off from your family because of something so little, Fern. Or from me. What if I need to call you someday? Or you need to call me?"

"I have minutes for things I *need* to make calls for. I don't call people to talk, though." Before, admitting that would've been embarrassing. It doesn't bother me now, though. He knows how tight money was for me.

He lays a hand across my cheek and pulls me closer to kiss my forehead. "Call your sister. Talk as long as you want. Call your mom and your dad if you want. But we're getting you a new phone before we pick Ronni up from Mom's." He helps me with my chair and nudges me toward the hallway. "The code is Ronni's birthday."

I retreat to my room for privacy. My hands shake, making it difficult to tap the correct numbers, but I manage.

"Hello?" Her voice sounds uncertain, but of course, she won't recognize the number.

"Ivy?" My voice cracks with the effort of holding back tears.

"Who is this?"

"It's Fern." Tears well in my eyes anyway, but I'm determined I won't waste any of our time crying.

"Fern? Oh, my God! Scott! Take the kids! It's Fern! Fern, hon? Is everything okay? You never call! Did you get a new number?"

"No, it's not my number. I'm uh . . . borrowing a phone from . . . a friend. I'm okay, Ivy. Better than I've been in a long time."

"It's so damn good to hear your voice!" Ivy sobs, testing my hold on my tears. "Have you talked to Mom yet?"

"No . . . I called you first. I'll call her later if I have time." I'm not ready to talk to Mom yet. I miss her, but it's hard to stick to my carefully crafted web of lies without feeling like the world's worst daughter.

She gasps. "You didn't steal a phone, did you?"

"No!" I giggle. "It's uh . . . Actually, that's why I'm calling. Are you busy?"

"Fern, the rest of the world can wait. You're my baby sister, and we haven't gotten to do this in years. Talk to me."

She listens patiently while I tell her about Mason. His brother is in on it, so I debate telling her about the contract. If anyone can keep a secret, it's Ivy. She'd be appalled, so I try to skip that.

Ivy knows me better than that, though, so she pokes and prods until I tell her everything. As predicted, she's utterly horrified. She spends a good thirty minutes trying to change my mind but finally accepts the inevitable, even though she thinks I'm crazy.

"You make sure he knows that if he hurts you in any way other than the impending heartbreak when this is over, I'll kill him. No one gets to hurt my baby sisters."

Her protectiveness makes me chuckle. It's a switch—she's the eldest, but I was always the protector. "I am perfectly capable of kicking his ass, remember? I took lessons for years."

"The horror!" she says in a perfect imitation of my grandmother. "Ladies don't hit, or kick, or . . . grunt *'hiya!'*"

Mason taps on my door and opens it just enough to poke his head inside. His smile is so beautiful it could be one of the wonders of the world. I shouldn't let myself notice that. Not when I'm in real danger of falling for my boyfriend. I'll never admit it, but Aaron isn't protecting my heart anymore. He's practically handing it over on a silver platter. "Sorry to bother you, pretty girl. I'm going to run an errand."

I pull on my poker face to keep from pouting. "Alright, just a second. Ivy? I've gotta—"

Mason shakes his head and saunters over to me. "You keep that. Call Len if you need me."

"But—"

He leans down and silences me with a kiss. "No 'buts.' I'll be back soon." He turns and walks away before I can argue.

"Oh, my," Ivy says in my ear. I'm too busy enjoying the view to respond.

***

I sit quietly, half-listening to Ronni chatter about her sleepover with her Gigi. She surprised me when we told her our plans. I expected her to be upset with us for picking her up early, but she seemed happy. Mason drives to a section of the graveyard near a familiar church and parks. He and Ronni bail out of the car, but I stay. I don't want to intrude upon their time with Vee.

Mason opens the door and holds out his hand for mine. "Coming?" he asks.

I shake my head. "I'll wait here. Take your time."

Ronni runs up to Mason and wraps her arms around his waist. "But I want you to come," she tells me. "Please?"

How do I say no to that? "Are you sure?" I ask Mason. I don't want to make this awkward for him.

Mason gives me that brain-melting smile. "Absolutely. C'mon, sweetheart." He reaches into the car and snags my hand where it rests in my lap. He helps me from the car but doesn't drop my hand once I'm out. Ronni grabs the other and leads the way, half dragging us along in her wake.

A tall oak casts Vee's grave in shadows, providing shade from the afternoon sun. Mason leads me to a concrete bench near the trunk, while Ronni sinks to the ground next to the paving over the grave and unzips her backpack, pulling out a bag of half-used sidewalk chalk. Without a word, she selects a piece and sets to work decorating the blank canvas in front of her.

It's shocking at first. But what better way for her to connect with her mother?

Mason moves a little closer and slips his arm around me, silently urging me to relax. I feel like I'm trespassing here. "She's done that since she was big enough to draw," he says, nodding toward the bag of chalk.

"I think it's sweet."

We watch quietly, enjoying the gentle breeze and the late afternoon sun while she colors flowers, hearts, and rainbows on every inch of the paving. Then, she puts her chalk away and stands. "Okay, I'm ready now," she says, turning to watch us expectantly. *But I'm not.*

I feel wrung out all of a sudden, like it's time for their funeral all over again. Mason pulls me to my feet when I fail to move again. Once again, they each claim one of my hands, but this time, I lead the way.

We don't have far to go. The church I noticed on our way in is where I said goodbye to my family. My heart beats harder and faster the closer we get. The world around us fades away. Their hands in mine keep me tethered to the earth, but all I see is the big brick building in front of me.

The interior hasn't changed. Same pews. Same wooden floor. I remember the hollow thuds of my high heels as I followed their caskets down the aisle that day.

"Can I look at the glass, Daddy?" Ronni asks, bringing me back to the present. She's pointing to the nearest stained-glass window.

He hesitates, his eyes bouncing between the two of us. Finally, he cups my face in his hands and locks eyes with me. "I'm here if you need me. But I understand if you want to do this by yourself."

I take a deep breath and let it out slowly. I don't know what I want. The thought of having him right there to lean on is enticing, but I don't want a crutch. I need to find the strength to do this alone. "I kinda do," I say in a voice that sounds nothing like my own. *That applies to so much in my life.* "I need to face this, but . . ."

"I get it, sweetheart. I'll be there in a heartbeat if you need me." He kisses my forehead and joins Ronni.

Slowly, I turn toward the aisle and lock eyes with a priest. He nods at me, but seem to understand that I want to be alone because he moves to follow Mason and Ronni. On trembling legs, I make my way to the front pew and collapse into the same place I sat last time I was here. I close my eyes and let the smell of dust and candle wax take me back to that day. Even Mrs. Williams' perfume wasn't strong enough to overpower it.

The words the priest read were meant to bring comfort. Closure. I was too numb from guilt and loss and medications to fully absorb them then. I can't remember them now. I'd know the man's voice anywhere, but what he said is forever lost to me.

I shift a little and the old wood creaks, adding another sensory layer to the memory. Aaron had a lot of friends here. And what family he had on his mother's side flew in from California. The place was standing room only. That many people can't be quiet, no matter how hard they try.

Stop distracting yourself. I'm only delaying the inevitable, dissecting memories of that day when I'm supposed to be making my peace with what happened. But imagining I've traveled back in time, and they're right there makes it easier. It's hard to say goodbye to someone who is already gone.

And when I open my eyes, they will be. I will stand up and walk away, knowing that I will always love them, and I will never forget them, but I have to live. And I choose to be happy. I choose to live a life, or at least a few years of one, with a man who is so good at acting like he adores me that it's hard to remember it's not real. And with a little girl who loves me as much as I love her. Her love for me makes the ache of knowing that her father will never feel the same bearable. Worth it.

For the first time since their deaths, I'm not sorry I survived. I'm going to walk out of here and live the life we wanted to the best of my ability. I'm going to make the world a better place in my own way. I'm going to be happy. I'm going to be . . . valued. Valued will do until Mason and I part ways. I'm going to help him raise Ronni to be a strong woman until it's time for me to move on.

I will mourn when I must, but I won't let grief and guilt control my life any longer, because they wouldn't want that for me.

"Goodbye," I whisper. The vision of flower-draped caskets shatters when I open my eyes. My legs still tremble when I stand, but it's different this time. I've cast off the weight holding me down, holding me back.

A floorboard creaks under my weight. Mason turns, offering me a small smile that could easily be mistaken for a grimace. Maybe it's a little of both. He knows what it's like to finally set yourself free. It's bittersweet, like our relationship.

Chapter 28
Fern

One Week Later

"Rainbow!" I groan. My head falls back into the headrest. My resolve is weakening with every pretty please with rainbows on top.

"Ronni . . ." There's a note of caution in Mason's voice, warning her again to drop it.

"But Daddy! Please! Just tonight, then I won't ask again for . . . two weeks!"

My head rolls his direction when we stop at an intersection. She's been begging since we got in the car after a pit stop for ice cream on our way home from roller-blading.

I've been burning for him since he whispered in my ear that he could watch me lick an ice cream cone all day long.

She's begging to sleep with us. Not him. Us.

And I'm caving.

"We can move Fern's stuff, too! With the three of us working, it won't take long at all, and you won't have to worry about finding time to do it!" She's been hinting around about it for a week now, since we got home from the graveyard. But I keep delaying. Having my own space makes it easier to remember what started all of this and how it'll end.

"Ronni," Mason repeats in the same tone. His knuckles are white on the steering wheel. Our eyes meet, his saying loud and clear he's every bit as anxious for bedtime as I am. That only makes things worse.

I wasn't even planning to sleep with him tonight. Sleep sleep, or *sleep* sleep. I've made a point to stay in my room when Ronni's home, though I know she thinks

I'm sleeping in her father's bed. Mason has made it clear that the choice is mine, and I'm welcome to join him any time, but actually doing it is a mental hurdle I haven't made it over yet. Once that starts, there's no nightly reminder that we're pretending. And what if we get caught?

Mason's warm hand grips my thigh, sliding higher and squeezing when he can't move it anymore. The bottom drops out of my heart for a second. It stalls before it quickens to a pace to rival a hummingbird's. *What is he thinking?* He's nearly fingering me over my jeans with his daughter in the backseat. It shouldn't be tripping my trigger, but it is. *The thrill of getting caught.*

He grins because he *knows* what he's doing to me. "I shouldn't negotiate with terrorists, but just this once . . ." he says slowly. "If Fern is all right with it."

No! What the hell are you doing? He was supposed to be the bad guy here!

"Please, Fern?"

My resolve is already shot. It's too hard to tell her no sometimes. "I suppose."

"I can? Really?"

"Just you hold your horses . . ." Mason says. "You ever harass me like that again, and the answer will be no for a month, Veronica Anne. Do you understand me?"

"Yes, Daddy," she whispers. I barely catch it over the music, but he nods. The man has bionic ears, I swear.

"And never again on a school night. I'm making an exception this once because it's a special occasion."

"It is? Why?"

"Because we have Fern."

That's it. I'm done. The man is going to kill me. He missed his calling. He was born to be an actor.

"Straight to your room," he tells her as soon as he turns the car off. "Get your things together for school tomorrow, and get yourself ready for bed."

She's out of the car in a blink. The Flash could learn a thing or two from her.

When the door closes behind us, Mason's hands close firmly around my hips, and he yanks me against him. I swallow a moan. I'm partial to that assertive streak of his. This close, I can't refute the evidence; the desire is still there, pressed against my belly. *It's like he's dangling a treat on the end of a fishing line.* I'm not falling for it, though. He's already yanked it out of my reach. Not that it was ever within my grasp tonight.

He lowers his lips to my ear until they're close enough to give me goosebumps when he whispers, "Once she's out, we're going to the other room, and I'm going to make you come again and again until you're too tired to move."

Yes, please. The little voice in the back of my head reminds me this is a horrible idea. We could get caught. At least that's the excuse I give him to hide my fears. But he makes me feel so good—not only in terms of physical gratification. Every time I surrender control to him, he treats me like something beautiful and priceless. When he surrenders to me, I become someone to be worshiped. Both are powerful and addictive experiences. It's hard to say no.

All the same, practicality wins out. "We shouldn't."

"Why?" He grazes my ear with his teeth, chuckling at my involuntary response. My mouth is saying stop, but I'm leaning closer to give him better access. I can't help myself with him.

I know what he'll say if I use Ronni as an excuse, but I try it anyway. "Because we're not—"

"Married? Engaged?"

My face burns with my embarrassment. That's not where I was going with that, so why did he go there? Does he think that's my real reason? Maybe it's better to let him believe that? I can't tell him I'm afraid of catching feelings for him if we keep it up. He's so good to me. It would be so easy to turn that into something it isn't. *The cuddle hormone . . .*

His big hands come to cup my face. "What's going on in here, hmm? You didn't hesitate last night. Or last weekend."

The mention of the hours we've spent shut in his room grabs me by the spine and gives me a shake, rattling my objections right from my brain. Only for a moment, though. "I don't know," I whisper. It's time for some truth. We promised to be honest, and I'm not. "I worry about what's going to happen when this means more to one of us than it does to the other."

He actually laughs at me. "Silly woman." Warm lips press a quick kiss to the tip of my nose. "Don't worry about the *what-ifs*. That's not going to happen."

"We can't know that! What if we get to the day we're supposed to sit and discuss the future of this . . . arrangement, and one of us is in love, but the other isn't and is ready to be out?"

Grinning, he darts forward to nip my bottom lip. "It's sex, Fern. It's not going to be a problem. Be happy right now. Let the future take care of itself. Let me take you to bed and take care of you."

"But Ronni—"

"Is a heavy sleeper."

The voice between my legs overrides the one in the back of my mind. She isn't willing to be overlooked anymore. I should have seen that coming after letting her have a visitor after years of forced isolation. Resistance is futile. I'll make it a week—tops—before I'm ready to beg him.

I finally have what I've wanted for years. Mason may not be the one I've longed for, but he's here, and he's mine. I can reach out and touch him anytime I want, and I'm trying to push him away. Seven years is a long time. Maybe he's right. Maybe it won't be a problem.

"Alright, you win," I whisper. Losing shouldn't feel like winning, but it does with him.

"I love it when you let me win." The grin on his face is so self-assured I kind of want to slap it off of him. He had me right where he wanted me. *It's a good thing he's cute.*

"At least you're smart enough to realize I'm letting you."

"Hey . . ." The grin fades away. He studies my face while his thumb strokes my lips. "No always means no. I don't care if I've had you a thousand times. I respected Felicity when she said no, and you can bet your ass I'll do the same for you. Just . . ." He sighs heavily and closes his eyes. "Tell me why okay? I can't fix something if I don't know it's broken."

Felicity really did a number on him. "Deal." That is easy enough to agree to.

"Daddy!" Ronni shouts from upstairs. "I'm ready for bed!"

He sighs and shakes his head. "We'll be right up, Rice Monster." With a smile, he tells me, "I need a kiss first."

One becomes two. Three. Four. When he asks for more, I lose count. One of his hands slides into my hair while the other grabs my ass to pull me closer. The last thing we need is for Ronni to find us like this, but I can't seem to find the capacity to pry my lips off his.

An irritated sigh is our first warning. "Daddy! Fern!"

Mason stops. "You told me to give her lots of kisses."

"Yeah, but—"

"You didn't shower."

"But—"

"No 'buts.' Go shower."

"Yes, Daddy." She sighs. The patter of running feet is the only sign I get that she listens. That and Mason's lips attaching themselves to mine again.

"That'll buy us twenty minutes," he whispers between one kiss and the next.

Mason

It's hard to lose myself in her kiss like I normally do with her fears ricocheting around my brain. How can she be afraid one of us will fall in love when we're both still very much in love with other people? It's ridiculous. There's no reason for us to deny ourselves. I meant it, we're good together. *Too good.* I'd keep her in bed all day if I could. I've got a lot of lost time to make up for, and so does she.

I don't mind admitting I'm greedy for her. I'm probably horrible for coaxing her into something she's unsure of. I need her, though. There, I said it, if only to myself. I didn't realize how true it was before. Felicity hurt me, but Fern is healing me.

Giving someone else—someone other than Ronni—so much power over my happiness is bad news, but I can't help myself this time. It was a conscious choice with Felicity, but Fern . . . It just happened. I didn't mean for it to.

She's so sweet, and she loves Ronni so much. She's done so much for both of us without ever asking anything more in return than her paycheck—more than I ever realized. It's so easy to lose myself in her because I was right before; she doesn't ask for more than I'm willing to give. There's not much I wouldn't give her, though.

Fern doesn't really want to stop this. She wouldn't be so willing if she meant it. She only needs the occasional reassurance this won't blow up in our faces. That's easy enough. I can't love her. It's not possible. Care deeply? That, I can do. She's mine now, and nothing and no one will ever hurt her again.

"Daddy?" Rice calls from upstairs.

Shit. I didn't mean to spend the entire twenty minutes kissing Fern. It makes me happy, though. "Coming," I call.

Fern's eyelashes flutter, and she leans in, searching for more. Her eyes are glassy, like a drunk's. She's drunk on kisses. *I did that.* That's how I know she doesn't actually mean it when she suggests we slow down. She's only saying it because she worries about what is socially acceptable. So long as my girls and I are happy, the rest of the world can kiss our asses.

***

"Fern?" Ronni says, raising her voice to carry into the other room.

Fern finally caved and consented to move her things to my room. She's been tense ever since and quickly shut herself in the bathroom to clean up for bed. But she's taking too long. Ronni's patience is shot. I tried to distract her with a cat video, but nothing can hold her attention.

Our bathroom door opens. Fern steps out, her eyes darting every which way but mine. "That's my spot, Rainbow. You're gonna have ta scoot."

Ronni giggles. "Nope. You're gonna have ta scoot! You're sleeping in the middle!"

What? No! That'll make it harder to sneak away.

Fern opens her mouth to argue, but Ronni proves that the stubborn little woman had just as much of a hand in raising her as I have and lifts her chin to an imperious angle. *That's all you, baby. I didn't teach her that one.* Fern closes her eyes, takes a deep breath, and shakes her head. She climbs up from the foot of the bed and settles between us, but she doesn't relax. While Ronni makes herself comfortable using Fern as a pillow, I turn off my lamp and pull up the covers. Having Fern in the middle works out well for me. Hiding a hard-on from my daughter while wearing sleep shorts is next to impossible.

The timing is terrible, but I want this as much as Ronni does. Every time we're together as a family, it just does something to me. There's no reason I can't have both of the things I want tonight, though. Once Ronni's sleeping, Fern and I can slip away, and I can keep my promise to her. When we're done, we'll come back here and keep our promise to my daughter.

I settle in, slipping an arm under Fern's neck and throwing the other over both of them. "Perfect. Good night ladies."

"I love you," Ronni says as she yawns.

"I love you, too," Fern and I say at the same time.

I like the sound of that. *Wait. What?* To Ronni. I like hearing her say that to Ronni. That's it.

Ronni's breathing indicates she'll be asleep in minutes if she isn't already. It won't be long until I can remind the little temptress next to me of my promise. My daughter's soft snore—more of a purr really—makes me smile. "Give her ten minutes, and we can move her."

In the meantime, I'm not going to risk Fern drifting off, too. I squeeze her silk-covered tit, and she stills under my hand, not even breathing. *I like her in silk.* I'll have to buy her more. Teasing her is a risk with Ronni asleep, but I know Fern can be quiet. Knowing she can't react adds to the fun.

Pinching her nipple makes her twitch. If we were alone, she would arch her back for me, pressing into my hands, begging for more. It didn't take long for us to learn to communicate without a word, and I've used that skill to plot a map of her body. A touch here gets one reaction, but a bite in the same spot drives her crazy.

Ronni sighs and stirs. I hold my breath, afraid of waking her, but she rolls over, away from Fern. I have to suppress a laugh. We don't have to wait after all. I quickly roll out of bed and reach back for Fern because she isn't moving fast enough, and because I want her in my arms. "Come on, you. We have things to do."

Chapter 29

Mason

Monday Evening

"**I**'m home, girls!" It's been a long day. I want to watch their faces light up with their pretty smiles and give them both a good squeeze.

"Daddy!" The warning thunder of running feet comes from the direction of the family room. She slides the corner into the kitchen and launches herself into my arms. "Did you have a good day? I missed you!"

"I missed you too, Rice. And yes, I did. Did you?" She nods and chatters my ear off about school while I search the kitchen, but Fern is nowhere to be seen. My smile threatens to slide off my face, but I refuse to allow it to budge. She's probably busy with something upstairs. If she's focused on something, she won't stop until it's done.

"Where's Fern?" I ask when Ronni has run out of things to tell me.

"She's in your office on her laptop looking at school stuff."

I do a double take. This is big. It could mean she's decided what she wants to do.

My stomach rumbles, reminding me that I never finished lunch. There are no mouthwatering scents to reassure my hungry stomach. That's unusual. Fern always starts dinner at five o'clock, and it's usually ready shortly after I walk in the door. Which is why I was counting on her being in the kitchen when I got home. "What's for dinner?"

"I don't know, Daddy. She went in after we got home and hasn't left. I've checked on her a couple of times now, but she seems really . . ." She trails off.

"Focused? Like there's nothing else around, just what she's reading?"

She nods. "She didn't ignore me or anything, but I didn't want to bother her. It seems important."

"It is, but you know nothing is more important to her than you are."

"And you!"

Right in the gut! " . . . And me," I say belatedly. "Let's go check on her, hmm?"

Her face is the first thing my eyes zero in on when I step into my office. Her eyes zoom back and forth while I watch her, but she doesn't notice me.

"Hey, pretty girl."

Fern jumps but smiles at me when she recovers. "Hi! Sorry! I didn't hear you come in."

I close the distance between us quickly and crouch for a kiss. "I noticed. I missed you today." *You have no idea how much.*

Her eyelashes flutter. When she glances toward Ronni, comprehension lights her eyes. "I missed you too." *We agreed not to lie, Fern . . .* "How was your day?"

"Good, but very long. I nearly called to invite you to lunch."

She chuckles nervously. "That would have been nice."

There's no hesitation this time, so she might actually mean that. "Tomorrow then? You name the place." If I coax her into coming back to the office after, she can meet Granddad as my girlfriend before the party. That'll take some of the stress out of it for both of us.

"Sure!" Her smile is so genuine there's no doubt in my mind she means it. Tomorrow is already shaping up to be a good day.

"What's this, then?" I ask, gesturing to the computer. It appears to be a list of course requirements for accounting. *Do nurses need classes in finance?*

"Well . . ." She bites her lip and drops her gaze to her knees. It makes me want to grab her and hug her because I don't want that Fern to make a comeback. "I think I'd like to try something else . . . Nursing was my dream when I was a kid, but I'm not the same person anymore. There are other ways to help people, and financial planning would let me help people who find themselves in the same situation I was in."

"Would you have hired a financial planner?" I ask, spotting a flaw in her plan right off the bat. It's a wonderful idea until you stop to consider the cost to the people who would need the help she wants to provide.

"No . . . But if one had offered to help for free . . ."

That's my Fern. My pride cannot be contained. Grinning, I grab her face and kiss her again. She's already thought this through, and I'm sure she'll be good at it. Why does she sound so timid, though? "So, you plan to take on some pro bono work?"

She nods shyly.

"That's wonderful. When do you want to enroll?"

Her shoulders heave with a sigh. "I thought I might start next semester."

This is perfect. She wouldn't agree to this if she were unsure about our arrangement. "Sounds good to me. Everything can go on your credit card. If they hassle you, call Darren. He'll get it sorted out for you. Okay?"

Decision made, she lets out a breathy little laugh and sags back into her seat. "Okay. Thank you."

"Anything, sweetheart." *And I do mean that.* "C'mere you." Her stress level wasn't evident to me until I witnessed it fading away. *How'd I miss it?* She's getting that hug now; she needs it. I pull her to her feet and wrap my arms around her. She doesn't resist, not that she ever really did. She melts and pushes onto her tiptoes to lay her head on my shoulder. "Now that that's settled, What's for dinner?"

"Oh, uh . . . Shoot! I'm so sorry! I lost track of time. It'll be just a little late and—"

"Fern," I cut her off patiently, "it's okay, darlin'. We can go out."

"I'm still sorry! I was going to grill pork chops and make—"

"Raincheck, baby. Get your shoes, ladies!"

Chapter 30
Fern

Tuesday

The visitor's parking lot at CFI is packed. The clock on the dash says eleven forty-eight a.m. when I finally find an empty spot. I've got twelve minutes to get inside, get my badge, and find Mason before he leaves for lunch.

The basket isn't heavy, but it's awkward. Running with it in high-heeled boots is even more awkward, but I've come this far, and nothing is going to ruin this. Mason is waiting on me. He doesn't know it, but I'm sure he'll be happy. *I hope he'll be happy.* This could all be a huge mistake.

My run of bad luck holds. There's a line four people deep at the reception desk. *Time to phone a friend.*

My hands are shaking when I get my phone from my pocket and navigate to the one number in my contacts I've never dialed.

"Hello?"

"Hi, Darren . . . This is Fern." *What if he doesn't know my name?* We've exchanged a handful of texts over the years because going through him to get a message to Mason was a Felicity-approved mode of communication. That doesn't mean he remembers me.

Before I can freak out and babble about working for Mason, he says, "Yes, it is." He sounds bored, and I can hear the clack of a keyboard in the background. I've never met the man, but I imagine him sitting at his desk with his phone wedged between his shoulder and his ear while he types away on something important for his boss. *Great, I'm bothering him, too.* "Mason told me you might call me instead. Where did you decide on?"

I take a deep breath and dive into my problem. Only it's not so much of a dive as it is a slow fall off a cliff, hitting a couple of protruding boulders on my way down. "Well . . . That's the thing . . . I'm downstairs, in line to get my visitor's badge. I brought lunch to him."

"Huh," he grunts. It almost sounds like he's laughing.

Oh shit . . . He thinks this is stupid. "Is something the matter?" Of course, this is stupid. Why would Mason want to eat in when he invited me out?

The sounds of keys clacking cut off. "Not at all. Merely an observation. Mason would take you *anywhere.* Any restaurant in town. That bitch—sorry—"

"Don't be. I call her worse."

Darren laughs for real this time, a loud belly laugh that probably made other people drop what they were doing to stare. "That bitch frequently insisted on dining at the most expensive restaurants in town, but you bring him lunch?"

My heart sinks. *I knew this was a bad idea!* Tears pool in my eyes. My voice is strained when I ask, "Is this a mistake?" What if he's insulted? Or maybe he wants to get out for a bit?

The elevator behind the reception desk dings and the doors whir open. There's only one man in it. I watch his lips move, and the voice in my ear says, "Miss Williams, he'll be thrilled."

"Oh." My relieved sigh is so big the woman in front of me turns to look.

Darren is a little on the short side and stocky. He gives off a dependable vibe, which makes perfect sense to me because he is. Mason frequently says he couldn't do what he does without Darren. Or me. Everything from his no-nonsense haircut to his polished Oxfords lends to that look. "Right this way," he says.

Hesitantly, I leave the line and stumble a few steps in his direction.

"Miss?" the receptionist calls. "You need a badge."

Darren covers the mouthpiece and says, "I've got this one, Nance."

"But—"

"I'll see to it she gets her ID." He holds out a hand and beckons me forward. "Come on, hon," he says into the phone, "don't worry about her. She thinks she's the sheriff here."

An indignant squawk pierces the silence of the lobby. "I heard that!"

He's still laughing with his whole body when the door slides closed behind me. "Welcome to Chambers Freight, International, Miss Williams. I'll take that," he says, sliding his arm through the handles of the basket. "It's nice to finally meet you. I'm Darren Markson, but you know that already. I'll need you to fill out some paperwork, but I'm fairly confident you're not here to cause any problems, so it can wait until you're finished with lunch."

"Thank you, Darren." I check my watch and sigh in relief. I have time. Plenty of time.

The elevator opens. He ushers me off and down the hall with a hand on the small of my back. "Miss Williams—"

"Please, call me Fern."

His face splits into a smile. "Fern, then." He places the basket on the floor by my feet. "This is the boss man's office. Normally, I'd call and tell him he has a visitor, but why don't you just knock? My desk is right over there," he points to the desk nearest Mason's door. "Swing by to fill out that paperwork before you leave, please." He walks away without waiting for an answer.

I do as he says and try not to fidget while I wait. The door opens, and I watch Mason's eyes go wide. "Surprise!" I say weakly.

"Second best surprise ever!" he says, sweeping me into a hug. He stiffens and clears his throat. "Sorry, Ronni will always be the best."

"Which is exactly as it should be." I don't think before I say it, the words sort of tumble out—word vomit, only less embarrassing.

Mason steps back and holds me at arm's length. There's a little furrow between his brows while his eyes roam over my face. He pulls me close and kisses me square on the mouth, surprising a squeak out of me. "Thank you for understanding that she always comes first," he whispers. "But you will always be first and a half."

"First and a half?"

"Yep. First is taken, but second isn't good enough for you."

There's a lump in my throat the size of the Rockies. "I'll take it," I somehow manage to get out. I shouldn't let him get to me like this. We promised to always be honest, but he can't mean that the way I want to take it right now. *I'm losing it. He's going to break me.*

I gulp down the lump and clear my throat. "Anyway . . . I uh . . ." I sigh. "Since you're probably busy with everything going on this weekend, I brought lunch to you."

He glances down at the basket by my feet. "I am *never* too busy for you, Fern. I love this, though. Thank you. Let me clear a spot."

He gives me another quick kiss before he grabs the basket and hurries back to his desk to move the papers.

"I smell food." Even without recognizing his voice, I wouldn't need to confirm the speaker's identity with my eyes. Austin always turns up wherever the food is. "Fern! Did you bring food?"

I turn anyway and smile at him. "Hey, Austin. Yes, I brought food."

His eyes latch onto the basket on his brother's desk, and he edges closer. "What are the chances you thought of me when you were planning this?"

Austin knows that I like to cook. I like to feed people, and I never pass up an opportunity to do so. But I also never pass up a chance to tease him. I let my eyes go wide and pout a little. "Oh, Austin! I'm so sorry!" He groans and hangs his head. I let him suffer for a second longer. "I only brought enough to feed a small army."

Austin lets out a whoop and does a happy dance Mason probably wishes he could've recorded.

"She said a small army," Mason says. "You eat enough to feed a large one."

"What's all this noise?" a teasing voice asks from the hall. There's a little roughness to the voice that hints at the age of the speaker. My stomach churns. I'm about to meet the Patriarch of the Chambers clan. *It's not like it's the first time . . .* Only it sort of is.

"Food!" Austin tells him as he ambles into the room.

"Yes, I smell that." Mr. Chambers chuckles. "Good food, too, if my nose still works right."

Mason steps around his desk again and strolls toward me. He's making a real effort to act casual, but I can tell he's anxious. Heck, if I can tell, everyone in the room probably can. "Granddad, you remember Fern, right?"

"Ronni's Fern?" Mr. Chambers asks. With a chuckle, he adds, "How could I possibly forget?"

My heart pounds louder than the drums at a rock concert. Mason turns me around with a hand on my shoulder and pulls me into his side. "That's the one. Only she's my Fern now."

"Well, I'll be," Mr. Chambers whispers. His keen eyes zero in on Mason's hand on my hip before they flit to my face and up to Mason's "Took ya long enough, son."

"W-what?" Mason asks. We're probably rocking identical looks of disbelief, which is probably why Mr. Chambers is laughing.

"I've wondered how long it was going to take you to realize that not just any-one will love your child as much as you do and to realize that there was someone who fit the bill right in front of you all along."

I think I'm gonna pass out. I lean on Mason a little harder than I probably should because he's leaning on me pretty hard too.

Mason clears his throat. "You aren't . . . You don't think . . ."

Mr. Chambers lifts his chin in an understanding nod. "You thought I'd object." It's not a question. He knows.

"Understatement of the century," I accidentally mutter out loud.

Mr. Chambers and Austin bust up laughing. *Glad they're amused . . .*

"Son," Mr. Chambers gasps between one laugh and the next, "if you'd pro-posed to that snotty little witch you've been wasting your time with all these years, I would have disinherited you."

Mason's arm falls away, and he turns his back to the room, scrubbing his face with his hands. "Are you telling me your ultimatum was a ruse to get me to dump Felicity?"

Blood pounds in my ears. If it was a trick, then what we're doing is pointless now. Mason doesn't need to get married—doesn't need me. Movement draws my eye to Austin, who is watching me closely. He only winks when I catch him. *What's that all about?*

Mr. Chambers scratches his chin. To his credit, he looks a little guilty. Only a little. "I stand by what I said. This is a family-run business. Yes, you have Ronni, but you need someone to come home to every night to help you put the stress of the day behind you. You need a partner to help you shoulder the load. Your daugh-ter can't do that for you.

"Your leaving her was a hoped-for side effect, but you beat me to it. *This* isn't what I intended," he says, gesturing at the two of us, though Mason can't see. "But I'm not disappointed, and I certainly don't object. I only hope, Miss Williams, that you know what you're getting yourself into. Mason shouldn't be looking for someone to replace what he had. Mason better be looking for someone permanent."

That's a hint if I ever heard one. His approval is supposed to make this easier, so why do I feel like he just dropped a mountain on my shoulders?

"I warned her," Mason whispers.

So, the old man was sort of playing him . . . Sneaky. Mason must be devastated, but I kinda wanna give the guy a hug for scheming to get Felicity of out Ronni's life, even if he scared me there for a second.

Mr. Chambers nods. "Good. I look forward to officially welcoming you to the family someday soon, Fern."

Mason turns on his heels and holds up a hand. "Hey, slow down, Granddad. We're just starting out, alright?"

Mr. Chambers waves a dismissive hand. "Now you kids listen to me, all of you," he glances at Austin, too. "I've seen a thing or two in my day, and I'm here to tell ya, dating a friend is either the worst decision you'll ever make, or the best one. Either way, it all happens fast. You either sink before you've made it out of the harbor, or it's all relatively smooth sailing. No one can say you weren't friends. When you've worked closely with someone long enough, they're your friend. Otherwise, you would have replaced them already."

"But most of the time they sink," Austin says, grinning our way.

Mason makes an unhappy sound, and I tense, ready to stop him from saying something he'll regret.

"Oh no," Mr. Chambers says. He winces and admits, "Well, yes. But these two, they're going to do fine. They have something most don't. They have Ronni."

"So, they'll stay together for the kid? How noble," Austin says.

"That's not what I mean at all. Love feeds love. And that, you can figure out on your own. I'm starving, and I'm going to be the lunchroom bully if I don't get out of here soon."

"Mr. Chambers, I brought enough to share," I tell him, trying to hide my blush. "With all of you," I say over Austin's protests.

"Martin, my dear. Mr. Chambers makes me sound old."

I smile because I'm not sure what to say. I'm still processing his easy acceptance of me.

Austin scoffs. "You *are* old."

Martin crosses his arms over his chest, drawing himself up to his full height. "Boy . . ."

Austin points at his grandfather. "See! That, right there! Only old men call grown men '*boy*.' You're only incriminating yourself!"

Mason scowls at his brother. "For the love of God, Austin, get your food so your mouth will be too busy to talk,"

Frowning at his outburst, I lay a hand on his cheek, hoping to calm him. "Play nice," I say under my breath.

"I don't want to play nice." He covers my hand with his and squeezes. "Austin is being a dick, and Granddad is going to scare you away."

"Language!" Austin gasps in mock horror at the same time I chuckle and whisper, "You said dick."

His laugh rings out. As a direct result, my smile widens until it hurts. I mentally pat myself on the back for successfully lightening the mood.

Austin takes Mason at his word and unpacks the basket in record time. Surprisingly, once his bowl is full of the chicken casserole I brought, he pushes it into my hands, saying, "Ladies first."

He dishes up a bowl for Martin next, who immediately shovels a bite into his mouth and nods his approval. "Wonderful! Thank you, dear. I hate to eat and run, but I was planning to work through lunch."

"It's okay!" After all, this was supposed to be a lunch date with Mason. Not Mason plus two. I didn't think about that when I made extras. I figured we'd take him a bowl as a sort of peace offering.

He leaves, and Austin follows him out without needing to be told. Once the door is closed behind them, Mason takes my bowl and sets it aside to give me a proper hello. "This is great. Thank you so much, baby." Cupping my face in his hands, he gives me a kiss that's not fit for public consumption.

When he finally frees my lips, I ask, "You don't mind?"

"Not at all. You can do this anytime. Tell me, though, how hungry are you? Because I could go for dessert first."

"I've always been an eat dessert first kinda girl . . ."

Faster than I can blink, I'm on his desk, and my boots are off.

Chapter 31
Fern

Saturday Evening

Between last-minute hairstyle changes and Saturday evening traffic, we're running behind. Ronni squeezes my right hand at the same moment her father does the same to my left. Almost as if they planned it. They didn't, but they both know I'm nervous. My breath grows a little shallower with every step we take closer to the venue rented for this evening's festivities. Mason's reassuring presence keeps me anchored, while Ronni's skipping steps promise a fun evening.

Mason warned me that the Chambers family always kicks off the holiday season with a bang, and he wasn't lying. There are people *everywhere*, and we haven't made it inside yet. The dinner is for the employees of CFI and their families, but I didn't comprehend how many people CFI employs here. *There's no way this is just headquarters.*

At least one news station covers the event, plus a handful of papers. Martin and Lola do a press conference beforehand to announce which charities the company will support the following year and answer questions for them. They're not allowed through the doors, but they're still packing up when we arrive. As we approach, they shout various forms of the same question over each other, each vying to get the scoop. We've been seen together numerous times, and local papers have noticed, but this is our first official outing as the family we will soon be. The thought makes my heart flutter. *Family.*

Inside is entirely different. Once I get over the sheer number of people packed into the space, I'm overwhelmed by how lovely the room actually is. Hundreds of strands of yellow and orange lights arc gracefully from one exposed truss to the next. Aside from the candles dotting every table, they're the only light in the vast room, giving it a warm and intimate atmosphere. Martin Chambers insists on treating his employees like family, and everything from the family-style dinner, to the way the tables are arranged, to the inviting decorations, feeds that goal.

I've never attended one of these before. Felicity made a point to rip my invitation in half the first year and throw it in the garbage while I watched. She didn't need to bother after that, but she always found a way to let me know I wasn't welcome.

Most of Mason's family greets us with hugs, even for me. Marilyn, his mother, only stares at me, though. I knew last weekend, when we picked Ronni up, that she was going to need some time to adjust.

This is the first time I've seen his grandmother, Lola, since we started 'dating.' She is every bit as lovely to me as she has always been. Seated between her and Mason, I almost feel like I belong here. We're interrupted by a constant stream of visitors because the Chambers' table is at the heart of the dining area, accessible to all. But, most of them don't acknowledge me other than a polite nod or a hello. This suits me fine. I'd prefer to fade into the background anyway.

After the dishes are cleared, Martin goes to the stage. His speech is a highlight reel of the company's year. But instead of being about how much money they've made, it's about the ways they've endeavored to make the world a better place—reducing emissions, planting trees, donations to local and worldwide charities. A slideshow plays while he speaks, scrolling through pictures of each event. There's one of Mason—covered in dirt and sweat—and his brother behind him, holding a shovelful of dirt over his head, already in the process of tipping it.

"And now, my friends, what is undoubtedly your favorite part of the evening! I know it's mine!"

The Chambers family all push their chairs back as if they heard some cue I missed, leaving me the only person seated at the table. Mason grabs my chair and pulls it back before he takes me by the elbow. "You too," he whispers. He holds me close to his side while we follow the rest of his family to the stage.

Someone bumps me, causing me to stumble. I glance to my other side in time to catch his mother's cold glare before she manages to turn it into the sweet smile that I'm more accustomed to seeing on her face. *What's up with that?* Maybe she thinks I bumped into her on purpose.

"We have a couple of new faces this year," Martin tells the room proudly. "Nicole had her third child earlier this year, so please welcome little Marnie." There's a smattering of polite applause, nothing loud enough to scare the baby, though. My stomach tumbles when it occurs to me that there's only one other person he could be referring to. "And Mason's new girlfriend is joining us this year as well. Fern has been a great friend to our family for years now, and I'm overjoyed to have her with us tonight."

While the crowd applauds again, I whisper in Mason's ear. "What's going on?"

He leans down to murmur, "You're going to help us pass out the advance bonuses."

"The what?"

He scowls at me. "Oh, come on, you get one every year! The advance on the Christmas bonus!"

I still have no idea what he's talking about, but it's obvious he thinks I should. With all eyes on the stage, this isn't the time to ask him to explain, so I smile and nod. He sees right through me. He opens his mouth but closes it when Martin presses a stack of envelopes into his hands.

"Off you three go," he says.

Ronni bounces on the balls of her feet and clasps her hands under her chin. "May I have my own? Please?"

Martin chuckles and gives her a smaller stack. There's a sticky note on top, with a number that corresponds to a table. "Of course, you may! Do you know what to do?"

She nods eagerly. "Yes, Grandpop."

"There was never a doubt in my mind," he says with another chuckle. His eyes twinkle when they move my way. "I hope you enjoy this part of the evening as much as I do, dear."

My smile isn't fake for him. He's always been so kind, even before I was Mason's 'girlfriend.' "I'm sure I will."

With a smile and a nod, he steps to the side to give Nicole and her husband, John, their envelopes. Mason's hand curls around my side again, and he uses it to propel me through the organized chaos that is every dining area everywhere when there are multiple tables.

Grabbing his hand to pull him to a stop, I push onto my tiptoes and whisper in his ear, "What exactly are we doing?"

"Granddad likes for us to personally pass these out instead of mailing or direct depositing them. It puts a personal touch on it and makes the employees feel appreciated."

I must admit it's brilliant. They could do exactly that, or even pay someone to pass them out, but they're taking the time to do it themselves because their employees matter to them. I had no idea they did this. I had no idea I've been getting a Christmas bonus. Where it ended up isn't a mystery to me. It sucks that it is to him, and he's going to expect me to explain later.

"Fern?"

Or not. "Can we not do this now?" I ask, pointedly glancing around at the audience.

He crosses his arms over his chest. *Shit.* He's not going to budge until he gets answers. He's stubborn like that.

I mimic him and tilt my chin up, one-upping him. "This isn't the place."

"We will discuss it in depth later tonight, but I want an answer now so you can't try to wiggle out of telling me later."

I take a deep breath and let it out in a rush. "We both know the answer to your question, Mason. If you trusted Felicity to give it to me, it met the trashcan." *Or, she forged my name and cashed it.*

He closes his eyes and turns his face to the ceiling. When he finally looks back at me, his eyes are a little pink. "I'm sorry, Fern. So damn sorry."

"Don't worry about it, Mason. You couldn't've known. Let's drop it, alright?"

Mason nods and consults the name on the top envelope before he leads the way to the appropriate person. I got a quick glance at the envelope. It quite clearly reads Jason Jackson, but Mason greets a woman first, kissing her hand when she lays it in his. "Kimberly! Thank you for the pictures of Blake. Where is he tonight?"

The man next to her—who must be Jason—offers Mason his hand, grinning like he just found out he's won a billion-dollar lottery. "He's with my mom," he explains.

"Fern, Jason is one of our Forklift Operators. Remind me to show you the pictures Kim sent of their little one. He's growing so fast!"

Jason chuckles. "You know all about how that goes. Gosh, Ronni has grown a foot since I saw her last."

I've always known he was a good man to work for, but experiencing how much he cares about the employees he probably doesn't speak to more than once or twice a month, and their families he sees less often, really drives it home. It makes the time he wasted with Felicity even harder to understand, though. How can someone so *good* endure someone like her for so long?

Mason

Between one table and the next, I lean down to whisper in Fern's ear. "Are you enjoying yourself?"

"Oh, yes! This is fun!" She smiles and wraps her hand around my upper arm.

"Good." I pull her to a stop and steal a quick kiss. Someone catches us and whistles, but I don't care. Granddad won't care as long as I don't cram my tongue down her throat.

I can't help myself when she looks at me like she is—like I'm some sort of god among men. I only wish I could decipher the emotion in her eyes tonight. There's something there that most definitely wasn't there before. It looks like a good thing, but that is yet to be determined.

She let me turn our task into a game of sorts. I provide her just enough information about the worker and their partner for her to feel comfortable greeting them without my help. She was nervous at first but relaxed quickly. Since she's doing most of the talking, I have more time to think.

I'm not so certain I'm not in danger of falling for her anymore. It would be an accident, but it would be so easy to do. *Would it be so bad?*

We're the last back to the stage, but that's all right. I have the most to prove here since I'll be taking over for Granddad soon. I need the employees to approve of me and support my position.

Granddad greets us both with a smile and a hug. "Good choice, son," he whispers in my ear. I'm not sure what he's referring to, but I think I agree with him.

"What do you mean?" I ask anyway.

"This time, you picked a partner instead of a cheerleader. Heck, I wouldn't even call the last one a cheerleader. She was more of a spectator."

Really, I didn't need him to tell me that. It's good to hear him express his approval again, though. "Thank you," I tell him all the same. "I'm glad you like her."

While we were talking, the room fell silent, waiting for Granddad to wrap up the evening. He always has something more to say. This year is no exception. Holding me by the shoulder, he leads me to the mic and takes his place in front of it.

"Ladies and Gentlemen, now that your bellies are full and hopefully your hearts are too, there's one last thing I'd like to say before I bid you all good evening." He stops for a second and surveys the room. His voice is a little more gruff than usual when he starts again. "Some of you, a lot of you, actually, will remember my son, Jack. He left us far too soon, but he left behind a legacy—three beautiful children that I'm proud to call family. They're beginning to leave their marks on the world, starting their own families, working to make this world a better place.

Their father would be every bit as proud of them as I am. Tonight, I'm pleased to announce that within three years, Mason here will be the new CEO of Chambers Freight International."

Thunderous applause rocks the room and steals my breath away. Marnie wakes and fusses, but I can barely hear her. My eyes drop to my feet in a way that probably comes across as humble to everyone else, but I'm scrambling to get my shit together. I wasn't expecting him to make the announcement tonight, and I certainly wasn't expecting this response. A quick peek behind me shows my family is applauding too, even Fern. Her smile is brighter than the sun and every bit as beautiful. It takes my breath away, simultaneously filling me with the strength I need to face the crowd again.

"Thank you," Granddad says, barely managing to make himself heard, even with the mic. "Mason still has some work to do to prove that he's ready, but I'm confident he'll rise to the challenge, just as he has every other he's ever been faced with."

Guilt proceeds to eat me alive. *You have no idea, Granddad.* There's nothing wrong with what I'm doing, though. Everyone is happy, that's what matters.

***

"We'll follow you home," Nicole babbles while she hugs me one more time. I promised I'd keep her kids for a night, and it's time to uphold my end of the deal.

Everything turned chaotic after Granddad's announcement. Everyone in the room insisted on shaking my hand and congratulating me—even my own family. I've haven't had a moment to spare Fern or Ronni since. I'm sure they understand, but I feel guilty for abandoning them.

"I'm so proud of you!" Nicole squeals for the tenth time. She bounces up and down and throws herself at me for another hug.

"Thanks, Nikki." My siblings' approval means everything to me. They could just as easily resent me. Neither of them has ever wanted this, though. "Let me find my girls, and we can go. Everyone else is on their way out anyway."

There are only a handful of guests left, but none of the family ever leaves until the last guest has gone home. Sometimes, one of us—usually Nicole since Felicity was such a diva—would take the kids and go home after the advances were all passed out. This year though, everyone was too excited.

The kids don't understand, but the general atmosphere of the room rubbed off on them. I was joking with Fern earlier and said the children would never sleep. It seems prophetic now. *There will be no celebrating tonight.*

Oddly enough, celebrating is the last thing on my mind. The pressure is on now. It was before, but it felt abstract because Granddad hadn't put a date on anything other than my impending marriage. *Within three years, this will be mine. If it takes that long.*

Nicole lets me go and cuffs me on the shoulder. "Your girls," she says. "That's so cute. I'm glad you're happy, Mase."

"I really am," I murmur while I search the room for a pair of brunettes. Finally, I spot them leaving the ladies' room. They're smiling and giggling, and it's one of the most beautiful sights I've ever beheld.

My little girl drops Fern's hand and runs the rest of the way once her searching eyes land on me. "Daddy!"

I'm ready for her, which is good because she leaps the last couple of feet. "Ronni! Did you have fun this evening?"

"Yes! So much fun! What was Grandpop talking about when everyone scared Marnie?"

"In a few years, I'll be taking over Grandpop's job," I say while I watch Fern's approach over her shoulder. My future wife walks at a much more sedate pace, smiling brightly at me and my daughter all the while.

"What will Grandpop do when you take his job?"

"Whatever he wants, Ronni. He'll be retiring."

"What's retiring?"

"It means he's old and he doesn't have to work anymore, shrimp," Nicole says with a wicked gleam in her eyes that goes well with the equally wicked smile on her face.

"Don't let him catch you saying that," I tell her, only half meaning it. He'd get a good laugh out of it. Fern stops next to me, so I shift Ronni to my hip though she's really too big for such things and use my now free arm to pull Fern to me for a kiss. "I'm sorry," I murmur between the first kiss and the second.

Between the second and third, she asks, "For what?"

"The chaos," I say between the third and the fourth.

"Get a room!" Ronni says.

"Good idea, Rice," I tell her while Fern and Nicole laugh. "Let's go home, ladies."

"We'll be right behind you," Nicole says.

Chapter 32

Fern

Thanksgiving Morning

"You're beautiful." Mason sounds a little surprised. I'm not sure if I should be offended or not. He looks positively edible in the plaid button-down and dark jeans Ronni picked for him to go with her sweater dress and my burgundy top with matching plaid accents. She insisted we coordinate for Aunt Nicole's annual family pictures. I didn't have the heart to tell her that Nicole probably wouldn't include me in them since I'm just the girlfriend.

"It's not too much?" For maybe the fiftieth time, I turn this way and that, examining the outfit from all angles in the full-length mirror in our closet.

The last time I was this nervous, I was telling Aaron I was pregnant. Maybe I went overboard with my makeup? Or my ponytail isn't nice enough? This isn't like last weekend when there were hundreds of other people. This is family only. This is when I find out if I'm really accepted.

"I can stay home, really. I'm used to it, Mason. I'll put up the tree, and you and Ronni can decorate it like you always do."

He comes up behind me and winds his arms around my waist. Eyes on mine in the mirror, he presses a kiss to the side of my neck. "You're going." Another kiss. "And you look perfect." Another kiss. "And when *we* get home, we'll make some hot chocolate, put the tree up, and decorate it as a family."

That sounds nice . . . Much better than my plan. I'm used to being alone at Thanksgiving, though. I've done the same thing every year for six years now. Rosa or one of the others would slip me something to eat the night before. I'd save it for my Thanksgiving lunch and bring it here to eat after I finished putting up their Christmas tree.

Felicity would always leave Mason's family's Thanksgiving early to go visit her family for a couple hours and claim she got home early enough to put the tree up so they could decorate it before Ronni's bedtime.

Never again will she take credit for things I did. It doesn't matter that I was aware of most of it. It still hurt when they praised her for the stupid little stuff she demanded that I do. She knew how to ensure my cooperation, too. *"If you don't, Ronni's day will be ruined."*

Another kiss. "We'll put Ronni to bed." Another kiss. "And then, we'll have a different sort of feast."

Oh yeah, much better than my plan for the day. "You win," I tell him. The last few weeks have been wonderful. I haven't felt so special in years. Each day feels like a dream I never want to wake up from.

"You always let me."

"At least you know I'm letting you." His laugh warms me all over. "Is it time to go? Or did you need something?"

He shakes his head. "Just coming to check on my beautiful girlfriend. Oh, and Ronni asked if you could make her hair like yours today."

"Like mine? It's only a ponytail . . ."

"Nah," he spirals his finger in midair, "she wants curls in her hair like yours instead of like mine."

"I don't have a curling iron." My curls are natural. I could easily mimic them with a curling iron. I did for my little sister, Sage, for years, but without one . . .

"She does." *And he probably knows how to use it.* I love that about him.

I push onto my toes to press my lips to his. Kissing him is so natural now, but I've had a lot to thank him for. His tongue teases my bottom lip in a way I've come to recognize as a promise of more to come later rather than a request for more now. It lights the spark that sends heat racing through my veins, ensuring that I'll be anticipating the moment he keeps that promise.

Once he's gone, I steal one last look in the mirror. I don't recognize myself anymore. My hair is shiny now that I'm not using the cheap shampoo from the motel where Maria cleans. My skin is brighter for the same reason. The lines around and between my eyes are smoothing out since I'm not always stressed or exhausted. I look like my old self. I look *happy.*

The little voice in the back of my head pipes up to warn me that I should enjoy it while it lasts. All at once, the beat-down shell of a person I was before peers back at me in the mirror. The thought feels more like a premonition than a stray subconscious reminder. A chill dances up my spine.

"Fern?" Ronni calls, pulling me from my thoughts.

I shake my head to clear it and smile brightly at my reflection in an attempt to regain the happiness from before. It halfway works, so I search Ronni out to style her hair.

Mason

"Mom! We're here!" I call once I've ushered my girls inside.

They're so damn cute today. After a relentless onslaught of pouts and puppy dog eyes, I relented and agreed that Ronni could ask Fern for a little makeup. Fern put something vaguely shimmery on Ronni's eyes and lips. I saw Fern put something on her eyelashes, but I could hardly tell the difference when she was done. Ronni got the Chambers eyelashes, long, thick, and dark without the help of makeup.

And Fern . . . She nearly took my breath away. That's a common occurrence, though. Watching her thrive just does something to me. She's so damn appreciative of everything I do for her; it's easy to want to do more.

"Oh, good! I thought I heard car doors," Mom calls from the direction of the family room. "Leave your shoes on! We're eating in the garden today."

"Yay!" Ronni cheers. She grabs Fern's hand and mine and pulls us along, which only works because my arms are longer, and Fern's steps become minuscule.

"Oh, Fern!" Mom cries warmly when we burst into the family room. "So good to see you again, dear! I didn't know you'd be joining us today."

"Hello, Marilyn," Fern greets my mother as she was told to years ago. "Good to see you again, too."

Confused, I shake my head at her. "I told you we were all three coming."

Her smile is a little too innocent. "Doesn't Fern make four?"

The atmosphere in the room shifts, clogging with tension. "No, Fern makes three. Unless there's something you haven't told me, baby." My joke only adds to the tension, and no one laughs.

"Oh," Mom says. Her shoulders slump, and she rolls her eyes. "You're still doing this. I figured you would've proven your point by now."

Nicole and John take up a loud discussion about Marnie's upcoming doctor's appointment, but I dismiss them.

"What's that supposed to mean?" I ask, trying and failing to keep my rising anger from my voice. Fern is visibly wilting beside me, though she's fighting tooth and nail not to react in any discernible way. That's just who she is. She hides her pain.

Mom plasters on a fake smile. "Nothing at all," she says, waving a careless hand.

Her answer doesn't case my temper. "It's obviously something, Mom."

She ignores me to smile at Ronni until her eyes land on the hand still clinging tightly to Fern's, and that smile fades. "Come give Gigi some love, darling!"

For whatever reason, Ronni doesn't go. She takes a tiny step back, bumping into our legs. To her credit, Fern won't let Ronni shield her. She puts her free hand on the small of Ronni's back and gives her a little push. All the same, Ronni's greeting isn't nearly as effusive as it usually would be for her Gigi. John and Nicole fare much better, but Ronni knows they like Fern.

Because I'm not the sort of asshole who is going to let my mother walk all over my girlfriend just because she spawned me, I pull Fern close to my side and kiss the side of her head. "Ignore her," I whisper for her ears only. "I'll take care of it." *As soon as I figure out what 'it' is.*

Fern smiles tightly, but her eyes are guarded. She's one pointed comment away from hiding behind her walls again.

"Mom?"

Mom sighs and turns her eyes to the heavens. "I'm sorry if I don't approve of you toying with my granddaughter's feelings to prove a point."

"I have no idea what you're talking about, Mother. I'm not toying with any-one's feelings, and I have no point to prove to anyone."

Mom shakes her head and closes her eyes, but when they open, she smiles brightly. "Come, sit dears," she says. She seems to be backing off now that I've shown her I won't tolerate whatever this is. I've got room to breathe.

I give Fern a little nudge toward an empty love seat, but she holds her ground. "Is there anything I can help with, Marilyn?" she asks eagerly.

I wish she wouldn't have, but I get it. She's trying to make peace. Mom's sud-den coldness is baffling. She's always liked Fern and should like her more now that we're together. Of course, she doesn't know that this time next year, Fern will be her daughter-in-law. *She'll find out soon enough.*

Mom sort of smiles, but it comes across more like she's in pain than anything. "No, I think not. Thank you, though. We're doing something different this year. I decided to have dinner catered. It won't be a traditional spread, but the caterers come highly recommended. It was actually Felicity's idea . . ." She glares at me, her eyes accusing me of ruining her plans.

You've got to be kidding me. That's what this is all about? Mom is still bitter about my breakup? She'll get over that once Ronni and I prove how happy we are.

Fern lets me steer her toward the love seat, and she perches on the edge. *She looks like a little bird, poised to fly away.* The thought gives me a chill. It feels like a warning. Fern is happy, though. This is a little bump in the road that we'll get straightened out soon enough.

"That sounds lovely," she tells Mom.

"Oh, don't encourage her," Austin grumbles from the top of the stairs. "I was looking forward to stuffing and a heaping plate of candied sweet potatoes."

Mom scoffs, clearly offended. "It never hurts to try something new."

Austin drops into a chair across from us and catches my eye before subtly tilting his chin toward upward. *That's my cue.*

"I'll be right back," I whisper to Fern. Before I leave her alone, I give her shoulder a squeeze and the side of her head a kiss. Nicole eyes me suspiciously. All the same, she jumps into a conversation with Fern to cover for me, because she's an awesome sister.

Chapter 33

Mason

Armed with pretty paper and tape, I realize I haven't wrapped a present in an embarrassing number of years. Felicity always did that for me, and before her, Mom. The Internet saves my ass, though. There's a how-to guide out there for everything.

Still, it takes twenty minutes and a lot of cussing before I send Austin a text, asking him to send Ronni up.

"What is it, Daddy?" she asks when she finds me.

"Did you know Fern's birthday was a few weeks ago?"

She nods.

"You did?" I'm amazed. I only found out after we'd signed the contract, and that was by accident.

"Yeah. She always brings me ice cream on her birthday. She says there's no one she'd rather celebrate with. Really though, I don't think she has anyone else to celebrate with . . . It always makes me sad."

How was I so oblivious? "Oh, Rice . . . Never again, okay? Next year, we'll have a cake and go out for dinner and everything. We're giving her a present this year, even though it's late." I step aside to show her the boxes on the bed behind me.

"Can we give it to her now, Daddy?" Ronni asks. Her blue eyes sparkle with excitement, and she's bouncing on the balls of her feet. *She loves Fern so much.*

I reach to muss her hair but stop short because it looks so nice today. "Yeah. I'll carry this one though, alright? The little one is kinda heavy, but I think you can manage. She's going to be so excited."

"I'm tough enough! Promise!"

Chuckling to myself, I tuck the long, narrow box under my arm and follow my daughter from the room. Fern is still on the love seat where I left her, surrounded by my family but oddly alone. Conversation flows around her, but none of it actually includes her. She's visible over the railing as soon as I step out of the guest room where I took refuge to wrap the boxes. She doesn't notice us, though. She looks so small tucked into the corner of the loveseat. *Like she wants to disappear.*

Austin is busy schmoozing his latest conquest, laying it on thick. She must have arrived while I was wrapping presents. I can't believe he invited her to meet the family. She'll be history in two weeks, tops. Nicole is busy with the baby. Granddad and Grandma have arrived, so the family is all here now. Mom is studiously ignoring Fern, going so far as to sit with her back to her while she discusses something with Granddad.

I wanted to save this for tonight. Austin was going to help me smuggle it out the same way he got it in. After the less-than-welcoming greeting from my mother, Fern could use a pick-me-up. Or maybe it's me who needs one because I feel guilty as hell. This will also give Mom proof that Fern is important to me. That's a lot for two gifts to accomplish, but they're not ordinary gifts.

"Fern! I got you something!" Ronni calls, grabbing everyone's attention before we clear the staircase if they weren't already tracking us and our odd cargo.

Fern's brow furrows. She shakes her head a little. "What for, Rainbow?"

"Your birthday!" Rice says proudly.

Fern's confusion multiplies. "Ronni, my birthday was weeks ago!"

"I know that. But I didn't have presents then. I have them now."

I'm about to pull a muscle trying to hold in my laughter. I expected Ronni to take all the credit, and I'm happy to let her because Fern will know better. Especially once she opens it. Making Ronni happy means more than fighting for recognition that doesn't amount to shit.

"Mine first!" Ronni says, shoving the smaller box into Fern's hesitant hands. She immediately lets out an '*oof*' and adjusts to the unexpected weight.

"Nope, mine first." She has to open them in order. Really, it doesn't matter, but the one will reveal the other, and I want this to be a surprise. I can picture her face when she sees it. She'll be so happy. No one will have any doubts about us after this.

"Okay, Daddy," Ronni says glumly.

Fern sits on the floor beside her and gives her a one-armed hug. Already congratulating myself, I place the awkwardly balanced box in front of her. "Happy birthday, Fern. I'm sorry it's late."

She smiles across the present at me, but it's tinged in sadness. "You didn't have to get me anything," she says softly. Her eyes say something different, but I'm not quite sure I understand it. It can't be what I want it to, but a guy can dream.

"Yeah, I did. Just open it. You'll see."

Tentatively, she tears one end of the paper where it's taped. The paper comes off quickly, and the lid to the box follows. She gasps softly and presses her trembling hands to her mouth.

After a few, quiet seconds, Ronni whispers, "Daddy! You said she'd be excited!"

"Give her a minute, Rice," I whisper back. "This is big. I promise, she's excited."

One hand slowly reaches out to caress the body of the beat-up electric guitar. Her fingers lovingly brush over the place where the letters, 'A.W. + F. C.' are scratched into the paint. She turns to the second package and rips the paper off the sticker-covered amp in a frenzy. The whites of her eyes are tinged pink from tears, making the irises a startling green that glows with an otherworldly light when she finally looks up at me. She shoots to her feet and launches herself over the guitar box, into my arms with enough force I stumble back a few steps. Austin's hand on my back might be the only thing that stops me from falling over backward into his lap.

"Thank you!" she says through the sobs she's shaking with the effort it takes to contain. "Thank you. Thank you. Thank you." It becomes a breathy little chant that sounds sweeter than any music. "How did you—" The tears finally get the better of her, and she cuts off.

"One of the papers you gave me a few weeks ago," I murmur into her sweet-smelling hair. By which I mean the thick binder of papers recounting every cent she owes, every payment she's made, and detailed information about where the money came from. The same stack of papers in which I found her birth certificate.

There were tear stains on the paper, smearing the ink in a couple of places, but I managed to puzzle it out. Aaron's guitar and amp were the second-to-last things she sold, the last being her wedding rings. I tried, but I couldn't get them back for her. She pawned them, but she sold the guitar and amp outright and listed the guy's name, phone number, his address at the time, and how much he gave for it. There was a whole list of things she sold, but something told me the guitar was important.

"He wasn't real keen on parting with it, but I can be persuasive." I paid him triple what he gave her, and I don't regret a single penny of it.

Her arms tighten around my neck to the point where my face will probably turn purple soon, but I don't give a damn. She's never hugged me. Not once. She'll hug me back, but this is the first time she's ever initiated. It's better than the reaction I expected.

"Hey!" Ronni shouts. "Where's my hug?"

"Oh, Rainbow." Fern giggles and lets me go to fall to her knees beside our daughter for the demanded hug. *Our daughter.* Fern didn't give birth to her, but Ronni wouldn't be who she is today without Fern. She's raised her every bit as much as I have, maybe even more. "Thank you so very much. It's the best present anyone has ever given me." She might be talking to Ronni, but her eyes are fixed on me. They shine with the light of a million fireflies, twinkling in a way I've never had the privilege of witnessing before, but I hope to see it again. Often. Daily.

"Why do you call her Rainbow? Her name is Veronica," my mother asks, effectively killing the moment. Her nasty tone surprises me. Mom is normally so sweet she makes sugar seem sour. Today though, someone has apparently salted her sugar.

Fern turns to smile at her over Ronni's head and explains, "Because she's cheerful enough to brighten even the darkest day. You can't help but smile anytime you see her. Just like a rainbow."

The rest of the room '*awww*'s' because even I have to admit that is the sweetest thing I've ever heard. I've often wondered why, but I never asked.

"You can't call me that, Gigi. Only Fern can." Ronni misses the glare my mother shoots Fern, who meets it with wide-eyed innocence. I'm proud of her for refusing to stoop to my mother's level. The rest of the family laughs at Ronni, though.

"That's not very nice, Veronica Anne," Fern says. She takes Ronni's face in her hands and looks her in the eye as she always does when she's imparting words of wisdom. "Rainbows don't belong to any one person, love. You can be your grandmother's rainbow, too. You have more than enough brightness to go around."

"But if everyone calls me Rainbow, it's not special anymore. I always want it to be special." *Right in the feels!* She got Fern right smack dab in the middle of hers too, because her eyes well up.

"Well," Mom sniffs, "I'd rather you be my sunshine, anyway. The sun doesn't need a storm." *Does she hear how petty she sounds?*

Ronni shrugs and disentangles herself from Fern's arms to turn to her grandmother. "That's fine, Gigi. I like that name, too. But Fern needed a rainbow when we met."

"Ronni?" Fern whispers, asking for clarification. I'd like some as well. Fern doesn't talk to our daughter about the bad shit in her life. How the hell does Ronni know that?

"Well, you did! You're my rainbow too! We both needed rainbows because I didn't have a mommy, and you lost your baby right before we met."

"Ronni, I never said that," Fern whispers. Tears pool in her eyes again.

I drop to my knees and reach for her. I don't know how the hell to fix this, but I'm ready to do it whenever I figure it out.

"Am I wrong?" Ronni asks her, her eyes bouncing between Fern and me.

"No, Ronni . . . I just . . . I never told you *when* I lost my baby."

Fern's answer to the question I asked her one night after tuck-in time echoes in my head. *"Why do you never talk to Ronni about your family? I don't mind . . ."*

The faraway look in her eyes gives me an uncanny sense of loneliness. "Because I don't ever want Ronni to feel like she's a replacement for what I lost. I don't want that to taint our relationship in any way. I love Ronni for herself, not because I needed someone to love."

"Oh!" Ronni says brightly, bringing me out of my flashback. She turns back to Fern. "I found it on the Internet at school! We were searching our names for fun, so I checked yours and Daddy's, too. Is the scar on your shoulder from the accident? I wanted to ask before, but you never talk about it, so I didn't." She reaches to delicately trace the exact place a thin white line peeks out from the edge of her sleeve when she's wearing a tee.

Fern looks my way, but she's looking right through me. "Yes."

I need to stop this, but I'm a loss as to how. I can't get after Ronni for it. She's not doing anything wrong. It's a painful subject, but she doesn't understand that people don't like to talk about the past. Though it hurts, I never deny her answers to her questions about mine.

"That's why the guitar says A.W., huh? It was your husband's? Aaron's?"

"Yes," Fern whispers.

It's not that I intended to keep Fern's past a secret from my family, but I didn't want them to find out like this. I wanted them to get to know Fern as my girlfriend and find out organically through discussion with her. There's no putting this cat back in the bag, though. Maybe Ronni will lose interest after a couple of questions.

"What's the 'C' for?" Ronni asks, pointing toward Fern's last initial on the guitar. She's oblivious to the bomb she dropped on all of us, but maybe that's for the best. "Your last name is Williams."

"Cunningham," Fern says robotically. It's as though she's not processing Ronni's questions or her answers. Answering questions for Ronni is probably so natural to her, she is doing it on autopilot. "It was my maiden name—my last name before I married Aaron."

Ronni tips her head to the side, her eyes alight with curiosity. "How old were you when you got married?"

"Uh, twenty?"

"Hey! Daddy was twenty when I was born! But he didn't marry my mommy."

She's not slowing down as I hoped she would. I've got to do something. I stand up and gesture toward the kitchen. "Yes, Rice. Why don't you go ask the caterers how much longer lunch will be?" It'll probably be another fifteen minutes, but it'll give Fern a breather I'm sure she desperately needs. That's the best I can come up with right now.

"Okay!" She pops to her feet and runs to the kitchen without a backward glance, probably hoping for some little treat more than she's interested in the wait.

"You okay?" I ask Fern, holding out a hand to help her up. She takes it, and I pull her into a hug when she's vertical again. "Let's take your guitar to the car." She doesn't owe anyone here an explanation. I look around at the others, who are all watching without trying to hide it, but they keep their questions to themselves.

"I'm fine," she whispers when I close the door behind us. "Just, wasn't expecting the inquisition."

Once her presents are safely stored, I lace my fingers through hers and lead her up the drive. "Sorry . . . I couldn't think of a way to make it stop."

"It's okay. I knew she'd find out someday . . . I figured I'd tell her about it when she was older. I didn't know Google was going to rat me out."

"Yeah . . . I'll be having a word with the school about that . . ."

"I should go," she says.

Surprised, I stop. I use our interlaced fingers to pull her back to me, turning her to face me in the process. Words fail me, so I kiss her. As always, she whimpers a little and melts. "Mom can get over it. I'm not going to let her run you off over whatever the fuck her problem is. You have every right to be here, Fern."

Chapter 34
Fern

shouldn't be here. The others probably spent the time we were outside talking about me. I'm sure Ronni helped fill in any blanks with whatever she read on the Internet. It was kind of a big story because the guy who hit us was some A-lister who just got out of rehab that day. He didn't survive the accident, either. After he hit our car, he veered into oncoming traffic and was hit by a trucker. His car spun, and he was hit by another. Traffic was stopped in both directions for miles. That's why they didn't get me to the hospital in time to save my baby.

Here I sit, though, sandwiched between Mason and Austin at the table. Ronni would be a welcome distraction, but she's sitting at a smaller table with her cousins. Mason's grandmother and grandfather are across from us. They both smile any time they happen to catch my eye. *At least not everyone here hates me.* Nicole's entire family is perfectly sweet, too. And Austin's girlfriend has been lovely when she's stopped flirting with him long enough to answer questions.

Mrs. Chambers, though . . . I wasn't expecting such a cold greeting. I've known her for years. I always thought she didn't have a mean bone in her body. *It must just be me.*

I didn't expect to be good enough for him in her eyes. He's her firstborn. Austin better watch out because he's the baby. If she's this way toward me, she'll be worse when he is actually serious about someone. Still, I didn't expect her to be so imperious about it. And she's been an absolute delight to Beth, Austin's date.

Everyone cheers when the chef, who specializes in cuisine from different parts of the world, and his team come through the doors carrying platters of food. The food might not be traditional, but when the last dish is set into place, Martin holds out his hands to his wife and daughter-in-law. His voice soft but authoritative, he says, "Let us pray."

He gives thanks for the food, the family, the unseasonably beautiful weather, safe travels, grandchildren, and great-grand-babies. But he doesn't stop there. "And, Father God, thank you for Beth and for Fern. These special ladies could be home with their families today, but they chose to be here as part of ours. We hope this is only the first of many such occasions they will join us for."

Mason and Austin both squeeze my hands while we all echo Martin's, "Amen." It's enough to bring a tear to my eye. As nice as it is to have his approval, I feel a little guilty. He'd be hurt to learn this thing Mason and I have is just a contract. *But is it really?*

Like the meal, our relationship might not be traditional. It's real, though. It's not what they think, but it's very real. I've finally accepted that and learned to live with it. It'll hurt that much more in the end, but, as I told Ivy, I'm going to enjoy it while it lasts.

Bowls and platters are passed around the table amid laughter and questions like, "What the heck is that?" It's easy to forget Marilyn's attitude. I'm even enjoying myself.

"Is that any good?" Austin asks, pointing with his fork at something we both have on our plates.

Laughing, I tell him, "Actually, yes. Don't ask me what it is, but yes."

"Ow!" Mason cries from my other side. His outburst startles me. He frantically smacks at the back of his neck.

"Are you okay?" I ask. He never shouts like that.

"Yeah, something bit me." He reaches to rub the spot, but I stop him.

"Don't! Rubbing it will only make it worse. Let me see."

His mother beats me to it and takes up twice her usual amount of space, ensuring there isn't room for both of us to examine the spot. *This is getting old.* I swear, it's Mrs. Williams all over again.

"It's just a little bump," she tells him. "Nothing to worry about."

I reach for his arm and squeeze it. I'm not going to double-check, it would come across as petty, but I'm still concerned.

"I'm okay," he whispers. "It burns, but . . ."

"Do you want me to check if I've got anything in my purse?" I have my EpiPens because I'm allergic to stings, but they're overkill if he's not allergic. His mother would be more concerned if he were. The little first aid kit I carry now that I drive Ronni around might have something else.

He glances at his mom and shakes his head. "Nah, I'm okay."

He picks up his fork again, so I reluctantly do the same. *I'm only paranoid.*

Plates are mostly cleared, and Ronni and the other children are making noise about dessert when Mason grabs my arm. "Fern?" he says softly.

His lips are swollen, and it's not from kisses. *Something isn't right.* "Mason? Are you okay?"

He breathes my name and grabs at his throat, panic burning in his eyes. "I . . . can't . . ."

My heart slams into overdrive. "Hey, look at me. Stay calm, okay? Deep, slow breaths." He's either choking or having an allergic reaction. I'm unaware of any allergies, though. He complies, and I listen, but he's not wheezing. "Is something stuck in your throat?"

He shakes his head frantically, still taking deep breaths and trying to stay calm because I asked him to.

The sting! I jolt to my feet and jump into action. "Call an ambulance!" I order his mother. Someone else shouts that they're on it. "Ronni! I need you to go get my bag. Now. Run."

"But I can't run—"

"Run, Ronni. Just this once. As fast as you can! Austin, help me lay him down. I don't want him sitting in case he passes out!" Austin jumps up and quickly lifts his brother to his feet, kicking the chair out of the way.

"What's going on?" he asks. I love him for following orders first and asking questions later, though.

"Allergic reaction." Mason's lips are swelling in earnest now and look slightly blue. "You're going to be fine," I tell Mason, forcing the words through my misgivings. *This is bad.* I clutch his hand in mine and listen to Ronni's running feet coming closer. She's panting when she skids to a stop next to me. "Dump it out, Ronni."

She doesn't hesitate this time. The contents of my purse are unceremoniously strewn across the ground. It's easier to find my EpiPen that way.

"Daddy?" she says. The waver in her voice hurts my heart, but I don't have time to comfort her.

I grab my Epi. "It's going to be fine," I tell her while I uncap it.

She calls to him again, then begins to cry. I glance up again as Lola steps in to comfort her granddaughter.

"Just keep breathing," I tell Mason. He complies, but he's coughing and wheezing now. Each breath is a struggle. I check the time and offer up a silent prayer that this will do the trick.

"What are you doing?" Marilyn shouts at me when I slam the tip of the EpiPen into the side of Mason's thigh.

I count to three before withdrawing it. "Austin, rub his leg, right here."

He hops over Mason and shoves my hand aside, leaving me free to check Mason's pulse.

"The ambulance will be here in ten," John says. "The operator had me put the phone on speaker so you can hear her," he tells me as he lays his phone on the ground by Mason's head.

His words register, but I'm too focused on Mason to respond. I might miss something if I'm distracted. I have always been good in an emergency. Lots of little accidents happened over the years I spent summers on my grandfather's farm, and I always kept my cool. This time, I can't. Mason's pulse is getting weaker, and he's still struggling to breathe. *This is bad.* The epinephrine isn't helping.

"Miss? Can you hear me?"

A hard shake clears my head, making room for my training to take over. "Yes. My name is Fern. My boyfriend was stung by something and showed signs of anaphylaxis after about ten minutes. It began with trouble breathing, his face was flushed, lips began to swell and turn blue. He is wheezing and coughing now. I administered epinephrine," I tilt my wrist to check the time, "two minutes ago. His pulse is getting weaker." *Eight minutes go to on the Ambulance. Hang in there, Mase.*

"Good, Fern. Do you know what stung him? Are you sure it was a sting and not a bite?" Ronni's wailing nearly drowns out the question. I don't have the heart to tell her to quiet down. She's just a kid, and he's her whole world. So much is riding on my promise.

I look up at his mother, hoping she can answer. I don't want to turn his head when he's struggling to breathe. But if it's something venomous, they need to know. *I should've thought of that before.*

Marilyn shakes her head numbly. "There was only one spot." Martin is holding her, but it's more like he's holding her back, and I appreciate that. I don't need more hands right now.

"Hold it," Austin says. He's crouched by Mason's feet, near where his chair was before it was kicked out of the way. He reaches into the grass and holds up a dead bald-faced hornet, its wings gingerly pinched between his fingers.

"Okay," the operator says once this information is relayed. "Whose EpiPen did you use? Do they have another?" She knows what I do. The first Epi isn't helping as it should be. Mason is only getting worse. There's only so much I can do to keep him going until help arrives.

"Mine. Yes, I carry a spare."

"Fern," Mason gasps between coughing fits. "I—" Whatever he thinks he needs to say is drowned out by another cough.

"Get Ronni out of here!" I say over my shoulder. There's no way in hell I'm going to let her lose her dad, but she doesn't need to see him like this. He can barely breathe now, but bless him, he's so calm. His eyes track my every move, glued to my face like I'm his lifeline.

Mason moves our clasped hands to his lips and presses a kiss to the back of mine.

"You're going to be fine," I say again. My voice doesn't sound like my own, though. I check the time. Two minutes to go, and I can hit him with another dose of epinephrine. "Just hold on, okay?"

He smiles at me, the barest twitch of his lips between coughs before his eyes roll back in his head.

"He's out!" I cry for the benefit of the operator. My fingers fly to his neck, but I can't find a pulse. "Someone go wait for the ambulance!"

"John already is," Nicole says in a watery voice.

"Austin, help. His shirt's gotta go." He pushes my hands away from the buttons. Instead, he grabs both sides of the collar and yanks, sending buttons flying everywhere. "Did you watch how I did the Epi?" I ask him. He nods, so I toss him the spare. "In one minute, hit him with that in the other leg." Something warm and wet falls onto my hand when I can't find even the faintest hint of a pulse. I don't have time to analyze, so I dismiss it. "No heartbeat. Starting chest compressions," I tell the operator. I don't recognize my own voice again. It's so . . . emotionless. But I'm dying inside. There's no time for me to fall apart. If I do, he's a goner.

Five minutes isn't all that long sometimes. Other times, it's forever. Performing CPR for five minutes feels like an eternity. Determination and desperation keep me going when I wear down. The burn in my arms is but a distant annoyance, something easily dismissed under the importance of my task. I won't lose Mason, too. *I couldn't save Aaron, but I can save him.*

Someone is talking to me, but it's not the operator telling me to adjust my pace, or to check for a pulse, so I ignore it. The family will have to understand. CPR is exhausting work, and no one else here is trained to take over.

I can't ignore it when someone deadlifts me like I'm a rag doll and hauls me away from him, though.

"No! Mason! No!" I scream and kick and fight to get back to him. I can't stop. Not yet. He's not breathing yet. If I stop, he'll die. I can't lose him. I won't. I can't survive it again.

Austin shouts my name in my ear. "You did it, Fern. The ambulance is here. You need to calm down, or they're going to sedate you!"

Shaking, I sag in his arms. *Oh, thank God.* Numbly, I watch them load him onto a stretcher. One of the EMTs straddles him and continues chest compressions even as they roll him around the house. When I move to follow, Marilyn shoulder checks me hard enough to knock me to my knees and runs after them without a backward glance, shouting that she has Power of Attorney.

"Come on," Austin says. He pulls me to my feet and dabs at my face with a napkin he must have grabbed from the table. "Granddad and Grandma are taking the kids. Nicole and John have Ronni and Mom. You're not diving anywhere right now, so you're stuck with me. Beth already called a ride."

"Thank you," I whisper. Now that everything is out of my hands, I'm falling apart at the seams. Austin stepping up to the plate helps me hold myself together, gives me a new purpose. I'm a bewildering jumble of exhausted, scared, hopeful, and numb, but I put one foot in front of the other. He's right, though; I wouldn't trust me to drive two feet down an empty street.

***

Austin's hand is warm on my shoulder. Nicole rushes to hug us both when we step into the waiting room. "He came around in the ambulance, but he's sleeping now," she tells us.

Relief hits me in the back of the knees with a two-by-four, and I sink to the dirty hospital floor without an ounce of care to be found. "Oh, thank God," I whisper. He'll be fine.

"Mom and Ronni are with him now. He was asking for you, though. They're limiting him to two visitors right now, but I'll have Mom come out so you can go in."

"No, you won't," Marilyn says from the hallway.

What? No! My stomach lurches. Bile climbs the back of my throat.

Nicole frowns. Her eyes dart between her mother and me. "What do you mean, Mom?"

I scramble to my feet so that I'm not blocking the door and sit next to John.

Marilyn waves away her daughter's question. "He's delusional. He nearly *died!* He doesn't know what he wants!"

He did die . . . I refused to let him stay that way.

"He wants to see his girlfriend!" Nicole says, digging her heels in.

"Oh, please!" Marilyn scoffs. "You're not really dating, right, dear?" My blood freezes to ice. *What does she know?* "He's paying you to pretend, to upset Felicity so she'll behave herself next time."

"N-no, ma'am." She's got it all wrong. Well, sort of. It has nothing to do with getting back at Felicity. "We're together."

Austin's voice is too loud. "Fern saved him, Mother. I don't know what you suddenly have against her after years of telling everyone how wonderful she is with Ronni, but if it weren't for her, we'd be planning a funeral right now."

Marilyn rounds on him before he's finished shouting at her. "And I will forever be grateful to her for it, but he is sleeping and doesn't need to be disturbed. Especially not by her. I can't believe the rest of you actually believe this sham. Felicity will be back. She always comes back."

Let her try!

Austin laughs bitterly. "You keep telling yourself that, Mom. That relationship was sinking long before she got caught cheating this time. Mason is happier with Fern than he's been since Vee passed. Why can't you accept that?"

Marilyn shakes her head. "He is a grown man, and I cannot control what he does with his life, but I don't have to approve. At any rate, they're only allowing family in to see him." She comes and pats me on the shoulder. I let her because slapping her hand away won't help anything. When I blink up at her, she smiles sweetly. "You may as well go home, dear. You know it's not that I don't like you. I only don't like the game you two are playing. You need to stop."

I'm helpless for an entirely different reason than before. I want to scream and beat the shit out of the heavy bag right now, but I don't have one of those handy. I *need* to see Mason. I need to talk to him and tell him things I just figured out. The promise I made to myself be damned, I nearly lost him. But his mother stands between us. And I know what happens next.

"Mom!" Austin shouts. Someone is going to come kick us all out soon if they don't calm down. "Do you *hear* yourself right now?"

Nicole is no better. "He asked for her! He wants to see her! I'd want to see John, no matter how bad I felt." Beside me, John folds one of my hands between both of his and squeezes, silently offering me support.

She ignores them all, and her smile never falters. "Mrs. Williams, you know you want to do the right thing. I can't force you to end this farce, but I suggest you pack your bags and get out of my son's home. I've called Felicity. I'm sure he'll come to his senses after they talk, and it'll be easier for all of you if you're already gone. Maybe that way, the three of you can work out a way for you to keep your job. You truly are good with Veronica. She'll be devastated if he has to replace you."

She's just like Mrs. Williams. No matter what I do, she'll never accept me. I'll never be good enough, even though Felicity set the bar low enough to step over without knowing it's there. Mason will defend me, as he did today, and it'll drive a wedge between them. *And it'll be my fault.*

"Mom, look at her!" Nicole says, trying again. "She's freaking wrecked! How can you be so cold?"

"Because she's just a rebound! This is Mason attempting to subdue Felicity. Once she settles down, they'll be perfectly happy together."

Austin and Nicole begin shouting over each other. Nicole pulls me to my feet and wraps an arm around me. "Come on, Fern. You have every right to be with him." She marches to the reception desk with me in tow. "I'm here to visit Mason Chambers," she says, so confident I feel like I should ask her for lessons. *If I had half her confidence, I could rule the world.*

The receptionist, whose name tag reads Sue, checks something on the computer and smiles at Nicole. "What's your relation to Mr. Chambers?"

"I'm his sister, Nicole," she says.

Sue turns to me. "And you?"

"This is his girlfriend," Nicole says quickly. "They've been together for years."

Sue frowns, glances at her computer, and sighs. "I'm sorry, family only."

"Oh, come on! They're practically married!"

"Nicole, it's fine," I say before she can conjure up any more lies. "When he wakes up, and they're sure he's stable, they'll let me in. He'll be home by dinner anyway."

"I'm sure it won't be long," Sue says.

I push Nicole toward the door. "Go on in. Ronni needs someone with her."

"Ronni needs *you*," she says. "But I'll go. Don't let Mom steamroll you."

"I'll be fine." I watch her go before I give Sue one last smile and leave. I don't go back to the waiting room, though. I don't want to give Marilyn the satisfaction.

Instead, I pace the halls and try to hold myself together. It's harder now that I'm alone. I had to be strong for Mason because he couldn't afford for me to break down. I had to keep it together in front of Austin. I'm down to me, and I'm too tired to do anything other than fall apart. *I've been too strong for too long.*

The problem with having time to do nothing but think and cry is the thinking part. This contract seemed harmless at first. It's anything but, though. Mason was upset with his mother before lunch. His siblings are upset with her now. Ronni won't understand what's going on, but she'll know something is wrong. And it all boils down to me.

Marilyn doesn't want to see the truth. Nothing we say will help. There's only one way to make it better. I agreed to marry him to protect Ronni, but now I'm hurting her. Leaving will hurt her more, but sometimes, you have to hurt to heal.

It's only been a few weeks. It's not too late to tell her that Mason and I are better off as friends. If we end this now, he can find someone else to fill his contract. I can pay him back at the same rate I was paying off my bills. He can stop paying me. I'll still see Ronni every day. Everyone will be happy.

Everyone else. Leaving will hurt, but it's for the best. I see that now. I'll call Desi. Or Monique. One of them will surely let me crash on their couch for a night or two while I figure out my next step. I have money set aside for a deposit and rent for a month. I just need a place to crash while I search.

Chapter 35

Mason

"Where's Fern?" I keep asking. They keep ignoring me, but Austin and Nicole exchange angry scowls every time. John bites his lip like there's something he'd like to say, but he's keeping it to himself. Mom . . . is forcefully cheerful. Yet again, no one answers.

"Damnit, where is Fern?" I don't know what the fuck is going on, but I'm fed up with their bullshit. My whole body hurts like I've been hit by a truck and drug behind it for a couple of miles. Especially my chest and the side of each thigh where she stabbed me with that pen thing. I'm alive, though. Better than the alternative.

The last thing I recall is Fern's worried eyes swimming in tears while she worked to keep my sorry carcass alive. I need her here. I need to thank her for keeping her promise. *I need to kiss her and make her promise she'll always be mine.*

Austin puts on his most winning smile and turns to our mother. "Yeah, Mom. Where is Fern?"

Mom glares at him before smiling anxiously at me. "Oh, I'm sure she's around somewhere. She was pacing when I saw her last. She doesn't like to sit still, does she? How are you feeling, dear?"

I ignore her last question. She won't like the answer right now, but I don't like hers. That makes us even. Something isn't right here, and I'm going to get to the bottom of it.

"No, she doesn't," I say instead. If Fern is in this damn building—and where else could she possibly be?—she should be here with me. I want her curled into my side, her head on my chest, pain from chest compressions be damned. I hit the call button and wait for a nurse. I don't care if they have to page Fern, I want her here. I will pay someone to hunt her down if I have to. That same chill I felt earlier when I noted that she looked like a bird on the verge of flying away rolls down my spine. *I won't let her.*

"Are you okay, Daddy?" Ronni asks for maybe the millionth time. Any time I make a little face, she asks. I'm probably making a lot of faces right now. Angry faces, but she doesn't discriminate.

"Yeah, Rice. Just worried about Fern."

"I'm sure she's fine," Mom says much too quickly.

"I'm sure she's fine as well, but I'll feel better once she's here." Some part of me knows she needs to see for herself that I'm okay. I would, if our roles were reversed. After what she went through with Aaron and Cassie, she has to be terrified. It's not the same, but she shouldn't be alone right now.

A nurse taps on the door and walks in. "What can I help you with, Mr. Chambers?"

"Well, this is kind of silly, but no one here seems to know where my girlfriend has wandered off to, and I'm worried about her. She was a bit of a mess the last time I saw her." Austin snorts at my joke. It's probably an understatement, but I wasn't conscious to see her lose it. *If* she did. I'll never tell her about the fear in her eyes every time she told me I'd be okay. The only thing she'll ever hear from me is how amazing and strong she was.

"Maybe she got turned around and ended up on the wrong floor," the nurse says with an understanding smile. "I'll keep an eye out. What does she look like?"

"She's short, with dark hair. It was in a ponytail last time I saw her. Green eyes. Burgundy top and dark blue jeans. Her name is Fern."

Her smile is quickly replaced with a frown that reveals more than I'm sure she'd like for it to. "Is her hair kind of curly?" the nurse asks.

I nod. "Big ringlets at the ends."

"I saw her about an hour ago. She was pacing in the radiology hallway. Poor thing was a hot mess, but I guess I would be too."

My mother cuts the nurse off before she can say anything more. "Why don't you let the nice lady get back to work, dear? Maybe Fern has gone home to rest."

I nod at the nurse, who smiles and leaves. Once the door is shut behind her, I turn to my mother.

"What. Did. You. Do?" Since I'm stuck in this bed, hooked up to every sort of monitor known to mankind, my words lose some of their bite. All the same, she flinches.

Mom rallies and plants her fists on her hips. "Oh, please! No one believes you're actually dating her. It's your way of getting back at Felicity!"

I understand now why Fern sometimes feels the need to lash out when her emotions are too big to express. It's never been my way, but my life has always been under my control, until now. The only thing I can reach is the big, plastic water cup they left me. It's empty because I woke with a mouth drier than the

Sahara, but I wouldn't care if it wasn't. I snatch it up and throw it as hard as I can at the wall across from me, where no one is standing. It hits with a satisfying thud and leaves a dent in the drywall I have no problem paying to fix. Everyone flinches. Ronni gasps and burrows deeper into her seat. *Fuck.*

My voice is amazingly reasonable when I ask, "Austin, would you take Ronni for something from the vending machines, please?"

"I've got this," John says quickly. He pops to his feet and holds out a hand for Ronni. She tries to argue, but he bribes her with ice cream from the cafeteria.

The door is still closing behind them when I turn to Mom. "I want answers."

She tries to look me in the eye, but she can't. "I told her the truth. That none of us buy this, and you're going to toss her aside like a used napkin when Felicity comes home. She probably took my advice and went to pack her things. I told her you'd let her keep her job that way."

My heart stops. I don't know why the monitors keep beeping like everything is fine. Fern won't listen to her, though, so everything *is* fine. She's too stubborn. She's here somewhere and doesn't know that I'm awake. It hasn't been that long. The sun is still high in the sky. But Fern would never leave to rest. She'd sleep in a chair first.

"Does anyone have my phone?" I need to call Fern. I need to hear her voice to get me through until I can see her face again—even if she's only five minutes away. The last time I saw it, I was afraid it was my last.

"Here," Nicole says, reaching into a pile by her chair that I recognize as my jeans and shoes.

She hands it over, and everyone waits with me while I listen to the phone ring again and again. *"You have reached mailbox number—"*

I don't wait to leave a message. I disconnect and dial again. And again. And again. She doesn't answer. There's no logical reason for me to believe something is wrong, but I do. Fern never ignores me.

The door opens, and I sigh in relief. *Finally!* "Fer—" The woman who steps through the door is *not* my Fern, and she is *not* welcome here. "What the fuck are you doing here?"

Felicity pouts at my tone. "Your mom called me." She flounces over to my bedside and leans in to kiss me. Eyeing her in disbelief, I dodge her attempts. She sniffs but plays it off as if nothing happened, per usual. "You look horrible, sugar."

Mom flinched under my glare earlier, but Felicity doesn't even twitch. "I died, thanks. I trust you remember where the door is, don't let it hit you in the ass on your way out. Or do, I don't care. Just get out."

"Mason James!" Mom says. I'm not five anymore, and my respect for her is dwindling every time she opens her mouth, so her rebuke has less of an effect than it usually would.

If I had something else to throw, I would do it.

Mom flinches again when my glare swivels her direction. It didn't have far to go because she jumped to hug that bitch the way she should have embraced Fern before lunch. "No! You are not doing this to me. I will not sacrifice my happiness for your preconceived notion of what my life should be like!"

Since Felicity's ears seem to be broken, I jab the call button hard enough to hurt my finger. I will have her ass tossed out of here if she won't leave.

The bitch powers up her pout in a way that always used to work for her. I'm immune now that I know the real Felicity Green. It doesn't stop her from trying, though. "Come on, Macie . . ." She reaches for me, but I dodge again, and she gets the hint. "He didn't mean anything to me, I swear! I love *you*, babe. Let me come home."

That God-forsaken nickname makes my blood boil. I fucking hate it when she calls me that. She knows it, too. "Am I speaking another language here? Get. Out. I *detest* you. You didn't love *me!* You loved my money! You're not welcome here. You're not welcome at my house. You're not welcome anywhere in my life. You cheated on me *twice*. You didn't have the balls to confront me when you thought I was cheating. Instead, you made Fern's life hell and tried to set me up to get someone pregnant. That someone would have been you, by the way. I was never unfaithful. *And* you planned to send my daughter off to school because she was an inconvenience to you."

Her normal bubble-headed blonde act dries up fast. She glares at me with such loathing that I hardly recognize her. "Oh, you think you're a fucking saint? Do you know what it was like having that bitch show up every day? I know who she looks like, Mason. I saw the pictures the first time I was there. I saw it the second she came walking in. You may have never fucked her, but I couldn't hold your attention when she was in the room! You never loved me; it's always been her."

That's why she thought I was cheating? Because Fern resembles Vee? She suspected us the entire time and never said a word? *What kind of man did she take me for?* It doesn't matter anymore. "You're right, I never loved you! But did it ever occur to you it was *Ronni* I was paying attention to? If you'd bothered to cultivate a relationship with my daughter, you might have realized that. Ronni is and will always be the most important person in my life. That's why you wanted to send her away; because you're not the kind to settle for runner up. Maybe you viewed Fern as a threat because of her relationship with Ronni, but don't you *dare* stand there and say I ever wronged you."

With a quivering bottom lip, she opens her mouth to argue, but nothing comes out. She can't defend herself. I gave her more than enough time to be a part of our family. She never tried.

One of the monitors I'm hooked to beeps angrily. *Good, that'll get a nurse in here sooner.*

As if on cue, the door bursts open, and three nurses rush in. "Mr. Chambers, is everything okay?" One stops inside the door while the other two rush to check me over. They said something about a possible relapse or something when I came to, but I'm breathing fine. *Pissed, but I'm fine.*

"No. If this . . . woman," I wave a hand at Felicity in case there's any confusion, "doesn't leave now, I will call the cops."

The nurse by the door frowns and holds out a hand to usher Felicity out. "Ma'am, you're going to have to come with me. Please, don't make me call security."

The other two nurses stop the beeping, and one scowls at me between glances at whatever monitor I set off. "Mr. Chambers, I need you to calm down, sir."

"I will when she's gone. Has anyone found my girlfriend yet?"

Felicity yanks her arm out of the other woman's grasp to whirl around. "*I'm* your girlfriend!"

One short, loud, bark of laughter tears from my throat. "You *were* my girlfriend. Actually, you were a shiny mistake I never should've made. I meant it when I told you to get out. Goodbye Felicity. Don't call."

The third nurse, the one who was here before, squeezes my shoulder. "Sir, I called downstairs earlier. She left. About twenty minutes ago."

Her words are a shock to my system that sends me bolt upright. "Fuck!" I yank at the leads they have attached to me, desperate for my freedom. I have to get out of here.

Two pairs of hands reach to stop me, and it takes them both. "Sir, please! You have got to calm down."

"No, I have got to get out of here. I need to find her. Now. Unhook this shit, I'm going home." I try to shake them off, but they're stubborn.

"Sir, that's—"

"Yes, I know, you advise against it. I don't care. I want to be discharged."

The nurses exchange a glance. "Mr. Chambers, if you don't calm down, we're going to have to sedate you. You're behaving irrationally."

My brother will have my back. He'll help me get out of here. "Austin—"

"Sorry, Mase. I'm on their side. It's not worth the risk. You can talk to her later."

"Not if she fucking leaves!"

My phone rings, blaring Fern's ringtone. "Oh, thank God." I sink back against the mattress and answer the phone. The nurses spring into action, reattaching the few wires I managed to shake off before they stopped me. "Fern! Where are you?"

"You don't sound like you're relaxing," she says. Her voice is rough from crying, and it breaks my heart.

The glimmer of hope her call gave me fades. *I can fix this.* "Well, I tried, but I've been too worried about you. They told me you left, but that can't be true. You just went out for some air, right? Come inside, sweetheart."

"Mason . . ."

My heart free falls into my toes. That one word sounds like the beginning of the end. "Fern," I whisper.

"Your mom—"

She can't see me, but I shake my head anyway. This can't be happening. "No. No, no, no. That doesn't—"

She sucks in a breath and lets it out, slow and shaky. "I'll pay you back. I promise."

"No, you won't. You're not doing this. You promised."

"When I made that promise, I thought I could keep it." She's crying. It's worse than I imagined. I need to get out of here. She needs me, and I'm stuck in here in a dress with no back, tied to a bed by flimsy wires.

"Whatever you're thinking of doing, don't, okay? We'll talk about this when I get home." My desperation is evident to my own ears, so the others have to catch it as well. I don't care. Whatever it takes to get through to her.

She tries to hide it but doesn't quite stifle a sniffle. "Your mom—"

Like magnets, my eyes are drawn to my mother, who cringes under the weight of my anger. It takes real effort to hold it back, but I refuse to let any of my anger toward my mother seep into my voice, lest Fern thinks it's directed at her. Nothing could be further from the truth. "I don't care what she told you! Please, wait until I get home." *I'm not too damn proud to beg.*

She sighs, a sign that I'm wearing her down. "It's easier this way, Mason. I'll come by when you've had a chance to recover. We can discuss payment, and if you want a new nanny, there are a couple people I'd recommend. I'd like to keep my job, though. We can tell Ronni—"

"No. I don't want any of that. I want you to stop this."

To my surprise, she snaps, "You don't understand! I can't do another bitter mother-in-law. It's not fair to any of us. Think of Ronni!"

"Fern! I'll fix it, I promise!" I'm too late. She's disconnected the call already. *I'm too late by hours. I should have made sure this was fixed before lunch.* The hand holding my phone falls to the bed. Desperate to do something, I spear my brother with a look. "Austin, I'm begging you. Go to my house and stop her. I don't care if you have to fucking sit on her until I get out."

He springs to his feet and rushes from the room without a word. I can always count on Austin to have my back, even when it doesn't seem like he does.

"Mom, you need to go. Now." Having her here is a constant reminder of everything wrong right now. If she'd been nicer . . . If she'd let Fern look at the sting . . . I could have my woman here with me right now, and life would be good. As good as possible, all things considered. I wouldn't be angry with her and on the verge of losing Fern.

"Mason James Chambers! I am your *mother!*"

"That's why I called you 'Mom.' You might be my mother, but you ruined the best thing that ever happened to me."

She smirks at me, which doesn't help her case any. "If that were true, she wouldn't have broken up with you over the phone."

Before I say another word, I take a deep breath and count to ten so that I don't lose my shit. "You don't understand what you've done," I say through clenched teeth, speaking as clearly and concisely as possible. I can't yell at my mother, no matter what she's done. I'd like to, but I can't. That's why she needs to go. If she stays much longer, I will. "You could've been happy for me and let me live my own life, but that wasn't good enough for you. Now you've ruined it!"

She throws a hand up to her chest, clutching her pearls again. "You can't blame me for wanting my son to be happy! You should be thanking me for talking her out of this mistake! But no! You threw away your chance to patch things up with Felicity for a *rebound.*"

"Mother," I sigh, praying for some patience to come my way. "I was happy. But that doesn't matter now, because you've managed to make her think our relationship would ruin my life by ruining my relationship with you, thereby robbing Ronni of her grandmother. Because her mother-in-law hated her!"

I can't believe I didn't spot the danger sooner. This all stems back to that bitter, hateful woman who ruined Fern's future out of spite. Fern is leaving me because she doesn't want to be put in that same situation again. She thinks Ronni and I would suffer from it. Today was a replay of her worst nightmare.

She's doing the only thing that seems logical to her. She was the root of the problem, so she's removing herself from the equation, believing we will go on without her and be perfectly happy.

But we're not. Somewhere in the past three weeks, that little woman wiggled her way into my heart. Now, a piece of it is missing. She has it, and she needs to come back. She can keep it, so long as I can keep her. That seems like a fair trade to me.

"What on God's green earth are you talking about?" my mother snaps. "I don't like this game you're playing, but I would never let anyone come between my family and me."

"Mom! There. Is. No. Game. The sooner you accept that, the happier we're all going to be." Sure, Fern and I omitted some of the truth, but we never lied. We never even pretended to be in love. We didn't have to pretend to be happy. That comes naturally to us because we're good together.

As patiently as I can, I give my mother a brief rundown of Fern's life up to this point. It's not my story to tell, but it's the only way. "She gave up her full scholarship to get a job to pay those bills," I add because they can't find that on the internet. "Now, Fern is leaving me because you don't like her."

"That's preposterous!" Tears well in Mom's eyes while I detailed what that Williams bitch did and they didn't go away. Even if she doesn't grasp the enormity of what she's done, she might at least be civil to Fern from now on. *If I can get her to stay.*

Chapter 36

Fern

It's harder to pack my things this time. All of *my* stuff is jumbled together with the things Mason bought me.

And I don't want to be doing this.

I don't want to go.

I didn't want to talk to him on the phone. I had to hear his voice, though. *I'd give anything for another hug.*

He has some luggage he wouldn't mind me borrowing until I come back to discuss where we go from here. I can't make myself do it, though. Using trash bags seems fitting after the way his mother made me feel today. *Maybe I'll just toss it all on the curb and walk away.*

No. I've clawed my way up before, I'll do it again. I will not let her do that to me.

The front door opens. My breath catches in my lungs. He *can't* be home. Even if he did insist on being discharged, the paperwork alone would take an hour to process.

"Fern?" Austin shouts.

I sigh in relief. I can handle him. He might be my friend, but it's nothing to him if I stay or go. Not really. Mason will find someone else. Someone he can learn to love, no matter what he says. I know he can do it.

"I'm here," I call back so he doesn't run to every room in the house yelling.

"Oh, thank God," he says when he skids to a stop in the doorway. "Just don't, okay? Wait until Mason gets home. Mom's being a dumbass. I'll be the first to say it, but don't let her come between you."

"It's better this—"

"Better for whom?" When I fail to answer, he presses the issue. "For you? For Ronni? For Mason? Who, Fern?"

"All of you," I mutter, my hands still busy folding, delaying the inevitable. I could cram everything in a Hefty bag and be out the door in five, but I'm neatly folding each article of clothing. "No one will notice I'm gone, except for Ronni. Hopefully, we can work something out for her, though."

"No, Fern. None of us. We almost lost my brother today. He's still here thanks to you, but you're going to kill him if you do this. You weren't there to see him the split second he realized you weren't coming. Don't do this, Fern. You're wrong about all of it."

I wish that were true. "I'm sorry, Austin. I don't see it that way. It'll take some adjusting, but it did when I moved in too. Better now than later, when leaving requires legal help."

"Tell me something. How long have you loved him?"

The shirt I was folding slips from my fingers. "What?" *How does he know?* What have I done to give myself away?

"Don't try to deny it. I'm not stupid. I was right there with you today. How long?"

I hang my head. My heart rises into my throat, making it hard to get the words out. "How long have I loved him, or how long have I known?"

His only reaction to his triumph is a soft chuckle that's over in a blink. "Either. Both."

I sigh and rub the side of my neck to ease the tension there. "I think I've loved him from the day we met," I confess, fighting back a fresh wave of tears. "Watching him with Ronni . . . I wasn't *in* love with him until . . . I'm not sure. Recently."

"I'm not blind, Fern. I knew you loved him, even if you didn't. Just like I knew he'd love you when he got out of his own damn way."

I want to believe him, but I can't. Mason doesn't love me. He never will, because he's not supposed to. That's the whole point of our contract, no feelings required. "You're wrong. He might love someone again someday, but it isn't now, and I'm not that person. That's why I can't do this anymore. Before, it didn't matter. But I deserve to be loved too."

What have I done? How could I let this happen to myself? Life was easier when I was content to love and be loved by a ghost. With renewed purpose, I snatch up the shirt I dropped. I need to get out of here before Felicity turns up. I know Mason won't take her back, but she'll try.

"I promised him I wouldn't let you leave."

"So tell him I was already gone."

He must consider it because I fold three shirts before he speaks again. "Where will you go?"

"I don't know. I'll call Monique or Desi."

He walks around me to flop onto the bed, putting his face in my line of sight for the first time since he arrived. "Stay with me. I swear that's not a come on. I have a guest room. He'll never forgive me if something happens to you, Fern."

I stop for a minute to think. Aside from Mason, Austin is probably my best friend in this city. Yeah, I've got Desi and Monique, but they don't know the truth about my life since the accident. It's not a tidy solution, but it works. Temporarily. I have to get as far out of Mason's life as I possibly can while still maintaining my relationship with Ronni. "You won't tell him?"

He holds up his hands, the gesture warning me to slow my roll. "I make no promises. I won't volunteer the information, but I won't lie if he asks."

I can live with that. Mason won't think to ask. Probably. I can reason with him if he finds out. Maybe. This is best for Ronni. That'll carry weight with him.

"Okay." I toss a few more things in the sack by my feet. "I'm ready."

Chapter 37
Fern

Thanksgiving Evening

How has it only been six hours since lunch? My head pounds with every beat of my racing heart. Dehydration from crying and the adrenaline crash are catching up with me, making me extra miserable. Mason's house is dark, save for the windows in the family room, which is typical for this time of night. We should be putting up the tree right now. *I may never get to do that again.*

Tears sting my eyes. I swipe at them, willing them away. I'm not going to cry. Anymore. I can't show weakness. Maybe it was an act, but Mason pretends to care, and he does it well. That'll make leaving this time harder. I knew it would hurt in the end, but I didn't expect the end to come so soon.

Austin stops the car at the front door and waits for me to get out first. He won't let me out of this—his condition for his hospitality. He doesn't want me to leave Mason hanging. Regardless, it's the right thing to do even though I'd rather hide at his place and pretend that nothing's wrong for a few days while I work up the courage. I don't want to do this, but I have to in order to move on. Like I told Mason, sometimes the things you want to do and the things you should do aren't the same.

I don't know if I should knock or go on it. This isn't my home anymore. Austin solves this for me and opens the door, swinging it wide for me to go in. My eyes dart to the corner where the Christmas tree goes. It isn't up yet, which breaks my heart. Ronni should be drinking hot chocolate and decorating it while her daddy rests and recovers in his favorite chair. She's big enough to do it by herself now.

Mason is in his favorite chair, though. He lurches to his feet when I step into the room. He's wearing the same clothes from lunch, with the addition of a white tee under his shirt since Austin tore the buttons off. "Fern! You're home!"

His greeting stomps all over the shards of my heart.

Movement draws my eye to the couch, where his sister sits holding Marnie. John is next to her, and Martin and Lola are seated opposite them. His mother is in my usual seat. Takeout boxes litter the coffee table where he and Ronni play board games in the evenings on the weekends. I only learned that after I moved in. It's just one more thing about him . . .

"Hi," I whisper roughly. Austin squeezes my shoulder on his way to his true love—food—but I keep my feet planted. At least here, I have an escape route. "How are you feeling?"

Mason waves away my concern but frowns at the space between us. *I've seen that before.* "Thankful. You look like you need a hug, baby," he says, holding his arms out slightly.

Without meaning to, I hug my middle and shake my head. He's right, but I can't let him do that, or I'll never leave. "Can we talk in the office, please?"

"As far as I'm concerned, we have nothing to talk about. Grab a seat. Have you had dinner? No one wanted to cook, but I ordered your favorite for you."

Why is he making this so hard? Once Austin got the call that Mason was released I made a list of things I needed to tell him. If I stick to the script, maybe I can get through this. I don't want to do it in front of his family. I don't want to give his mom this victory. But I will since he won't cooperate. "The laptop is—"

"Don't do this."

"—on your desk, where it always is. Keys are next to the garage door. Len knows a consignment shop that will sell the clothes and send you a check."

He sighs my name and rakes a hand through his hair, which looks as if he's repeating the gesture for the millionth time today.

"I uh, owe you for a few things you replaced, but I took nothing more than I came with." *Less actually.* My hands shake when I reach for the cell phone in my back pocket. It's like a lifeline, my last connection to my family. Without my old phone and laptop, I have no way to communicate with them, no way to see the touched up photo of my daughter Nicole sent me last week. I won't ask to keep it, though. I don't want to owe him more than necessary. I can go to the library to email my family and see my picture.

Crossing the room with determined steps, I hold the phone out to him. He barely spares it a glance, his eyes focused on mine. "I'd also appreciate it if you'd tell my family I'll be in touch when I can so they won't be worried. And I'll pay you at the same rate I was paying before—every cent I can spare every week. You can deduct my wages from what I owe." I hold my breath, hoping he won't contradict me. It's audacious of me to presume he'll let me keep my job, but he doesn't say a word.

Losing my patience, I grab his wrist, yank his hand up, and slap the phone in his palm, making sure to curl his fingers around it because he doesn't. It was a mistake, though, because fingers like vice grips close around my wrist, holding me in place.

This is harder than I imagined possible. I thought he'd understand, maybe even agree. *He would if he knew.* "I think that's everything. I'll go tell Ronni goodnight and be out of your hair."

"No." The pressure on my wrist increases, reminding me that I'm not taking a step without his permission.

Tears crash down my cheeks. *Here it comes.*

He reaches around and shoves the phone back into my pocket. "You can go upstairs and put your things back where they belong, Fern. You're not doing this to me."

Someday, someone is going to knock that stubborn streak out of him . . . "It's for the best, Mason."

"The best for whom?"

Everyone but me. "You. Ronni. Your family."

Fingers, gentle this time, curl around my chin and adjust the tilt until we're face to face, because his is only a hairsbreadth away. "Let me stop you right there. Mom and I have had what you call a *come to Jesus.*" Several people in the room choke on a laugh.

Too little, too late. "You can't force anyone to accept me."

"I didn't *force* anything, I helped her understand." A soft, suspiciously sniffle-like noise comes from my left, where his mother is seated, but I ignore her. "And Ronni promises she'll never forgive her if you don't come back."

My breath catches in my throat. "She doesn't mean that!"

"Oh, I wouldn't be so sure . . . Stop bullshitting me, woman. In your defense, after what Cassandra Williams put you through, you have a perfectly good reason for second thoughts. You should know I won't let anyone mistreat you, though. So, what gives?" I don't answer, so he tugs at the arm he's still holding. "Come on, there must be something else. What did I do?"

Why would he assume that it's him? The haunted look resurfaces. It's been weeks since I've seen such sadness in his eyes—the day at the furniture store. Sad doesn't even begin to cover it. It's more like he's losing someone he loves. "Mason, no! You didn't do anything. You're . . . you're wonderful."

"Trying to patch my ego?" he asks, mischief crinkling the corners of his eyes. He gives me another little shake. "What is it?"

I've never had a problem owning up to anything in my life until now. I do something wrong? I'll be the first to admit it. This time though . . . It hurts. I can pretend it's because of the audience, but the truth is, it was going to either way. *Ivy was right. There's nothing but heartache here.* "I broke the rules," I whisper.

He smirks at me. "There were two rules, Fern. I know where you've been every day and night, so I know you didn't cheat. What did you do?"

He catches my face in both hands to prevent me from looking away. Once his eyes snag mine again, I'm stuck as surely as a fish on a hook. "I did the one thing I never thought I'd do again."

"What's that?" Those baby blues shine with triumph while he watches me squirm. He smiles like he has a secret and can't decide if he wants to share it or tease me with it.

My heart tries to choke me again. "I fell in love," I barely even whisper around the knot in my throat.

"I know you did."

"What?"

He releases me to reach for his back pocket, producing a folded paper that he deftly opens. It's our contract. Holding it between us, he rips it in half and in half again. He doesn't stop until it's confetti that rains down on the floor.

Watching him destroy it is painful. I was hoping he'd find a way to use it to convince me to stay. Instead, he's giving up now that he understands I'm giving more than he can.

Though I'm nodding, there are tears in my eyes again. "I deserve to be loved too," I whisper for his ears only.

"Of course you do." He reaches for his front pocket, and I expect him to offer the handkerchief he carries, *"because I have a daughter who cries at dead vermin on the road."* But he drops to his knee and holds up a ring.

I freeze, afraid to even blink and shatter this illusion. It's as beautiful as it is cruel. This could've been my future. *Wait, why does he have a ring?*

"And I love you, too. Marry me? Not because of that," he nods toward the confetti on the ground, and the whole family, except Austin, gasps. "Because you love me, and I love you, and we've spent the last six years being a family without even knowing it. Marry me, and be here for the good parts too."

My head spins. Blood pounds in my ears. *Is this for real?* I hardly hear myself say, "They're all good parts." Even sneaking in here every year to put up the tree for Ronni was a good part. The days she was sick, and I would clear my schedule to take care of her because Felicity wouldn't even set foot in the house. Those were good too.

"Is that a yes?"

It's on the tip of my tongue, but it dies there. *What if he doesn't mean it? What if he's still pretending? What if he was* never *pretending?* I may never know. "You mean it?" I whisper raggedly. Trying to hold back tears is making it hard to speak. I can't elaborate, because if I do, I'm going to bawl.

He understands, though. He always does. "I've been trying to tell myself I didn't for a week now. Watching you today, when you were too busy trying to keep me alive to keep your guard up . . . I knew it. And I realized that you love me, too. I tried to say it then, but I couldn't. I love you. No contracts. No catch. I don't want you to marry me because of our agreement. I want you to marry me because you love me, and you want to be mine—ours—forever."

Be theirs? Oh yes, in a heartbeat. He's right. I've always been theirs. I was too blind before to see that they *both* own a piece of my heart. Still, I hesitate. How can I be sure?

"How many times does the man have to ask, Fern?" The voice reminds me so much of my sister's it makes me homesick. *I wish she were here.* That's impossible, though. My eyes dart toward the speaker and land on Ivy's gorgeous smile, where she waits at the foot of the stairs, watching me. "Hi, baby sis," she says with a grin and a little wave.

I cover my mouth to try and hold back the weird half-sobbing, half-laughing sound I'm making. *I can't believe this!* I look down at Mason and move my hand to ask, "You brought me my sister?"

He smirks and hugs one shoulder to his ear. "I was afraid I'd need the big guns."

He nearly falls over when I drop to my knees to hug him. Strong arms surround me, promising to take me with him if he goes. Maybe I'm a fool, but he wouldn't bring her all the way here from Nebraska if he didn't care. "Yes! I love you, yes."

"Thank God," he whispers before he clears his throat. "There's a slight correction to be made, though."

Concerned, I sit back on my heels and look at him. He's smiling, so it can't be too bad. All at once, I'm engulfed from behind by a pair of arms that are most definitely not Ronni's. Ronni doesn't have freckles and loose skin. More arms join the party.

"Mom? Dad?" I'm already sobbing.

"I brought your whole family. The timing is a little off, and we were supposed to be decorating the tree, but we're all here."

Over his mother's sobs, I ask, "You've been planning this?"

"Since the day you called Ivy on my phone. I didn't know it was going to be real, but I wanted them to be here."

"Wait, one more minute," someone says from the hall, drawing our attention to where Sage is fighting with everything she's got to hold Ronni back.

"Rainbow!" I whisper.

She twists in Sage's arms and is free. "Mommy!" she yells as she barrels across the room to launch herself into my arms.

I'd know Mason's arms anywhere, so I know when he joins in, hugging Ronni between us, right where she belongs.

Epilogue

Mason

Christmas Eve, one year later

The rings on Fern's hand sparkle in the twinkle lights on the tree, the only light in the room save for the fire. She and Nicole joke and toss balls of ripped wrapping paper at each other in mock outrage as they work together to clean up the mess from the first Christmas Eve gift exchange between the families of Cunningham and Chambers and the following movie. It was Fern's idea, and just enough to tide the kids over until tomorrow morning. They looked so cute in their matching pajamas, drinking hot chocolate while they watched *How the Grinch Stole Christmas* in our family room.

"Alright, everyone!" Fern says, raising her voice to be heard over the gaggle of giggling kids on the floor as she shoves the last wad of paper in the garbage sack. "When I was growing up, we had a tradition."

"Ohhh!" Her mother coos excitedly from my favorite chair—my old favorite chair. There's no room to snuggle both of my girls in it, so I've found I prefer the couch.

"What's that?" Ronni asks excitedly. We didn't do this last year, but last year Fern's family wasn't here for Christmas.

"Every year, my mom would read *Twas The Night Before Christmas*. This year, I thought I'd read a special version of it." The kids all cheer because they love story time with Fern almost as much as they love it when I read. She doesn't do all the voices, but she gets so animated it's adorable. "Alright then! Cuddle up!"

They shoot to their feet and dog pile their parents. Ronni nearly lands a knee in places I'd rather she not , since I have plans to seduce my little storyteller later. I promised her a baby months ago, and I have yet to deliver. *No pun intended.* If you're going to be a failure at something, what a way to go. But I'd rather give her what she asked for.

Ronni settles in with her head on my shoulder, none the wiser that I was already cringing, ready for the pain. Fern glances around at her audience and nods, but her smile is nervous. I'd recognize that smile anywhere because it was the first one I saw when she walked down the aisle. It didn't last long, though before her eyes found mine, and the nerves melted away.

"Here we go! 'Twas the night before Christmas, and all through our house, all the creatures were stirring, right down to the mouse!"

"Mommy!" Ronni giggles, melting my heart. "That's not how the story goes!"

"Shhh, I told you, it's special, just listen!" I'm not sure what she's up to, but she's not nervous anymore. Ronni slides off my lap to cuddle with Austin, too. She's very conscious of the fact that he has no children of his own and tries to include him in things like this. It's sweet.

"The stockings are hung by the chimney with care."

My eyes dart to our fireplace, where pictures of Vee, Aaron, and Cassie watch over us every day from the mantle.

"And this year, a fourth one proudly hangs there."

Luckily, Ronni moved, or I would have dumped her off on the floor when I shoot to my feet. Is she saying . . . ? Several of the others gasp, latching onto what I heard as well. It could be a coincidence, though.

"Daddy, are you okay? Did you get stung again?" Ronni asks, concern tightening her voice. All eyes are on me now.

"He's fine, Rainbow," Fern says with a smile. Blithely, she continues her story, stealing everyone's attention once more. "The family was snuggled all warm in their beds, until the littlest woke them with demands to be fed."

No way! She's only four steps away, but I run it and sweep her into my arms. Ronni loudly demanding to know what's going on, but everyone else is too busy hugging each other to pay her any attention. "I like this story," I murmur to my wife before I crush her lips with mine.

"Ronni, where'd you put the envelope I gave you earlier?" Nicole asks her.

"You're in on this?" I ask, whirling around with Fern still clutched to my chest to glare at my sister. I was too wrapped up in watching my wife before to notice her camera on a tripod, positioned to catch the entire room.

Nikki shrugs. "She needed a partner in crime who could record. Just so happens, I'm a photographer."

There's the sound of paper being ripped. Ronni's sweet voice fills the room as she reads, "This certificate hereby declares that one Veronica Anne Chambers will be promoted to . . . Big Sister! Effective July!" She jumps off the couch and squeals, "I'm gonna be a sister!"

"I'm sorry," Aspen, our eldest niece, deadpans, causing the adults in the room to dissolve into giggles.

Ronni doesn't stop jumping or squealing, though. Until, "Oh!" Something falls to the floor. She picks it up and studies it. "What's this? It looks like a white jelly bean!"

Fern is laughing now because I won't let her go. Not even to charge back to the couch for the sonogram pictures our daughter is holding. "That jellybean is your baby brother or sister," I tell her, awe tinging my voice. Disappointment knifes through my heart on the tail end of that revelation. "You had your first appointment without me?"

"Nah." Fern laughs at the confusion on my face. "I have a friend in the radiology department who owed me a solid. I asked her to put them in the envelope for me, so even I haven't seen them yet. She's the only one who has."

I loosen my hold, letting her slide down my body so I can hand her the pictures. While she's marveling over them, I drop to my knees. "Hello, little jellybean," I whisper to the baby growing inside her. She lets me press my lips to her abdomen like I did the first night we made love. The first time I marveled over the beautiful miracle that is her belly after carrying her daughter. And now, it's my baby there. Satisfaction hits me on a primal level.

While Fern fields questions from our family about how far along she is—ten weeks!—and morning sickness—not yet—Ronni and I take turns kissing her belly like a couple of fools and whispering to each other and the baby. For so long, it was only the two of us. But two became three, and now, there are four. Our dreams are coming true.

"Well," my mom says, her voice pitched to carry over the excited babble. I can tell from the way she says it, the way she draws it out, she's about to crack a joke. "I guess she really does love him if she's willing to put up with morning sickness."

I look up to find Fern grinning. It didn't happen overnight, but the two of them are very close now. Mom wasn't the one dragging her feet, either. After I proposed and the kids were in bed, we all sat down and had a long talk. A lot of truths came out, and it wasn't easy for any of us. Despite Mom's tearful apology and her jumping through hoops to make it up to Fern, Fern was slow to trust her again. Not that I blame her.

Fern combs her fingers through my hair and hugs my face to her belly. "Yeah, I kinda do," she jokes right back.

"Daddy!" Ronni says, highly affronted by something. "Why didn't you tell me?"

"What do you mean, Rice? I just found out too."

"You didn't tell me you were planting seeds in Mommy's belly button! I would have helped!"

Fern's body stiffens in my arms. I've learned that children have a way of saying the most embarrassing things during the most unfortunately timed lulls in conversation. This is no exception. I feel eyes on me—lots and lots of eyes. I sneak a peek at Fern, unsurprised by her gape of horrified stupefaction. It's probably a mirror of my own.

"If you're putting them in her belly button, you're doing it wrong," Austin mutters.

"What are you talking about, Uncle Austin?" Ronni asks. "Everyone knows that's where babies come from! And it worked! But I would have helped!"

"I'm sure you would have, Rice," I say, trying to fight back the wave of embarrassment. She keeps digging this deeper. "It was a secret."

"Oh," she pouts. "No one knew?"

"No one . . ."

"Daddy! That's naughty! What if Mommy didn't want you to?"

"Oh, I don't think Mommy minded one bit," Austin mutters. The adults in the room laugh. If he doesn't knock it off, I'm going to knock his teeth down his throat. *My father-in-law is right fucking* there!

"I didn't mean it was a secret from Mommy, too," I say before she can question Austin. "We uh . . . Didn't want anyone else to know we were planting seeds."

"Where do you get baby seeds?" Mallory asks.

Austin chokes on a laugh and coughs so hard I'm afraid he'll puke. I'm only scared because I'll have to clean it up. I'm not going to let my pregnant wife clean up vomit. She might be a sympathy puker, and she'll spend enough time doing that all too soon. Otherwise, he deserves it. *Asshole.*

"It's a secret, Mallie!" I rush to say. "Only men who want to be daddies know. And if we tell, they won't give us any more seeds." *Pulled that out of my ass.* "What do you think, Ronni, will it be a boy or a girl?"

"I want a sister!"

I don't care either way, so long as mama and baby are healthy. I climb to my feet and hug my girls, with Ronni and the jellybean in the middle, right where they're supposed to be. "I can live with that."

A note from Cara

Thank you for reading I Kinda Do! If you enjoyed reading it as much as I enjoyed writing it, I hope you'll consider taking a moment to leave a review and share your thoughts. Reviews are magic fairy dust readers use to help good books fly. Your review could help other readers decide to read I Kinda Do and the other stories in the Tarnished Hearts series.

My newsletter is a great way to stay up-to-date with the newest releases. If you haven't already signed up, you can do so on my website, caradsmith.com. You'll get a free short story about the day Ronni, Fern, and Mason met when you sign up, and there are sure to be more short stories made available to subscribers along the way!

Acknowledgments

First and foremost, thank you to my little family for not giving up on me. I know it's been a process, and I know the timing was less than ideal, but we made it. Each book I finish is a dream come true and I couldn't do it without you. Isaac, thank you for being (mostly) patient with me while I work. I'm sorry for all the times I forgot to get your chocolate milk when you asked so nicely.

Thank you to Kelsey and Katie for not laughing at me when I said I was going to publish a book. Also, thank you for answering my random-as-all-get-out questions, sometimes at weird times of the day. For being patient with me when I was losing my marbles over various parts of the process, and for taking a chance on being my first readers.

Thank you to Nancy, Dawn, and May for not running away when I warned you that I have no idea what I'm doing, and for helping me make this story what it is today.

Last, but not least, thank you, Mom and Dad for always having my back.

Follow Cara

My website:
www.caradsmith.com

Facebook:
www.facebook.com/CaraSmithAuthor

Instagram:
www.instagram.com/caradsmith

Also by Cara Smith

Tarnished Hearts:
*Hired—Newsletter bonus short story
I Kinda Do—Mason and Fern
*Surprise!—Deleted Epilogue
Right By You—Gabe and Tara
Dare To Love—Austin and Jamaica
(TBD)Tarnished Hearts 3.5—Noel and Colton
It's Not You—Ryan and Trista
A Second Glance—Chris and Heidi

Each book in the Tarnished Hearts series is a stand-alone, meaning each story is self-contained and they can be read in any order. Some jokes, conversations, and references might make a little more sense if you read them in the order in which they were written, but it is not necessary. Each story has a guaranteed HEA.

*Find these on my website.

Right By You (Tarnished Hearts Book Two) is coming soon! Find out the truth behind Gabe and Tara's divorce. Can he manage to stay by her side the second time around?